*Passion is
the ultimate
temptation…*

"You're in pain and I can help you."

Alistair looked at Helen, his eye cynical. "Why would you care?"

Did he think she'd back away at his harsh words?

She leaned into his face, still holding his hand. "What kind of woman do you think I am? Do you think I let just any man kiss me?"

His eye narrowed. "I think you're a nice woman. A kind woman."

The patronizing answer nearly drove her to violence. "A nice woman? Because I kissed you? Because I let you touch me? Are you mad? No woman is that nice, and certainly not I."

He simply looked at her. "Then why?"

"Because." She took his face in her palms. "I *do* care. And so do you."

And she set her lips against his. Deliberately. Softly. Putting all her longing, all her loneliness into the gesture. She started the kiss lightly, but he tilted his head beneath hers, angling and opening his mouth, and somehow she found herself on his lap.

She'd been waiting for this for days now, and the reality set her limbs to trembling . . .

Please turn the page for raves
for Elizabeth Hoyt and her novels . . .

"A wonderful story."

—JandysBooks.com

"Hoyt masterfully throws you into the setting, characters, and plot . . . A skillfully wicked and sensuous tale, guaranteed to capture your attention and heart."

—BookPleasures.com

"Fans of Georgian romances will relish this fine tale."

—*Midwest Book Review*

"This story will grab you and not let you go until the last page is turned. Hoyt's unique storytelling style . . . makes you think, makes you smile, and also keeps your curiosity piqued as you move along the story."

—HistoricalRomanceWriters.com

"A great series."

—GoodBadandUnread.com

"Funny and heartbreaking, sexy and poignant . . . wrenching and riveting reading . . . Jasper and Melisande are full, vibrant characters. I loved the unusual setting, the intriguing and complex characters, the emotional struggles and connections, the lush love scenes, the mystery . . . all in all, a remarkable book."

—LikesBooks.com

"Falls firmly into the 'love it!' category . . . Our hero and heroine's relationship leaps off the page. Watching the two try to sort each other out while uncovering their true selves was wonderful."

—Rakehell.com

more . . .

"4½ Stars! I continue to be blown away by Elizabeth Hoyt. [She] writes the most remarkable characters. I couldn't have been happier at how the story was told and how it ended."

—TheBookBinge.com

To Taste Temptation

"Hoyt . . . is firmly in control of her craft with engaging characters, gripping plot, and clever dialogue."

—Publishers Weekly

"4½ Stars! Hoyt's new series . . . begins with destruction and ends with glorious love. She begins each chapter with a snippet of a legend that beautifully dovetails with the plot and creates a distinct love story that will thrill readers."

—Romantic Times BOOKreviews Magazine

"4½ Stars! There's an interesting suspense embedded in this book . . . The sensuality is breathtaking and the reader is carried into the headiness of growing love . . . I loved this book, the high quality of the writing, the engaging plot, and, most of all, the character development. A terrific novel . . . highly recommended."

—TheRomanceReadersConnection.com

"[A] brilliant start to a sexy new historical romance series. I thoroughly enjoyed this story of action, mystery, and steamy romance. Her love scenes are scorching hot . . . Hang on to your seat and have a cold glass of water handy."

—FreshFiction.com

more . . .

The Serpent Prince

"Exquisite romance . . . mesmerizing storytelling . . . incredibly vivid lead characters, earthy writing, and an intense love story."
—Publishers Weekly

"Wonderfully satisfying . . . delightfully witty . . . with just a touch of suspense. Set in a lush regency background, Elizabeth spins a story of treachery, murder, suspense, and love with her usual aplomb."
—RomanceatHeart.com

"Delectably clever writing, deliciously complex characters, and a delightfully sexy romance between perfectly matched protagonists are the key ingredients in the third book in Hoyt's superbly crafted, loosely connected Georgian-era Prince trilogy."
—Booklist

"With an engrossing plot centered on revenge and a highly passionate romance between Simon and Lucy, *The Serpent Prince* delivers a steamy tale that packs an emotional punch. The three-dimensional characters, high drama, and sensuous love story make it a page-turner."
—RomRevToday.com

The Leopard Prince

"4½ Stars! TOP PICK! An unforgettable love story that ignites the pages not only with heated love scenes but also with a mystery that holds your attention and your heart with searing emotions and dark desire."
—Romantic Times BOOKreviews Magazine

"The new master of the historical romance genre."
—HistoricalRomanceWriters.com

"An exhilarating historical romance."
—*Midwest Book Review*

"4½ Stars! Absolutely fantastic . . . filled with witty dialogue and sparkling characters."
—TheRomanceReadersConnection.com

"A refreshing historical romance . . . Elizabeth Hoyt weaves a superb tale that will keep you reading long into the night."
—Bookloons.com

The Raven Prince

"A sexy, steamy treat! A spicy broth of pride, passion, and temptation."
—CONNIE BROCKWAY,
***USA Today* bestselling author**

"Hoyt expertly spices this stunning debut novel with a sharp sense of wit and then sweetens her lusciously dark, lushly sensual historical romance with a generous sprinkling of fairy-tale charm."
—*Chicago Tribune*

"Will leave you breathless."
—JULIANNE MACLEAN, author of *Portrait of a Lover*

OTHER TITLES BY ELIZABETH HOYT

The Raven Prince

The Leopard Prince

The Serpent Prince

To Taste Temptation

To Seduce a Sinner

ELIZABETH HOYT

To Beguile A Beast

FOREVER

NEW YORK   BOSTON

Copyright © 2009 by Nancy M. Finney
Excerpt from *To Desire a Devil* copyright © 2009 by Nancy M. Finney.
All rights reserved. Except as permitted under the U.S. Copyright Act
of 1976, no part of this publication may be reproduced, distributed,
or transmitted in any form or by any means, or stored in a database or
retrieval system, without the prior written permission of the publisher.

Cover illustration by Alan Ayers
Hand lettering by Ron Zinn

Forever
Hachette Book Group
237 Park Avenue
New York, NY 10017
Visit our Web site at www.HachetteBookGroup.com

Forever is an imprint of Grand Central Publishing. The Forever name and
logo is a trademark of Hachette Book Group Inc.

Printed in the United States of America

First Printing: May 2009

10 9 8 7 6 5 4 3 2 1

For my husband, Fred, and the twenty marvelous years we've had together . . . even if they did come with rocks in my downstairs sink.

Acknowledgments

Thank you to Eileen Dreyer, who answers even the most gory and bizarre medical questions with aplomb; to my agent, Susannah Taylor, who has nerves of steel even when the deadline is *this* close; to my editor, Amy Pierpont, whose editorial suggestions are always spot-on; to her wonderful assistant, Alex Logan; to the spectacular GCP sales team, including Bob Levine; to the super GCP publicity department, including Melissa Bullock, Renee Supriano, and Tanisha Christie; to the amazing GCP art department, particularly Diane Luger for my wonderful covers and sexy stepbacks (rhoar!); and last, but certainly not least, to my copy editor, Carrie Andrews, who has once again unraveled my more creative use of English grammar.

Thank you all!

Prologue

Once upon a time, long, long ago, a soldier was hiking home through the mountains of a foreign land. The way was steep and rocky, black and twisted trees clung to the edges of the path, and a cold wind blew bitterly against his cheeks. But the soldier didn't hesitate in his stride. He had seen places both more fearsome and stranger than this, and few things had the ability to make him shiver anymore.

Our soldier had fought most bravely in his war, but many soldiers fight bravely. Old, young, fair of face, and those who misfortune stalks, all soldiers go to battle the best that they are able. Often it is more a matter of luck than justice that determines who shall live and who shall die. So, in his courage, his honor, his very virtue, our soldier was perhaps no better than thousands of his fellows. But in one respect, our soldier was very different. He could not tell a lie.

Because of this, he was called Truth Teller. . . .

—from TRUTH TELLER

Chapter One

*Now dark began to fall as Truth Teller made the crest
of the mountain and saw a magnificent castle, black
as sin. . . .*
—from TRUTH TELLER

SCOTLAND
JULY 1765

It was as the carriage bumped around a bend and the decrepit castle loomed into view in the dusk that Helen Fitzwilliam finally—and rather belatedly—realized that the
whole trip may've been a horrible mistake.

"Is that it?" Jamie, her five-year-old son, was kneeling
on the musty carriage seat cushions and peering out the
window. "I thought it was 'sposed to be a castle."

"'Tis a castle, silly," his nine-year-old sister, Abigail,
replied. "Can't you see the tower?"

"Just 'cause it has a tower don't mean it's a castle,"

Jamie objected, frowning at the suspect castle. "There's no moat. If it *is* a castle, it's not a proper one."

"Children," Helen said rather too sharply, but then they *had* been in one cramped carriage after another for the better part of a fortnight. "Please don't bicker."

Naturally, her offspring feigned deafness.

"It's pink." Jamie had pressed his nose to the small window, clouding the glass with his breath. He turned and scowled at his sister. "D'you think a proper castle ought to be pink?"

Helen stifled a sigh and massaged her right temple. She'd felt a headache lurking there for the last several miles, and she knew it was about to pounce just as she needed all her wits about her. She hadn't really thought this scheme through. But, then, she never did think things through as she ought to, did she? Impulsiveness—hastily acted on and more leisurely regretted—was the hallmark of her life. It was why, at the age of one and thirty, she found herself traveling through a foreign land about to throw herself and her children on the mercy of a stranger.

What a fool she was!

A fool who had better get her story straight, for the carriage was already stopping before the imposing wood doors.

"Children!" she hissed.

Both little faces snapped around at her tone. Jamie's brown eyes were wide while Abigail's expression was pinched and fearful. Her daughter noticed far too much for a little girl; she was too sensitive to the atmosphere adults created.

Helen took a breath and made herself smile. "This will be an adventure, my darlings, but you must remember what I've told you." She looked at Jamie. "What are we to be called?"

"Halifax," Jamie replied promptly. "But I'm still Jamie and Abigail's still Abigail."

"Yes, darling."

That had been decided on the trip north from London when it became painfully obvious that Jamie would have difficulties *not* calling his sister by her real name. Helen sighed. She'd just have to hope that the children's Christian names were ordinary enough not to give them away.

"We've lived in London," Abigail said, looking intent.

"That'll be easy to remember," Jamie muttered, "because we *have*."

Abigail shot a quelling glance at her brother and continued. "Mama's been in the dowager Viscountess Vale's household."

"And our father's dead and he isn't—" Jamie's eyes widened, stricken.

"I don't know why we need to say he's dead," Abigail muttered into the silence.

"Because he mustn't trace us, dear." Helen swallowed and leaned forward to pat her daughter's knee. "It's all right. If we can—"

The carriage door was wrenched open, and the coachman's scowling face peered in. "Are ye getting out or not? It looks like rain, an' I want to be back in th' inn safe and warm when it comes, don't I?"

"Of course." Helen nodded regally at the coachman— by far the surliest driver they'd had on this wretched journey. "Please fetch our bags down for us."

The man snorted. "Already done, innit?"

"Come, children." She hoped she wasn't blushing in

front of the awful man. The truth was, they had only two soft bags—one for herself and one for the children. The coachman probably thought them desolate. And in a way, he was right, wasn't he?

She pushed the lowering thought away. Now was not the time to have discouraging thoughts. She must be at her most alert and her most persuasive to pull this off.

She stepped from the rented carriage and looked around. The ancient castle loomed before them, solid and silent. The main building was a squat rectangle, built of weathered soft rose stone. High on the corners, circular towers projected from the walls. Before the castle was a sort of drive, once neatly graveled but now uneven with weeds and mud. A few trees clustered about the drive struggled to make a barricade against the rising wind. Beyond, black hills rolled gently to the darkening horizon.

"All right, then?" The coachman was swinging up to his box, not even looking at them. "I'll be off."

"At least leave a lantern!" Helen shouted, but the noise of the carriage rumbling away drowned out her voice. She stared, appalled, after the coach.

"It's dark," Jamie observed, looking at the castle.

"Mama, there aren't any lights," Abigail said.

She sounded frightened, and Helen felt a surge of trepidation as well. She hadn't noticed the lack of lights until now. What if no one was home? What would they do then?

I'll cross that bridge when I come to it. She was the adult here. A mother should make her children feel safe.

Helen tilted her chin and smiled for Abigail. "Perhaps they're lit in the back where we can't see them."

Abigail didn't look particularly convinced by this theory, but she dutifully nodded her head. Helen took the bags and marched up the shallow stone steps to the huge wooden doors. They were within a Gothic arch, almost black with age, and the hinges and bolts were iron—quite medieval. She raised the iron ring and knocked.

The sound echoed despairingly within.

Helen stood facing the door, refusing to believe that no one would come. The wind blew her skirts into a swirl. Jamie scuffed his boots against the stone step, and Abigail sighed almost silently.

Helen wet her lips. "Perhaps they can't hear because they're in the tower."

She knocked again.

It was dark now, the sun completely gone, and with it the warmth of day. It was the middle of summer and quite hot in London, but she'd found on her journey north that the nights in Scotland could become very cool, even in summer. Lightning flashed low on the horizon. What a desolate place this was! Why anyone would willingly choose to live here was beyond her understanding.

"They're not coming," Abigail said as thunder rumbled in the distance. "No one's home, I think."

Helen swallowed as fat raindrops pattered against her face. The last village they'd passed was ten miles away. She had to find shelter for her children. Abigail was right. No one was home. She'd led them on a wild-goose chase.

She'd failed them once again.

Helen's lips trembled at the thought. *Mustn't break down in front of the children.*

"Perhaps there's a barn or other outbuilding in—" she began when one of the great wood doors was thrown open, startling her.

She stepped back, nearly falling down the steps. At first the opening seemed eerily black, as if a ghostly hand had opened the door. But then something moved, and she discerned a shape within. A man stood there, tall, lean, and very, very intimidating. He held a single candle, its light entirely inadequate. By his side was a great four-legged beast, far too tall to be any sort of dog that she knew of.

"What do you want?" he rasped, his voice low and husky as if from disuse or strain. His accent was cultured, but the tone was far from welcoming.

Helen opened her mouth, scrambling for words. He was not at all what she'd expected. Dear God, what was that thing by his side?

At that moment, lightning forked across the sky, close and amazingly bright. It lit the man and his familiar as if he was on a stage. The beast was tall and gray and lean, with gleaming black eyes. The man was even worse. Black, lank hair fell in tangles to his shoulders. He wore old breeches, gaiters, and a rough coat better suited for the rubbish heap. One side of his stubbled face was twisted with red angry scars. A single light brown eye reflected the lightning at them diabolically.

Most horrible of all, there was only a sunken pit where his left eye should have been.

Abigail screamed.

THEY ALWAYS SCREAMED.

Sir Alistair Munroe scowled at the woman and children on his step. Behind them the rain suddenly let down in a wall of water, making the children crowd against their mother's skirts. Children, particularly small ones, nearly always screamed and ran away from him. Sometimes even grown women did. Just last year, a rather melodramatic young lady on High Street in Edinburgh had fainted at the sight of him.

Alistair had wanted to slap the silly chit.

Instead, he'd scurried away like a diseased rat, hiding the maimed side of his face as best he could in his lowered tricorne and pulled-up cloak. He expected the reaction in cities and towns. It was the reason he didn't like to frequent areas where people congregated. What he didn't expect was a female child screaming on his very doorstep.

"Stop that," he growled at her, and the lass snapped her mouth shut.

There were two children, a boy and a girl. The lad was a brown birdlike thing that could've been anywhere from three to eight. Alistair had no basis to judge, since he avoided children when he could. The girl was the elder. She was pale and blond, and staring up at him with blue eyes that looked much too large for her thin face. Perhaps it was a fault of her bloodline—such abnormalities often denoted mental deficiency.

Her mother had eyes the same color, he saw as he finally, reluctantly, looked at her. She was beautiful. Of course. It would be a blazing beauty who appeared on his doorstep in a thunderstorm. She had eyes the exact color of newly opened harebells, shining gold hair, and a magnificent bosom that any man, even a scarred, misanthropic recluse such as himself, would find arousing. It was, after all, the natural reaction of a human male to a human female of obvious reproductive capability, however much he resented it.

"What do you want?" he repeated to the woman.

Perhaps the entire family was mentally deficient, because they simply stared at him, mute. The woman's stare was fixated on his eye socket. Naturally. He'd left off his patch again—the damned thing was a nuisance—and his face was no doubt going to inspire nightmares in her sleep tonight.

He sighed. He'd been about to sit down to a dinner of porridge and boiled sausages when he'd heard the knocking. Wretched as his meal was, it would be even less appetizing cold.

"Carlyle Manor is a good two miles thataway." Alistair tilted his head in a westerly direction. No doubt they were guests of his neighbors gone astray. He shut the door.

Or rather, he tried to shut the door.

The woman inserted her foot in the crack, preventing him. For a moment, he actually considered shutting her foot in the door, but a remnant of civility asserted itself and he stopped. He looked at the woman, his eye narrowed, and waited for an explanation.

The woman's chin tilted. "I'm your housekeeper."

Definitely a case of mental deficiency. Probably the result of aristocratic overbreeding, for despite her lack of mental prowess, she and the children were richly dressed.

Which only made her statement even more absurd.

He sighed. "I don't have a housekeeper. Really, ma'am, Carlyle Manor is just over the hill—"

She actually had the temerity to interrupt him. "No, you misunderstand. I'm your *new* housekeeper."

"I repeat. I. Don't. Have. A. Housekeeper." He spoke slowly so perhaps her confused brain could understand the words. "Nor do I wish for a housekeeper. I—"

"This is Castle Greaves?"

"Aye."

"And you are Sir Alistair Munroe?"

He scowled. "Aye, but—"

She wasn't even looking at him. Instead, she had stooped to rummage in one of the bags at her feet. He stared at her, irritated and perplexed and vaguely aroused, because her position gave him a spectacular view down the bodice of her gown. If he was a religious man, he might think this a vision.

She made a satisfied sound and straightened again, smiling quite gloriously. "Here. It's a letter from the Viscountess Vale. She's sent me here to be your housekeeper."

She was proffering a rather crumpled piece of paper.

He stared at the paper a moment before snatching it from her hand. He raised the candle to provide some light to read the scrawling missive. Beside him, Lady Grey, his deerhound, evidently decided that she wasn't getting sausages for dinner any time soon. She sighed gustily and lay down on the hall flagstones.

Alistair finished reading the missive to the sound of the rain pounding steadily on his drive. Then he looked up. He'd met Lady Vale only once. She and her husband, Jasper Renshaw, Viscount Vale, had visited his home uninvited a little over a month ago. She hadn't struck him at the time as an interfering female, but the letter did indeed inform him that he had a new housekeeper. Madness. What had Vale's wife been thinking? But then it was near impossible to fathom the workings of the female mind. He'd have to send the too-beautiful, too-richly-dressed housekeeper and her offspring away in the morning. Unfortunately, if nothing else, they were protégés of Lady Vale, and he couldn't very well send them off into the dark of night.

Alistair met the woman's blue eyes. "What did you say your name was?"

She blushed as prettily as the sun rising in spring on the heath. "I didn't. My name is Helen Halifax. *Mrs.* Halifax. We are becoming quite wet out here, you realize."

A corner of his mouth kicked up at the starch in her tone. Not a mental deficient after all. "Well, then, you and your children had better come in, Mrs. Halifax."

THE TINY SMILE curving one side of Sir Alistair's lips startled Helen. It drew attention to a mouth both wide and firm, supple and masculine. The smile revealed him as not the gargoyle she'd been thinking him, but a man.

It was gone at once, of course, as soon as he caught her looking at him. In an instant, his expression turned stony and faintly cynical. "You'll continue to get wet until you come in, madam."

"Thank you." She swallowed and stepped into the dim hall. "You're most *kind,* I'm sure, Sir Alistair."

He shrugged and turned away. "If you say so."

Beastly man! He hadn't even offered to carry their bags. Of course, most gentlemen didn't carry the belongings of their housekeepers. Even so, it would've been nice to at least offer.

Helen grasped a bag in each hand. "Come, children."

They had to walk quickly, almost jogging, to keep up with Sir Alistair and what appeared to be the only light in the castle—his candle. The gigantic dog padded along at his side, lean, dark, and tall. In fact, she was very like her master. They passed out of a great hall and into a dim passage. The candlelight bobbed ahead, casting eerie shadows on grimy walls and high, cobwebbed ceilings. Jamie and Abigail trailed on either side of her. Jamie was so tired that he merely trudged along, but Abigail was looking curiously from side to side as she hurried.

"It's terribly dirty, isn't it?" Abigail whispered.

Sir Alistair turned as she spoke, and at first Helen thought he'd heard. "Have you eaten?"

He'd halted so suddenly, Helen nearly trod on his toes. As it was, she ended up standing much too close to him. She had to crane her neck to look him in the eye, and he held the candle near his chest, casting the light diabolically over his face.

"We had tea at the inn, but—" she began breathlessly.

"Good," he said, and turned away. He called back over his shoulder as he disappeared around a corner, "You can stay the night in one of the guest rooms. I'll hire a carriage to send you back to London in the morning."

Helen gripped the bags higher and hurried to catch up. "But I really don't—"

He'd already started up a narrow stone stair. "You needn't worry about the expense."

For a second, Helen paused at the bottom of the stair, glaring at the firm backside steadily receding above them. Unfortunately, the light was receding as well.

"Hurry, Mama," Abigail urged her. She'd taken her brother's hand like a good older sister and had already mounted the steps with Jamie.

The horrid man stopped at the landing. "Coming, Mrs. Halifax?"

"Yes, Sir Alistair," Helen said through gritted teeth. "I

just think that if you'll only *try* Lady Vale's idea of having a—"

"I don't want a housekeeper," he rasped, and resumed climbing the stairs.

"I find that hard to believe," Helen panted behind him, "considering the state of the castle I've seen so far."

"And yet, I enjoy my home the way it is."

Helen narrowed her eyes. She refused to believe anyone, even this beast of a man, actually *enjoyed* dirt. "Lady Vale specifically instructed me—"

"Lady Vale is mistaken in her belief that I desire a housekeeper."

They'd finally reached the top of the stairs, and he paused to open a narrow door. He entered the room and lit a candle.

Helen stopped and watched him from the hall. When he came back out, she met his gaze determinedly. "You may not *want* a housekeeper, but it is patently obvious that you *need* a housekeeper."

The corner of his mouth quirked again. "You may argue all you want, madam, but the fact remains that I neither need you nor wish to have you here."

He gestured to the room with one hand. The children ran in ahead. He hadn't bothered moving from the doorway, so Helen was forced to sidle in sideways, her bosom nearly brushing his chest.

She looked up at him as she passed. "I warn you, I shall make it my purpose to change your mind, Sir Alistair."

He inclined his head, his one good eye glittering in the light of the candle. "Good night, Mrs. Halifax."

He shut the door gently behind him.

Helen stared at the closed door a moment, then glanced

about her. The room Sir Alistair had led them to was large and cluttered. Hideous long drapes covered one wall, and a huge bed with thick carved posts dominated the room. A single, small fireplace sat in a corner. Shadows masked the other end of the room, but the outlines of furniture crowded together made her suspect that it was being used as storage space. Abigail and Jamie had collapsed on the huge bed. Two weeks ago, Helen wouldn't have let them even touch something that dusty.

But then two weeks ago, she'd still been the Duke of Lister's mistress.

Chapter Two

Truth Teller stopped and stood before the black castle. Four towers loomed, one at each corner, rising high and ominous to the night sky. He was about to turn away when the great wooden doors creaked open. A beautiful young man stood there, clad in robes of gold and white and wearing a ring with a milky-white stone upon his forefinger.

"Good evening, traveler," said the man. "Won't you come in out of the cold and wind?"

Well, the castle was foreboding, but snow was blowing around him, and Truth Teller didn't mind the thought of a hot fire. He nodded and entered the black castle. . . .

—from TRUTH TELLER

It was dark. Very, very dark.

Abigail lay in the big bed and listened to the darkness in the castle. Beside her, Jamie was snoring in his sleep. He was right up against her, squishing himself as close as possible, his head shoved into her shoulder, his hot breath blowing on her neck. She was nearly at the edge of the bed. Mama breathed softly on her side of the bed. The rain had stopped, but she could hear a steady drip from the eaves. It sounded like a little man walking up the wall, each measured step growing closer. Abigail shivered.

She had to pee.

Perhaps if she lay still, she'd go back to sleep. But then there was the fear of waking to a wet bed. It'd been a very long while since she'd wet the bed, but she still remembered the shame the last time it had happened. Miss Cummings, their nurse, had made her tell Mama what she'd done. Abigail had nearly thrown up her breakfast before she could make her confession. In the end, Mama hadn't been cross, but she'd looked at her with worry and pity, and that had almost been worse.

Abigail hated to disappoint Mama.

Sometimes Mama looked at her with a sad expression, and Abigail knew: She wasn't quite right. She didn't laugh like other girls, didn't play with dolls and have lots of friends. She liked to be by herself. Liked to think about things. And sometimes she worried about the things she thought about; she simply couldn't help herself. No matter how much it disappointed Mama.

She sighed now. There was no use for it. She'd have to use the commode. She shifted quietly and peered over the edge of the great bed, but it was too dark to see the floor. Poking out a foot from the covers, she slowly slid until she could touch the floor with just one toe.

Nothing happened.

The wood floor was cold, but there were no mice or spiders or other horrible insects. At least, not nearby. Abigail took a breath and slid fully from the bed. Her night rail caught and hiked up, baring her legs to the cold. Above, Jamie mumbled and rolled toward Mama.

She stood and shook down her night rail, then crouched and pulled the commode out from under the bed. She scooped up her skirts and squatted over the commode. The sound of her water hitting the commode was loud in the room, drowning out the dripping footsteps from the eaves.

She sighed in relief.

Something creaked outside the bedroom door. Abigail froze, her stream still trickling into the tin commode. Flickering light crept under the door. Someone stood in the hallway. She remembered Sir Alistair's horribly scarred face. He'd been so tall—taller, even, than the duke. What if he'd decided to toss them from his castle?

Or worse?

Abigail held her breath, waiting, her thighs burning from crouching over the commode, her bottom growing cold in the night air. Outside the door, someone hawked— a long, scratching, liquid gurgle that turned Abigail's stomach—and spat. Then boots scraped against the floor as he moved away.

She waited until she could no longer hear the footsteps, and then she leapt up from the commode. She shoved it away and scrambled into the bed, yanking the covers over her and Jamie's head.

"Wassit?" Jamie muttered, slumping against her again.

"Shh!" Abigail hissed.

She held her breath, but all she heard was the suck-ing sounds Jamie made as he jammed his thumb into his mouth. He wasn't supposed to do that anymore, but Miss Cummings wasn't here to scold him. Abigail wrapped her arms tightly around her little brother.

Mama had said that they'd had to leave London. That they could no longer stay in their tall town house with Miss Cummings and the other servants she'd known all her life. That they had to leave pretty dresses and picture books and lovely sponge cake with lemon curd behind. Leave everything Abigail knew, in fact. But surely Mama hadn't realized how awful this castle would be? How dark and dirty the halls or how scary the master? And if the duke knew how terrible this place was, wouldn't he let them come home?

Wouldn't he?

Abigail lay in the dark listening to the little man climbing the walls and wished she were safe at home in London.

HELEN WOKE THE next morning to the sun shining dimly through the window. She'd made sure to pull the curtains the night before so they wouldn't sleep past first light. If one could call a single feeble ray struggling through a grimy windowpane first light. Helen sighed and scrubbed at the pane with a corner of the curtain, but she only managed to make the dust swirl greasily on the glass.

"This is the dirtiest place I've ever seen," Abigail observed critically as she watched her brother.

There were several stuffed chairs crowded into the far end of the room, as if a long-ago chatelaine had stored them there and then forgotten them. Jamie was leaping from chair to chair. Each time he landed, a small cloud of dust puffed from the cushion. Already a film of dirt covered his little face.

Oh, God, how was she to do this? The castle was filthy, its master a nasty, rude beast of a man, and she hadn't a clue what to do first.

But then, it wasn't as if she had any choice. Helen had known what kind of man the Duke of Lister was when she left him. The kind who didn't let go of anything that belonged to him. He may not have lain with her for years, and he may've taken other mistresses in that time, but Lister still considered her his mistress. His *possession*. And the children were his possessions as well. He had fathered them. Never mind that he'd hardly said two words to the children over the years or that he'd never formally acknowledged them.

Lister kept what was his. Had he any suspicion that she was going to flee with Abigail and Jamie, he would've taken them from her; she had no doubt at all. Once, nearly eight years ago, when Abigail was only an infant, Helen had talked about leaving him. She'd returned to her town house from an afternoon's shopping expedition to find Abigail gone and the nursemaid in tears. Lister had kept the baby until the next morning—a night that still haunted Helen in her dreams. By the time he'd come to her door in the morning, Helen had been nearly ill with worry. And Lister? He'd sauntered in, the baby on his arm, and explained quite clearly that if she hoped to keep her daughter by her side, she must resign herself to their relationship. She was his, and nothing and no one could alter that.

So when she had made the decision to leave Lister, she'd known that she would be burning her bridges behind her. Lister must never find her if the children were to be kept safe. With the help of Lady Vale, she'd escaped London in a borrowed carriage. She'd changed that carriage at the first inn on the road north and had continued renting different carriages as often as possible. She'd kept to the less traveled roads and tried to attract as little attention as possible.

It'd been Lady Vale's idea for Helen to present herself as Sir Alistair's new housekeeper. Castle Greaves was well away from society, and Lady Vale had been sure Lister would never think to look for her here. In that respect, Sir Alistair's domain was the perfect hideaway. But Helen wondered if Lady Vale had any notion of just how wretched the castle was.

Or how stubborn its master.

One step at a time. It wasn't as if she had anywhere else to go. This was the path she'd decided on, and she must make it work. The consequences of failure were simply too unthinkable to contemplate.

Jamie landed awkwardly and slid off a chair in an avalanche of dust.

"Stop that, please," Helen snapped.

Both children looked at her. She didn't often raise her voice. But then, until a week or so ago, she'd had a nursemaid to take care of the children. She'd seen them when she'd wanted to—at bedtime, for tea in the afternoon, and for walks in the park. Times when both she and they had been in pleasant frames of mind. If Abigail or Jamie became tired or angry or out of sorts, she'd always had the option of sending them back to Miss Cummings. Unfortunately, Miss Cummings had been left behind in London.

Helen inhaled, trying to calm himself. "It's time we were at our work."

"What work?" Jamie asked. He got up and started kicking a cushion that had slid to the floor with him.

"Sir Alistair said we were to go away again this morning," Abigail stated.

"Yes, but we'll convince him otherwise, won't we?"

"I want to go home."

"We can't, darling. I've already told you so." Helen smiled persuasively. She hadn't told them what Lister would do if he caught them. She hadn't wanted to frighten the children. "Sir Alistair does need someone to clean his castle and put it back in order, don't you think?"

"Ye-es," Abigail said. "But he said he liked his castle all dirty."

"Nonsense. I think he's just too retiring to ask for help. Besides, it's our Christian duty to help those in need, and it seems to me that Sir Alistair has a very large need indeed."

Abigail looked doubtful.

Helen clapped her hands together before her too-perceptive daughter could make any more objections. "Let's go down and order a splendid breakfast for Sir Alistair and something for ourselves. After that, I'll consult with the cook and maids on how best to set about cleaning and managing the castle."

Even Jamie perked up at the thought of breakfast. Helen opened the door, and they crowded into the narrow corridor outside.

"I think we came this way last night," Helen said, and set off to the right.

As it turned out, that *wasn't* the direction Sir Alistair

had led them, but after a few more wrong turns, they found themselves on the ground floor of the castle. Helen noticed Abigail dragging her heels as they tramped to the back of the castle and the presumed direction of the kitchens.

Abigail suddenly halted. "Do I have to greet him?"

"Who, dear?" Helen asked, although she knew perfectly well.

"Sir Alistair."

"Abigail's afraid of Sir Alistair!" Jamie sang.

"Am not," Abigail said fiercely. "At least, not very. It's just . . ."

"He startled you and you screamed," Helen said. She looked about the dingy walls of the hallway, searching for how to reply to her daughter. Abigail could be so sensitive. The slightest criticism sent her brooding for days. "I know you feel awkward, sweetheart, but you must think of Sir Alistair's feelings as well. It can't be very nice to have a young lady scream at the sight of you."

"He must hate me," Abigail whispered.

And Helen's heart squeezed painfully. It was so difficult being a mother sometimes. Wanting to shield one's children from the world and their own weaknesses, and at the same time needing to instill honor and proper behavior.

"I doubt he feels anything as harsh as hate," Helen said gently. "But I think you shall have to apologize to him, don't you?"

Abigail didn't say anything, but she gave a single jerky nod, her thin face looking pale and worried.

Helen sighed and continued in the direction of the

kitchens. Breakfast, in her opinion, generally made things better.

But as it turned out, there was very little to eat in Castle Greaves. The kitchen was a vast, terribly ancient room. The plastered walls and groined ceiling had once been whitewashed, but the color was a dingy gray now. A cavernous fireplace, much in need of sweeping out, took up one whole wall. Judging from the dust on the pots piled in the cupboards, not much actual cooking was done here.

Helen looked about the room in dismay. A single dirty plate lay on one of the tables, evidence that someone had eaten a meal here recently. Surely there must be a pantry with food somewhere? She began opening cupboards and drawers in a state of near panic. Fifteen minutes later, she examined her booty: a single sack of mealy flour, some oats, tea, sugar, and a handful of salt. She'd also found a small dried up piece of streaky bacon hanging in the larder. Helen was staring at the supplies, wondering what could possibly be made for breakfast out of them, when the full horror of her situation finally dawned on her.

There was no cook.

Indeed, she hadn't seen any servants this morning. Not a scullery maid or footman. Not a bootblack boy or a parlor maid. Had Sir Alistair *any* servants at all?

"I'm hungry, Mama," Jamie moaned.

Helen gazed blindly at him a moment, still dazed by the magnitude of the job ahead of her. A small voice was screaming at the back of her mind, *I can't do this! I can't do this!*

But she had no choice. She *must* do this.

She swallowed, threw a blanket over the screaming

voice in her mind, and rolled up her sleeves. "We'd better set to work, then, hadn't we?"

ALISTAIR PICKED UP an old kitchen knife and broke the seal on a thick letter that had arrived just this morning. His name was scrawled on the outside in a large, looping, nearly illegible hand that he recognized immediately. Vale was probably writing to exhort him once again to come to London or some other such nonsense. The viscount was a persistent man, even when shown no encouragement at all.

Alistair sat in the largest of the castle towers. Four tall windows spaced evenly around the curved outside walls let in a wonderful amount of light, making the tower perfect for his study. Three wide tables took up most of the room. Their surfaces were covered with open books, maps, animal and insect specimens, magnifying glasses, paintbrushes, presses for preserving leaves and flowers, various interesting rocks, bark, bird nests, and his pencil sketches. Against the outer walls, between the windows, were glass cases and shelves holding more books, maps, and various journals and scientific papers.

Beside the door was a small fireplace, lit even though the day was warm. Lady Grey was getting on in years, and she enjoyed warming herself on the little rug in front of the fire. She sprawled there, taking her morning nap as Alistair worked behind the largest table, which also served as his desk. Earlier they'd gone on their morning ramble. They no longer walked as far as they used to, and Alistair had been forced to slow his stride in the last couple of weeks to let Lady Grey keep pace. Soon he'd have to leave the old girl behind.

But he'd worry about that another day. Alistair unfolded the letter and perused it as the fire gently crackled. It was early in the morning, and he had no doubt that his unexpected guests of the night before were still sleeping. Despite her claim to be a housekeeper, Mrs. Halifax struck him as more of a society lady. Perhaps she was here on a wager, some other aristocratic lady daring her to beard the revoltingly scarred Sir Alistair in his castle den. The thought was a terrible one, making him ashamed and angry at the same time. But then he remembered that she'd been genuinely shocked by his appearance. That at least wasn't part of some game. And in any case, Lady Vale was not the type of frivolous woman to play such tricks.

Alistair sighed and tossed the letter on the table before him. No mention of Vale's wife's scheme to send him a supposed housekeeper. Instead, the letter was full of Vale's news about the Spinner's Falls traitor and the death of Matthew Horn—a false trail abruptly cut short.

He lightly traced the border of his eye patch as he gazed out the tower window. Six years ago in the American Colonies, Spinner's Falls was the place where the 28th Regiment of Foot had fallen in an ambush. Nearly the entire regiment had been massacred by Wyandot Indians, allies of the French. The few survivors—including Alistair—had been captured and marched through the woods of New England. And when they'd made the Indian camp . . .

He dropped his hand to touch a corner of the letter. He'd not even been a member of the 28th. His was a civilian position. Charged with discovering and describing the flora and fauna of New England, Alistair had been three months from returning to England when he'd had the misfortune of walking into Spinner's Falls. Three months. Had he stayed behind with the rest of the British army in Quebec as originally planned, he wouldn't even have been at Spinner's Falls.

Alistair carefully refolded the letter. Now Vale and another survivor, a Colonial named Samuel Hartley, had evidence that the 28th had been betrayed at Spinner's Falls. That a traitor had given the French and their Wyandot Indian allies the day when they'd pass by Spinner's Falls. Vale and Hartley were convinced that they could find this traitor and eventually expose and punish him. Alistair tapped the letter gently against his desk. Ever since Vale's visit, the thought of a traitor had begun to fester in his mind. That such a man was still free—still *alive*—while so many good men were dead was unbearable.

Three weeks ago, he'd finally taken action. If there was a traitor, he'd almost certainly dealt with the French. Who better to ask about the traitor than a Frenchman? He had a colleague in France, a man named Etienne LeFabvre, who he'd written and asked if he had heard any rumors about Spinner's Falls. Since then, he'd been waiting impatiently for a reply from Etienne. He frowned. Relations with France were terrible, as usual, but surely—

His thoughts were interrupted by the opening of the tower door. Mrs. Halifax entered carrying a tray.

"What the hell're you doing?" he rasped, surprise making his words harsher than he'd intended.

She stopped, her wide, pretty mouth turning down with displeasure. "I've brought you your breakfast, Sir Alistair."

He refrained with effort from asking what she could've

possibly brought him for breakfast. Unless she'd caught the castle mice and fried them up, there wasn't much of anything to eat. He'd dined on the last of the sausages the night before.

She glided forward and made to set the tray on a rather valuable Italian tome on insects.

"Not there."

At his command, she froze, half-bent.

"Ah, just a moment." He hastily cleared a space, stacking papers on the floor beside his chair. "Here will do."

She set the tray down and uncovered a dish. On it reposed two ragged slices of bacon, crisped within an inch of their lives, and three small, hard biscuits. Beside the plate was a large bowl of porridge and a cup of inky black tea.

"I would've brought up a pot of tea," Mrs. Halifax was saying as she busied herself arranging the dishes on his desk, "but you don't seem to have one. A teapot, that is. As it was, I was forced to boil the tea in a cooking pot."

"Broke last month," Alistair muttered. What scheme was this? And was he expected to consume this dreck in front of her?

She looked up, all rosy cheeks and sparkling blue eyes, damn her. "What did?"

"The teapot." Thank God he'd put on his eye patch this morning. "This is most, ah, *kind* of you, Mrs. Halifax, but you needn't have bothered."

"No bother at all," she blatantly lied. He knew full well the state of his kitchen.

He narrowed his eye. "I expect that you'll want to leave this morning—"

"I shall just have to get another, shan't I? A teapot, I

mean," she said as if she'd suddenly gone deaf. "The tea just doesn't taste the same boiled in a cooking pot. I think ceramic teapots are the best."

"I shall order a carriage—"

"There are people who prefer metal—"

"From the village—"

"Silver's quite dear, of course, but a nice little tin teapot—"

"So you can leave me in peace!"

His last words emerged as a bellow. Lady Grey raised her head from the hearth. For a moment, Mrs. Halifax stared at him with large, harebell-blue eyes.

Then she opened her lush mouth and said, "You *can* afford a tin teapot, can't you?"

Lady Grey sighed and turned back to the warmth of the fire.

"Aye, I can afford a tin teapot!" He closed his eye a moment, irritated that he'd let her draw him into her babble. Then he looked at her and took a breath. "But you'll be leaving just as soon as I can—"

"Nonsense."

"What did you say?" he rasped very gently.

She raised her impertinent chin. "I said *nonsense*. You obviously need me. Did you know that you have hardly any food in the castle? Well, of course you *know,* but really it will not do. It will not do at all. I shall do some shopping as well when I go to the village for the teapot."

"I don't *need*—"

"I do hope you don't expect us to live on oats and streaky bacon?" She set her hands on her hips and glared at him in an entirely becoming manner.

He frowned. "Of course I—"

"And the children need some fresh vegetables. I expect you do as well."

"Don't you—"

"I'll go to the village this afternoon, shall I?"

"Mrs. Halifax—"

"And that teapot, do you prefer ceramic or tin?"

"Ceramic, but—"

He was talking to an empty room. She'd already closed the door gently behind her.

Alistair stared at the door. He'd never been so completely routed in all his life—and by a pretty little slip of a woman he'd thought half-witted the night before.

Lady Grey had raised her head at Mrs. Halifax's exit. Now she lay it back down on her paws and seemed to give him a pitying look.

"At least I got to choose the teapot," Alistair muttered defensively.

Lady Grey groaned and turned over.

HELEN CLOSED THE tower door behind her and then couldn't resist a small grin. Ha! She'd definitely won *that* round with Sir Beastly. She hurried down the tower stairs before he could come to the door and call her back. The stairs were old stone, worn and shallow, and the walls of the tower were bare stone as well until she came to a door at the bottom of the stairs. This led to a narrow hall that was dim and musty but at least paneled and carpeted.

She hoped that Sir Alistair's breakfast wasn't too cold, but if it was, it was his own fault. It'd taken her a while to find him this morning. She'd been all over the gloomy upper floors of the castle until it had finally occurred to her that she should try the towers. She should've thought he'd be lurking in an old tower like something out of a tale meant to terrify children. She'd braced herself before opening the door so that she wouldn't react to his appearance. Fortunately, he'd worn an eye patch this morning. But he still let his black hair hang around his shoulders, and she didn't think he'd shaved in a week or more. His jaw had been quite shadowed with stubble. She wouldn't be at all surprised if he kept it that way to intimidate people.

And then there had been his hand.

Helen paused at the memory. She hadn't noticed his hand last night, but this morning when she'd opened the door to the tower, he'd been holding a sheet of paper between his middle two fingers and thumb. His forefinger and little finger were missing on his right hand. What caused such a horrible mutilation? Had he been in some accident? And had this terrible accident also scarred his face and cost his eye? If so, he wouldn't welcome her pity or even sympathy.

She bit her lip at the thought. Her last sight of Sir Alistair gave her a twinge of remorse. He'd been surly and unkempt. Rude and sarcastic. Everything she'd expected after the night before. But there was something else. He'd sat at that huge table, barricaded behind his books and papers and mess and he'd looked . . .

Lonely.

Helen blinked, gazing around the dim little passageway. Well, that was just silly. He'd make a terribly cutting remark if she told him her impression of him. She'd never met a man less likely to take kindly to the concern of another human being. And yet, there it was: He'd seemed lonely to her. He lived all alone, far from civilization in this great dirty castle, his only company a big dog. Could anyone, even a man who seemed to dislike people, be truly happy in such a circumstance?

She shook her head and began marching toward the kitchen again. There was no place in her life at the moment for such sentimental thoughts. She couldn't afford to be swayed by soft emotions. She'd done that once and look where it'd gotten her—fleeing in fear with her children. No, better to be pragmatic about the castle and its master. She had Abigail and Jamie to consider.

Helen rounded the corner and heard shouting from the castle kitchen. Good Lord! What if a tramp or some other villain had invaded the kitchen? Abigail and Jamie were in there alone! She picked up her skirts and ran the rest of the way, bursting into the kitchen quite out of breath.

The sight that met her didn't do anything to calm her fears. A stubby little man was waving his arms and shouting at the children, who were arrayed before him. Abigail held an iron skillet in both hands, resolute, though her face was pale. Behind his sister, Jamie hopped from one foot to the other, his eyes wide and excited.

"—all of you! Thieves and murderers, a-stealin' into places you don't belong! Hangin's too good for you!"

"Out!" Helen bellowed. She advanced on the creature haranguing her children. "Out, I say!"

The little man jumped and whirled at the sound of her voice. He wore a greasy waistcoat over too-big breeches and patched stockings. His hair was a graying ginger, and it stood out in a frizzy cloud on either side of his head.

He had bulging eyes, but he narrowed them at the sight of her. "Who're you?"

Helen drew herself up. "I am Mrs. Halifax, Sir Alistair's

housekeeper. Now, you must remove yourself from this kitchen, or I shall be forced to call Sir Alistair himself."

The little man gaped. "Dinna talk nonsense, woman. Sir Alistair doesn't have a housekeeper. I'm his man. I'd *know* if he had one!"

For a moment, Helen stared at the repulsive creature, nonplussed. She'd begun to think Sir Alistair hadn't any help at all. Indeed, that prospect, dim as it had been, was preferable to the nasty manservant in front of her.

"What is your name?" she finally asked.

The little man threw out his thin chest. "Wiggins."

Helen nodded and folded her arms. The one thing she'd learned in her years in London was not to show fear before bullies. "Well, then, Mr. Wiggins, Sir Alistair may not've had a housekeeper in the past, but he has one now, and I am she."

"Go on with you!"

"I assure you it's true, and what's more, you'd best get used to the idea."

Wiggins scratched his rear end contemplatively. "Well, if'n it's true, you got a wagon load of hard work on yer hands."

"Indeed." Helen softened her tone. The little man had no doubt been startled to find strangers in the castle kitchen. "I hope I can count on your help, Mr. Wiggins."

"Ur," he grunted noncommittally.

She let it go for the moment. "Now. Would you care for some breakfast?"

"Naw." Wiggins shuffled to the hall. "Hisself will be wantin' ta see me and give me his orders for the day, won't he?"

He stomped out of the kitchen.

Abigail set the iron skillet on a table. "That man smells."

"He does indeed," Helen said. "But we shouldn't hold that against him. However, I want you both to stay out of his way when I'm not by your side."

Jamie nodded vigorously, while Abigail merely looked worried.

"Well, enough of that," Helen said briskly. "Let's do the washing up, and then we'll start on the kitchen."

"*We're* going to clean this kitchen?" Jamie gaped at the cobwebs hanging from the ceiling.

"Of course." Helen said it confidently, ignoring the flutter of trepidation in her stomach. The kitchen was *very* dirty. "Now. Let's go fetch some water to wash with."

They'd found the old pump in a corner of the stable yard just this morning. She'd pumped one bucket of water then, but she'd used it all up in making breakfast. Jamie carried the tin bucket as they all tramped out to the stable yard. Helen grasped the pump handle and gave an encouraging smile to the children before hauling it up with both hands. Unfortunately, the pump was rather rusted, and it took a great deal of effort to work it.

Ten minutes later, Helen pushed sweaty hair off her forehead and eyed the half-full bucket.

"It's not very much," Abigail said dubiously.

"Yes, well, it'll do for now," Helen panted. She took the bucket and returned to the kitchen, the children trailing behind.

She set the bucket down and bit her lip. The water had to be heated to wash the dishes, but she'd let the fire go out since breakfast. Only a few embers still glowed in the fireplace ashes.

Mr. Wiggins entered the kitchen as she was standing and staring at the hearth in dismay. The little man looked from her to the pitiful bucket of water and grunted. "Had a grand start, have ye? Why, th' kitchen's so clean it near blinds me eyes t' look at it. Well, never fear. Yer stay is fixin' to be short. Hisself is sendin' me to fetch a carriage from th' village."

Helen straightened in dismay. "I'm sure that won't be necessary, Mr. Wiggins."

The little man merely snorted and left.

"Mama," Abigail said quietly, "if Sir Alistair is sending for a carriage for us to go home in, maybe we don't have to clean the kitchen after all."

Helen felt sudden weariness sweep over her. She wasn't a housekeeper. She didn't know how to clean a kitchen or even know enough to keep the fire burning, it seemed. What was she doing, attempting a task this insurmountable? Perhaps Sir Alistair was right.

Perhaps she should admit defeat and take the carriage away from the castle.

Chapter Three

The black castle was cavernous and gloomy, with winding passages leading into more passages. Truth Teller followed the beautiful young man, and although they walked for long minutes, they did not meet another soul. Finally the young man led Truth Teller to a great dining hall and set before him a meal of roasted meat and fine bread and all manner of exotic fruit. The soldier ate everything gratefully, for it had been years since his vittles had been so fine. All the while Truth Teller ate, the young man sat and smiled and watched him. . . .
— from TRUTH TELLER

Helen let her head loll against the carriage side as they swept around a bend, and the castle disappeared from view.

"It was a very dirty castle," Abigail said from across the carriage.

Helen sighed. "Yes, my love, it was."

A very dirty castle with a surly master—and she'd let them both defeat her. She'd seen movement in the high tower window as they'd tramped out to the waiting rented carriage. No doubt Sir Beastly had been gloating over her rout.

"Our house in London is much nicer," Abigail said. "And maybe the duke will be happy that we've come back."

Helen closed her eyes. *No. No, he wouldn't.* Abigail obviously thought that they'd be returning home to London now, but that wasn't an option. Lister wouldn't welcome them with open arms. He'd steal the children from her and toss her into the street.

And that was if she was lucky.

She looked at Abigail and tried to smile. "We won't be going back to London, dearest one."

Abigail's face fell. "But—"

"We'll just have to find another place to stay." *And hide.*

"I want to go home," Jamie said.

A headache started at her temple. "We can't go home, sweetheart."

Jamie's lower lip protruded. "I want—"

"It's simply not possible." Helen inhaled and then said in a quieter voice, "I'm sorry, my darlings. Mama has an aching head. Let's discuss this later. For now, all you need to know is that we must find another place to stay."

But where else could they go? Castle Greaves might've been filthy and its master impossible, but as a hiding place it'd been perfect. She patted her skirts, feeling for the little leather bag that hung under them. Inside were some coins and quite a few jewels—the nest egg she'd saved from

Lister's gifts. She had money, but finding a place where a single woman with two children wouldn't excite comment was going to be difficult.

"Shall I read to you from the fairy-tale book?" Abigail asked very quietly.

Helen looked at her and tried to smile. Her daughter really was a dear sometimes. "Yes, please. I think I'd like that."

Abigail's face smoothed in relief, and she bent to rummage in the soft bag at her feet.

Beside her, Jamie bounced on his seat. "Read from the story about the man with the iron heart!"

Abigail drew out a bundle of papers and very carefully paged through them until she came to the place she wanted. She cleared her throat and began reading slowly. "Once upon a time, long, long ago, there came four soldiers traveling home after many years of war. . . ."

Helen closed her eyes, letting her daughter's high clear voice wash over her. The fairy-tale "book" she read from was actually a bundle of loose papers. The original book was written in German, and Lady Vale translated the tales for her friend, Lady Emeline Hartley. When the viscountess had sent Helen and her children north, she'd requested that Helen transcribe it so that she might eventually have the translation bound for Lady Emeline. All the long journey into Scotland, Helen had read the stories to the children, and now they were familiar favorites.

Helen glanced out the window. Outside, the purple and green hills rolled by, bringing them closer to the little village of Glenlargo. If she was still Sir Beastly's housekeeper, she could've bought groceries there. Something more appetizing than moldering bacon and oats.

Oh, if only she wasn't so terribly useless! She'd spent her entire adult life as the plaything of a rich gentleman. She'd never been trained in anything practical.

Except that wasn't quite true. Once upon a time, before Lister, before she'd broken ties with her family, when she was still young and innocent, she used to help her father as he made his rounds. Papa had been a doctor—quite a successful one—and sometimes when he visited patients, she had accompanied him. Oh, not to help with the doctoring—that was considered too distasteful a task for a young girl—but she'd kept a little notebook in which she'd written his thoughts on the various patients they attended, kept a calendar of appointments, and made lists.

Lots of lists.

She'd been Papa's helper, his organizer of lists. The one who kept his life and business in order. It hadn't been a big job, but it had been an important one. And, now that she thought about it, wasn't that really what most housekeepers were? Certainly they needed to know how to clean and run a house, but didn't they often delegate these jobs to *other* people?

Helen sat up so suddenly that Abigail stuttered to a stop. "What is it, Mama?"

"Hush, darling. Let me think. I have an idea." The carriage had reached the outskirts of Glenlargo. It was a tiny village in comparison to London, but it held everything a small, isolated community needed: shops, craftsmen, and people who could be hired.

Helen half stood in the swaying carriage and pounded on the roof. "Stop! Oh, stop the carriage!"

The carriage jerked to a stop, nearly throwing her back on the seat.

"What are we doing?" Jamie asked excitedly.

And Helen couldn't help but grin at him. "It's time to enlist reinforcements."

ALISTAIR SPENT THE afternoon in his tower writing—or at least trying to write. Like many previous days, the words simply refused to form. Instead he filled a basket with crumpled sheets of paper, each covered in the crossed-out attempts at an essay on badgers. He couldn't even find the first sentence. Writing had once been as easy as breathing for him, and now . . . now he feared he would never again finish an essay. He felt like a broken fool.

When four o'clock came and he noticed that Lady Grey had wandered from the tower, he took it as a good excuse to abandon his wretched attempts and go looking for the dog. Besides, he hadn't eaten anything since that execrable morning meal.

The castle was silent as he made his way down the winding tower stairs. It was nearly always silent, of course, but last night, when Mrs. Halifax and her children had occupied his home, it had seemed less dead. He shook his head at the morbid thought. He'd watched the woman leave this morning and had rejoiced at once again being virtually alone—Wiggins hardly bothered him at all. It was good to be alone. Good to not be interrupted at work.

When he could work.

Alistair scowled as he reached the hallway, and strode to his own rooms first. Lady Grey liked to nap in a spot of sunlight under the windows in the afternoons. But his rooms were as he'd left them this morning: empty and untidy. He frowned at his unmade bed, the coverlet and sheets trailing on the floor. Hmm. Perhaps a housekeeper wouldn't have been such a bad idea after all.

He returned to the hall and called, "Lady Grey!"

No scratch of claws on stone floor heralded her approach.

Most of the other rooms were closed off on this floor, so he proceeded to the next. Here there was an old sitting room he sometimes used. He looked, but Lady Grey wasn't lying on either of the overstuffed settees. Farther down the hall was the room he'd given to Mrs. Halifax. He glanced in and didn't learn anything besides the fact that her bed had been made. She might not've ever been here at all, so forlorn did the room look. From outside he thought he heard the sound of her carriage pulling away again. Fanciful nonsense. He continued his search. On the main floor, he checked all the rooms without success, ending in the library.

"Lady Grey!"

He stood staring at the dusty library a moment. There was a patch of afternoon sun where a curtain had fallen and never been replaced, and sometimes she would nap here. But not today. Alistair frowned. Lady Grey was over a decade old and noticeably slowing down.

Dammit.

He turned and strode toward the kitchen. Lady Grey didn't usually go there without him. She and Wiggins didn't get on, and the kitchen was where the manservant hung about most often. In fact—

He halted abruptly at the sound of voices. High, childish voices. He wasn't being fanciful now—there were children in his kitchen. And the odd thing—the completely unexpected thing—was that his first emotion was gladness. They hadn't left him after all. His castle wasn't really dead.

Of course, that was followed very quickly with outrage. How dare she defy his command? She should be halfway to Edinburgh by now. He'd order another carriage, and he'd pack her pretty arse on it himself if he had to this time. There was no room in his castle, in his life, for a too-attractive housekeeper and her pair of brats. Alistair started forward, his intent focused, his stride firm.

And then the childish voices clarified into words.

". . . *can't* go back to London, Jamie," the girl was saying.

"Don't see why not," the boy replied in a mutinous voice.

"Because of *him*. Mama said so."

Alistair frowned. Mrs. Halifax couldn't return to London because of a man? Who? Her husband? She'd presented herself as a widow, but if her husband was still alive and she'd fled him . . . Dammit. The man might've hurt her. There were very few things a woman could do if she married badly, but fleeing her husband was one of them. This put a different angle on things.

Which wasn't to say that he had to welcome her back with open arms. Alistair felt a wicked smile curve his lips.

He sobered and entered the kitchen. The children were at the far end of the room, squatting by the hearth. At his appearance, they both rose hastily, turning guilty faces toward him. Revealed between them was Lady Grey, lying before the small fire. She was on her back, her large paws in the air. She turned a sheepish face toward him, her ears flopping comically upside down, but she made no move to rise. Why should she? Quite obviously she'd been receiving the adoration of the children.

Humph.

The boy stepped forward. "'Tisn't her fault, really! She's a nice dog. We were just petting her. Don't be angry."

What kind of ogre did this child think him? Alistair scowled and advanced toward them. "Where is your mother?"

The boy glanced over his shoulder at the outside kitchen door and backed up a step as he talked. "In the stable yard."

What was she doing in the stable yard of all places? Bathing his gelding, Griffin? Winding daisies in his mane? "And what are you two doing here?"

The girl moved around her brother so that her body shielded his. She stood very stiff, her thin little chest nearly quivering with tension. "We came back."

He cocked an eyebrow at her. She looked like a martyr ready for the torch. "Why?"

She looked at him with her mother's blue eyes. "Because you need us."

He halted his advance. "What?"

She drew in a breath and spoke carefully. "Your castle is dirty and awful, and you need us to make it nice."

ABIGAIL STARED UP at Sir Alistair's face. Sometimes, on the carriage ride to Scotland, they'd passed huge stones, planted upright in fields, standing all by themselves. Mama had said they were called *standing stones* and that some ancient people had put them there, but no one knew why. Sir Alistair was like one of those standing stones—large and hard and sort of scary. His legs went on for miles, and his shoulders were wide and his face . . . She swallowed.

He had a dark beard that was patchy, because it didn't grow on the scars on one side of his face. The scars ran through his beard, red and ugly. He'd covered his empty eye socket today with an eye patch. She was grateful for the eye patch, otherwise she might not have been able to look him in the face at all. His one eye was light brown, the color of tea without milk, and he looked down at her like she was an insect. A beetle, perhaps. One of those horrid black ones that scuttled away when someone overturned a rock.

"Huh," Sir Alistair said. He cleared his throat with a grating, rumbling sound. Then he frowned. When he frowned, the red scars twisted on his cheek.

Abigail looked down. She wasn't sure what to do next. She should apologize to him for screaming at him last night, but she didn't quite have the courage. Her new apron was pinned to her bodice, and she plucked at it. She'd never worn an apron before, but Mama had bought one for herself and one for Abigail in the village. She said they'd need them if they were to set the castle kitchen to rights. Abigail didn't think cleaning a castle would be nearly as fun as Mama was trying to pretend.

She peeked up at Sir Alistair. The corners of his mouth were turned down, but oddly his frown wasn't half as frightening as it'd been the night before. She cocked her head. If Sir Alistair hadn't been a very big, very stern sort of gentleman, she might've thought that he didn't know what to do next, either.

"There was hardly any food in the pantry this morning," she said.

"I know." His mouth went flat.

Jamie had gone back to the big gray dog by the fire. He'd been the one to see her when they'd come in the kitchen. He'd run over to pet the dog, despite Abigail's warnings. Jamie adored dogs of all kinds, and he never seemed to think that they might bite him. Abigail always thought about being bitten when she saw a strange dog.

She had a sudden longing for home, in London, where she knew everyone and where everything was familiar. If they were at home right now, she and Jamie would be having tea and bread with Miss Cummings. Although she'd never been very fond of Miss Cummings, the thought of her pinched, narrow face and the bread and butter she always served made Abigail's chest ache. Mama said they might never return to London.

Now Sir Alistair was frowning down at the big dog as if he might be cross with her.

"Mama'll be in soon," Abigail said to distract him.

"Ah," he said. The old dog put a paw on his boot. Sir Alistair glanced up at Abigail, and she stepped back. He was so stern-looking. "What are your names?"

"I'm Abigail," she said, "and that's Jamie."

"We're to have tea when Mama comes in," Jamie said. He didn't seem at all nervous at Sir Alistair's presence. But then he was blissfully rubbing the dog's ears.

Sir Alistair grunted.

"And eggs and ham and bread and jam," Jamie recited. He often forgot things, but not things that had to do with food.

"She's going to make some for you as well," Abigail said cautiously.

"She isn't a very good cook," Jamie said.

Abigail frowned. "Jamie!"

"Well, she isn't! She's never done it before, has she? We always—"

"Hush!" Abigail whispered fiercely. She was afraid that Jamie was about to say that they'd always had their own servants. He was so stupid sometimes, even if he was only five.

Jamie looked at her with wide eyes, and then they both looked at Sir Alistair.

He was hunched down, scratching the dog under her chin. Abigail noticed that his hand was missing two fingers. She shivered in disgust. Maybe he hadn't heard them?

Jamie rubbed his nose. "She's a right nice dog."

The dog tilted her head and waved a great paw in the air as if she'd understood Jamie.

Sir Alistair nodded. "That she is."

"I've never seen one so big." Jamie began stroking the dog again. "What kind is she?"

"A deerhound," Sir Alistair said. "Her name is Lady Grey. My ancestors used hounds like her to hunt deer."

"Coo!" Jamie said. "Have you ever hunted deer with her?"

Sir Alistair shook his head. "Deer are rare in these parts. The only thing Lady Grey hunts anymore is sausages."

Abigail carefully bent and touched Lady Grey's warm head. She made sure to stay far enough away from Sir Alistair so that she didn't accidentally brush him. The dog licked her fingers with a long tongue. "She's still a nice dog, even if it's only sausages she hunts."

Sir Alistair turned his head so he could see her out of his good eye.

Abigail froze, her fingers clutching Lady Grey's wiry fur. She was so close to him that she could see lighter bits of brown like a star around the center of his eye. They were almost gold-colored, those bits. Sir Alistair wasn't smiling, but he wasn't frowning anymore, either. His face was still horrible to look at, but there was something almost sad about it, too.

She drew in her breath to say something.

At that moment, the outside kitchen door blew open. "Who's ready for tea?" Mama asked.

HELEN STOPPED SHORT at the sight of Sir Alistair kneeling with her children by the hearth. *Oh, dear.* She'd rather hoped he'd not discover their return until after she'd made some tea. Not only might a meal pacify him, but she could also use a bite or two before confronting Sir Beastly. Shopping was much harder work than she'd first supposed.

But a respite was not to be. Sir Alistair rose to his feet slowly, his worn boots scraping on the hearth's flagstones. Goodness! She'd seen him just this morning, but already she'd forgotten how tall he was—how big in general, really, especially standing next to Abigail and Jamie— and how intimidating. That was probably why she was just a little bit short of breath.

He smiled, and the expression made the back of her neck tickle. "Mrs. Halifax."

She swallowed and tilted her chin. "Sir Alistair."

He prowled toward her, athletic, male, and rather dangerous. "I confess your presence in my kitchen is something of a surprise."

"Is it?"

"I believe"—he circled behind her, and she twisted her neck to try and keep him in her sight—"that I dismissed you just this morning."

Helen cleared her throat. "About that—"

"I'm almost certain, in fact, that I saw you leave in a carriage."

"Well, I—"

"A carriage I hired to take you away." Was that his breath against the back of her neck?

She turned, but he was several paces away, by the fireplace now. "I explained to the driver that you'd made a mistake."

"*I* made a mistake?" His gaze dropped to the basket she carried in her hands. "You've been to the village, then, madam?"

She tilted her chin. No use letting him intimidate her. "Yes, I have."

"And you've bought eggs and ham and bread and jam." He stalked straight toward her, his long stride eating up the few feet between them.

"Yes, I have." She shied away—entirely inadvertently! —and found herself against the kitchen table.

"And what sort of mistake did you tell the carriage driver *I'd* made?" He plucked the basket from her hand.

"Oh!" She reached for her basket, but he carelessly held it up out of reach.

"Tut, tut, Mrs. Halifax. You were about to tell me how you convinced the driver to bring you back here." He took the ham out of the basket and set it on the kitchen table. "Did you bribe the man?"

"Certainly not." She watched him worriedly as he placed the bread and jam beside the ham. Was he angry? Amused? The problem was she simply couldn't tell. She expelled an exasperated breath. "I told him that you were confused."

He looked at her. "Confused."

If the table hadn't been at her back, she might've fled. "Yes. Confused. I said I only needed the carriage to do my shopping in Glenlargo."

"Is that so?" He'd emptied the basket by now and was examining the contents laid out on the table. Besides the jam, ham, bread, and eggs, she'd purchased tea, a lovely brown-glazed teapot, butter, four nice round apples, a bunch of carrots, a wedge of creamy yellow cheese, and a herring.

He turned his gaze to her. "What a magnificent feast. Did you use your own money?"

Helen blushed. Naturally, she'd had to use her own money. "Well, I—"

"How very generous of you, madam," he rasped. "I don't think I've ever heard tell before of a housekeeper using her own funds for her master."

"I'm sure you'll repay me—"

"Are you?" he murmured.

She set her hands on her hips and blew a lock of hair out of her eyes. This afternoon had been the most trying of her entire life. "Yes, I'm sure. You'll repay me because I begged and bullied that wretched driver into stopping in Glenlargo. Then I had to find the shops, wheedle the baker to reopen his shop—he closes at noon, would you believe?—bargain the butcher down from his quite scandalous prices, and tell the grocer I wasn't going to buy wormy apples." She didn't even mention the task that'd taken up most of her time in the village. "And after that I had to persuade the carriage driver into bringing us back here and helping me unload the carriage. So, yes, the very least you could do is repay me!"

A corner of those wide sensuous lips twitched.

Helen leaned forward, on the verge of violence. "And don't you dare laugh at me!"

"I wouldn't dream of it." He reached for a knife in a drawer. "Abigail, can you put the kettle on for tea by yourself?" He began to slice the bread.

"Yes, sir." Abigail jumped to help.

Helen let her arms fall, feeling a bit deflated. "I want to try it again. The housekeeping, I mean."

"And I, as the master of the house, am to have no say in the matter, I see. No, don't touch that." This last was directed at her as she began to unwrap the ham. "It'll have to be boiled, and that'll take hours."

"Well, really."

"Yes, really, Mrs. Halifax." He glanced at her with that light brown eye. "You can butter the bread. I'm assuming, of course, that you are capable of buttering bread?"

She didn't bother replying to that insulting remark but merely took up a butter knife and began applying butter. His mood seemed to have lightened, but he still hadn't indicated if he'd let her and the children stay. Helen bit her lip, darting a sideways glance at him. He looked perfectly content slicing bread. She blew out a breath. Easy for him to be at ease; he didn't have to worry if he'd have a roof over his head tonight.

Sir Alistair didn't speak again for a bit but sliced and handed her bread to butter. Abigail had brought out the tea, and now she rinsed the new teapot with hot water before filling it. Soon they all sat down to a meal of tea, buttered bread, jam, apples, and cheese. It wasn't until Helen bit into her second slice of bread that she realized how very odd this might look to anyone walking in. The master of the castle eating with his housekeeper and her children in the kitchen.

She glanced at Sir Alistair and found him watching her. His long black hair fell over his brow and eye patch, giving him the appearance of a surly highwayman. He smiled—not very nicely—and she was put on the alert.

"I've been wondering something, Mrs. Halifax," he rasped in his broken voice.

She swallowed. "Yes?"

"What, exactly, was your position in the dowager Viscountess Vale's household?"

Damn. "Well, I did do some housekeeping."

Technically true since Lister had set her up in her own house. Of course, she'd had a paid housekeeper. . . .

"But you weren't the official housekeeper, I'm thinking, or Lady Vale would've said so in her letter."

Helen hastily took another bite of bread so she could think.

Sir Alistair watched her in that disconcerting way, making her quite self-conscious. Other men had stared at her before, she was considered a beauty, and it was only false modesty not to admit the fact. And, of course, as the Duke of Lister's mistress, she'd been an object of curiosity. So she was used to being stared at by men. But Sir Alistair's gaze was different. Those other men had looked at her with lust or speculation or crass curiosity, but they hadn't been looking at her really. They'd been looking at what she represented to them: physical love or a valuable prize or an object to be gawked at. When Sir Alistair stared at her, well, he was looking at *her*. Helen the woman. Which was rather disconcerting. It was almost as if she were naked before him.

"You certainly weren't the cook," he murmured now, interrupting her thoughts. "I think we've established that."

She shook her head.

"Perhaps you were a type of paid companion?"

She swallowed. "Yes, I think you might call my position that."

"And yet I've never heard tell of a companion who was allowed to keep her children with her."

Helen glanced at the children across the table. Jamie was intent on devouring an apple, but Abigail looked back and forth between Helen and Sir Alistair with a worried expression.

Helen threw the abominable man her best smile along with a conversational bomb. "Have I told you about the two footmen, three maids, and the cook I hired in town today?"

MRS. HALIFAX WAS the most astonishing woman, Alistair reflected as he deliberately set down his teacup. She was bent on staying at Castle Greaves, despite his inhospitality; on buying teapots and food; on, in fact, becoming his housekeeper of all things; and now she'd hired an entire staff of servants.

She quite took his breath away.

"You've hired half a dozen servants," he said slowly.

Her brows drew together, making two small lines in her otherwise smooth forehead. "Yes."

"Servants I neither want nor need."

"I think there can be no question that you need them," she replied. "I've dealt with Mr. Wiggins. He seems unreliable."

"Wiggins *is* unreliable. He's also cheap. Your servants will expect to be paid well, won't they?" Grown men had been known to flee when he spoke thus.

But not she. She tilted up her softly rounded chin. "Yes."

Fascinating. She appeared to have no fear of him. "What if I don't have the money?"

Her beautiful blue eyes widened. Had that thought never occurred to her? That a man who lived in a castle might not have servants because he couldn't afford them?

"I . . . I don't know," she stammered.

"I do have the money to hire servants if I wished to." He smiled kindly. "I don't."

Actually, Alistair supposed he could be called rich, if the reports from his man of business were to be believed. Investments he'd made before he set off for the American Colonies had done very well. Then, too, his book describing the flora and fauna of New England had been a rather spectacular success. So, yes, he had money to hire a half dozen servants—or dozens more if he cared. Ironic, really, considering that he'd never set out to make a fortune.

"Why not hire servants if you have the money?" She seemed honestly perplexed.

Alistair leaned back in his ancient kitchen chair. "Why

should I spend my money on servants that are useless to me?" He didn't add, servants who would no doubt loiter in the halls to stare at him and his scars.

"Cooks aren't useless," Jamie objected.

Alistair raised his eyebrows at the lad. Jamie sat across from him, his elbows flat on the table, a slice of bread with jam between his hands.

"Indeed?"

"Not if they can make steak pie," the boy pointed out. He had jam smeared on either side of his face. There was jam on the table in front of him as well. "Or custard."

Alistair felt his mouth quirk. Warm custard, fresh from the oven, had been a favorite of his as well when he'd been Jamie's age. "Can this cook make steak pie and custard?"

"I believe so," Mrs. Halifax said primly.

"Pleeease may we keep the cook?" Jamie's eyes were wide and earnest.

"Jamie!" Abigail chided. Her eyes weren't pleading at all. Interesting.

"I don't think Mama can make a steak pie. Do you?" Jamie whispered hoarsely to his sister. "At least not a proper one."

Alistair glanced sideways at Mrs. Halifax. A pretty blush was creeping up her cheeks. It had spread down as well; disappearing under a gauze fichu she had wrapped about her neck and tucked into her elegant bodice. She caught his gaze, her eyes wide and blue and a little sad. The sight of those eyes, even more than the tender skin at her throat, caused him a sudden and altogether unwelcome jolt of desire.

Alistair pushed back from the table and surged to his

feet. "I'll give the cook—and you, Mrs. Halifax—a week in which to prove yourselves. One week. If I'm not convinced of the usefulness of cooks and housekeepers by then, you'll all go. Understand?"

The housekeeper nodded, and for a moment he felt a tiny twinge of guilt when he saw her stricken look. Then his mouth twisted at his own idiocy. "If you'll excuse me, madam, I have work to do. Come, Lady Grey."

He slapped his thigh and the dog got slowly to her feet. He strode from the kitchen without a backward glance.

Damnable woman! Coming to his castle and questioning and demanding and taking his time when all he wanted was to be left alone. He took the tower stairs two at a time and then had to pause and wait for Lady Grey. She was climbing the stairs slowly and stiffly as if her legs pained her. The sight made him even angrier. Why? Why did everything have to change? Was it too much to ask to be left to write his books in peace?

He sighed and climbed back down the stairs to Lady Grey. "Come on, lass." He bent and gently scooped her against his chest. He could feel her heartbeat under his hands and the trembling in her legs. She was heavy, but Alistair held the big dog in his arms as he ascended the tower stairs. Once in the tower, he knelt and set her in her favorite place on the rug before the fire.

"Nothing to be ashamed of," he whispered as he stroked her ears. "You're a brave lass, you are, and if you need a bit of help up the stairs, well, I'm glad to oblige."

Lady Grey sighed and laid her head on the rug.

Alistair stood and walked to the tower window that overlooked the back of the castle grounds. There was an old garden there, terraced in steps that led down to a stream. Beyond, rolling purple and green hills met the horizon. Vegetation overgrew the garden, falling down the buttressing walls and crowding the paths. It hadn't been tended in years. Not since he'd left for the Colonies.

He'd been born and raised in this castle. He didn't remember his mother, who had died giving birth to a stillborn baby girl when he wasn't quite three. His mother's death might've infused the castle with gloom, but though she'd been well loved, it hadn't. He'd grown up running wild over the hills, fishing with his father in the stream and arguing history and philosophy with Sophia, his older sister. Alistair smiled wryly. Sophia had usually won the arguments, not only because she was the older by five years, but also because she was the better scholar.

Back then, he'd thought that eventually he, too, would marry. He'd bring his bride to the castle and raise another generation of Munroes, just like all his ancestors. But that hadn't happened. He'd been betrothed at three and twenty to a girl named Sarah, but she'd died of a fever before they could wed. Grief had kept him from forming another alliance for years, and then somehow his studies had taken precedence. He'd traveled to the Colonies when he was eight and twenty and had stayed there three years before returning, a prematurely aged one and thirty.

And after he'd returned from the Colonies . . .

He traced the eye patch on his cheek as he gazed out at his countryside. It'd been too late by then, hadn't it? He'd lost not only his eye, but also his soul. What remained was not fit for civilized company, and he knew it. He stayed far from other people to protect himself and, perhaps more importantly, to protect them. He'd seen sorrow, smelled death's rotting breath, and knew that savagery lurked close beneath the thin veil of society. His very face reminded others that the basic animal was very near. That it might pounce on them as well.

He'd been resigned, content if not boisterously joyful. He had his studies; he had the hills and his stream. He had Lady Grey to keep him company.

And then *she* had arrived.

He didn't need an officious, too-beautiful housekeeper to barge into his home and life. He didn't need her changing his retreat. He didn't need this sudden desire that hardened his muscles and made his skin itch with irritation. She would be appalled—*revolted*—if she knew what she did to him physically.

Alistair turned from the window in disgust. Soon enough, she'd tire of playing housekeeper and find some other place to hide from whatever—or whoever—she was running from. In the meantime, he would make sure she didn't keep him from his work.

"It's been over a fortnight," Algernon Downey, the Duke of Lister, said in an even, controlled voice. "I ordered you to hire the best men in London. Why can't they find one woman traveling with two children?"

He swung around on the last syllable and pinned Henderson, his longtime secretary, with a cold stare. They were in Lister's study, an elegant room newly redecorated in white, black, and dark red. It was a room appropriate for a duke and the fifth richest man in England. At the far end, Henderson sat in a chair before Lister's spacious desk. Henderson was a dry little man, mainly bones and sinew, with a pair of half-glasses perched on his forehead.

He had an open notebook on his knee and a pencil with which to record notes in one shaking hand.

"I admit it is very distressing, Your Grace, and I do apologize," Henderson said in his whispery voice. He thumbed through his notebook as if to find the answer for his own incompetence there. "But we must remember that Mrs. Fitzwilliam has no doubt chosen to disguise herself and the children. And, after all, England is a very large place."

"I'm well aware of how large England is, Henderson. I want results, not excuses."

"Of course, Your Grace."

"My resources—my men, money, contacts—should have found her by now."

Henderson gave several quick birdlike bobs of his head. "Naturally, Your Grace. Of course, we have been able to trace her as far as the road north."

Lister made one sharp cutting motion with his hand. "That was nearly a week ago. She may've laid a false trail, gone west to Wales or Cornwall, or for all we know, caught a ship for the Colonies. No. This is simply unacceptable. If the men we have on her now can't find her, then hire new ones. Immediately."

"Quite, Your Grace." Henderson licked his lips nervously. "I shall see that it is done at once. Now, as to the duchess's trip to Bath . . ."

Henderson droned on about Lister's wife's travel plans, but the duke hardly listened. He'd been the Duke of Lister since the age of seven; his title was centuries old. He sat in the House of Lords and owned vast estates, mines, and ships. Gentlemen of all ranks respected and feared him. And yet one woman—the daughter of a quack physician, no less!—thought she could simply leave him, and what was more, take his bastard offspring with her.

Unacceptable. The entire thing was simply unacceptable.

Lister strolled to the tall windows of his study, which were draped in white and black striped silk. He'd have her found, have her and his children brought back, and then he would impress upon her how very, very stupid it was to cross him. No one crossed him and lived to gloat about it.

No one.

Chapter Four

When Truth Teller could eat no more, the beautiful
young man showed him to a large, handsomely
decorated room and bade him good night. There the
soldier slept without dreaming and in the morning
woke to find his host standing beside his bed.
"I have been looking for a brave fellow to do me a
task," said the young man. "Are you such a fellow?"
"Yes," said Truth Teller.
The beautiful young man smiled. "That we
shall see. . . ."
—from TRUTH TELLER

Mrs. McCleod, the new cook, was a tall dour woman who
hardly spoke, Helen reflected the next afternoon. The
woman had once cooked for a great house in Edinburgh,
but she hadn't liked the rush and noise of the city and
had retired to the nearby town of Glenlargo where her
brother was the baker. Privately, Helen wondered if Mrs.
McCleod hadn't become bored with the slow life of Glen-

largo and her brother's bakery, for she certainly accepted the job as cook quickly enough.

"I hope the kitchen meets with your approval," she said now, twisting her apron in her hands.

The cook was nearly the height of a man, and her face was wide and flat. She was expressionless, but her large reddened hands moved lightly and swiftly as she rolled out pastry on the kitchen table. "Hearth needs sweeping."

"Ah, yes." Helen looked nervously at the giant fireplace. She'd been up at the crack of dawn, scrubbing the kitchen as best she could in preparation for the cook, but she hadn't had time to clean the fireplace. Her back ached terribly now, and her hands were raw from the hot water and harsh lye soap. "I'll have one of the maids do it, shall I?"

Mrs. McCleod expertly flipped the pastry into a pie plate and began trimming the edges.

Helen swallowed. "Well, I have other matters to attend to. I'll return in an hour or so to see how you're getting on, shall I?"

The cook shrugged. She was arranging vegetables and pieces of meat in the pie.

Helen nodded, just to give the appearance that she knew what she was doing, and went into the hallway. There she took out a small notebook and tiny pencil. They'd been the first items she'd bought in Glenlargo yesterday. Opening the notebook, she flipped to the third page and wrote, *clean hearth*. This notation was at the bottom of what was becoming a rather long list that included among other things *air library, clear ivy from windows in sitting room, polish hall floor,* and *find the good silverware.*

Helen put away the notebook and pencil, smoothed her hair, and continued on her way to the dining room. This, she'd decided, would be the first room to be completely set to rights in the castle. That way, Sir Beastly could enjoy a properly cooked dinner tonight and, more importantly, realize how very useful it was to have a housekeeper. She hadn't actually seen the master of the castle all morning. When she'd brought his breakfast to the tower room, he'd yelled through the door to leave it outside. She very much hoped he wasn't going to sulk in his tower and then throw them all out of the castle in a fit of ill temper tonight. All the more important to have the dining room at least cleaned.

But when Helen rounded the corner into the dining room, the sight that met her eyes was pure chaos. One of the maids was shrieking and covering her head with her apron. The other maid brandished a broom as she chased a bird about the room. Jamie and Abigail were helping the maid with the broom, and the two footmen—young lads from the village—were doubled over with laughter.

For a moment, Helen gaped in horror. *Why?* Why must every single thing be so hard? Then she shook herself. Aching back, difficult servants, filthy castle, it simply didn't matter. *She* was the one in charge here. If she couldn't bring order to this scene, no one else would do it. And if she couldn't bring order, then Sir Alistair would dismiss her and the children in the coming week. It was as simple as that. She hurried to the windows that lined the far wall of the dining room. They were made of ancient diamond-paned glass, and most were immovable, but she found one with a catch and shoved it open.

"Chase it over here," she called to the maid with the broom.

The girl, a sturdy redhead who obviously had a level

head on her shoulders, obediently did so, and several frantic minutes later, the bird found freedom.

Helen slammed the window shut and latched it.

"Now, then." She turned to her troops and took a breath. "What happened?"

"It came out the chimney!" Jamie exclaimed. He was so excited his hair was on end, and he was quite red in the face. "Nellie was sweeping it"—he pointed to the maid now removing her apron from her face—"and the bird fell down with a heap of soot."

A large mound of soot and what looked like an ancient bird's nest lay on the hearth.

"Gave me ever such a turn, mum," Nellie concurred.

"And then you stood there and yelled like a banshee while it flew about the room." The red-headed girl had the broom over one shoulder like a musket and her other hand on her hip.

"Oh, will ye now be holdin' it over me, Meg Campbell, that ye know how to chase a bird with a broom?" Nellie shot back.

The maids started arguing, while the footmen guffawed.

Helen felt a headache begin to pound at her temple. "Enough!"

The cacophony of voices silenced and all eyes turned toward her.

"You"—Helen pointed at the tallest footman—"go to the kitchen and sweep out the fireplace."

"But that's a lass's job," the boy objected.

"Well, you're doing it today," Helen said. "And mind it's well swept and scrubbed."

"Aw," the tall footman groaned, but he went from the room.

Helen turned to the remaining servants. "Meg, come help me polish the dining table. You two"—she gestured to the other maid and the shorter footman—"finish cleaning that chimney. We have to get it clear if we're to have a fire in here tonight without setting the room ablaze."

They worked all through the afternoon, cleaning, sweeping, polishing, and even taking the rugs and curtains out to beat them in the wind. By six o'clock, the dining room was as neat as a pin and a fire roared in the fireplace, though it did still smoke a little.

Helen looked about, one hand massaging the ache at the small of her back. What a tremendous chore! She'd never take a housemaid's work for granted again. At the same time, she couldn't help a pleased smile spreading over her face. She'd set her mind to it, and she'd done it! Helen thanked the maids and the two rather worn footmen and sent them off to the kitchen for a well-deserved cup of tea.

"What shall we do now, Mama?" Abigail asked. The children had been wonderful workers all afternoon. Even Jamie had helped polish the windows.

Helen smiled at them. "Now we go wash up so that we can properly greet Sir Alistair when he comes down for his supper."

"And we'll eat in the dining room with him!" Jamie exclaimed.

Helen felt a pang. "No, dear, we'll have a lovely supper in the kitchen."

"But why?" Jamie asked.

"Because Mama's the housekeeper, and it's not proper

for us to eat with Sir Alistair," Abigail said. "We're servants now. We eat in the kitchen."

Helen nodded. "That's right. But the meat pie will taste just as good in the kitchen, don't you think? Now, let's tidy up, shall we?"

But forty-five minutes later, when Helen and the children again came down the stairs, Sir Alistair was nowhere to be found.

"I think he's still in his tower," Abigail said, frowning at the ceiling overhead as if she could see the master of the castle four floors above. "Perhaps he sleeps up there, too."

Both Helen and Jamie glanced instinctively up at the ceiling. Mrs. McCleod had said that she planned supper for seven o'clock. If Sir Beastly didn't appear soon, his supper would be cold, and, more importantly, he might offend the only qualified cook for miles and miles.

That decided it. Helen turned to the children. "Darlings, why don't you go to the kitchen and see if one of the maids can make you tea?"

Abigail looked at her. "But what will you do, Mama?"

Helen straightened her fresh apron. "Fetch Sir Alistair from his den."

THE KNOCK ON the tower door came just as Alistair lit the candles. The light was fading, and he was in the midst of trying to record his observations on badgers. This was for his next great work: a comprehensive listing of the flora and fauna of Scotland, England, and Wales. It was a huge undertaking, one that he felt without vanity would place him in the ranks of the great scientists of his age. And today he'd been able to write for the first time in weeks—months, if he was honest with himself. He'd eagerly begun the work over three years ago, but for the last year or more, his work had slowed and faltered. He'd been beset by a sort of lethargy that made writing extremely difficult. Indeed, for the last few weeks he'd made barely any progress at all.

Today, however, he'd risen knowing exactly what to put down in his manuscript. It was as if a breath of reviving wind had been blown into his lungs by some unseen god. He'd spent the day in intense writing and sketching, accomplishing more than he had in months.

So when the knock interrupted his labors, he was not pleased.

"What?" he growled at the door. It was bolted so a certain female couldn't just swan in at will.

"Your supper is ready," she called back.

"Bring it here, then," he replied absently. Sketching a badger's nose could be quite difficult.

There was a short silence, and he thought for a moment that she'd gone away.

Then she rattled the doorknob. "Sir Alistair, your supper is laid upon the table downstairs in the dining room."

"Nonsense," he shot back. "I've seen my dining room. It hasn't been used in near a decade, and it's filthy. It's not fit for man or beast to eat in."

"I've spent all this day cleaning it."

That gave him pause, and he stared suspiciously at the tower door. Had she really spent the day scrubbing out his dining room? It'd be a Herculean task if so. For a moment, he felt a flicker of guilt.

Then he regained his good sense. "If what you say is true, Mrs. Halifax, and I really have a newly cleaned dining room, I thank you. I'm sure at some point I may even use it. But not tonight. Go away."

The silence this time stretched for so long that he was convinced she'd gone away. He'd returned to sketching the badger and was working on the difficult bit around the eyes when a great *thump!* shook the door. Alistair's hand jerked and the pencil tore through the paper.

He scowled at the ruined sketch.

"Sir Alistair." Mrs. Halifax's voice came through the door, sounding very much as if she might be gritting her teeth. "Either you come out at once and eat the delicious supper that Mrs. McCleod spent all day cooking in the dining room that I and the other servants spent all day cleaning, or I shall instruct the footmen to break down this door."

Alistair raised his eyebrows.

"I have scrubbed and polished, beaten and swept all the day long," Mrs. Halifax continued.

He set his pencil down, rose from his chair, and approached the door.

"And I think it only common courtesy to—" she was saying as he opened the door. She stopped, mouth agape, and looked up at him.

Alistair smiled and leaned a shoulder against the door frame. "Good evening, Mrs. Halifax."

She started to back up a step but then caught herself, although her wide blue eyes were wary. "Good evening, Sir Alistair."

He loomed over her to see if she would flee. "I understand you have supper waiting downstairs for me."

She clutched her hands but stood firm. "Yes."

"Then I shall be pleased to dine with you."

Her eyes narrowed. "You can't dine with me. I'm your housekeeper."

He shrugged and slapped his thigh for Lady Grey. "I dined with you yesterday."

"But that was in the kitchen!"

"It's proper for me to eat with you in my kitchen but not in my dining room? Your logic escapes me, Mrs. Halifax."

"I don't think—"

Lady Grey passed them and started down the stairs. Alistair gestured for the housekeeper to precede him. "And I expect your children to dine with us as well."

"Abigail and Jamie?" she asked as if she might have other offspring about the place.

"Yes."

She was below him on the stairs, but she shot a look over her shoulder that clearly stated that she thought he'd gone mad. And perhaps he had. Children never dined with adults, at least not in his level of society.

His beautiful housekeeper was still protesting when they made the hall outside the dining room, although Alistair was fairly sure she'd given up the idea of dining in the kitchen by then. Her objections were merely stubbornness now.

He nodded to the children when he saw them hovering in the hall. "Shall we go in?"

Jamie readily ran into the dining room, but Abigail frowned and glanced to her mother for guidance.

Mrs. Halifax pursed her lips, looking uncommonly disapproving for such a lovely woman. "We're to eat with Sir Alistair tonight. But this will be the only time."

Alistair took her arm firmly, leading her into the dining room. "On the contrary, I expect you and the children to dine with me every night that you stay in Castle Greaves."

"Huzzah!" yelled the boy. He had already found a place at the table.

"You can't!" hissed Mrs. Halifax.

"It is my castle, madam. Allow me to remind you that I do here as I please."

"But the other servants will think . . . will think . . ."

He looked down at her. Her harebell-blue eyes were wide and pleading, and perhaps he should've taken pity on her.

But he didn't. "They'll think what?"

"That I am your mistress."

Her lips were red and parted, her hair smooth and golden, the skin of her neck and breast so white and pure it might've been made from the wings of doves.

The irony was enough to kill him.

His mouth twisted. "Madam, I care not what others think, about me or anyone else. I should've thought that was obvious by now. You may either leave my castle this very night, or you may stay and dine with me tonight and every evening henceforth. It's your choice alone."

Alistair pulled out her chair with a thump and watched to see if worry for her own reputation would finally drive her away.

She inhaled, her sweet bosom swelling above the square-cut neckline of her dress. She'd left off the fichu tonight, and he damned the loss. Yards of creamy skin seemed to be revealed in the fichu's absence. He could feel the blood rushing through his veins, pounding to that most earthly part of him.

"I'll stay." She lowered herself to the chair he held.

He gently pushed it in for her and bowed over her golden head. "I am filled with joy."

*   *   *

BEASTLY, BEASTLY MAN!

Helen glowered from beneath her brows as she watched Sir Alistair round the table and sit at his own place. He didn't have a worry about society or the consequences of flaunting it, and as a result, he'd put her in an untenable position purely on a whim it seemed! She inhaled and beckoned to Tom, the taller of the two footmen. He'd been standing in the corner gawking at their byplay all this while.

"Fetch dishes and silverware for myself and the children," she ordered.

Tom hurried out of the room.

"Mrs. McCleod's made meat pie," Jamie confided to Sir Alistair.

"Indeed?" Sir Beastly replied to her son as gravely as if he spoke with a bishop.

Helen frowned at the polished table in front of her. Lister had never been interested in anything Jamie or Abigail had ever said.

"Yes, and it smells won-*der*-ful." Jamie drew the last word out to emphasize the ambrosia that awaited them.

Despite working all afternoon, Jamie was bouncing with energy. Helen couldn't help but smile at him, though she worried whether his exhaustion was merely waiting for bedtime. There had been several times on the ride north when Jamie had fallen apart with tiredness at the end of the day. It made putting him to bed rather wearying. Nursemaids, too, were something she'd never take for granted again.

Sir Alistair sat at the head of the rectangular table as was proper. Jamie was to his right, Abigail to his left, and Helen was at the foot, blessedly as far away from the master of the castle as she could be. Jamie's face barely cleared the table.

If they were to do this every night, Helen would have to find something he could sit on to make him higher.

"Mama said we weren't to eat with you." Abigail's blue eyes were shadowed by worry.

"Ah, but this is my castle, and I set the rules within it," Sir Alistair replied. "And I wish for you and your brother and your lovely mother to dine with me. Is that to your liking?"

Abigail knit her brow in thought before answering. "Yes. I like eating in the dining room. We polished the table and beat the carpet today. You wouldn't believe the cloud of dust that came out of it. Nellie, the maid, coughed so hard I thought she'd choke."

"And there was a bird in the chimney!" Jamie said.

Sir Alistair looked toward the fireplace. It was surrounded by old carved stone with a painted wood mantel. "What color was the bird?"

"It was black, but its belly was pale and it was ever so fast," Jamie replied.

Sir Alistair nodded as Tom returned with more plates and silverware. "Probably a swallow. They nest in chimneys sometimes."

Meg and Nellie bustled in carrying trays of food. Meg cast quick curious glances as she handled the food while Nellie gaped at Sir Alistair's scarred face until Helen caught her eye and frowned. Then Nellie ducked her head and went about her work. Besides the meat pie, there were new peas, carrots, fresh bread, and stewed fruit. For a minute, there was silence as the maids retreated.

Sir Alistair looked at the table. The dishes of food steamed, and the glasses sparkled in the candlelight. He raised his glass of wine and nodded at her. "I commend you, madam. You've set a feast out of thin air and managed to clean this dining room as well. I would think it impossible if the result were not here before my eyes."

Helen found herself smiling foolishly. For some reason, his words warmed her far more than the practiced flowery rhetoric she'd once received in London ballrooms.

He watched her over the rim of his glass as he drank, and she didn't know where to look.

"Why?" Jamie asked.

Sir Alistair's gaze was diverted to her son, and Helen took a deep breath, wishing she could fan herself.

"Why what?" the castle's master asked.

"Why do swallows sometimes nest in chimneys?" Jamie asked.

"That's a silly question," Abigail stated.

"Ah, but no question is silly to a naturalist," Sir Alistair said, and for a moment Abigail looked crushed.

Helen opened her mouth to defend her child.

Then Sir Alistair smiled at Abigail. It was only a quirk at the corner of his mouth, but the child relaxed and Helen closed her mouth.

"Why should a swallow nest in a chimney?" Sir Alistair asked. "Why there and not somewhere else?"

"She wants to escape the cat?" Abigail guessed.

"She's warmed by the fire," Jamie said.

"But there hadn't been a fire in that chimney in ages," Abigail objected.

"Then I don't know why." Jamie gave up the question and forked up a piece of meat pie instead.

But Abigail still frowned. "Why should a swallow nest in the chimney? It seems a silly thing to do—and dirty."

"Your idea that the swallow wants to bring up its young

where the cat can't get them is a good one," Sir Alistair said. "Perhaps also the swallow nests where no other bird is nesting."

Abigail stared hard at Sir Alistair. "I don't understand."

"Birds—and animals—must eat and drink just like us. They must have space to live and grow. But if another bird, particularly one of its own kind, is nearby, that bird might wish to fight it. The bird guards its own manor."

"But some birds like to live together," Abigail said. Her brows were drawn together stubbornly. "Sparrows are always together in a flock, pecking at the ground."

"Always?" Sir Alistair buttered a piece of bread. "Do they nest together as well?"

Abigail hesitated. "I don't know. I've never seen a sparrow's nest."

"Never?" Sir Alistair darted a look at Helen, his brows slightly raised. She shrugged. They'd always lived in London. The birds of the city must nest somewhere, but she didn't recall seeing them. "Ah. Then I shall have to show you some nests."

"Coo!" Jamie exclaimed—regrettably with his mouth full.

Sir Alistair tilted his head toward the boy, his eye gleaming. "Sparrows have solitary nests, but you are quite correct, lass. Some birds and animals do congregate together and even raise their young in a group. For instance, I am writing my findings on badgers at the moment, and they like to live all together in a mass of burrows called a *sett*."

"Can you show us a badger, too?" Jamie asked.

"They're quite shy," Sir Alistair said as he cut into his slice of meat pie. "But I can show you a sett nearby, if you like."

Jamie's mouth was full of peas, but he nodded enthusiastically to show he'd like a trip to a badger sett.

"Is that what you do up in your tower?" Helen asked.
"Write about badgers?"

He looked at her. "Yes, among other things. I'm writing
a book about the animals, birds, and flowers of Scotland
and England. I'm a naturalist. Didn't Lady Vale tell you
before she sent you to me?"

Helen shook her head, avoiding his gaze. The truth
was, there hadn't been much time for Lady Vale to tell
her anything. When Helen had gone to Melisande, she'd
been fleeing Lister and had feared she was being followed.
Melisande had suggested Sir Alistair because he lived in
Scotland—far away from London—and Helen had jumped
at the idea. She'd been desperate.

"Have you written many books?" She felt foolish that
she hadn't thought about what he might be doing up in his
cluttered study.

"Only one." He sipped his wine, watching her. "*A Brief
Survey of the Flora and Fauna of New England.*"

"But I've heard of that." She looked up at him in surprise. "It's all the rage in London. Why, I saw two fashionable ladies nearly come to blows over the last copy in a
bookseller on Bond Street. It's considered de rigueur for a
complete library. You wrote that book?"

He inclined his head ironically. "I confess it."

Helen felt strange. The book in question was very elegant, a portfolio-sized volume filled with full-page hand-
colored illustrations. She would never have dreamed in a
thousand years that Sir Alistair could write something so
beautiful.

"Did you illustrate the book as well?"

"In a way—the engravings are based upon my sketches," he said.

"It's lovely," she said truthfully.

He raised his glass but didn't comment, his eye watching her.

"I want to see the book," Jamie said.

Abigail had stopped eating. She didn't echo Jamie's plea, but it was quite obvious she was curious as well.

Sir Alistair inclined his head. "I suppose there must be a copy about somewhere in the library. Shall we go see?"

"Huzzah!" yelled Jamie again, this time fortunately having swallowed the food in his mouth.

Sir Alistair looked across the table at Helen, cocking the eyebrow over his eye patch at her. It looked very much like a challenge.

ALISTAIR ROSE FROM his newly polished dining room table and walked around it to help Mrs. Halifax from her chair. She stared up at him, suspicious at his courtesy, so he held out his arm just to flummox her.

She laid her fingertips on his sleeve as if touching a hot pot. "We don't wish to take your time. I know you're busy."

He cocked his head to better see her. She wasn't getting away that easily. "Alas, I have no pressing matters at the moment, ma'am. Take a candle."

She didn't reply but merely nodded, though a small frown played about her mouth. She picked up one of the candles from a sideboard. Alistair led her toward the library, the children trailing behind. He was conscious of her fingers so lightly pressed against his arm and of her warmth as she walked beside him. Women, especially beautiful ones, didn't often venture so near to him. He could smell the soap she'd used to wash her hair—a light lemon scent.

"Here we are," he said as they made the library door.

He opened the door and went in. Mrs. Halifax immediately separated herself from him, not surprisingly really, but he felt the loss. Maudlin idiocy, that. He should be used by now to women running from him. He didn't comment but took her candle and began lighting the ones in the room.

This had been his father's library and his grandfather's before him. Unlike many great house libraries, this one was actually used and the books read and reread. It was a rectangular room on an outside wall with some of the largest windows in the castle. The windows were hidden behind long, dusty curtains that hadn't been drawn for years. All except the one curtain that had fallen, letting in Lady Grey's afternoon ray of sunlight. The remaining walls were covered, floor to ceiling, with bookshelves, each crammed to overflowing with volumes. At one end of the library was a small fireplace. Two decrepit chairs and a small table sat before it.

He finished lighting the candles and turned back. The children and Mrs. Halifax were still clustered by the door. A corner of his mouth kicked up. "Come in. I know it isn't as beautifully clean as the dining room now is, but I don't think you'll come to actual harm."

Mrs. Halifax muttered something under her breath and frowned at one of the chairs by the fireplace. The chair was lopsided; it had a broken leg and was propped up by two books. Abigail was running her finger along a bookshelf and inspecting the dust collected on her fingertip.

But Jamie ran to a globe of the world and peered at it. "I can't see England."

The globe was nearly obscured by dust.

"Ah." Sir Alistair took out his handkerchief and wiped off the globe. "There. Now England's revealed, and so is Scotland. Here we are." He pointed to the area north of the Firth of Forth.

Jamie squinted at the globe and then looked up. "Where's your book?"

Alistair glanced about the library, frowning. He hadn't had occasion to look at his own writing in quite some time. "Over here, I think."

He led the way to a corner in which several oversized volumes were piled on the floor.

"These ought to be put on a shelf," Mrs. Halifax muttered. "I can't believe you keep your own book on the floor."

Alistair grunted before rummaging in the pile with Jamie. "Ah, here it is."

He laid the book out on the floor and opened it. Jamie promptly threw himself down on his stomach to peer closely at the pages, and Abigail sat by his side to look.

"You must have spent many years in New England." Mrs. Halifax was standing behind her children, looking at the book over their shoulders. "Mind the pages when you turn them, Jamie."

Alistair strolled to her side. "Three years."

She looked up at him, her blue eyes startlingly bright in the candlelit room. "What?"

"Three years." He cleared his throat. "I spent three years in New England recording the information in that book."

"That's a very long time. Did not the war interfere with your work?"

"On the contrary. I was attached to regiments in His Majesty's army the entire time."

"But wasn't that dangerous?" Her brows were drawn together in concern.

For him.

He looked away. Her eyes were too beautiful for this dingy room, and he regretted the impulse to bring her and the children in here. Why lay himself open like this, let them see into his life, his past? This was a mistake.

"Sir Alistair?"

He didn't know what to say. Yes, it'd been dangerous— so dangerous that he'd left behind an eye, two fingers, and his pride in the woods of North America—but he couldn't tell her that. She was merely making conversation.

He was saved from having to reply by Jamie looking up suddenly from the book. "Where's Lady Grey?"

The deerhound hadn't followed them into the library.

Alistair shrugged. "Probably fell asleep by the fire in the dining room."

"But she'll miss us," Jamie said. "I'll go get her."

And he hopped up before anyone could say a word and scurried from the room.

"Jamie!" Abigail called. "Jamie, don't run!" And she was off as well.

"I'm sorry," Mrs. Halifax said.

He frowned at her in surprise. "What for?"

"They can be so impetuous."

Alistair shrugged. He wasn't used to children, but these ones were rather interesting to have about.

"I—" she began, but she was interrupted by a single shrill scream.

Alistair was out the door without waiting for Mrs. Halifax. He ran down the hallway. The scream wasn't repeated, but he was sure it'd come from the dining room. Perhaps Abigail had seen a spider. But when he rounded the dining room door, he knew it was something else entirely.

Lady Grey lay by the fireplace as he'd predicted, but Jamie knelt over her, frantically patting her side, and Abigail stood still and pale with her hands pressed to her mouth.

No.

He slowly walked to the fireplace, Mrs. Halifax trailing behind. Abigail simply stared at him, silent tears running down her face.

But Jamie looked up as he neared. "She's hurt! Lady Grey is hurt. You must help her."

Alistair knelt by the old dog and placed his palm on her side. She was already growing cold. It must've happened as she slept, while they ate supper, as he'd shown Mrs. Halifax his library, completely oblivious.

He had to clear his throat. "There's nothing I can do."

"Yes!" the boy cried. His face was red, tears glittering in his eyes. "Yes! You must!"

"Jamie," Mrs. Halifax murmured. She tried to grasp her son's arm, but he wrenched it from her grasp and threw himself on the dog.

Abigail ran from the room.

Alistair placed a hand lightly on the boy's head. It quivered under his palm as the child sobbed. Lady Grey had been a gift from Sophia, many, many years ago, before he'd left for the Colonies. He hadn't taken her with him;

she had been a young dog back then, and he feared that the long sea voyage would prove too cramped for her. But when he'd returned home, broken, his life no longer what he'd thought it would be, Lady Grey had been here. She'd galloped down the drive to greet him, had stood with her paws upon his shoulders as he'd rubbed her ears, and she'd grinned, tongue lolling. She'd walked by his side when he'd wandered the heath, lay by the fireside as he'd written his book. Come to nuzzle his hand when he'd woken in the dark of night, drenched in sweat from hideous dreams.

Alistair swallowed with difficulty. "Good dog," he whispered huskily. "That's a good lass."

He stroked her side, feeling the rough, cooling fur.

"Help her!" Jamie reared up and hit at the hand that had touched his head. "*Help* her!"

"I cannot," Alistair said, choking. "She's dead."

Chapter Five

The beautiful young man led Truth Teller into the courtyard of the castle. An ancient knot garden lay here, formed of yew shrubs and decorated with statues of knights and warriors. A small cage of swallows was at one corner, the birds beating their wings hopelessly against the bars. In the center of the knot garden was a great iron cage. Dirty straw was scattered in the cage, and in the back huddled a large thing. It was a dull black color with rotting scales and stringy hair. It stood eight feet tall and had huge horns that curved down to its great shoulders. The thing's eyes were yellow and bloodshot. At the sight of the young man, it leapt at the bars and snarled with a mouth filled with dripping fangs.

The beautiful young man merely smiled and turned to Truth Teller. "Are you afraid now?"

"No," said Truth Teller.

His host laughed. "Then you shall be this monster's guard. . . ."

—from TRUTH TELLER

She'd made a ghastly mistake. Helen stroked Jamie's sweaty head that night and berated herself. Jamie had cried himself to sleep, desolate over Lady Grey's death. On the other side of the bed, Abigail was silent. She hadn't made a sound since that single shrill scream in the dining room. Now she lay on her side, facing away from Jamie, her body a slight lump under the covers.

Helen closed her eyes. What had she done to her darlings? She'd taken her children from the safety of their home in London, from all they knew, all that was familiar to them, and brought them to this strange, dark place where sweet old dogs died. Perhaps she'd been wrong. Perhaps she could've endured Lister and the hopeless, imprisoned life she'd led as his forgotten mistress, if only for the sake of her children.

But no. She'd known these last years that it was only a matter of time before she offended him in some way and she would wake up to find the children gone. If nothing else, that had been the primary driving reason to leave the duke: she could not live without Abigail and Jamie.

She opened her eyes and got up, drifting to the dark windows. The view was less than comforting, though. The ivy on the outside walls so overgrew the windows that the moon was but a glittering speck. There was a small table under the window that she'd made into a desk to transcribe Lady Vale's fairy-tale book. She touched the papers there. She really ought to work on it some more, but she was too restless tonight.

She glanced back at the children. Jamie was in exhausted slumber, and Abigail hadn't moved. Just in case she was still awake, Helen rounded the bed and bent over her daughter.

She touched her shoulder lightly—not enough to wake her if she slept—and whispered, "I'm going for a walk, darling. I'll return before too long."

Abigail's closed eyelids didn't move, but nonetheless Helen suspected she wasn't asleep. She sighed and kissed her daughter's cheek before leaving the room and shutting the door carefully behind her.

The corridor was dim, of course, and she really had no notion of where she could go. The castle didn't lend itself to a meditative stroll. Still, she was restless and had to move somehow. Helen wandered down the hall, her single candle casting flickering light against the walls. The castle had five main floors. The bedroom she shared with the children was on the third, along with several rooms that once must've been quite nice bedrooms and sitting rooms. Helen trailed her fingers idly along the carved paneling of the hall. She'd have to have the maids dust and polish the old wood eventually, but this floor was low on her list of things to be put to rights.

She stopped suddenly and shuddered. She was making plans—*future* plans—for the castle when she might not even be here tomorrow. She had no doubt that Lister had men searching for her and the children at this very moment. The knowledge made her skin prickle in fear, made her want to flee at once. But she'd attended shooting parties in the country and knew what happened to the bird that flew when the beaters came close. They were shot from the sky. No. Better to keep her nerve and stay here at this hiding place she'd found.

She shivered and started down a staircase at the end of the hall. The treads were even and strong, but they were bare. Did Sir Alistair have the funds for a proper carpet?

Perhaps she could hang a painting or two on the landing. She'd found quite a cache of paintings just today. They were all leaning on their sides and covered with a cloth in one of the closed rooms on the second floor.

The stair led to the back of the castle, quite near the kitchens. She hesitated when she made the ground floor. Light was coming from the kitchen. It couldn't be any of the new servants. The maids and footmen made the journey to and from the village daily. Mrs. McCleod would eventually live in, but she'd taken one look at the cook's quarters and stated that they'd need to be cleaned before she could move in. The light in the kitchen meant that either Sir Alistair was having a late snack or Mr. Wiggins was lurking there. Helen shivered. She hadn't the fortitude to take on the nasty little man at the moment.

That decided, she turned to the front of the castle. The dining room was dark as she passed it, and for a moment she wondered what Sir Alistair had done with the big dog's body. She'd left the castle's master there in the dining room when she'd gone to take care of Jamie and Abigail. When she'd last glimpsed him, he'd been crouching silently over the dog. His eyes had been dry, but every bone in his body had projected grief.

Helen looked away from the dining room. She didn't want to feel sympathy for Sir Alistair. He was a disagreeable man who'd gone out of his way to make it plain he didn't want her here. She'd like to think that he didn't care for anyone or anything. But that'd been clearly disproved, hadn't it? He might wear the mask of an unfeeling ogre, but underneath he was a man. A man who could be hurt.

She was at the front of the castle now, by those great doors where first they'd entered. She had to set down the candle to pull back the heavy bolt and wrench the door open. Sir Alistair had performed these jobs without any sign of strain. Obviously he had some muscles under that old hunting coat he habitually wore. An image of the master of the castle without any clothing at all suddenly sprang up in her too-fertile mind, and Helen halted, startled and oddly warmed. Good Lord! Had she truly become a wanton? Because imagining Sir Alistair nude only aroused her curiosity: Did the man have hair on his chest? Was his belly as flat as it looked? And while she was standing here in the darkness, she might as well think it—was his manhood long or short? Thick or narrow?

A wanton, indeed.

Helen inhaled, shaking the crude thoughts away, and set her candle on the stone step of the castle. The moon was high enough to see a little in the dark as her eyes adjusted. The group of trees by the drive rustled softly in the wind, their tops waving against the night sky. Helen shivered. She should've brought a wrap.

There was a kind of path that led around the side of the castle, and Helen began picking her way. She rounded the back of the castle, and the moon shone, full and fat, on the hills in the distance. Its light was as nearly bright as day, and as she tore her eyes from it, Helen belatedly saw that she wasn't alone. A tall male figure was silhouetted against the sky, like an ancient monolith, grim and still and lonely. He might've stood thus for centuries.

"Mrs. Halifax," Sir Alistair rasped as she started to turn away. "Have you come to torment me even in the night?"

"I'm sorry," Helen murmured. She could feel a flush start on her cheeks, and she was grateful for the dark, not only to hide her blush, but also to keep him from seeing the expression on her face. Her wayward imagination conjured up that same hazy picture of him nude. *Oh, dear!* "I didn't mean to intrude."

She turned to go back around the castle, but his voice halted her.

"Stop."

She peered at him. He still faced the hills, but he'd turned his head toward her.

He cleared his throat. "Stay and talk with me, Mrs. Halifax."

It was an order, spoken in commanding tones, but Helen thought perhaps there was a hint of a plea underneath the gravel in his voice, and that decided her.

She wandered closer to where he stood. "What would you like to talk about?"

He shrugged, his face averted again. "Don't women always have something to babble about?"

"You mean fashion and gossip and other terribly unimportant things?" she asked sweetly.

He hesitated, perhaps thrown off balance by the iron underlying her tone. "I'm sorry."

She blinked, sure she had misheard him. "What?"

He shrugged. "I'm not used to the company of civilized people, Mrs. Halifax. Please forgive me."

It was her turn to feel uncomfortable. The man was obviously grieving the death of his loyal companion; it was unkind of her to snap at him. In fact, considering she'd made her living for the last fourteen years by catering to the needs of a man, it was rather out of character for her.

Helen pushed that strange thought aside and wandered a little closer to Sir Alistair, trying to think of a neutral topic of conversation. "I thought the meat pie at dinner was quite good."

"Yes." He cleared his throat. "I noticed that the boy ate two slices."

"Jamie."

"Hmm?"

"His name is Jamie," she said, but without any censor.

"Quite. Jamie, then." He shifted a little. "How is Jamie?"

She looked blindly at her feet. "He cried himself to sleep."

"Ah."

Helen stared out at the moonlit landscape. "What a wilderness this is."

"It wasn't always." His voice was low, the gravel making it rumble in a sort of comforting way. "There used to be gardens that led to the stream."

"What happened to them?"

"The gardener died and another was never hired."

She frowned. The ruined terrace gardens were silvered in the moonlight, but she could see that it was terribly overgrown. "When did the gardener die?"

He tilted his head back, gazing at the stars. "Seventeen . . . no, eighteen years ago?"

She stared. "And you've never hired a gardener since then?"

"There seemed no need."

They stood in silence then. A cloud drifted across the moon. She wondered suddenly how many nights he had stood thus, alone and lonely, looking out over the ruin of his garden.

"Do you . . ."

He tilted his head. "Yes?"

"Forgive me." She was glad the darkness masked her expression. "You've never married?"

"No." He hesitated, and then said gruffly, "I was engaged, but she died."

"I'm sorry."

He made a movement, perhaps a halfhearted shrug. He hardly needed her sympathy.

But she couldn't leave it alone. "No family, either?"

"I have an older sister who lives in Edinburgh."

"But that's not too far away. You must see her often."

She thought wistfully of her own family. She hadn't seen any of them—her sisters, brother, mother, or Papa—since she'd gone to Lister. What a price she'd paid for her romantic dreams.

"I haven't seen Sophia in years," he replied, interrupting her thoughts.

She looked at his dark profile, trying to make out his expression. "You're estranged?"

"Nothing so formal." His voice had grown cold. "I simply don't choose to travel much, Mrs. Halifax, and my sister sees no reason to visit me."

"Oh."

He pivoted slowly, facing her. His back was to the moon, and she couldn't see his expression at all. He seemed suddenly bigger, looming over her more closely—and more ominously—than she'd realized.

"You're very curious about me tonight, Mrs. Halifax," he growled. "But I think I'd rather discuss you."

THE MOONLIGHT CARESSED her face, highlighting a beauty that needed no additional ornamentation. But her loveliness didn't distract him anymore. He saw it, admired it, but he could also see past the surface camouflage to the woman beneath. A vivacious woman who, he suspected, was not used to labor yet had spent the day cleaning his filthy dining room. A woman not used to fending for herself but who had still managed to push her way into his home and his life. Interesting. What motivated her? What life had she left behind? Who was the man she was hiding from? Alistair watched Mrs. Halifax, trying to see the expression in her harebell-blue eyes, but the night shielded them from him.

"What do you want to know about me?" she asked.

Her voice was even, almost masculine in its directness, and the contrast to her extremely feminine form was surprising. Fascinating, actually.

He cocked his head, considering her. "You've said that you're widowed."

Her chin lifted. "Yes, of course."

"For how long?"

She looked away, hesitating for a fraction of a second. "Three years this fall."

He nodded. She was very good, but she was lying. Did the husband still live? Or did she run from another man? "And what did Mr. Halifax do?"

"He was a doctor."

"But not a successful one, I take it."

"Why do you say that?"

"If he'd been successful," he pointed out, "you wouldn't have to work now."

She lifted a hand to her forehead. "Forgive me, but the topic distresses me."

No doubt he was supposed to feel pity for her at this

point and give up the chase, but he had her cornered, and his curiosity urged him on. Her distress only made him more eager. He stepped closer, so close that his chest nearly touched her shoulder. His nose caught the scent of lemons from her hair. "You were fond of your husband?"

Her hand fell and she glared up at him, her tone tart. "I loved him desperately."

His mouth curved in a smile that wasn't very nice. "A tragedy, then, his death."

"Yes, it was."

"You were married young?"

"Only eighteen." Her eyes dropped.

"And the marriage was happy."

"Extremely happy." Her voice was defiant, the lie transparent.

"What did he look like?"

"I . . ." She wrapped her arms about herself. "Please, might we change the subject?"

"Certainly," he drawled. "Where did you live in London?"

"I've told you." Her voice was steadier now. "I was in Lady Vale's household."

"Of course," he murmured. "My mistake. I keep forgetting your vast experience in running a household."

"It's not vast," she whispered. "You know that."

For a moment, they were silent and only the wind whistling around the corner of the castle gave voice.

Then she said very quietly, with her face still turned away, "It's just that I . . . I need a place to stay right now."

And something inside him surged in triumph. He had her. She couldn't leave. It made no sense, this feeling of triumph. He'd been urging her to go ever since she'd arrived, but somehow the knowledge that she had to stay, and that as an honorable gentleman he had to *let* her stay, filled him with contentment.

Not that he let it show. "I confess, Mrs. Halifax, that I am surprised by one thing."

"What is that?"

He bent closer, his mouth nearly brushing her lemon-scented hair. "I would've thought a lady of your beauty would be besieged by suitors."

She turned her head, and their faces were suddenly only inches apart. He felt her breath brush across his lips as she spoke. "You find me beautiful."

Her voice was curiously flat.

He cocked his head, eyeing the smooth brow, the lush mouth, and the fine wide eyes. "Devastatingly so."

"And you probably think beauty sufficient reason to marry a woman." Her tone was bitter now.

What had the mysterious Mr. Halifax done to his wife? "No doubt most men do."

"They never think of a woman's disposition," she muttered. "Her likes and dislikes, her fears and hopes, her very soul."

"Don't they?"

"No." Her beautiful eyes had grown dark and tragic. The wind blew a curling lock of hair across her face.

"Poor Mrs. Halifax," he mocked softly. He gave in to impulse and raised his left hand—his unmaimed hand—and stroked the lock of hair back away from her face. Her skin was as fine as silk. "How terrible to be so lovely."

A frown creased her unblemished brow. "You said *most men*."

"Did I?" He let his hand drop.

She looked up at him, her eyes were quite perceptive now. "Don't you consider beauty to be the most important criteria in a wife?"

"Ah, but you've forgotten my aspect, I'm afraid. It's in the natural order of things that a lovely wife will either stray or come to hate an ugly husband. A man as revolting as I would be an idiot to attach himself to a beautiful woman." He smiled into her mesmerizingly lovely eyes. "And I am many things, Mrs. Halifax, but an idiot is not one of them."

He bowed and turned to stride back into the castle, leaving Mrs. Halifax, a lonely, desperately tempting siren, behind him.

"WHEN WILL WE go home?" Jamie asked the next afternoon. He picked up a rock and threw it.

The rock didn't go very far, but Abigail frowned, anyway. "Don't do that."

"Why not?" Jamie whined.

"Because you might hit someone. Or something."

Jamie looked about the old stable yard, empty except for themselves and a few sparrows. "Who?"

"I don't know!"

Abigail wanted to throw a rock herself, but ladies didn't do such things. And besides, they were supposed to be beating an old rug. Mama'd made one of the footmen put up a line across a corner of the yard, and a row of rugs now hung from it, all waiting to be beaten. Abigail's arms were sore, but she took a swing at the rug anyway with the broom she held. It felt almost good to hit the rug. A great cloud of dust flew out.

Jamie squatted to pick up another rock. "I want to go home."

"You've already said that over and over again," Abigail said irritably.

"But I do." He stood and threw the rock. It hit the stable's wall and clattered onto the gray stones that paved the stable yard. "We never had to beat rugs at our old house. And Miss Cummings took us to the park sometimes. There's nothing to do here but work."

"Well, we can't go home," Abigail shot back. "And I told you—"

"Oy!" The voice came from behind them.

Abigail looked over her shoulder, still holding the broom.

Mr. Wiggins was trundling toward them, his ginger hair waving in the breeze as his stumpy arms waved in the air. "Watcha doin', throwin' rocks about like that? Are you soft in the head?"

Abigail straightened. "He's not soft—"

Mr. Wiggins snorted like a surprised horse. "If'n throwin' rocks about that could hit anybody, includin' me, isn't soft in th' head, I don't know what is."

"You don't talk that way!" Jamie said. He'd stood and his hands were balled by his sides.

"Don't tawk whot?" Mr. Wiggins mimicked their accent. "Whot're yew, a soft-headed London ponce?"

"My father's a duke!" Jamie shouted, red-faced.

Abigail froze, horrified.

But Mr. Wiggins merely threw back his head and laughed. "A duke, eh? Then what does that make you? A dukeling? Ha! Well, dukeling or not, don't throw them stones."

And he walked off, still chuckling.

She waited, holding her breath until he was out of sight; then she swung on her brother, whispering furiously, "Jamie! You know we weren't to say anything about the duke."

"He called me a ponce." Jamie's face was still red. "And the duke *is* our father."

"But Mama said we mustn't let anyone know that."

"I hate it here!" Jamie put his head down like a bull and ran out of the stable yard.

Or at least he started to. At the corner of the castle, he stumbled headlong into Sir Alistair coming the other way.

"Whoa, there." Sir Alistair caught Jamie easily in both hands.

"Let me go!"

"Certainly."

Sir Alistair raised his hands and Jamie was free. But having gained his freedom, he didn't seem to know what to do next. He stood in front of the castle's master, his head bowed, his lower lip protruding.

Sir Alistair watched him for a moment, and then looked at Abigail with one eyebrow raised. His hair was about his face, his scars shone dully in the sunlight, and his jaw was still stubbled, but he wasn't nearly as terrifying as Mr. Wiggins.

Abigail shifted from one foot to the other, still holding the broom. "We were beating the rugs." She gestured weakly to the line of rugs behind her.

"So I see." Sir Alistair looked back at Jamie. "I was going to the stable to fetch a shovel."

"What for?" Jamie grunted.

"I'm going to bury Lady Grey."

Jamie hunched his shoulders and kicked at the cobblestones.

Everyone was silent a moment.

Until Abigail licked her lips and said, "I-I'm sorry."

Sir Alistair looked at her from his one eye, and his expression wasn't friendly at all, but Abigail gathered all her courage and blurted it out before she let her fear and embarrassment freeze her. "I'm sorry about Lady Grey and I'm sorry that I screamed."

He blinked. "What?"

She took a deep breath. "The first night when we came. I'm sorry I screamed at you. It wasn't very nice of me."

"Oh. Well . . . thank you." He glanced away then and cleared his throat, and there was another silence.

"May we help you?" Abigail asked. "Bury Lady Grey, I mean."

Sir Alistair frowned, his brows drawn together over his eye patch. "Are you sure you want to?"

"Yes," Abigail said.

Jamie nodded.

Sir Alistair looked at them a moment and then nodded. "Very well, then. Wait here."

He went into the stables and then came back out with a shovel. "Come on."

He set off toward the back of the castle without another glance toward them.

Abigail put down her broom, and she and Jamie trailed him. She darted a look at Jamie. He had tears at the corners of his eyes. He'd cried for quite a long time the night before, and the sound had made her chest hurt. She frowned and watched the path. It was rocky and bumpy; Sir Alistair was leading them down through the old garden toward the stream. It was stupid because they hadn't known Lady Grey all that long, but Abigail felt like crying, too. She didn't even know why she'd asked to come along to help bury the dog.

Below the gardens was a bit of a grassy meadow. Sir Alistair tramped through it and as they neared the stream, Abigail could hear the rush of water. Farther up, there were some rocks in the stream and the water boiled about them, frothing white. But below the garden, the water had calmed, pooling in the shade of some trees. At the base of one was a lump bundled in an old rug.

Abigail looked away, feeling her throat ache.

But Jamie went right up to the bundle. "Is this her?"

Sir Alistair nodded.

"It seems silly to waste a good rug," Abigail muttered.

Sir Alistair looked at her out of his one light brown eye. "She liked to lie on that rug before the fire in my tower."

Abigail glanced away, feeling ashamed. "Oh."

Jamie squatted and stroked the faded rug as if it were the fur of the dog beneath. Sir Alistair set his spade and began digging beneath the tree.

Abigail wandered closer to the stream. The water was clear and cool. A few leaves floated lazily on the surface. She knelt carefully and looked at the rocks at the bottom. They seemed quite close, yet she knew they were a yard or more away.

Behind her, Jamie asked, "Why're you burying her here?"

She could hear the sound of the spade scraping against

earth. "She liked to ramble with me. I'd come here to fish, and she'd take a nap under that tree. She liked it here."

"Good," Jamie said.

Then there was only the sound of Sir Alistair digging. Abigail leaned over the pool and trailed her fingers in the water. It was shockingly cool.

Behind her the digging stopped, and she could hear the rug sliding. Sir Alistair grunted. She put her face closer to the pool, watching a water weed waving below. If she were a mermaid, she'd sit on those rocks far below and tend a garden of water weeds. The stream would flow all about her, and she wouldn't be able to hear a thing from the world above. She'd be safe. Happy.

A fish flashed silver among the rocks and she straightened.

When she turned around, Sir Alistair was smoothing a mound of earth over Lady Grey's grave. Jamie had a tiny white flower he'd plucked from the meadow, and he laid it on the grave.

Her brother turned to her, holding out another flower. "Do you want one, Abby?"

And she didn't know why, but her chest suddenly felt as if it would burst from within her. She'd die if that happened.

So she turned and ran back up the hill to the castle, as fast as she could, with the wind against her face until it blew all the thoughts from her mind.

IN THE EARLY years, when she'd still been naive and in love, Helen had sat up many nights waiting in case Lister should deign to visit her. And many nights she'd finally given up her vigil to retire alone and lonely. She was past those nights of waiting now—years past them. So it was particularly aggravating that she found herself that evening at midnight pacing the dim library in her chemise and wrap and waiting for Sir Alistair's return.

Where was the man?

He hadn't appeared for supper, and when she'd made the climb to his tower, she'd found it deserted. In the end, after waiting until the roast duck was completely cold, she'd had to eat without him, just her and the children in the now-clean dining room. When she'd questioned the children over the cold duck and congealed sauce, Jamie had told her about burying the dog earlier in the afternoon. Abigail had merely pushed her peas about her plate and then asked to be excused early, saying she had a migraine. Her daughter was too young to have migraines, but Helen had taken pity on the girl and let her retire in peace. That was another concern entirely—Abigail and her secretive, sad little face. Helen wished she knew what she could do to help her daughter.

She'd spent the rest of the evening consulting with Mrs. McCleod about meals and refurbishing the kitchen. Then she'd made Jamie take a bath by the kitchen fire, which had resulted in a puddle that needed mopping up before she'd put him to bed. The entire time she'd done these chores, she'd kept an ear half-cocked, listening for Sir Alistair's return. All she'd heard for her troubles was Mr. Wiggins stumbling to the stables drunk as a lord. Sometime after that, it'd begun raining.

Where was he? And more to the point, why did she care? Helen halted by the pile of books where his great album of birds and animals and flowers of America still lay. She set her candle on a long table against the wall, bent, and hauled the big tome to the table's surface. A small cloud of dust stirred and she sneezed. Then she moved the candle close enough to illuminate the pages without dripping wax on them and opened the book.

The frontispiece was an elaborate hand-colored illustration of a classical arch. Through the arch, a lush forest, blue sky, and a pool of clear water could be seen. To one side of the arch stood a beautiful woman in classical drapery, obviously an allegory. She held out her hand, inviting the viewer to enter the arch. On the other side of the arch was a man in sturdy buckskin breeches and coat, on his head a floppy hat. He had a pack over one shoulder and carried a magnifying glass in one hand and a walking stick in the other. Beneath the picture was the caption, THE NEW WORLD WELCOMES HIS MAJESTY'S BOTANIST ALISTAIR MUNROE TO DISCOVER HER WONDERS.

Was the little man supposed to be Sir Alistair? Helen peered closer. If so, it didn't look a thing like him. The illustration had a cupid's bow mouth and plump pink cheeks and looked rather like a woman in man's clothing. She wrinkled her nose and turned the page. Here was the title page, which read in elaborate script A BRIEF SURVEY OF THE FLORA AND FAUNA OF NEW ENGLAND BY ALISTAIR MUNROE. On the next page were the words,

The Dedication
To His Most Serene Majesty
GEORGE
By the Grace of God
KING OF GREAT BRITAIN, &c
If it please him
I dedicate this book and my work.

yr humble servant, &c.
Alistair Munroe
1762

She traced the letters. It must have indeed pleased the
king, for she remembered hearing that the author had
been knighted soon after the publication of this book.
Helen turned several pages more and then stopped, inhal-
ing sharply. When they'd looked at this book yesterday
evening, she'd not paid it too much attention. The children's eager heads had obscured the pages as she stood
above. But now . . . .

Before her was a full-page illustration of a flower with
long curving petals on a bare branch. The blooms were ex-
travagant and multiple, clustered together, and they were
exquisitely hand-colored a sort of lavender pink. Beneath
the flower was a branch with a flower dissected to show
the different parts. Beside that was a branch with leaves
opening. On one leaf lay a gaudy black and yellow but-
terfly, each leg and antenna drawn in meticulous detail.
Beneath the engraving were the words, RHODODENDRON
CANADENSE.

How could he be so surly, so *uncivilized* and yet be the
artist who'd drawn the original pictures for this book? She
shook her head and turned another page. The library was
quiet, save for the sound of rain pelting against the windows. The lush illustrations drew her in, and she stood for
what might've been minutes or hours, mesmerized by the
illustrations and words, turning the pages slowly.

Helen didn't know what broke the spell—certainly not
a sound, because the falling rain masked all sounds from
without—but she looked up after a while and frowned.

The candle had burned down to a sullen nub, and she picked it up carefully before going to the library door. The hall was deserted and dark, the rain drumming against the great front doors. There was no reason at all for what she did next.

She set the candle on a table and wrenched at the doors. For a moment, they stubbornly held, and then they gave, groaning reluctantly. The rain immediately blew in, soaking her nearly from head to toe. Helen gasped at the cold shock and peered into the darkness of the drive.

Nothing moved.

What a silly fool she was! She'd gotten soaked for nothing. Helen began to push the doors closed again when she saw it: a long shadow emerging from the trees beside the drive. A man on horseback. She felt overwhelming relief, and then the sight drove her mad.

She half stumbled down the step, her hair immediately flattened to her skull by the rain, and screamed all her hours of worry at him. "What are you doing? Do you think I scrub and dust and plan a meal all day long just so you can cavalierly miss it? Don't you know that the children waited for you? Jamie was disappointed at your absence. And the duck was cold—quite, quite cold. I don't know if I shall be able to apologize to Mrs. McCleod enough, and she the only cook for miles!"

He was leaning a bit over the horse, his hat gone, and the shoulders of his old hacking coat were shining with wet. He must be entirely soaked through. He turned a deathly white face at her, and a corner of his mouth curved mockingly. "Your welcome home is most gracious, Mrs. Halifax."

She caught the horse's bridle and stood blinking in the

rain. "We made a deal, you and I. I would sit with you at your dining table and you—*you!*—would appear at the evening meal. How dare you make a pact with me and then break it? How dare you take me for granted?"

His eyes closed for a moment, and she saw the lines of weariness incised into his face. "I must apologize yet again, Mrs. Halifax."

She scowled. He looked ill. How long had he been riding in this downpour? "But where have you been? What was so important that you must go gallivanting off in this storm?"

"A whim," he sighed, his eyes closing. "A whim merely."

And he fell from the horse.

Helen screamed. Fortunately, the horse was well trained and didn't start and trample him. He'd fallen to his back, and as she bent over his still form, something stirred under his coat. A small black nose and then a whimpering little head poked from the wet folds of material.

Sir Alistair sheltered a puppy under his coat.

Chapter Six

*Every day Truth Teller guarded the monstrous
thing at the center of the yew knot garden. It was
monotonous work. The creature sulked in a corner
of its cage, the swallows endlessly fluttered, and the
statues merely stared dumbly.*

*In the evening, before the sun set, the beautiful
young man would come and relieve Truth Teller, and
he always asked the same question: "Have you seen
aught to frighten you today?"*

And every evening Truth Teller replied, "No. . . ."
—from TRUTH TELLER

"Mr. Wiggins!" Helen screamed into the blowing rain.
"Mr. Wiggins, come help me!"

"Hush," Sir Alistair moaned, having apparently recovered from his faint. "If Wiggins isn't fast asleep, he's dead drunk. Or both."

She scowled at him. He was lying in a puddle, the

puppy huddled against his chest, both man and beast shivering with cold. "I need help to get you inside."

"No"—he heaved himself to a sitting position—"you don't."

She took his arm and pulled hard, trying to help him up. "Stubborn man."

"Stubborn woman," he muttered back. "Don't hurt the pup. I paid a shilling for him."

"And nearly died bringing the beast home," she panted.

He lurched to his feet, and she wrapped her arms about his chilly chest to steady him. The position put her head under his arm, her cheek against his side. He laid a heavy arm over her shoulders. "You are a lunatic."

"Is this any way for a housekeeper to talk to her master?" His teeth were chattering, but he balanced the puppy in the crook of his other arm.

"You may dismiss me in the morning," she snapped as she helped him awkwardly up the step. For all his sarcasm, he leaned heavily on her, and she could feel the ragged heave of his chest against her cheek. He was a big, stubborn man, but he must've been riding in the rain for hours.

"You forget, Mrs. Halifax, that I've tried and failed to dismiss you since the night you arrived at my door. Watch it." He'd fallen against the doorframe, pulling her off balance.

"If you'd just follow my lead," she gasped.

"What a very bossy woman you are," he mused as he staggered through the doorway. "I can't think how I managed without you."

"Neither can I." She propped him against the wall and

shoved the door shut. The pup whimpered. "It'll serve you right if you catch an ague."

"Oh, how dulcet is the feminine tone," he murmured. "So soft, so gentle, even enough to rouse the protective urge in any man."

She snorted and led him toward the stairs. They were leaving a trail of water that would have to be cleaned on the morrow. Despite his sardonic words, he was pale and shivering violently, and she truly was afraid he'd catch a deathly chill. She'd seen strong men laid low by fever before, when helping her father on his rounds. They'd be laughing and alive one week and dead within days.

"Watch the step," she said. He was tall enough, heavy enough, that if he started to fall, she wasn't altogether sure she could keep him from tumbling down the stairs.

He merely grunted, and that worried her more—did he no longer have the strength to argue with her? Her mind leapt ahead as she helped him slowly up the stairs. She'd have to get hot water, perhaps make tea. Mrs. McCleod had left a kettle near the banked kitchen fire last night—perhaps she had again tonight. She'd get him to his room and then run down for the kettle.

But he was shuddering in waves by the time they made the hallway outside his room. The puppy was in danger of being flung from his arm.

"You may leave me here," he grunted when they reached his door.

She ignored him and pushed the door open. "You're an idiot."

"Several imminent scientists in Edinburgh and the continent would beg to differ."

"I doubt they've seen you half-dead and clutching a wet puppy."

"True." He staggered toward the bed. His room was huge. A bed with massive posters squatted between heavily draped windows, the coverlet trailing on the floor. On one wall was a large ancient fireplace, made of the same rose stone as the rest of the castle. For a moment, Helen wondered if this room had been used continuously by the master of the castle since it was built.

Then she shoved the thought from her mind. "Not the bed. You'll get it wet."

She guided him toward the fireplace. A single enormous chair sat before the cold hearth. Sir Alistair sank into it, shuddering, while she bent and stirred the fire. A feeble ember still glowed there. Carefully she heaped coals upon it and blew until the fire caught. Rainwater ran down her face from her hair and dripped to the floor. She shivered, but she wasn't nearly as cold as he.

She stood and faced Sir Alistair. "Take off those clothes."

"Why, Mrs. Halifax, such daring." His words were slightly slurred as if he'd been drinking, though she had detected no alcohol on his breath. "I had no idea you had designs upon my person."

"Humph." She picked up the shivering puppy and placed it near the fire, where it sat in a forlorn wet heap. She'd worry about the dog later. At the moment, its master took precedence.

Helen stood and started peeling the soaking coat from Sir Alistair's shoulders. He leaned forward to help her, but his movements were clumsy. She flung the wet coat on the hearth, where it began to steam. Then she knelt before him and worked the buttons through the soaking fabric of his waistcoat. She could feel him watching her, his eyes heavy-lidded, and her heartbeat could not help but speed up. She got the waistcoat undone, pulled it off, and threw it on top of the coat. When she started on the buttons of his shirt, she was conscious that her breath was coming harder. She concentrated, staring at the white translucent material plastered to the hard planes of his chest. Crisp hair was shadowed under the cloth. She could feel his hot breath on the top of her head. This position was too intimate.

She determinedly drew off his shirt before she could stop and think about it, but she still faltered when his nude torso was revealed. His body was ever so much lovelier than her imaginings. The wide strong slopes of his shoulders led to surprisingly thick muscles on his arms, and his chest was broad and covered with dark curling hair on the upper part. Brown-red nipples peaked through the hair, hard and pointed and shockingly bare. His taut belly had only a fine line of dark hair that circled his navel before widening below and then disappearing into the waistband of his breeches. She'd stretched out one hand toward that seductive line of hair before she'd even realized her own movement.

Helen snatched back her wayward hand, hid it in her skirts, and said briskly, "Stand up so we can get the rest of these clothes off you. You're nearly blue with cold."

"Mrs. Halifax, your regard alone is enough to heat m-me," he drawled as he stood. The rakish words were only marred by the chattering of his teeth.

"Humph."

She knew that her entire face was enveloped in a fiery blush, but she still needed to get those wet breeches off him. She began on the buttons, waving his fumbling hands away when he tried to help her. He swayed as she got the last button undone, and suddenly she was no longer worried about her flush or what he might think of her.

"Get to the bed," she ordered.

"Bossy woman," he muttered, but his words were slurred again, and he shuffled toward the massive bed.

Once there, she had him lean against the mattress as she stripped his boots, breeches, hose, and smallclothes from him. She had only a glimpse of long hairy legs and a dark patch of fur at their apex before she was shoving him into the bed and heaping the covers on top of him.

She expected some sardonic comment from him then—perhaps along the lines of her hurry to get him into bed—but he merely closed his eyes. And that forbearance shot a bolt of pure fear through her. She stopped only to scoop the puppy up and plop him beneath the covers next to the man, and then she was running to the kitchen.

Thank God! Mrs. McCleod had indeed left a kettle warming by the banked kitchen fire. Helen quickly made tea and took the pot, a cup, and plenty of sugar along with an ancient metal bed-warming pan back up to Sir Alistair's bedroom. When she entered, panting from the quick climb up the stairs, his body was a still mound beneath the covers, and her heart gave a painful jolt.

But then he stirred. "I was beginning to wonder if the sight of my naked body had caused you to flee the castle."

She snorted as she laid her full tray on a table beside the bed. "I'm the mother of a small boy. I've seen a naked male body many times, I assure you. I bathed Jamie just tonight."

He grunted. "I'd hope that my form would be some-what different than a boy's."

She cleared her throat to say primly, "There are some differences, of course, but the similarities are still there."

"Humph." She knew he watched her as she took the warming pan to the fire and scooped in glowing coals. "Then undressing me gave you no more worry than bathing wee Jamie."

"Naturally not," she said with what she thought was admirable aplomb.

"Liar," he rasped softly.

She ignored that and brought the hot pan back to the bed. "Can you move over?"

He nodded, his face weary and lined. He managed to inch over on the mattress, and she threw back the covers to use the warming pan on the sheets. She tried hard, but it was impossible not to see the long line of his bared leg, hip, and side. Heat uncurled in her belly. Hastily, she averted her eyes.

When she finished, he rolled back and grunted, his eye closing. "Feels good."

"Good." She set the pan on the hearth and hurried back. "Try and sit up so you can take some tea."

His eye opened, surprisingly sharp and focused on her bosom. "You're soaked through, Mrs. Halifax. You need to attend to yourself."

She glanced down and saw that her chemise and wrap were nearly transparent. Her pointed nipples were outlined quite clearly against the thin fabric. Goodness! But modesty hardly mattered at the moment. "I'll attend to myself as soon as you're settled. Now sit up."

"I shall repay you for your officiousness later," he

warned, but he heaved himself against the pillow until he was half upright.

"You do that," she replied as she heaped sugar into the cup and then poured steaming tea in it.

"I don't think sugar will help your tea, Mrs. Halifax," he drawled behind her.

"Oh, hush." She turned and caught his gaze focused on her bottom. "It's hot and sweet, and that's what you need now. Drink."

She held the cup for him and he sipped, wincing. "Your tea could take the rust off iron. Do you mean to kill me?"

"Yes, that's exactly what I'm trying to do," she murmured soothingly. A small corner of her heart seemed to tug at his gruff words. He was so stubborn, so surly, and at the moment he needed her so much. "Take some more."

He sipped from the cup again, his gaze all the while on her face, steady and disconcerting. Her fingers trembled as she watched his strong throat work. She hastily took the cup away and set it on the tray.

"Thank you, Mrs. Halifax," he said. His eye was closed, and he'd sunk into the bed, but there was color in his face again. "I think I shall survive the night without you."

She frowned. "Perhaps I should heat a brick or bring more tea."

"God, please no more tea. You may retire for the night. Unless"—he opened his light brown eye and glanced at her sardonically—"you'd like to join me?"

Her eyes widened involuntarily at the blunt invitation, and for a crucial moment, she didn't know what to say or do. Then she whirled and left the room, his laughter echoing behind her as she rushed to her own bedroom.

*   *   *

PERHAPS IT WAS the memory of his housekeeper's lush breasts outlined in wet fabric the night before. Perhaps it was the lemon scent of her hair that seemed to linger like a ghostly presence in his rooms. Or perhaps it was simple biological need catching up with him. In any case, Alistair woke the next morning with the vision of her lush, red lips wrapped about his achingly hard prick. An overly vivid erotic dream, but alas, his flesh did not know the difference between reality and fantasy.

Alistair groaned and threw back the covers. His head, and indeed his entire body, ached most horribly, but still his cock was proudly erect. He contemplated that clayish part of himself. What an irony that even the most intellectual man could be reduced to this throbbing base need solely because of plump lips and a round white bosom. His prick bobbed at the vivid image of Mrs. Halifax. Proud. Argumentative.

Entirely naked.

He swallowed and touched himself, running his fingers up hot flesh made iron, surrounding the aching head in his fist. His foreskin was already pulled back by the swelling of his cock, and his seed gleamed between his fingers. His imaginary Mrs. Halifax knelt before him and cradled her own white breasts in her hands. She lifted them, offering them, at once wanton and shy, her lower lip caught between her teeth. He squeezed the head of his cock, feeling the shaft of pleasure shoot to his balls. Her breasts were big and bonny, overflowing her little hands. She took her red nipples between thumb and forefinger and pinched them hard, giving him a wicked look. He groaned and fisted down, pulling gently. If she pushed those soft mounds together, if he leaned forward and thrust his cock between her sweet, hot breasts . . .

Beside him came a small canine whimper.

He instinctively jerked and grabbed for the covers. "Shit!"

Then he remembered and let his body flop back on the pillows. He looked down. The puppy cringed against the bedding, half buried in the sheets that had covered him.

"It's all right, laddie," Alistair said. "It's not your fault I'm a daft man." Nor was it the puppy's fault that he still remained erect and aching.

But then he'd woken many a morning in this state. And since he'd returned from the Colonies, he'd had naught but his own hand to satisfy his animal desires. Once, several years ago, he'd reached a point of such frustration that he'd journeyed into a wretched section of Edinburgh. There he'd sought out the services of a woman paid to relieve men of their erotic urges. But when the whore he'd settled on saw his face in the candlelight of her rented room, she'd asked for a higher price. He'd left, humiliated and disgusted with himself, the whore shouting curses behind him. He'd never repeated that awful experience. Instead, he'd settled for his own hand whenever base lust overcame his reason.

The puppy bumbled out from the covers at the sound of his voice, its rear end wiggling in delight. It was a brown and white spaniel with floppy ears and a speckled nose. The puppy had come from a litter belonging to a farmer living just beyond Glenlargo. Saddling Griffin and riding out in search of a puppy yesterday had been a whim. The sight of Jamie scattering petals on Lady Grey's grave had stayed in his mind, nagging him for hours yesterday. Even more disturbing was Abigail running so determinedly away from the burial. Poor lass, so stiff and unlikable. Not sweet and biddable as a girl should be. He snorted softly. In a way she reminded him of himself.

The puppy stretched on too-large paws, his round belly nearly touching the bed, and yawned. No doubt he would need to relieve his bladder soon and, being a baby, wouldn't care where he did it.

"Hold on, laddie," Alistair muttered.

He rose, joints creaking, and began dressing, but he'd only managed smallclothes before his door suddenly opened. For the second time that morning, he grabbed for the sheets. The puppy spun and yelped at the intruder.

Alistair sighed, biting back a curse, and looked into startled harebell-blue eyes. "Good morning, Mrs. Halifax. Had you thought to knock before you entered?"

Those beautiful eyes blinked and she frowned. "What are you doing out of bed?"

"Attempting to find my breeches, if you must know." He propped a fist on his hip, thanking providence that he still wore his eye patch from the night before. "If you'll leave me in privacy, I can greet you more fully attired."

"Humph." Instead of leaving, she bustled past him and set her tray on the table next to his bed. "You need to get back in bed."

"What I *need*," he rasped, very aware that his cock had sprung back to life at her entrance, "is to dress and take the puppy out."

"I've brought you some warm milk and bread," she replied blithely, and then stood in front of him, arms folded, as if she actually expected him to eat pap.

He regarded the bowl on his bedside table. It was half

full of milk. Soggy bits of bread floated on top, a thoroughly revolting mess.

"I've begun to wonder, Mrs. Halifax," he said as he dropped the sheets and reached for the puppy, "if you've decided on a deliberate campaign to drive me mad."

"What—?"

"Your insistence on disturbing my work, hiring servants I do not need, and in general disrupting my life cannot be all accident."

"I didn't—!"

He set the puppy in front of the bowl as she sputtered. The puppy stuck its face and one paw in the bowl and began to eat, spilling milk and bread lumps on the table. Alistair looked at his housekeeper.

Who'd found her voice. "I *never*—"

"And then there's the problem of your attire."

She looked down at herself. "What's wrong with my attire?"

"This dress"—he flicked the lace at her bosom, brushing against warm, soft breasts as he did so—"is too fashionable for a housekeeper. Yet you persist in swanning about my castle in it, in an attempt to distract me."

Her cheeks reddened, making her blue eyes sparkle with indignation. "I have only the two dresses, if you must know. It isn't my fault that you find them objectionable."

He took a step toward her, his chest nearly touching the dress in question. He wasn't sure anymore if he was trying to drive her away or lure her closer. The scent of lemons was heady in his nostrils. "And what of your insistence on barging into my rooms without so much as a knock?"

"I—"

"The only conclusion I can come to is that you wish to see my body unclothed. Again."

Her eyes dropped—perhaps inevitably—to where his smallclothes tented over his rampant cock. Her lush, beckoning lips parted. God! This woman drove him insane.

He couldn't help but bend his head toward her, watching those plump red lips as she licked them nervously. "Perhaps I ought to assuage your curiosity."

HE MEANT TO kiss her, Helen knew. The intent was in every line of his face, in the sensuous look of his eye, in the determined pose of his body. He meant to kiss her, and the awful part was that she wanted him to. She wanted to feel those sometimes sarcastic, sometimes hurting lips on hers. She wanted to taste him, to inhale his male scent as he tried her. She actually began to lean toward him, to tilt her face up, to feel the racing of her heart. Oh, yes, she longed for him to kiss her, perhaps more than she longed for her next breath.

And then the children rushed into the room. Actually, it was Jamie mainly, running as always, with his sister following more slowly behind. Sir Alistair cursed rather foully under his breath and turned to clutch the sheets about his waist. He needn't have bothered, though, for all the attention the children paid him.

"A puppy!" Jamie cried, and lunged for the poor creature.

"Careful," Sir Alistair said. "He hasn't . . ."

But his warning came too late. Jamie lifted the dog, and at the same time, a thin stream of yellow liquid poured onto the floor. Jamie stood there, mouth open, holding the puppy in front of him.

"Ah . . ." Sir Alistair stared blankly, his magnificent chest still bared. Helen sympathized with the man. Half killed by cold the night before, not even dressed this morning, and already invaded by incontinent dogs and running children.

She cleared her throat. "I think—"

But she was interrupted by a giggle. A sweet, high, girlish giggle that she hadn't heard since they'd left London. Helen turned.

Abigail was still standing by the doorway, both hands clapped over her mouth, giggles spilling forth from between her fingers. She lowered her hands.

"He peed on you!" she crowed to her poor brother. "Peed and peed and peed! We ought to call him Puddles."

For a moment, Helen was afraid that Jamie would burst into tears, but then the puppy wriggled and he drew the little animal to his chest, grinning. "He's still a grand puppy. But we oughtn't to call him Puddles."

"Definitely not Puddles," Sir Alistair rumbled, and both children started and looked at him as if they'd forgotten him.

Abigail sobered. "It's not our dog, Jamie. We can't name him."

"No, he's not your dog," Sir Alistair said easily, "but I need help naming him. And at the moment, I need someone to take him out on the lawn and make sure he does the rest of his business there instead of the castle. Do I have any volunteers?"

The children jumped to the task, and Sir Alistair had barely nodded before they were out of the room. Suddenly she was alone again with the master of the castle.

Helen bent to wipe at the puddle on the floor with the cloth she'd brought from the kitchen along with the pap. She avoided his eyes. "Thank you."

"What for?" His voice was careless as he flipped the sheets back on the bed.

"You know." She looked up at him and realized her vision had blurred with tears. "Letting Abigail and Jamie take care of the puppy. They . . . they needed that right now. Thank you."

He shrugged, looking a bit uncomfortable. "It's little enough."

"Little enough?" She stood, suddenly irritated. "You almost killed yourself getting that dog. It was more than little enough!"

"Who says I got the dog for the children?" he growled.

"Didn't you?" she demanded. He liked to act the beast, but underneath she sensed a different man entirely.

"And if I did?" He stepped closer and gently grasped her shoulders. "Perhaps I deserve a reward."

She had no time to think or debate or even anticipate. His lips were on hers, warm and slightly rasping from the stubble on his chin, and oh, they felt good. Masculine. Yearning. She hadn't been wanted like this in so long. Hadn't been kissed by a man since she couldn't remember. She leaned into him, her hands on his bare upper arms, and that was wonderful, too, the feel of his hot, smooth skin beneath her fingers. He opened his mouth over hers and probed gently with his tongue, and she opened, welcoming him in. Happily. Wonderfully. Easily.

Perhaps too easily.

This was her one great fault: a tendency to act too

soon. To fall in love too fast. Giving everything of herself only to regret her impulsive passion later. She'd thought Lister's kisses lovely, too, once upon a time, and what had that led to?

Nothing but despair.

She drew away, panting, and looked at him. His eye was half-closed, his face flushed and sensuous with a darkened beard of whiskers.

She tried to think of something to say. "I . . ."

In the end, she merely pressed her fingers to her lips and ran from the room like the greenest virgin.

"ROVER," JAMIE SAID. He was squatting in the grass behind the castle, watching as the puppy sniffed at a beetle he'd found.

Abigail rolled her eyes. "Does he look like a Rover to you?"

"Yes," Jamie said, and then added, "Or perhaps Captain."

Abigail carefully lifted her skirts and found a bit of dryish grass to sit in. Most everything was soaked from the storm the night before. "I think Tristan would be nice."

"That's a girl's name."

"Is not. Tristan was a great warrior." Abigail frowned a little, not entirely sure of her facts. "Or something. Certainly not a girl, anyway."

"Well, it sounds like a girl's name," Jamie said stoutly.

He picked up a twig and held it in front of the puppy's nose. The puppy bit the twig and took it from him. He flopped on the ground, back legs splayed behind him, and started chewing the twig.

"Don't let him eat it," Abigail said.

"I'm not," Jamie said. "And, anyway—"

"Oy!" a familiar voice called. "Wot have you there?"

Behind them stood Mr. Wiggins. His head blotted out the morning sun, and the red hair standing up around his face seemed to be on fire. He swayed just a little on his feet and frowned down at the puppy.

"He's Sir Alistair's dog," she said quickly, afraid he'd try to take the dog. "We're watching him for Sir Alistair."

Mr. Wiggins squinted, his little eyes nearly disappearing into wrinkles in his face. "Lowly work for a duke's daughter, innit?"

Abigail bit her lip. She'd so hoped that he had forgotten Jamie's words from the day before.

But Mr. Wiggins was thinking about other matters. "Juss make sure it don't piss in the kitchen. Have enough work about here as it is, don't I?"

"He—" Jamie started, but Abigail interrupted him.

"We won't," she said sweetly.

"Huh." Mr. Wiggins grunted and walked off again.

Abigail waited until he'd disappeared into the castle; then she rounded on her brother. "You mustn't say anything to him again."

"You're not the master of me!" Jamie's lower lip trembled, and his face was growing red.

Abigail knew that these were signs of an imminent fit of screaming or crying or both, but she pressed, anyway. "It's important, Jamie. You mustn't let him tease you into saying things."

"I didn't," he muttered, which they both knew was a lie.

Abigail sighed. Jamie was still very young, and this

was the best she'd get out of him. She held the puppy out. "Would you like to hold Puddles?"

"He's not Puddles," he said, but he took the puppy and squished it against his chest, hiding his face in its soft fur.

"I know."

Abigail sat back on the grass and closed her eyes, feeling the sun on her face. She ought to tell Mama what Jamie'd said. She ought to go right now and find her. But then Mama would become cross and worried, and it'd spoil this new happiness. Maybe it wouldn't matter, anyway.

"Puddles hasn't seen the stables," Jamie said beside her. He seemed to have recovered his good temper. "Let's show him."

"Very well."

Abigail stood and trailed her brother across the wet grass toward the stables. The day was lovely, after all, and they had a sweet puppy to take care of. Something made her look back over her shoulder in the direction that Mr. Wiggins had gone. He was nowhere to be seen, but black clouds hovered in the distance, ominous and low, threatening the sunshine.

She shivered and ran to catch up with Jamie.

"THEY SAY WHEATON will propose another soldiers' pension bill this next parliament," the Earl of Blanchard said, leaning back in his chair until Lister feared he'd break it.

"The man never gives up," Lord Hasselthorpe said with contempt. "I predict we'll dismiss it with hardly any debate. What do you say, Your Grace?"

Lister contemplated the glass of brandy he held in

his hand. They were in Hasselthorpe's study, a pleasant enough room, even if it was done in purple and pink. Hasselthorpe was a sober man with a cool head on his shoulders and the ambition of obtaining the prime minister's seat—perhaps very soon—but he had a nitwit for a wife. She'd probably done the decorating.

Lister looked at his host. "Wheaton's bill is pure nonsense, of course. Think what a pension for every idiot who's ever served in His Majesty's army would cost this government. But there may be some popular support for the thing."

"Come, sir, you don't truly believe it might pass?" Blanchard looked aghast.

"Pass, no," Lister said. "But there may be a fight. Have you read the pamphlets circulating on the street?"

"The rhetoric of pamphleteers is hardly sophisticated," Hasselthorpe scoffed.

"No, but they do sway the coffeehouse regulars." Lister frowned. "And recent events in the Colonies during the war with the French have brought the fate of the common soldier to the forefront of people's minds. Atrocities such as the massacre at Spinner's Falls make some wonder if our soldiers are paid enough."

Hasselthorpe leaned slightly forward. "My brother was killed at Spinner's Falls. The idea of the massacre being used as some bully point in a pamphleteer's spouting makes me sick, sir."

Lister shrugged. "I agree. I merely point out the opposition we will face to defeating this bill."

Blanchard made his chair creak again as he went into a long ramble about drunken soldiers and thieves, but

Lister was distracted. Henderson had cracked the door to the room and poked his head in.

"If you'll excuse me," Lister said, interrupting whatever Blanchard was babbling about.

He barely waited for the other gentlemen's nods before rising and going to the door. "What?"

"I beg your pardon, Your Grace, for disturbing you," Henderson whispered nervously, "but I have news about a certain lady's flight."

Lister glanced over his shoulder. Hasselthorpe's and Blanchard's heads were together, and in any case, it was doubtful they could hear him. He turned back to his secretary. "Yes?"

"She and the children were sighted in Edinburgh, Your Grace, not much more than a week ago."

Edinburgh? Interesting. He wasn't aware that Helen knew anyone in Scotland. Had she found someplace in Edinburgh to stay, or was she traveling on from there?

He focused once more on Henderson. "Good. Send a dozen more men. I want them to scour Edinburgh, find out if she's still there, and if she isn't, where the hell she went."

Henderson bowed. "Very well, Your Grace."

And Lister allowed himself a very small smile. The distance between the hunter and the prey had narrowed. Soon, very soon, he'd hold Helen's sweet neck between his hands.

Chapter Seven

One evening as Truth Teller guarded the monster, the
young man did not come at the expected hour. The
sun lowered and set, the shadows lengthened in
the yew knot garden, and the swallows stopped
fluttering and found perches in their cage. When
Truth Teller peered at the monster, he saw something
pale behind the bars. Curious, he walked closer,
and to his astonishment saw that the monster had
disappeared. In its place lay a nude woman, her long
black hair spread around her like a cloak.

At that moment, the beautiful young man ran
panting into the castle courtyard, crying, "Go!
Go now!"

Truth Teller obediently turned to leave, but his
master called behind him, "Have you seen aught to
frighten you today?"

Truth Teller paused but did not turn around.

"No. . . ."

—from TRUTH TELLER

She was avoiding him. By midmorning, when a tray of tea and biscuits were delivered to his study by one of the new maids instead of his maddening housekeeper, Alistair was sure of it. Had he repulsed her with that kiss? Frightened her with his clear intent? Well, to hell with it. This was his castle, dammit; *she* was the one who'd insisted on disturbing his peace. She couldn't hide from him now. Besides, he reasoned as he ran down the tower stairs, it was past time to inquire about the morning mail.

When he entered the kitchen, he saw Mrs. Halifax huddled with the cook over a steaming pot on the hearth, and she didn't see him at first. Near the hall door he'd just entered, the boy and girl played with the puppy. No other servants were in sight.

"Are you come for luncheon?" Jamie asked, clutching the wiggling puppy to his chest. "We're to feed Puddles a bowl of milk soon."

"Mind you take him out afterward," Alistair muttered. He started for the hearth. "And *do* think of another name for the pup."

"Yes, sir," Abigail called behind him.

Mrs. Halifax looked up as he neared, and her eyes widened as if startled by the sight of him. "Can I get you something, Sir Alistair?"

There was wariness in her gaze. *Or maybe she was simply appalled that she'd let such a disgusting beast near her,* a mocking voice taunted.

The thought made him frown as he said, "I came for my mail."

The cook muttered something and bent over her pot. Mrs. Halifax glided to a nearby table, where a small bundle of letters lay. "I'm sorry. I should've had them sent up." She held out the bundle.

He took it, his fingers brushing briefly against hers and then frowned down as he shuffled the letters. A reply from Etienne wasn't there, of course—it was much too soon—but he'd hoped it would be nonetheless. Alistair had been brooding over the Spinner's Falls traitor since Vale's letter. Or perhaps it was Mrs. Halifax's advent and the knowledge of all he'd lost along with his face in that terrible massacre.

"Were you expecting a letter?" Mrs. Halifax interrupted his dark thoughts.

He shrugged and tucked the letters in a pocket. "A missive from a colleague in another country. Nothing terribly important."

"You correspond with gentlemen abroad?" She tilted her head as if intrigued.

He nodded. "I exchange findings and ideas with other naturalists in France, Norway, Italy, Russia, and the American Colonies. I have a friend exploring the wilds of China right now and another somewhere in deepest Africa."

"How wonderful! And you must travel as well to visit these friends and explore yourself."

He stared at her. Was she mocking him? "I never leave the castle."

She stilled. "Truly? I know you like the castle, but surely you must travel sometimes. What of your work?"

"I haven't traveled since returning from the Colonies." He could no longer meet those wide blue eyes, and he glanced away, watching the children play with the puppy by the door. "You know what I look like. You know why I stay here."

"But . . ." Her brows knit before she took a step toward him, forcing him to meet her solemn gaze once more. "I know it must be hard to go out. I know people must stare. It must be awful. But to shut yourself up here forever . . . you don't deserve such a punishment."

"Deserve?" He felt his mouth twist. "The men who died in the Colonies didn't deserve their deaths. My fate has nothing to do with whether or not I *deserve* it. It's simply fact: I am scarred. I frighten little children and the sensitive. Therefore, I stay in this castle."

"How can you bear to live the rest of your life thus?"

He shrugged. "I don't think of the rest of my life. This is simply my fate."

"The past can't be changed. I understand that," she said. "But can't one accept the past and still continue to hope?"

"Hope?" He stared at her. She argued her case too intensely for it not to be personal in some way—but in what way he wasn't certain. "I don't understand your meaning."

She leaned toward him, her blue eyes serious. "Don't you think about the future? Plan for happy times? Strive to better your life?"

He shook his head. Her philosophy was entirely foreign to his way of thinking. "What point in planning for a future when my past will never change? I am not unhappy."

"But are you happy?"

He turned to the door. "Does it matter?"

"Of course it matters." He felt her small hand at his

arm. He swiveled to look at her again, so bright, so pretty. "How can you live your life without happiness, or even the hope of happiness?"

"Now I know you mock me," he growled, and wrest his arm free.

He strode from the kitchen, deaf to her protest. He knew she didn't have it in her to be so cruel, but her very honesty was in some ways more harsh than mocking laughter. How could he think of a future when he had none, when he'd given up all faith of one nearly seven years ago? Even the thought of resurrecting that optimism filled him with a kind of horror. No, better to flee the kitchen and his too-perceptive housekeeper than to face his own weakness.

HELEN WAS OUT front sweeping the step that afternoon when a rumbling made her look up. A great carriage and four was coming down the drive, and the sight was so strange—as she'd already become used to the castle's isolation—that all she could do was stand there and gape for a moment. Then fear slammed her heart into her ribs. Dear God, had Lister found them?

By rights, Meg or Nellie should be sweeping the step, but the maids were busy turning over the first-floor sitting room. So she'd gone after the step herself following luncheon, maddened by the sight of the weeds growing between the cracks. Which left her standing in a rumpled apron armed only with a broom. She didn't even have time to try and hide the children.

The carriage rolled majestically to a stop and a be-wigged footman jumped down to set the step and open the door. A very tall lady emerged, bowing her head to clear the carriage roof. Helen nearly dropped to the ground in relief. The lady wore an elegant cream dress with a striped underskirt and a lace cap topped by a straw hat. Behind her was a shorter, plump lady, all in lavender and yellow with a great frilly cap and bonnet framing her jolly red face. The tall lady straightened and frowned at Helen through a pair of formidable and rather odd spectacles. They were large, entirely round, and had thick black frames with an X between the eye pieces.

"Who," the woman said, "are you?"

Helen curtsied, rather well she thought, considering she was holding a broom. "I'm Mrs. Halifax, Sir Alistair's new housekeeper."

The tall lady raised her eyebrows skeptically and turned to her companion. "Did you hear that, Phoebe? Chit says she's Alistair's housekeeper. Does it seem likely to you that he's hired a housekeeper?"

The shorter, plump lady shook out her skirts and smiled at Helen. "Since she said she's the housekeeper, Sophie, and since she was sweeping the step as we arrived, I think we must assume that Alistair has indeed obtained a housekeeper."

"Hmm," was all the tall lady said to that. "You might as well show us in, girl. I doubt Alistair has a decent room, but we're staying nonetheless."

Helen felt her face warm. It'd been quite a while since she'd last been called a girl, but the lady didn't seem to mean anything by it.

"I'm sure I can find something," she said, not sure at all. If she set the maids to cleaning two of the spare rooms right away, they might be ready by nightfall. *Might.*

"Perhaps we ought to introduce ourselves," the shorter lady murmured.

"Should we?" wondered her companion.

"Yes." Was the firm reply.

"Very well," the taller lady said. "I am Miss Sophia Munroe, Sir Alistair's sister, and this is Miss Phoebe McDonald."

"How do you do?" Helen curtsied again.

"Very pleased to meet you," Miss McDonald beamed, her plump, red cheeks shining. She seemed to have forgotten that Helen was a servant.

"Won't you come this way?" Helen said politely. "Um . . . is Sir Alistair expecting you?"

"Of course not," Miss Munroe said promptly as she stepped inside the castle. "If he was, he wouldn't be here." She took off her hat and frowned around the hall. "He *is* here, isn't he?"

"Oh, yes," Helen said, taking both ladies' hats. She looked about the hall and finally laid them on a marble table. Hopefully it wasn't too dusty. "I'm sure he'll be quite pleased to know you've come to visit."

Miss Munroe snorted. "Then you're more sanguine than I."

Helen thought it best not to reply to that comment. Instead, she led her guests to the sitting room that she'd set the maids to cleaning, crossing her fingers that things had progressed since luncheon.

But when she opened the door, Tom the footman was sneezing explosively, his head covered in an enormous dusty cobweb, and both Meg and Nellie were giggling uncontrollably. The servants straightened at her entrance, and Nellie slapped a hand over her mouth to contain her laughter.

Helen sighed and turned back to the ladies. "Perhaps

you'd prefer to wait in the dining room. It's the only entirely neat room in the castle, I'm afraid—barring the kitchen."

"Not at all." Miss Munroe swept into the room and stared critically at the moth-eaten row of stuffed animal heads that lined one wall. "Phoebe and I can direct matters here whilst you fetch Alistair."

Helen nodded and left the servants behind with the ladies. As she mounted the stairs, she could hear Miss Munroe barking orders. She hadn't seen Sir Alistair since their argument this morning in the kitchen. The truth was that she'd been avoiding him, she'd even sent Meg up with his luncheon instead of delivering it herself. In fact, she realized as she made the third floor, she wasn't completely sure that Sir Alistair was lurking in his tower room. For all she knew, he'd decided to take one of his rambles.

But when she knocked at the door to the tower, Sir Alistair's deep voice rasped, "Come."

She opened the door and stepped into the tower. Sir Alistair was at the biggest table, bent over a book with a magnifying glass in his hand.

He spoke without looking up. "Have you come to distract me from my work, Mrs. Halifax?"

"Your sister has arrived."

He glanced up sharply at that. "What?"

She blinked. He'd shaved. His unscarred cheek was quite smooth and rather nice-looking, actually. She mentally shook herself. "Your sister—"

He surged around the table. "Nonsense. Why would Sophia come here?"

"I think she's merely—"

But he was already striding past her. "Something must be the matter."

"I don't think anything's wrong," she called as she trailed him.

He didn't seem to hear, descending the stairs rapidly. She was panting by the time they'd made the lower hall, but he wasn't out of breath at all.

He stopped and frowned. "Where did you put her?"

"In the sitting room with the ugly animal heads," Helen gasped.

"Wonderful. She's sure to say something about that," Sir Alistair muttered.

Helen rolled her eyes. It wasn't as if she could leave his sister waiting in the *drive*.

Sir Alistair strode ahead and burst into the sitting room. "What's happened?"

Miss Munroe turned to him and frowned through her odd spectacles. "Grandfather's hunting trophies have moldered completely. They should be thrown out."

Sir Alistair scowled. "You didn't travel all the way from Edinburgh to critique the state of Grandfather's hunting trophies. And what are those things on your face?"

"These"—Miss Munroe touched her ugly spectacles— "are Mr. Benjamin Martin's visual glasses, which he has developed scientifically to reduce the damage that light has upon the eye. I had them shipped all the way from London."

"Good God, they're ugly."

"Sir Alistair!" Helen gasped.

"Well, they are," he muttered. "*And* she knows it."

But his sister was smiling tightly. "Exactly the reaction I'd expect from a philistine such as yourself."

"So you traveled all the way here just to show them to me?"

"No, I came to see if my only brother was still alive."

"Why wouldn't I be alive?"

"I haven't received an answer to my last three letters," his sister shot back. "What was I to think but that you lay rotting somewhere in this old castle?"

"I answer all your letters." Sir Alistair frowned.

"Not the last three you haven't."

Helen cleared her throat. "Would anyone care for tea?"

"Oh, that would be lovely," Miss McDonald said from beside Miss Munroe. "And some scones, perhaps? Sophie loves scones, don't you, dear?"

"I loathe—" Miss Munroe began, but then stopped abruptly. If Helen didn't know better, she'd swear that Miss McDonald had pinched her. Miss Munroe drew in a breath and admitted, "I could take some tea."

"Good." Helen nodded to Meg, who, with the rest of the servants, had been standing watching the argument. "Please ask Cook for some tea and see if she has any scones or cakes to go with it."

"Yes, mum." Meg hurried from the room.

Helen stared pointedly at the remaining servants until they followed reluctantly.

"Won't you offer your sister a seat?" Helen murmured to Sir Alistair.

"I've got work to do," he grumbled, but said, "Please sit, Sophia, Phoebe. You, too, Mrs. Halifax."

"But—" she started, then thought better of her objection when he turned his one eye to glare at her. She sat primly in an armless chair.

"Thank you, Alistair," Miss Munroe said, and lowered herself to one of the settees.

Miss McDonald sat beside her and said, "It's so nice to see you again, Alistair. We were disappointed that you couldn't come for Christmas. We had a lovely roast goose, quite the biggest I've ever seen."

"I never come for Christmas," Sir Alistair muttered. He chose a chair next to Helen, making her rather self-conscious.

"But perhaps you should," Miss McDonald chided gently.

Her words seemed to be much more effective than Miss Munroe's strident ones. Sir Alistair's high cheekbones actually looked a little ruddy. "You know I don't like to travel."

"Yes, dear," Miss McDonald said, "but that's not sufficient reason to ignore us. Sophie was quite hurt when you never even wrote her a Christmas letter."

Beside her, Miss Munroe snorted, looking far from hurt.

Sir Alistair frowned and started to open his mouth.

Helen feared what he might say and hastily addressed Miss McDonald. "I understand you live in Edinburgh?"

That lady beamed. "Yes, indeed. Sophie and I have a lovely Whitestone house with a view of the city. Sophie belongs to quite a few scientific and philosophical societies, and we can attend a lecture, a demonstration, or a salon nearly every day of the week."

"How lovely," Helen said. "And you must be interested in science and philosophy, too, Miss McDonald?"

"Oh, I have an interest," she replied, smiling, "but not the avocation that Sophie has."

"Nonsense," Miss Munroe barked. "You do quite well for an untrained mind, Phoebe."

"Why, thank you, Sophie," Miss McDonald murmured, and twinkled conspiratorially at Helen.

Helen hid a smile. Miss McDonald seemed to know exactly how to handle her formidable friend.

"Did you know that Sir Alistair is working on another wonderful book?" she asked.

"Really?" Miss McDonald clapped her hands. "Can we see it?"

Miss Munroe arched an eyebrow at her brother. "Glad to hear you're working again."

"It's still in the early stages yet," he muttered.

The maids returned with the tea things at that point, and for a moment all was chaos as they set up.

Sir Alistair took advantage of the bustle to lean toward Helen and murmur, "Wonderful?"

She felt her cheeks heat. "Your book *is* wonderful."

His brown eye searched her face. "You've read it, then?"

"I haven't—not all of it—but I looked through part of it last night." She felt her breath catch at the intensity of his gaze. "It was fascinating."

"Was it?"

He was watching her mouth now, his eye narrowed and intent, and she wondered if he was remembering their kiss. She'd vowed not to repeat it. Involving herself with this man would be yet another example of rushing into folly without a thought for the danger. But as he raised his gaze and met her eyes, she knew.

Dangerous as it was, this folly was beginning to look very tempting, indeed.

* * *

AFTER TEA, ALISTAIR spent the remainder of the afternoon in his tower, not only because he wanted to finish the section on badgers, but also because he feared that if he lingered much longer near his seductive housekeeper, he might do something truly foolish. And besides, he was certain Sophia was harrying the help to clean the castle. He would be smart to stay well away from that.

So it was evening before he saw Mrs. Halifax again. He'd just come from his rooms, having remembered to clean up before dinner and even pull out a decent coat and breeches so his sister wouldn't scold too badly. Mrs. Halifax had also decided to wear her best, it seemed. He paused at the bottom of the stairs, watching her before she saw him. She'd worn the same blue frock every day since she'd come to the castle, but tonight she had on a green and gold gown, much too rich for a housekeeper, and what was worse, it revealed even more of her creamy bosom. Suddenly Alistair was glad that he'd taken the time to club his hair back and shave.

She turned and saw him at that moment, and for a second she paused, her blue eyes wide and vulnerable, her lovely cheeks pink and innocent. He should simply turn and remount the stairs. Lock himself in his tower and order her from his castle and his life. She hoped for some starry future, and he knew he had none.

Instead he strolled toward her. "You seem to have everything well in hand for dinner, Mrs. Halifax."

She looked distractedly into the dining room. "I think it'll do. Let me know if the service isn't properly done. Tom's still learning about serving soup."

"Oh, but you'll be there to observe," he said, taking her

arm. "Have you forgotten our bargain to dine together? You were quite adamant about my part last night."

"But your sister!" Her cheeks flamed. "She'll think that . . . that . . . you *know*."

"What she'll think is that I'm eccentric, and *that* she already knows." He watched her sardonically. "Come, Mrs. Halifax, this is no time for missish nerves. Where are your children?"

She looked, if possible, even more scandalized. "In the kitchen, but you can't—"

He beckoned to one of the maids. "Fetch Mrs. Halifax's children, please."

The maid hurried off. He arched an eyebrow down at his housekeeper. "There. You see. Quite simple."

"Only if one disregards all propriety," she muttered darkly.

"There you are, brother," Sophia's brisk voice came from behind them.

Alistair turned and bowed to his sister. "As you see."

She finished descending the stairs. "Wasn't sure you'd come down for dinner. And quite neat, too. I suppose I should be honored. But then"—she eyed Mrs. Halifax's hand on his arm—"perhaps your pretty toilet wasn't for me."

Mrs. Halifax tried to withdraw her hand, but Alistair placed his firmly over hers, preventing her. "Your favor is always uppermost in my mind, Sophia."

She snorted at that.

"Sophie," Phoebe chided from behind her. She shot an apologetic look at him. Poor Phoebe McDonald was always smoothing things over in his sister's wake.

Alistair was just opening his mouth to point out just

that—perhaps unwisely—when Jamie came rushing around the corner, nearly cannoning into Sophia.

"Jamie!" Mrs. Halifax cried.

The boy skidded to a stop and stared at Sophia.

Behind him came his sister, more sedate as always. "Meg said we were to come to dinner."

Sophia looked down her long nose at the girl. "Who are you?"

"I'm Abigail, ma'am," she said, curtsying. "This is my brother, Jamie. I apologize for him."

Sophia arched an eyebrow. "I'll wager you do that quite a lot."

Abigail sighed, sounding world-weary. "Yes, I do."

"Good girl." Sophia *almost* smiled. "Younger brothers can be a chore sometimes, but one must persevere."

"Yes, ma'am," Abigail said solemnly.

"Come on, Jamie," Alistair said. "Let's go into dinner before they form a Society for Bossy Older Sisters."

Jamie headed into the dining room with alacrity. Alistair took his habitual seat at the head of the table, seating Sophia to his right as was proper, but ensuring that Mrs. Halifax was to his left. He pulled out her chair for her pointedly when she tried to make a break for it and hide at the other end of the table.

"Thank you," she muttered rather ungraciously as she sat.

"You're quite welcome," he murmured gently as he pushed the chair in overly hard.

Sophia was busy instructing Abigail on the proper placement of her water glass and so missed their byplay, but Phoebe watched them curiously from the other side of Mrs. Halifax. Damn. He'd forgotten how observant the little woman was. He nodded at her and received a wink in reply.

"So you've begun writing again," Sophia said as Tom brought in a tureen of clear soup with a maid to serve it.

"Yes," Alistair replied cautiously.

"And this is the same work?" she demanded. "The one about the various birds and animals and insects in Britain?"

"Yes."

"Good. Good. I'm glad to hear it." She waved away the basket of bread Abigail was attempting to pass her. "No, thank you. I never eat yeasted breads after luncheon. I hope," she continued, turning on him again, "that you'll do a proper job of it. Richards made a hash of it with his *Zoölogia* a few years back. Tried to show that chickens were related to lizards, the idiot. Ha!"

Alistair leaned back to let the maid set a bowl of soup before him. "Richards is a pedantic ass, but his comparison of chickens and lizards was quite reasonable in my opinion."

"I suppose you think badgers are related to bears as well?" Sophia's spectacles glinted dangerously.

"As a matter of fact, the claws of both have a striking resemblance—"

"Ha!"

"And," he continued unperturbed, as they had, after all, been arguing like this since childhood, "when I dissected a badger carcass last autumn, I found similarities in the bones of the skull and forearms as well."

"What's a carcass?" Jamie asked before Sophia could set into him.

"A dead body," Alistair explained. Beside him, Mrs.

Halifax choked. He turned and solicitously thumped her on the back.

"I'm quite fine," she gasped. "But might we change the subject?"

"Certainly," he said kindly. "Perhaps we ought to discuss dung instead."

"Oh, Lord," Mrs. Halifax muttered beside him.

He ignored her, turning to his sister. "You won't believe what I found in the dung of a badger the other day."

"Yes?" Sophia asked with interest.

"A bird beak."

"Nonsense!"

"Indeed, it was. A small one—perhaps a titmouse or a sparrow—but a bird's beak most certainly."

"Surely not a titmouse. They don't come to the ground that often."

"Ah, but it's my judgment that the bird was already dead when ingested by the badger."

"You promised no more dead bodies," Mrs. Halifax burst out.

He looked at her and had a hard time not laughing. "I promised no more *badger* carcasses. This is a *bird* carcass we speak of."

She frowned at him, beautifully, of course. "You're being didactic."

"Yes, I am." He smiled. "What're you going to do about it?" Out of the corner of his eye, he saw Sophia and Phoebe exchange a raised-eyebrow glance, but he ignored them.

Mrs. Halifax tilted her nose in the air. "I just think you should be more polite to the woman who oversees the making of your bed."

His eyebrows shot up. "Are you threatening to place toads in my bed, madam?"

"Perhaps," she said loftily, but her eyes laughed at him.

His gaze dropped to her mouth, lush and wet, and he felt his loins turn to iron. He said low so no one else could overhear, "I would pay more attention to the threat were it something else you placed in my bed."

"Don't," she whispered.

"Don't what?"

"You know." Those harebell-blue eyes met his, wide and vulnerable. "Don't tease."

Her murmured words should've made him feel ashamed. But, like the basest cad, it only heightened his interest. *Careful,* a voice whispered. *Don't let the woman seduce you into thinking you can give her what she wants.* He should listen to that voice. Should obey and turn away from Mrs. Halifax before it was too late. Instead he leaned forward, beguiled despite himself.

LATER THAT EVENING, Miss Munroe lifted her dish of tea, pinned Helen with a piercing gaze, and asked, "How long has my brother employed you as his housekeeper?"

Helen swallowed the sip of tea she'd just taken and replied cautiously, "Only a few days."

"Ah." Miss Munroe sat back and stirred her tea vigorously.

Helen turned to her own tea, somewhat disconcerted. It was hard to tell whether that "ah" had been approving, disapproving, or something else entirely. After dinner they had retired to the sitting room, now cleaned—well, at least cleaner than it had been before. The maids had labored over it all afternoon and even had a fire crackling in the old stone fireplace. The stuffed animals still stared down out of rather gruesome glass eyeballs, but they no longer had trails of cobwebs hanging from their ears. That was a definite improvement.

Jamie and Abigail had stayed in the sitting room only long enough to make their good nights. When Helen had put them to bed and returned, Sir Alistair had been in discussion with Miss McDonald at the far end of the room. Miss Munroe had sat waiting by the door. If Helen was a suspicious sort, she'd wonder if Miss Munroe had been lying in wait for her.

Now she cleared her throat. "Sir Alistair said he hadn't seen you in quite some time?"

Miss Munroe scowled over her tea. "He hides himself away here like a leper."

"Perhaps he feels self-conscious," Helen murmured.

She glanced to where Sir Alistair and Miss McDonald were in conversation. Instead of tea, he drank brandy from a clear glass. He tilted his head toward the older lady, listening gravely to whatever she was saying. His clubbed hair exposed his scars, but it also civilized his countenance. Studying his profile, she realized that without the scars, he was a handsome man. Had he been used to female attention before he'd been maimed? The thought disconcerted her, and she looked away from him.

Only to find Miss Munroe watching her with an inscrutable expression. "It's more than self-consciousness."

"What do you mean?" Helen frowned into her tea, thinking. "Abigail screamed when she first saw him."

Miss Munroe nodded once, sharply. "Exactly. Children who don't know him fear him. Even grown men have been known to look askance at him."

"He doesn't like making *others* uncomfortable." Helen looked into Miss Munroe's eyes, seeing a spark of approval there.

"Can you imagine?" Miss Munroe mused softly. "Having a face that made you the center of attention wherever you went? Having people stop and stare and be afraid? He can't just be himself, can't just fade into a crowd. Wherever he goes, he's made aware of himself. He never has a moment of respite."

"It would be hellish." Helen bit her lip, a wave of unwanted sympathy washing over her, threatening to drown her good sense. "Especially for him. He's so gruff on the outside, but on the inside I think he's more sensitive than he likes to let on."

"Now you begin to understand." Miss Munroe sat back in her seat and stared broodingly at her brother. "It was actually better when he first returned from the Colonies. Oh, his wounds were fresher then, more shocking, but he hadn't yet realized, I think. It was a year or two before he knew that it would always be like this. That he was no longer an anonymous man but a freak."

Helen made a small sound of dissent at the harsh word.

Miss Munroe looked at her sharply. "It's true. It does him no good to gloss over it, to pretend that the scars aren't there or that he's a normal man. He is what he is." She leaned forward, her gaze so intense that Helen wanted to look away. "And I love him more for it. Do you hear me? He was a good man when he went away to the Colonies. He came back an extraordinary man. So many think that bravery is a single act of valor in a field of battle—no forethought, no contemplation of the consequences. An act over in a second or a minute or two at most. What my brother has done, is doing now, is to live with his burden for *years*. He knows that he will spend the rest of his life with it. And he soldiers on." She sat back in her chair, her gaze still locked with Helen's. "*That* to my mind is what real bravery is."

Helen tore her eyes away from the other woman and stared blindly down at the teacup, her hand trembling. Earlier, in the kitchen, she'd not fully understood his burden. To tell the truth, she'd thought him a bit of a coward for hiding in his dirty castle. But now . . . To live an outcast to humankind for years and to understand fully that damnation—as surely such an intelligent man as Sir Alistair must—yes, that would take real fortitude. Real bravery. She'd never thought before about what Sir Alistair endured, what he would endure for the rest of his natural life.

She looked up. He still talked to Miss McDonald, his face in profile to her. His scars were all hidden from this angle. His nose was straight and long, his chin firm and somewhat pronounced. His cheek was lean, his eye heavy-lidded. He looked like a handsome, clever man. Perhaps a bit weary this late in the evening. He must've felt her gaze. He turned, fully revealing his scars now, welted and red and ugly. His eye patch hid his missing eye, but the cheek under it sagged.

She stared at his face, at *him,* seeing both the hand-some, clever man, and the scarred, sardonic recluse. The air felt thin in her lungs, and her chest labored to take in more, but still she stared, forcing herself to see all of him.

All of Sir Alistair. What she saw should have repelled her, but instead she felt an attraction so intense it was all she could do not to rise and go to him at once.

He slowly raised his glass of brandy and saluted her before drinking, still watching her over the rim.

Only then could she tear her gaze away, gasping to fill her lungs with air. Something had happened in those few seconds when she'd held his eyes. It was as if she'd seen into his soul.

And perhaps as if he'd seen into hers.

Chapter Eight

Now, all the next day, Truth Teller thought of what he'd seen, and as the shadows grew long in the courtyard, he went to the cage of swallows and opened the door. Immediately they flew out and swarmed the evening sky. When the beautiful young man came into the courtyard, he gave an angry shout. He drew a fine silk bag and a little gold hook from his robes and gave chase to the swallows, running from the castle as he followed them. . . .
—from TRUTH TELLER

Alistair woke the next morning before dawn, as was his usual custom. He stirred the fire, lit a candle, splashed about in the frigid water in the basin on his dresser, and hurriedly got dressed. But when he walked out into the hallway, he paused in indecision. When Lady Grey had been alive, they'd take their morning rambles at this time, but now she was gone and the new, still unnamed puppy was too little to ramble.

He wandered, feeling vaguely irritable and sad, to the window at the end of the hall. Mrs. Halifax had been here. The window was suspiciously clean on the inside, although the ivy still half covered the outside. Hazy peach light was just beginning to illuminate the hills. It was going to be a sunny day. A perfect day for rambling, he thought morosely. Or a day for . . .

The wayward thought crystallized, and he made for the stairs. On the floor below, no light shone beneath the door of the room of his sister and Miss MacDonald. Oh, it'd been years since he'd gotten the drop on Sophia. Alistair banged on the door.

"What is it?" she shouted from within. Like him, she woke at once, fully alert.

"Time to rise, sleepyhead," he called.

"Alistair? Have you lost what mind you have?" She stumped to the door and flung it open. Sophia wore a voluminous gown, her graying hair in long braids.

He grinned at her grumpy expression. "It's summer, the day is sunny, and the fish are running."

Her eyes widened, and then narrowed in excited comprehension. "Give me half an hour."

"Twenty minutes," he called over his shoulder. He was already making for Mrs. Halifax's room around the bend.

"Done!" Sophia shot back, and slammed her door.

Mrs. Halifax's door was equally dark, but that didn't stop Alistair from rapping loudly on the wood. From within came a muffled groan and a thump. Then all was quiet. He knocked again.

Bare feet pattered to the door and it cracked open. Abigail's pale little face peered out.

Alistair looked at her. "Are you the only one awake?"

She nodded. "Mama and Jamie take forever to wake up."

"Then you'll have to help me."

He gently nudged open the door and strode into the room. It was a big room, once used for storage, and he'd forgotten the great ugly bed it held. Jamie and Mrs. Halifax still lay there, a corner of the covers thrown back where Abigail had obviously slept. The puppy was in a ball on top of the sheets, but he rose at Alistair's entrance and stretched, pink tongue curling. Alistair went to the head of the bed and reached to shake Mrs. Halifax awake, but then paused. Unlike his sister, the housekeeper slept with her hair unbraided and loose. It flowed in a mass of soft tangled silk over her pillows. Her cheeks were pink, her rosy lips parted as she breathed deeply. For a moment, he was mesmerized by her vulnerability and his own tightening groin.

"Are you going to shake her?" Abigail asked from behind him.

God! What a lecher he was to have these thoughts in front of a little girl. Alistair blinked and leaned forward to grasp his housekeeper's shoulder, soft and warm beneath his hand. "Mrs. Halifax."

"Mmm," she sighed, and shrugged her shoulder.

"Mama!" Abigail called loudly.

"What?" Mrs. Halifax blinked, blue eyes staring, puzzled, into his. "What is it?"

"You have to get up," Abigail said as if speaking to the hard of hearing. "We're to go . . ." She turned and looked at Alistair. "*Why* are we waking so early?"

"We're going fishing."

"Huzzah!" Jamie yelled, popping up from the other side of his mother. Either he wasn't as slow to wake as his sister thought or the mention of fishing had galvanized him.

Mrs. Halifax moaned and pushed a lock of hair from her forehead. "But why must we rise so early?"

"Because"—Alistair leaned close to whisper in her ear—"this is when the fish rise."

She groaned, but Jamie was on his knees beside her now, bouncing on the bed and chanting, "Come on, come on, come on!"

"Very well," his mother said, "but Sir Alistair must leave us so that we may dress." The flush on her cheeks had deepened as if she'd finally realized her state of undress.

For a moment, Alistair's gaze challenged hers. She appeared to be wearing a thin shift beneath the covers, and he was tempted to stay until she was forced to rise. To see her loose, quivering breasts beneath the delicate cloth, to watch her hair swing about her bare shoulders.

Madness, pure madness.

Instead he inclined his head, his eye never leaving hers. "Twenty minutes." And he scooped up the puppy and left the room before any other insanity could detain him.

The puppy lay docilely in his arms as he ran down the stairs and to the kitchen. He surprised Mrs. McCleod stirring the morning fire. One of the maids sat at the kitchen table yawning when he entered. She squeaked at the sight of him.

Mrs. McCleod straightened. "Sir?"

"Can you pack some bread and butter and cheese?" He

looked vaguely around the kitchen. "Maybe some fruit and cold meat? We're going fishing."

Mrs. McCleod nodded gravely, her broad, reddened face perfectly impassive at his sudden demands. "Aye, I can."

"And a large breakfast when we return." Alistair frowned. "Have you seen Wiggins?"

The maid snorted. "Probably still abed, that one." She flushed and straightened when Alistair looked at her. "I-I'm sorry, sir."

Alistair waved away her apology with the hand not holding the puppy. "Tell him that the stables need cleaning when you see him."

Wiggins was a lazy bastard, he thought as he strode into the morning sunshine. How lazy he'd never quite realized until the other servants had appeared. No, that wasn't right. He placed the puppy in the dew-spangled grass. He'd always known that Wiggins was a terrible worker; he'd just never given a damn before.

Alistair frowned as he watched the puppy yawn and tilt his nose to sniff the morning breeze. Wiggins was a problem that'd soon need to be dealt with, but not, thank God, this morning.

"Come on, lad, do your business," he murmured to the pup. "Best to learn to do it out here right away. God only knows what Mrs. Halifax would do if you shat in the castle."

As if understanding the command, the puppy squatted in the grass.

And Alistair threw back his head and laughed.

*   *   *

MAMA STOPPED AS they came out of the castle kitchen, and for a moment Abigail didn't know why. Then she dodged around Mama and she saw. Sir Alistair stood in the sunshine with the puppy at his feet and his hands on his hips and he was laughing. Loud, deep, man-laughter such as Abigail had never heard before. She'd hardly ever seen the duke, but she couldn't remember him laughing like this. She doubted that the duke *could* laugh like this. He was too stiff somehow. Surely he'd break something if he tried.

Sir Alistair's laughter was strange and wonderful and the very best thing she'd ever heard. Abigail glanced up at her mother and wondered if she felt the same. She must, because her eyes were wide and her lips were curved in a startled smile, too.

Jamie darted around them and ran to where Sir Alistair and the puppy stood.

"I'm still dreaming," said a voice.

Abigail started and turned.

Miss Munroe stood in the doorway to the kitchen, her eyes somehow softened behind her funny spectacles. "I haven't heard Alistair laugh in years."

"Truly?" Mama asked. She was looking at Miss Munroe as if she'd asked something else. Something more important.

Miss Munroe nodded once. She raised her voice to call to Sir Alistair. "Where are your fishing things, brother? I trust you don't expect us to catch trout with our bare hands?"

"Ah, there you are, Sophia. I'd begun to think you'd decided to stay abed."

Miss Munroe snorted in a not-very-ladylike way. "With the commotion you caused this morning? Hardly."

"And Miss McDonald?"

"You know Phoebe likes to sleep in."

Sir Alistair grinned. "The fishing poles are in the stables. I can fetch them with the children. I've asked Mrs. McCleod for a picnic basket. Perhaps you ladies can see if it's ready."

He was already turning toward the stables without waiting for a reply, so Abigail ran to catch up with him.

Jamie picked up the puppy in his arms. "I've never been fishing before."

Sir Alistair glanced down at him. "Haven't you?"

Jamie shook his head.

"Ah, but this is the sport of elegant gentlemen everywhere, my lad. Did you know that King George himself fishes?"

"No, I didn't." Jamie skipped a step to keep up with Sir Alistair's long strides.

Sir Alistair nodded. "He told me so himself when I took tea with him."

"Do dukes fish, too?" Jamie asked.

"Dukes?" Sir Alistair peered curiously down at Jamie.

Abigail's heart froze.

Then Sir Alistair said, "Dukes fish as well, I have no doubt. A good thing I'm here to teach you. And your sister." He smiled at Abigail.

Abigail felt her chest swell, and a smile seemed to take over her face; she couldn't stop it if she wanted to.

They entered the dim stables and tramped to a door in

the corner. Sir Alistair wrenched it open and rummaged about inside.

"Here we are," he grunted, and brought out a pole longer than he was tall. He leaned it against the wall and bent to the little room again. "I think . . . Yes, these will do." Four more poles appeared.

He backed from the storage room and held out an old basket with a leather handle and hinges. "Can you carry this, Abigail?"

"Yes," she said stoutly, though the basket was heavier than it looked. She wrapped both hands around the handle and lifted it against her chest.

Sir Alistair nodded. "Good lass. And this one for Jamie." He handed a smaller basket to her brother to carry. "All right, then."

He shouldered the poles, and they tramped back toward the castle where Mama and Miss Munroe were waiting for them.

"Mama, did you know that King George fishes?" Jamie asked. He held the puppy under one arm and grasped the basket in the other hand.

"Does he?" Mama looked rather suspiciously at Sir Alistair.

"Indeed he does." Sir Alistair took Mama's arm with his free hand. "Every day and twice on Mondays."

"Hmm," was all Mama said, but she looked happy.

Happy for the first time since they'd left London, Abigail thought as she skipped her way across the dewy grass.

FISHING APPEARED TO be a pastime that involved a lot of waiting around, Helen mused a half hour later. One attached a small hook, cleverly disguised in feathers, to the end of a string and then pitched it into the water, hoping to trick a fish into biting the hook. One would not think that fish were so silly as to confuse feathers and a hook for a fly alighting on the water, but apparently fish were foolish creatures. Or perhaps they were simply very nearsighted.

"Think of your wrist," Sir Alistair was saying. "Let it flick like the tail of a fish."

Helen arched an eyebrow and looked over her shoulder at him. He stood farther up the bank, watching her critically, apparently quite serious in his instruction. She sighed, faced forward, and thought of her wrist as she flicked the tall pole in her hand. The end of her line bobbed up in the air, doubled back on itself, and became entangled in a branch overhead.

"Damn," she muttered under her breath.

Abigail, who'd successfully cast her line thrice already, giggled. Miss Munroe politely didn't say anything, although Helen thought she saw the woman roll her eyes. And Jamie, who'd already lost interest in learning to "flick" and was now hunting dragonflies with the puppy, didn't even notice.

"Here." Sir Alistair was suddenly right beside her, his long arms reaching over her head.

His breath was warm against her cheek as he worked the line free of the branch. Helen stood very still. She was trembling inside, but he seemed not at all affected by their nearness.

"There," he said as the fly came undone from the branch. He stood behind her and reached forward and around her to demonstrate how to hold the pole. The light touch of his hands was devastating as he positioned her to his liking.

Keep your mind on the task, Helen scolded herself, and tried to look intent. She'd realized very early on that whilst she didn't mind standing on a stream bank for long moments on end, she would never be a great fisherwoman.

Abigail, surprisingly, was another story. She had listened to Sir Alistair's instructions with all the gravity of an apprentice learning an ancient and mystical art. And when she had correctly flicked the line to the middle of the stream for the first time, her pale little face lit up with proud joy. That, if nothing else, was well worth rising before the crack of dawn and tramping about in the wet grass.

"Do you have it now?" Sir Alistair rasped in her ear.

"Yes, uh, quite." Helen cleared her throat.

He turned his head slightly, and his good eye met hers from only inches away. "I can instruct you further, if you wish, on how to properly manipulate the pole."

Her cheeks flamed even though his voice had been too low for anyone else to overhear. "I think I have a sufficient grasp of the concept."

"Do you?" His eyebrow arched as his eye gleamed at her diabolically.

She slid her hand slowly up the pole and smiled sweetly. "I am a quick learner, sir."

"Yes, but I'm sure you wish to become an expert. Proper practice is in order, I think." He leaned fractionally closer, and for a wild moment she thought he meant to kiss her, here in the open, in front of the children and his sister.

"Alistair!" Miss Munroe shouted.

Helen started guiltily, but Sir Alistair merely murmured, "Perhaps later."

"Alistair, I have a fish!"

He finally turned at that news and sauntered over to where his sister was wrestling with her line. Jamie, too, was attracted by the excitement, and for a few minutes no one paid attention to Helen as she got her breathing back under control.

When she looked about again, Sir Alistair was trading jibes with his sister over the size of her fish. He didn't notice that Helen's little feathered fly had drifted into the shallow water almost at the bank of the stream, where no doubt there were very few fish. The bright blue sky arched overhead, gauzy clouds drawn across its expanse. The stream bubbled along, the bright water revealing smooth rocks at the bottom. The banks were green with fresh grass, and on this side there was a small copse of trees where Lady Grey had been laid to rest. It was quite lovely, Sir Alistair's stream, a magical spot where ordinary cares didn't seem to have sway.

Sir Alistair gave a sudden shout, and a silver fish leapt out of the water, dangling from the string on his pole. Jamie came running to see, Abigail jumped up and down, and Miss Munroe exclaimed and helped catch the string. In the excitement, Helen dropped her pole into the stream.

"Oh, Mama," Abigail said mournfully when the fish had been safely stowed inside a rather tatty-looking basket. "You've lost your pole."

"Not to worry," Sir Alistair said. "It's probably caught on the bank just past the copse. There's a bit of a whirlpool there. Sophia, mind the children, please, while Mrs. Halifax and I fetch her pole."

Miss Munroe nodded, already watching her line intently, and Sir Alistair took Helen's arm to help her up the bank. Even that small touch, his strong fingers wrapped around her upper arm, made her breath grow short. *Silly,* she chided herself. *He's only being polite.* But he didn't let go of her arm once they'd made the top of the bank, and she began to be suspicious. He led her swiftly along the grass, saying nothing. Perhaps he was cross that he'd had to leave his pole to help her fetch hers. She was foolish, she thought morosely, losing her pole like that.

They made the copse of trees and turned to the stream bank, completely hidden from the children and Miss Munroe.

"I'm sorry," Helen began.

But without saying a word—without any warning at all, in fact—he yanked her against his chest and captured her mouth with his. A great involuntary shudder shook her frame. She hadn't realized how much she'd been waiting for this, unconsciously anticipating when he'd make his next move. Her breasts were mashed against the hard plane of his chest, and his hands grasped her arms as his mouth moved with fierce determination on hers. Oh, it was lovely.

So lovely.

She tilted her head, melting against him like warm custard over apple pie. Her skirt was a simple one, without panniers, and if she moved closer, maybe, just maybe, she might feel that most male part of him. It'd been so long since she'd been wanted. So long since she'd felt the flash of desire.

His hot lips parted over hers, and his tongue demanded entrance to her mouth. She opened willingly, eagerly even. To be wanted like this was intoxicating. He claimed her like a conquering knight, and she welcomed him. His hand moved, drifting over her laced stomach and up to where her breasts were covered only by the thin material of her dress. She waited, breathless with anticipation, distracted even from the heat of his mouth, for that hand to act. He didn't disappoint. His fingers dipped tenderly beneath the edge of her gauzy fichu, stroking, probing, tickling, and teasing her flesh. Her nipples had tightened to almost painful arousal, and, oh, how she wished that she could fling aside her clothing and let his hot palms cover her breasts.

She must've made some sound, for his mouth broke from hers, and he murmured so low that she had to strain to hear, "Hush. They can't see us, but they might hear."

He stared at his hand, still inserted under her fichu. She couldn't help it—she arched to his gaze. He shot a smoldering look at her. Then he closed his eye and bowed his head over her bosom. She felt his tongue, hot and wet, probe the edges of her dress.

Dear God.

From up the bank, Jamie's high voice called, "Mama, come see this bug!"

Helen blinked. "Just a moment, darling."

"I can't get enough of you," Sir Alistair muttered low.

A streak of desire shot through her.

"Mama!"

He straightened and swiftly smoothed her fichu, his hands sure and steady. "Stay here."

He slid down the bank and deftly caught the fishing

pole, which was indeed spinning lazily in a whirlpool. He mounted the bank again and took her elbow casually. "Come."

And she wondered as they walked back to Jamie and the others, did he not feel the same incredible yearning when they kissed?

Madness, pure madness, Alistair thought as he resumed his fishing spot. Mrs. Halifax was dipping her line into the stream in an entirely ineffectual way downriver from him, but he didn't trust himself to go and help her. What was he about, kissing his housekeeper? What must she think of him, a great, ugly beast of a man, forcing himself on her as he had? Surely she was appalled and distressed.

Except she hadn't seemed particularly appalled or distressed as she'd opened her sweet mouth to his tongue and pressed her body against him. The memory had his cock rearing eagerly and nearly made him drop his fishing pole in the water. He caught Sophia's suspicious gaze at that moment. God only knew what she'd say if he lost his pole. Something cutting, no doubt.

He cleared his throat. "Mrs. McCleod packed some bread and such for us, I believe."

That got Jamie's immediate attention. He came scampering over with the puppy, and Mrs. Halifax set aside her fishing pole only too eagerly to go digging in the basket. "Lovely! There's a ham and some bread and fruit. Oh, and a meat pie and some small cakes." She looked up at him. "What would you like?"

"Some of everything," Alistair called back. He watched her out of the corner of his eye. She was smiling at her son and chatting as she put together plates of food, and every once and a while, she'd dart a quick little glance at him when she thought he couldn't see.

What was it about her? She was beautiful, yes, but that if anything would normally be a deterrent for him. Beautiful women merely made him more conscious of his own repulsiveness. She was different somehow. Not only had she seemed to have recovered from her shock at his appearance, but she also made *him* forget what he looked like. With her, he was simply a man flirting dangerously with a woman.

The feeling was intoxicating.

Abigail made a frustrated sound, and he moved to where she was trying to untangle her line. "Here, let me help you."

"Thank you," the girl said.

He glanced down at her solemn face. "You can go get some food if you wish."

But she shook her head. "I like this. I like fishing."

"You seem to have an aptitude for it."

She eyed him suspiciously. "Aptitude?"

He smiled. "You're good at it."

"Really?"

"Yes."

She gripped her pole fiercely. "I've never been good at anything."

It was his turn to eye her. Perhaps he should offer some platitude, wave away her self-doubt, but he couldn't find it in him to make light of her distress.

She glanced over her shoulder at her mother. "I disappoint Mama. I'm not . . . not as *right* as other girls."

Alistair frowned. Abigail was unusually solemn for a

little girl, but he knew that Mrs. Halifax loved her daughter. "I think that you're right enough."

Abigail's brows knit and he knew he hadn't said quite the right thing. He opened his mouth to try again when he was called by the picnickers.

"Here's your food, Sir Alistair," Jamie said.

Mrs. Halifax held out a plate, carefully avoiding his gaze. Alistair nearly groaned. Her attempt at discretion drew more attention than outright flirtation would. He glanced over her head as he walked to where she sat and met Sophia's gaze beneath raised eyebrows.

Alistair accepted the plate and sent a stern look at Sophia as he murmured to Mrs. Halifax, "Thank you. I did not mean for you to give up your fishing to serve the rest of us."

"Oh, it isn't any bother. I don't believe I'm particularly clever at the pastime, anyway."

"Ah, but practice makes perfect," he drawled.

Her face jerked up at that, her eyes narrowing with suspicion.

He felt his mouth quirk. If only they weren't so public, they—

"Oh! My line!" Abigail shrieked.

Alistair turned and saw her pole bent nearly at a right angle, her line taut and disappearing under the water. "Hold it, Abigail!"

"What should I do?" Her eyes were as big as saucers, her face gone white.

"Just hold it steady, don't pull."

He was by her side now. Abigail had both feet braced on the riverbank and was arching backward using all her slim strength to keep the pole in her hands.

"Steady," he murmured. The line was jerking through the water in circles. "He's wearing himself out, that fish of yours. You're bigger, stronger, and smarter, too, than the fish. All you have to do is wait him out."

"Shouldn't you help her?" Mrs. Halifax asked.

"She hooked the fish," Sophia said stoutly. "She can land it, too, never you fear."

"Aye, she can," Alistair said quietly. "She's a brave lass."

Abigail's face was set in determined concentration. The line was moving more slowly now.

"Don't let go your hold," Alistair said. "Sometimes one fish is a wee bit smarter than the rest of his family and pretends to be tired, only to jerk the pole from your grasp."

"I won't let go," the little girl declared.

Soon the movement slowed to nearly a stop. Alistair reached out and caught the line, swiftly lifting a sparkling fish from the water.

"Oh!" Abigail breathed.

Alistair held up the fish, flopping on the end of the line. It wasn't the biggest fish he'd ever seen, nor was it the smallest. "A very fine trout indeed. Wouldn't you agree, Sophia?"

Sophia solemnly inspected the catch. "The finest, I declare, that I've seen in quite some time."

Abigail's cheeks tinged a faint pink, and Alistair realized she was blushing. Pretending he hadn't noticed, he caught the fish and, kneeling, showed her how to remove the hook from its mouth.

She watched intently and then nodded as he placed her

fish with the others in the basket. "I'll do it myself next time."

And a strange emotion welled in his chest, so foreign that it took him several seconds to identify it: pride. Pride in this prickly, determined child.

"Yes, you will," he said, and she grinned at him.

And over her head, her mother smiled at him as if he'd handed her an emerald necklace.

Chapter Nine

Truth Teller turned to the monster's cage, and there
already lay the woman.
He walked close to the bars and asked,
"Who are you?"
The woman drew herself wearily to her feet and
spoke. "I am the Princess Sympathy. My father is
the king of a great city to the west. I lived in halls of
crystal, wore clothes woven from gold and silver, and
had my slightest wish granted."
Truth Teller frowned. "Then why—?"
"Hush." The lady leaned forward. "Your master
is coming. He has caught the swallows, and if he
finds you talking to me, it will anger him."
And Truth Teller had no choice but to go inside
the castle, leaving the lady caged. . . .
—from TRUTH TELLER

By that afternoon, Helen was wishing she could take a
nap. Abigail and Jamie didn't seem at all tired from their

early morning adventure. In fact, they'd eagerly accompanied Miss Munroe and Miss McDonald on an expedition to go hunting for badgers. Helen, however, was yawning as she climbed the stairs to Sir Alistair's lair.

She hadn't seen him since morning. He'd been closeted in his tower all this time, and she'd just about run out of patience. What had he meant by those kisses? Had he simply been playing with her? Or—awful thought!— had he lost interest after tasting her twice? The questions had nagged her since that morning until she felt she must find the answers.

Which was perhaps why she carried some tea and scones to him now.

The tower door was partially ajar, and instead of knocking, she simply leaned her shoulder against it and pushed. It opened silently. Sir Alistair sat at his accustomed table, oblivious to her presence. She stood and stared. He was drawing something, his head bent to the paper in front of him, but that wasn't what had caught her attention.

He drew with his maimed right hand.

He held the pencil between his thumb and the two middle fingers of his right hand, the hand itself held in an awkward hook. Just looking at him, Helen's hand ached in sympathy, but he continued to make small, precise movements. He'd obviously been using his hand thus for many years. She thought about what it must've been like, returning maimed from the Colonies and having to relearn how to draw. How to write. Had he been humiliated at having to practice a craft every schoolboy had mastered? Had he been frustrated?

Well, of course he'd been frustrated. Her mouth curved in a tiny smile. She knew something about Sir Alistair now. He would've broken pencils, torn up paper, been angered beyond bearing, and somehow he would've stubbornly kept at it until he could once again reproduce the fine drawings she'd seen in his book. He must've done so because she saw the result in front of her now—a scholar working on his manuscript.

She started forward, but as she did so, he exclaimed and dropped the pencil.

"What is it?" she asked.

His head jerked up and he glowered at her. "Nothing, Mrs. Halifax. You may leave the tea on that table."

She set her tray down on the table indicated but ignored his demand to leave. Instead she hurried over to him. "What's wrong?"

He was rubbing his right palm with his other hand and muttering about females who wouldn't listen.

She sighed and took his right hand gently in hers, surprising him enough that he abruptly fell silent. His forefinger was a reddened stump under an inch long. His little finger had been amputated at the first knuckle. The remaining fingers were long with slightly broader tips, the nails well shaped. They were beautiful fingers on what had once been a handsome hand. She felt a streak of sorrow pierce her middle. How had something so beautiful come to be mutilated?

She swallowed down the lump in her throat and said huskily, "I don't see an injury."

He glanced sharply at her, and her eyes widened as she realized her faux pas. "A recent injury, I mean."

He shook his head. "It's merely a muscle cramp."

He tried to withdraw his hand from hers, but she hung

on. "I'll see if Mrs. McCleod can warm a salve for you later. Tell me exactly where the cramp is."

She held his hand between both of hers and massaged his broad palm with her thumbs, pressing firmly. His hand was warm, the skin smooth. He had calluses at the base of his fingers as if from some type of physical work.

"There's no need—"

She looked up, suddenly angry. "Why isn't there need? You're in pain and I can help you. It seems to me that there's every need."

He looked at her, his eye cynical. "Why would you care?"

Did he think she'd back away at his harsh words? Run with girlish tears on her face? She wasn't a girl—hadn't been one since the age of seventeen.

She leaned into his face, still holding his hand. "What kind of woman do you think I am? Do you think I let just any man kiss me?"

His eye narrowed. "I think you're a nice woman. A kind woman."

The patronizing answer nearly drove her to violence. "A nice woman? Because I kissed you? Because I let you touch me? Are you mad? No woman is that nice and certainly not I."

He simply looked at her. "Then why?"

"Because." She took his face in her palms, the left side of his face bumpy and ragged under her hand, the right side smooth and warm. "I *do* care. And so do you."

And she set her lips against his. Deliberately. Softly. Putting all her longing, all her loneliness into the gesture. She started the kiss lightly, but he tilted his head beneath hers, angling and opening his mouth, and somehow she found herself on his lap with his tongue in her mouth.

Not that she protested. She'd been waiting for this for days now, and the reality set her limbs to trembling. She'd been a mistress, a bought woman, for all of her adult life, but this was something beyond her experience. A sharing, an exploring. She was an equal in this place with this man, and somehow the knowledge that she was as accountable as he, as involved as he, made her all the more aroused. Her fingers actually shook against the wool fabric of his coat as he explored her mouth with his tongue. Sweetly, darkly, erotically. Until she feared that she might meet her culmination simply from his lips.

She drew her head back, gasping. "I—"

"Don't stop me," he murmured. His hands were on the laces of her bodice, rapidly pulling them free. "Let me see you. Let me touch you."

She nodded and watched him. Stopping was the very last thing on her mind. His face was intent, his one eye entirely focused on the task of opening her bodice. She could feel a blush start at her throat. It'd been years since Lister had bedded her, and even then she didn't remember this intensity, this single-minded purpose. What if she disappointed him? What if she was unable to please him?

Her bodice parted, and he drew it off her, laying it absently on the table along with her fichu. His gaze never left her bosom. He began working on her stays.

She cleared her throat. "Can I—"

"Let me." His eye flicked up to hers. "Do you mind?"

She shook her head, biting her lip. She held very still as her stays drew apart. His fingers brushed her bare skin, but he didn't pause. She was conscious of each breath she drew into her lungs, of his own even breathing, of his unwavering gaze. Then her stays were off, and he drew her shift down her shoulders until she was bared to the waist.

He simply stared.

She raised her hand without thought, instinctively moving to cover herself.

He caught her wrist and drew it to her lap. "Don't," he whispered. "Let me look at you."

She closed her eyes then, because she could no longer bear the sight of his gaze taking her in.

"You're beautiful," he murmured. "Beautiful enough to drive a man insane."

He traced the forefinger of his left hand from the rapid pulse at her throat, down, down to the swell of one breast. She waited, her breath nearly stopped. He drew his finger slowly to her nipple and circled it, making it pucker.

She swallowed.

"I want this," he said.

She opened her eyes to see him staring at her intently, his mouth hardened into an arrogant, flat line.

His gaze flicked up to capture her own. "I want all of you."

Her mouth went dry. "Then take me."

He reached behind her and shoved aside the mess on his desk. She heard pencils skitter and drop to the floor and the thump of a book. Then he grasped her about her waist, lifting to set her on the heavy table.

"Take off your skirts." He rose suddenly from his chair and strode to the tower door, locking it.

When he returned to her, she was still fumbling at

the ribbons at her waist. He pushed her hands aside and began working at them himself. She felt a wild spurt of joyous laughter start in her mouth, but she tamped it down ruthlessly. Instead, she reached up and around his head and drew the tie from his hair. The heavy dark locks fell forward against his lean cheeks, wild and untamed, and she threaded her fingers through them, reveling in the intimacy.

He didn't even seem to notice her gesture, so intent was he on removing her remaining clothing. A moment later, he flung aside her skirts. She was left in just her stockings and shoes and would've felt more than a little silly if he wasn't so grave as he drew them off. Then she was naked, sitting with her bare bottom on his wooden table, and he was looking at her as if she were Aphrodite come to life. It was a heady feeling, being regarded thus. Heady and frightening at the same time, for she was no Aphrodite. She was simply a woman past her third decade. A woman who'd had only one other lover in all her life.

"Alistair," she whispered.

He shrugged out of his coat. "Aye?"

She didn't know how to put her concern into words. "I don't . . . that is, I'm not very experienced with . . . with . . ."

A corner of his mouth kicked up. He was only in shirtsleeves now. "Helen, lass, dinna fret."

And he brought his mouth to her breast, sucking strongly, warmly, on her tender nipple. She arched her back in reaction, catching his head, holding it close to her breast. She stroked her fingers into his silky hair. Maybe he was right. Maybe she shouldn't worry. Maybe she should, for this short while, merely feel.

He switched to her other breast, holding her in the curve of his left thumb and forefinger. He thumbed the damp nipple he'd just left, starting twin flickers of desire in her. She widened her legs, trying to pull him closer, but he was solid and heavy and wouldn't move until he was ready.

A small whimper of frustration escaped her lips.

He raised his head, his cheekbones flushed, and his eye gleaming roguishly. "Is this what you want?"

He held her gaze as he trailed his hand down over her trembling belly and into the curling hair at the juncture of her thighs.

"Alistair!" she gasped. "I don't know if—"

"Don't you?" he murmured, his gaze growing heavy. "Don't you know, Helen?"

And as she watched his face, mesmerized, embarrassed, and hotly aroused, he touched her *there*. Her lips parted in soundless wonder. His thumb rubbed her in gentle circles. His fingers softly petted her, parting, stroking, exploring.

"Oh," she gasped.

"Look at me," he whispered. "Keep your eyes on me."

He entered her with his finger, slowly, smiling when her eyes widened. He withdrew the finger and thrust again, his thumb keeping up the soft circling at her center. Her eyelids drooped. She felt hot. She was afraid she might make some awful animal sound if he continued, and at the same time she didn't want him to stop.

"Helen," he crooned. "Bonny Helen. Come and cover my fingers with your sweet dew."

Her head fell back, lolling restlessly on her shoulders. It was as if she were in a dream. She was a wanton, a lovely desirable wanton, and he was a man worshipping her. She felt his hot mouth on her throat, kissing, tonguing, and it began. Little tremors that built to a shaking, pounding rush of heat and pleasure—so much pleasure that for a time she lost herself entirely.

When she opened her eyes long moments later, he was watching her, his hand still softly stroking.

"Did you like that?" he asked, his voice more tender than she'd ever heard it.

She could only nod, heat rushing to her cheeks.

"Good." He withdrew his hand and unbuttoned the flap of his breeches. "Let's see if we can do that again, shall we?"

She just had a glimpse of pubic hair and dark flesh—a good deal larger than she'd expected—and then he stepped between her legs. He kissed her. Gently. Lightly. But her focus was on what was going on *down there*. He nudged her, and she inhaled at his heat, at the broadness of—

She broke the kiss and said breathlessly, "I don't—"

"Shh," he murmured. He nibbled at the corner of her mouth. "It's simple biology, really. I am made for inserting myself in you. You are made for receiving me. Thusly."

"But—"

He thrust, the crown of his penis parting her folds, opening and stretching her. Her eyes flew wide open.

He was watching her with a demonic gleam in his eye. He smiled slightly and thrust again. She felt him invading her, entering her.

"You see?" he purred. "So simple."

He ground his hips one more time, and the base of his penis met her mound. He was completely seated within her. She'd never felt a fullness like this. He swallowed and she knew suddenly that he was not nearly as sanguine as he pretended. His cheeks had flushed, his eye narrowed, and his mouth curved almost in a sneer.

"An interesting fact you may not know," he said in a low, gravelly voice, "is that once the male has ventured so far, it is almost impossible . . . ah!" His head tilted back, his eye closing as she clenched internally. He opened his eye, his mouth now curved down in savage determination. "*Impossible* for him to stop."

He withdrew fractionally and surged into her again. "He is compelled to complete the act as if"—he thrust again, this time harder, firmer—"his very life depended on it."

She smiled and wrapped her legs about him. He braced one hand on the table beside her hip, the other on her bottom and set a demanding rhythm. The table shook and thumped and something glass toppled over the edge and shattered on the floor.

And she didn't care. The laughter bubbled up in her throat again, and this time she let it free. She threw back her head and laughed as Sir Alistair made love to her with his strong, quick, determined body. She grinned at the ceiling in pure joy and felt his heavy cock sliding and rubbing against her, filling her full, and she'd never felt so light.

So free.

And then another wave hit, catching her by complete surprise and tossing her high, sailing on a crest of pure, exquisite pleasure. And at its peak she looked down and saw him, thrusting still faster into her, his broad shoulders bunched and tensed, his hairline gleaming with exertion. He arched back his head and shouted. And then he went still, trembling and jerking within her, his face gone curiously smooth.

She didn't recognize the expression on his face at first, and then she realized: it was peace.

AH, GOD, IT'D been a good long while since he'd last coupled with a woman—not since before Spinner's Falls, in fact. He'd forgotten how heady the feeling was. Actually, Alistair thought as he panted against Helen's neck, he didn't remember it ever having been this sweet. This glorious. He smiled, holding warm woman flesh against himself. Perhaps some things did improve with age.

She wriggled a little under him, as if the table was too hard for her soft arse. He straightened and looked at her. Her face was flushed, her eyes slumberous, and the surge of ridiculous masculine pride that went through him was probably only natural. What man wouldn't feel pride at having pleasured such a woman?

"Oh," she said softly. "Oh, that was . . . um . . ."

A grin tugged at his mouth. She sounded dazed.

"Wondrous?" he suggested, kissing the corner of her mouth.

She sighed. "Um . . ."

"Blissful?" He palmed a plump, heavy breast, sliding his fingers over the delicate rose nipple. Breasts were rather marvelous, all things considered, and Helen's were particularly fascinating. Made one wonder why they couldn't be uncovered and free all the time, civilized ideas of modesty be damned. Of course, then other men might ogle them, and *that* wouldn't do at all. He palmed her other breast as well. No, best to keep them covered. That made the private unveiling all the more exciting.

His eye narrowed at the thought, and he looked at her speculatively. She'd let him couple with her again, wouldn't she? If he was lucky. In fact, if she let him wait just a few minutes more, he was certain he could perform at least once more this afternoon.

As if she'd heard his thought, she suddenly straightened. "Oh, goodness! They'll be back from their walk soon."

"Who?" he demanded, loath to give up his handfuls of breast.

"Your sister and the children," she said impatiently.

She wriggled again and his limp cock slipped rather ignominiously from her sheath. He sighed. Not right now, then. He bent and gave each breast a farewell kiss and then straightened and rapidly buttoned his breeches. When he finished, Helen was still trying to dress without much success.

"Let me," he said, and gently nudged aside her fingers from her stays. He laced her, hiding those magnificent breasts, and then helped her don the rest of her clothes, all the while considering how to phrase the demand.

He smoothed the fichu at her bosom and inhaled. "Helen—"

"Where are my shoes?" She suddenly bent, searching under his table. "Do you see them?"

"Here." He fished them out of his coat pockets where he'd absently stowed them before. "Helen—"

"Oh, thank you!" She sat in his chair to slip them on.

He frowned down at her impatiently. "Helen—"

"Does my hair look all right?"

"Lovely."

"You're not looking."

"Yes, I am!" The words came out a good deal more forcefully than he'd meant. He closed his eye, damning himself for a fool. When he looked up, she was staring at him inquisitively.

"Are you all right?"

"Yes," he ground out, and then took a deep breath. "Helen, I want to see you again."

Her brows knit as if in faint confusion. "Well, of course we'll see each other again. I do live here, you know."

"That's not what I meant."

"Oh." Her harebell-blue eyes widened, and he briefly considered just taking her again on the table, good manners be damned. He didn't have trouble communicating with her when they made love. "Ohhh."

He suppressed his impatience. "Well?"

She took a step toward him until her breasts—those sweet breasts!—nearly touched his chest. Her face was still a little flushed, very prettily pink, and her eyes sparkled. She stood on tiptoe and kissed him chastely on the mouth, but when he moved to deepen the embrace, she darted away.

She walked to the tower door and paused to look back at him over her shoulder. "Perhaps later this evening?" She slipped out the door, closing it quietly behind her.

"BUT I DON'T like fish," Jamie said as they trudged home from their ramble with Miss McDonald and Miss Munroe. "I don't see why we should have it for supper."

"Because otherwise it's a waste to catch them," Abigail said. She was out of breath, because Puddles had decided to stop walking and now she and Jamie took turns carrying him. "If we didn't eat the fish, it'd be a sin."

"But I didn't catch them!" Jamie objected.

"Sad, isn't it?" Miss McDonald said cheerfully. "How one is doomed to eat the catch even when one is completely innocent of the fishing?"

"Phoebe," Miss Munroe grunted, "you're demonstrating the wrong attitude."

"Personally," Miss McDonald whispered loudly to Jamie, "I make sure to fill up on bread and soup. Can't stand fish myself."

"Phoebe!"

"Now if only they could learn to hook a good Yorkshire pudding, I'd be quite content to dine on the catch," Miss McDonald mused.

Jamie giggled and Abigail felt a small smile tug at her lips. They hadn't found any badgers on their ramble, but it'd been quite fun, anyway. Miss Munroe was very stern, but she knew all kinds of interesting things, and Miss McDonald was funny.

"Ah, here we are," Miss Munroe said as they came within sight of the castle. "I'm for tea and some muffins, I think. Who's with me?"

"I am!" Jamie exclaimed at once.

"Excellent." Miss Munroe beamed at Jamie.

"What shall I do with Puddles?" Abigail looked down at the sleeping puppy in her arms.

"We need to think of a better name for that dog," Miss McDonald muttered.

"Has he a bed in the kitchen?" Miss Munroe asked.

"We've found an old coal box," Jamie replied.

"Mmm. Best line it with some straw and a blanket if you have it," Miss Munroe said.

"I'll go look in the stables," Abigail said.

"Good girl," Miss Munroe said. "We'll save a muffin for you in the sitting room."

The others went inside the castle while Abigail continued around the side to the stables.

"Maybe we can find an old blanket or coat for you," she whispered to the sleeping puppy in her arms. Puddles's soft ear twitched as if he heard her even in his sleep.

The stables were dark compared to the sunshine outside. She stood quietly inside the door for a moment, letting her eyes get used to the dimness. There were several empty stalls at this end. Abigail started down the main aisle. Sir Alistair's big horse, Griffin, and the little dogcart pony were stabled at the other end. That was probably where she'd find fresh straw. She heard a snort and the thump of a hoof as she neared the far end of the stable, and then she heard something else. A man muttering.

Abigail stopped. Puddles squirmed as she squeezed him too tightly to her chest. The horse snorted again, and then Mr. Wiggins backed out into the aisle from a stall, holding something in his arms. Abigail tensed to run, but before she could do so, the little man whirled and saw her.

"What're you doin'?" he growled low. "Spyin' on me? Are ye spyin' on me?"

And she saw that the thing in his arms was a big silver platter. Abigail shook her head and stepped back, helplessly staring at the platter.

Mr. Wiggins's eyes narrowed to evil slits. "You tell anyone—hisself included—and I'll slit your throat, ye hear? I'll slit your throat and your Mam's and your wee little brother's, too, ye hear me?"

Abigail could only nod frantically.

He took a step toward her, and suddenly her legs worked again. She turned and fled down the aisle of the stables, running as fast as she could. But behind her she could still hear Mr. Wiggins shout.

"Don't you tell! You hear me? Don't you tell!"

LISTER STARED MOODILY out his study window. "I should go north myself."

Behind him, Henderson sighed. "Your Grace, it's only been a few days. I doubt the men we sent have even reached Edinburgh yet."

Lister swung on his secretary. "And by the time they do and send word, she'll have had plenty of time to flee overseas."

"We've done everything we can."

"Which is why I should go north myself."

"But, Your Grace . . ." Henderson seemed to search for words. "She's only a demimondaine. I had not thought our emotions were this engaged."

"She is mine and she left me." Lister stared hard at the secretary. "She defied me. No one defies me."

"Naturally not, Your Grace."

"I've decided." Lister went back to the window. "Make the arrangements. I leave for Scotland on the morrow."

Chapter Ten

The next evening, Truth Teller again loosed the
swallows, and once again the beautiful young man
pursued them out of the courtyard. Truth Teller stood
and watched as the sun set and the monster took the
form of the fair princess.

Then he asked, "How has this been done to you?"

The lady sighed sadly. "The man you serve is a
powerful sorcerer. He saw me one day as I rode in
the forest with my court. That night he came to my
father's castle and demanded my hand in marriage.
I refused him, for the sorcerer is an evil man and
I wanted nothing to do with him. But the sorcerer
became enraged. He stole me from my father's house
and brought me here. He put a spell on me so that
by day I am that repulsive beast. Only by night am
I myself again. Go now so that he does not find you
talking to me."

And again Truth Teller was forced to depart. . . .

—from TRUTH TELLER

The letter from France came late that afternoon. Alistair was so distracted by what had happened earlier with Helen and what might happen later that night with her that he nearly didn't notice it among the papers the footman brought up. He subscribed to several journals and news sheets from London, Birmingham, and Edinburgh, and they had a tendency to arrive all at once in the week. But at the bottom of the pile lay a very battered missive, looking as if it had come by way of the Horn of Africa, which, considering England's present relations with France, was entirely possible.

Alistair took up the letter and slit it open with a sharp knife he'd earlier used to dissect a meadow vole. He read the letter, pausing to carefully reread several passages, and then tossed it onto his crowded desk. He got up to pace restlessly to the windows and gaze out. Etienne phrased his words with circumspection, but his message was clear. He'd heard rumors from those in the French government that there had indeed been an English spy who'd given away the position of the 28th Regiment of Foot, leading to the slaughter at Spinner's Falls. What was more, the rumors specified that the spy was a titled Englishman. Alistair drummed his fingers restlessly on the windowsill. *That* was new information.

Etienne wrote that he could commit no more to paper but that he could speak to Alistair in person. Even now, he was preparing to set sail on a ship that would dock in London in a fortnight's time. If Alistair wished to meet the ship, Etienne could give more specific information at that time.

Alistair traced the scars on the left side of his face. To finally know that this was done apurpose by someone made his chest swell with a cold and determined rage. It made no logical sense. Catching a traitor wouldn't heal his face. But even knowing it was illogical couldn't stop the beast within. By God he wanted the Spinner's Falls traitor to pay.

A knock came at the tower door, and he turned absently. "Yes?"

"Dinner is served, sir," one of the maids called before clattering back down the stairs.

Alistair walked to his table and picked up Etienne's letter. He stared at it a moment, muttered a curse, folded it, and stuck it in an already full drawer. He needed to think on this before he moved, perhaps inform Vale of the new information, but for now dinner awaited him.

As he neared the dining room, he could already hear Jamie's high tones as he made some comment about fish. The mere sound sent his mouth to curving. Strange how the sound of a child's voice—something that would've irritated him a fortnight ago—now made him smile. Was he really so mercurial? The thought made him uneasy, and he pushed it away. Why think about the future when the present held much better delights?

When he walked into the dining room, he found that the others had all sat down. Helen had unaccountably taken a seat as far away as possible from his own chair at the head of the table. She was pointedly not looking at him, and a faint flush tinged her cheeks. She would never be a great liar, and he had the contrary urge to kiss her right then and there in front of his sister and Helen's children. Instead he strode to his own seat, avoiding Sophia's speculative gaze, and sat. Sophia was to his right tonight with Miss McDonald on her other side. Jamie sat for some unknown reason to his left. Abigail sat on the far side of her brother, looking oddly subdued. Her mother was on the other side of Abigail, far enough away that he'd practically have to hoist a flag to communicate with her.

One of the footmen brought in a steaming platter of fish.

"Ah, lovely," Alistair said, rubbing his hands together in anticipation. He'd not had fresh trout for several months, despite it being a favorite of his. "Here's a nice big fish for you." He forked up the largest of the trout and deposited it on Jamie's plate.

"Thank you," Jamie droned, his chin sinking onto his thin little chest as he stared at the fish on his plate.

Miss McDonald coughed into her napkin.

Alistair raised his eyebrows at his sister. "Something the matter?"

"No, nothing," Sophia said, frowning at her companion. "But perhaps Jamie would prefer just a wee bit of fish to begin with."

Alistair looked at Jamie. "Is that so?"

The boy nodded miserably.

"Then I shall eat your fish and you shall have my empty plate," Alistair said, switching the plates. "Have some of the bread instead."

Jamie perked up visibly at the suggestion.

"Bring in some marmalade or jam," Alistair instructed the footman sotto voce. "What about you, Abigail? Do you care for fish?"

"Yes," she whispered, and she did take a fish when the platter was offered, but then she merely poked it with a fork.

Alistair exchanged a glance with Helen. Helen shook her head, looking baffled.

Perhaps the chit was feeling unwell. Alistair frowned and sipped his wine. There was a surgeon in Glenlargo, but the man was more bloodletter than healer, and Alistair wouldn't trust himself with the man, let alone a child. In fact, the nearest good doctor might not be any closer than Edinburgh. If Abigail was truly ill, he'd have to take her there himself. Childhood illnesses could be so debilitating—and so often fatal. Damn. Perhaps he shouldn't have woken the children so early this morning. Had the stream been too cold? Had Abigail overexcited herself? It'd always struck him as a singularly silly theory that females could excite themselves into illness, but now, with a small female child under his roof, he realized how very inadequate his knowledge of children was.

"Are you ill?" he asked Abigail, perhaps a little sharply, as both Helen and Sophia turned to look at him.

But the child merely blinked and shook her head.

Alistair snapped his fingers at the footman. "Bring in a *very* small glass of wine, please."

"Yes, sir." The footman left the room, but Alistair never took his eye from Abigail.

Sophia cleared her throat. "We saw a hawk and two rabbits on our ramble, but no badgers. Are you sure that there is a sett nearby?"

"Yes," Alistair said absently. Was Abigail paler than normal? She was such a fair-complexioned child to begin with; it was hard to tell.

"Well, we'll have to wait for our next visit to look for it again." Sophia sighed.

He glanced at her in surprise. "What?"

The footman returned with the glass of wine, and Alistair indicated the girl. She stared in surprise at the tiny glass filled with ruby liquid.

"Have some of that," he said gruffly. "It'll fortify your blood." He turned and scowled at his sister. "What do you mean? Are you leaving so soon?"

"Early tomorrow," his sister confirmed.

"Sophie has a meeting of the Edinburgh Philosophical Society tomorrow," Miss McDonald said. "Mr. William Watson has traveled from London especially to demonstrate his Leyden electrical jar. If we are lucky, we'll be able to experience the phenomenon of electricity ourselves."

"Watson says that if a dozen people stand in a circle with linked hands, the electrical ether will travel around the circle equally," Sophia said. "Sounds preposterous to me, but if it does happen, I don't want to be the one to miss out."

"But you just got here," Alistair growled. When Sophia and Miss McDonald had first arrived, he'd been annoyed, but now he felt unaccountably put out at their sudden defection.

"You can always come with us, brother." Sophia raised her eyebrows in challenge behind her spectacles.

Abigail suddenly grew very still.

"I think not," Alistair muttered, eyeing the child. What ailed her?

"But you can at least come visit us next Christmas," Miss McDonald ventured.

Alistair didn't reply. Christmas was a long way away. He glanced at Helen, who inexplicably blushed. Why plan for the future when it held no joy for him? Better to stay here and enjoy Helen while she let him. His lonely dreary future could wait.

THAT NIGHT, HELEN found herself sneaking up the castle stairs like a thief. Or a woman intent on an assignation, which, as it happened, she was. It had seemed to take hours for the children to fall asleep, even after she'd read them all four of the fairy tales. Abigail in particular had tossed and turned. She'd also insisted on taking the puppy into bed with her and her brother, and nothing Helen said would dissuade her. When she'd fallen asleep, she'd been hugging the little animal to her cheek. Fortunately, the puppy hadn't seemed to mind.

Helen frowned now as she tiptoed down the dark upper corridor. She'd thought that Abigail was beginning to relax at the castle. She'd seemed so happy that morning fishing. But now she was more morose than ever. The frustrating thing she'd learned about her daughter over the years was that it was no good badgering her to tell her what was the matter. Abigail needed to take her own time to reveal what was troubling her. Of course, that didn't mitigate the motherly guilt Helen felt at not knowing what was bothering her child.

Sometimes she'd watched other little girls, pretty, carefree, talkative little girls, and wondered why her own child was so moody and sensitive. And then she would look into Abigail's pale, worried little face and a wave of love would wash over her. This was her daughter, difficult or not. She could no more stop loving her than cut off her own arm.

Helen paused outside Alistair's room.

Love—physical and emotional—had been her life's

downfall. Was she merely letting herself sink back into debauchery by seeking Alistair out? She knew most would certainly think so. But there was a fundamental difference between what she intended to do with Alistair and what she'd had with Lister. She'd never been in control with Lister. He'd been the one to set the pace, to make all the decisions. However arrogant and surly Alistair might seem, he wasn't making any decisions for her.

This was her choice and hers alone.

Taking a deep breath, she gently knocked at the door. Silence. She fidgeted, rubbing one cold slippered foot over the other. Perhaps he hadn't heard. Perhaps he wasn't even here. Perhaps he'd gone to his tower for the night or forgotten her promise this afternoon or changed his mind. Good Lord! How embarrassing if—

The door suddenly swung open, and Alistair grabbed her by the arm and pulled her inside his room.

She gave a startled squeak.

"Shh!" He frowned down at her even as he untied her wrapper.

The room was dim; only a few candles were lit, and the fire had died to embers. Alistair wore a blue and black striped banyan that was frayed about the cuffs. His dark hair was down, and she noticed that his cheeks were damp.

He'd shaved for her.

The realization sent a shiver of delight through her middle. She stood on tiptoe to run her fingers through his hair and found it just a little wet. He'd bathed for her as well.

"I love your hair," she murmured.

He blinked. "You do?"

She nodded. "Yes."

"Well, that's . . ." He frowned as if unable to think of what to say.

"And I love your throat." She pressed a kiss right there, feeling the beat of his pulse beneath her lips. He wasn't wearing a shirt beneath the banyan, and his chest was delightfully available.

"Would you, ah, like some wine?" he asked. His voice had deepened as she trailed kisses down the loose V of the banyan.

"No."

"Ah." He quickly stooped and picked her up in his arms. "Just as well, I suppose. I don't want any, either."

He took three giant strides and deposited her on his great bed. She sank a little, and then he made the bed dip more by setting his knee on the mattress.

She sat up and placed a restraining palm on his chest. "Take this off."

His brows shot up.

"Please," she said sweetly.

He huffed but rolled off the bed to discard the banyan. And there was his chest, as lovely as she remembered it. Broad and strong and hairy, but this time was better than the last time she'd glimpsed his chest—the night he'd brought home Puddles—because *this* time she could touch it as well.

And she intended to.

When he made to mount the bed again, she shook her head at him.

He paused. "No?"

She flicked her fingers imperiously at his lower anatomy. "The breeches as well, please."

That made him scowl.

So she simply removed her wrap. Underneath she wore her chemise. She let her shoulder drop, and the sleeve slid down.

He stared hard at her half-revealed breast and hastily removed his breeches. He paused, his fingers at the waist of his smallclothes, to look at her.

She arched an eyebrow and slowly pulled the ribbon on the neckline of her chemise. The neck opened, fully revealing that one breast.

He inhaled and shucked his smallclothes, stockings, and shoes. Then he straightened, nude and gloriously engorged.

Helen swallowed, staring at that part of his anatomy. It was just as well that she hadn't gotten a full view this afternoon, because he was larger than Lister—*considerably* larger. His penis stood proudly erect, magnificent veins vining about the shaft, the head gleaming and almost purple. Below, his balls were tight and heavy between muscled thighs.

She sighed.

He cleared his throat. "I believe it's your turn."

"Oh!" She'd quite forgot the game they'd been playing. She hastily knelt on the bed and drew her chemise over her head.

His gaze immediately dropped to her chest, and a wicked smile twisted the corner of his mouth. "There they are."

She glanced down at herself. "Are you referring to my bosom?"

He strolled forward and placed a knee on the bed. "I am."

She frowned a little. "You sound rather . . . possessive."

"Indeed." He leaned down and licked a nipple, making her inhale sharply. "You have the most splendid breasts I have ever seen."

"Thank you," she said rather breathlessly. "Am I allowed to comment on portions of your anatomy as well?"

"Mmm," he murmured against her breast, sending little shivers down her spine. "Although I don't know what you'd find to interest you. My body isn't beautiful like yours."

"Of course it is," she said in surprise.

He arched an eyebrow skeptically. "My body is big and ugly and hairy—like all men."

"Your body is big and beautiful and, yes, hairy. And I don't know about most men, but to me it's quite lovely." She ran her hand down his chest. "Lovely and hairy. I like the way your hair is so thick here"—she patted his chest—"and then thins *here*"—she trailed her fingers over his stomach—"and then it thickens again down here, where—"

But she wasn't allowed to finish. Even as she grasped that most masculine part of him, he took her shoulders and pushed her back in the bed, kissing her quite masterfully. When he raised his head to inhale, she looked at him with mock reproach.

"I hadn't finished."

"Well, I was about to," he muttered.

She smiled and gently squeezed the penis she still held.

His eye closed for a moment and then opened, brighter

than before. "And if you want this to last more than a minute, you'll desist doing that."

He gently pried loose her hand and shoved a muscular thigh between her legs. She could feel the hair on his leg rubbing against her moist flesh. She swallowed and arched up, grinding her pelvis against him.

"Witch," he whispered against her neck.

He pressed down more firmly, holding her nearly immobile as he licked across her chest to a breast. This he took into his mouth and suckled leisurely, as if he had all the time in the world to savor her.

Helen squirmed.

"Stop that," he growled, his voice vibrating against her damp skin.

"But I want to move," she gasped.

"But I want to taste your nipples," he retorted, and moved to the other breast.

She looked down, seeing only dark skin and darker hair moving over her white body. A shiver of erotic anticipation shook her. "I think you are obsessed with breasts."

"No," he murmured, levering himself up a little so he could cradle both her breasts in his big hands. He flicked her nipples idly as he talked, and she bit her lip. "I have an obsession with *your* breasts. I want to lick them, suck them, perhaps"—he leaned down to scrape his teeth over the curving side of one sensitive breast—"bite them."

"Bite?" she squeaked.

He smiled, slowly and wickedly. "Mmm. Bite."

And he lowered his head to take her nipple very gently between his teeth. She held her breath, the threat making her clench internally. He looked into her eyes, his hair falling forward like a pirate about his face, and raked his tongue against the tip of her nipple.

Her breasts had always been extremely sensitive. Helen could feel her breath coming quicker and quicker as he tortured that nipple. But when he closed his eye and sucked it into his mouth, drawing strongly, she clenched her thighs around his big leg and held on.

For long, passionate minutes, he licked and sucked and bit at her nipples until they were swollen, red, and glistening with his saliva. She moved agitatedly beneath him, entirely aroused yet unable to fulfill quite yet.

He reared up over her and studied what he'd done to her. His high cheekbones had a flush across them, his eyelid drooped lazily, and his lips were reddened from his ministrations yet were held in an almost cruel line.

"You look like a pagan sacrifice," he growled low. "Prepared and laid out for some god to"—he leaned close and whispered in her ear—"*fuck*."

She moaned at the forbidden word. No one had ever talked to her thus, made love to her thus. She was in a frenzy of neglected need.

"Touch me," she begged, trying to widen her legs so that part of her could rub against his thigh.

He tilted his head, studying her as if she were a particularly interesting specimen. Only the rock-hard length of his cock, pressing against her thigh, belied his dispassion.

"I don't know if you're ready," he murmured.

She glared. "I'm ready."

"Are you?" He licked the side of her neck, sending anxious shivers along her oversensitive skin. "I wouldn't want to engage you too soon. You might not experience the full effect of our lovemaking if I did."

"You," she panted half-hysterically, "are a *devil*."

He grinned almost boyishly. "Am I?"

"Ye-sss." Her assent ended in a moan because he'd shifted suddenly, bringing his penis in direct contact with her drenched folds. "Oh."

"You like that?" he inquired solicitously.

She could only nod as he slowly drew himself through her. He thrust with a small, controlled movement, his cock tunneling against her. She swallowed, not even caring about the wet, squishing sounds they made.

"Then," he purred, "perhaps you are ready. For *this*."

And he reared back and shoved himself full-length inside her. She arched her neck at the shock, the thrill, of being filled so suddenly.

Then he was hitching himself up her, pushing apart her legs to their widest point and grinding himself down on her. Down on her clitoris.

Oh, bliss!

She was incoherent, past speech, past thought, past humanity. All her being was centered there, experiencing, receiving, his exquisite lovemaking. She didn't even know when she started to come. It was one long, endless implosion of heat. She trembled uncontrollably.

And somewhere—sometime—during all this, she heard him growl and opened her eyes. He was on straight arms, levered above her, watching her as he made love to her. But now there was no way to mistake his expression for disinterest. Now his upper lip curled back in an erotic sneer. Now his face shone with effort and sweat. Now his one eye gleamed with dark intent.

Masculine intent.

As she watched, he speeded his thrusts until the bed

thumped against the wall. She spread her legs farther and wrapped them high over his hips, watching his struggle until his face twisted as if in agony. A cry ripped from his throat, and he jerked against her one last time.

And she felt his strength fill her with warmth.

ALISTAIR THREW OUT an arm early the next morning, reaching for something he wanted on an instinctual level, and it wasn't until he came fully awake that he realized both that it was Helen he searched for and that she was not there. He sighed and scrubbed his face with one hand. He still wore the eye patch from the night before, and it itched. He tore it off and flung it aside and then just lay there in the half light of morning.

His bed smelled of sex and Helen.

She'd left sometime the night before. He'd been so exhausted from their lovemaking that he wasn't even entirely sure when. Of course, she'd had to leave. There were the children to think of, propriety, and his sister still in the castle, but damn, he wished she were here now. Not just so that he could make love to her again—although he wanted that, too—but he also wanted to lie with her. To feel her warm curves against his body. To hold her in his arms while he slept and to wake to find her still there.

While she let him. Because although she'd never said anything, he knew she wasn't the type of woman who could live simply for the moment. Sooner or later, she would start to wonder about the future, perhaps question if she could spend it with him. And then, inevitably, she would discover that he had no future to offer her.

Then she would leave him.

Lowering thought. He pushed it aside, at least for the

moment, because he'd learned that there was no use fighting fate. Eventually she would leave him; eventually he would mourn her, but not today. He threw back the covers, washed, retied the eye patch carefully, and dressed. Sophia had said that she'd be leaving this morning, and he fully expected her to be downstairs, impatiently waiting while her bags were loaded into the carriage.

The hallway downstairs was deserted, however, when he stepped into it. He checked the front drive, but although the carriage did wait there, his sister was nowhere about. Perhaps she was taking breakfast. He strode back into the castle and made his way to the dining room, where he found one of the maids laying out silverware. She curtsied when she saw him.

"Is Miss Munroe about?" he asked.

"She hasn't come down, sir," the maid replied.

Alistair grinned. Sophia had overslept—a rarity and an occasion for ribbing. "Go up, please, and rouse her and Miss MacDonald. My sister wanted to make an early start this morning."

"Yes, sir." The maid curtsied again and scurried from the room.

Alistair found a basket of warm rolls on the sideboard and took one; then he wandered into the hallway again. He wanted to be present when his sister made her belated entrance. He munched on the bun, strolling down the hall toward the kitchens, and then he heard it. The sound sent a prickling chill down his back and turned the bun in his mouth to ashes.

Weeping. A child weeping.

Helen hadn't gotten to this part of the castle yet, and there were several unused rooms off the ancient hallway.

He strode from door to door until he located that forlorn sound, and then he pushed it open. The room was dim, dust motes floating in the feeble ray of sun creeping in from a dirty window. At first he couldn't see her, until she moved and whimpered.

Abigail crouched in a corner, next to a sheet-draped settee, the puppy clutched in her arms.

He started forward slowly, not sure of the problem or if he could do anything about it. Out of the corner of his eye, he saw Wiggins sneaking from the other door at the far end of the room.

Red washed over his vision.

He had no memory of moving, no memory of intent, but when next he was aware, he had Wiggins's scrawny neck in his grasp, and he was throttling the life from the man and knocking his head against the flagstones in the hallway.

"Alistair!"

Someone close by called his name, but he was interested only in the foul, reddening face in front of him. How dare he? How dare he touch her? He wouldn't again. Never, *never* again.

"Alistair!"

A soft, feminine palm was laid against his scarred cheek. Gentle pressure turned his head. Then he was staring into harebell-blue eyes. "Don't, Alistair. Let him go."

"Abigail," he rasped.

"She's fine," Helen said slowly. "I don't know what he said to her, but he didn't physically harm her."

That, finally, was the only thing that restored reason to his brain. He abruptly let go, straightening and backing up a step. Only then did he see that Sophia and Miss

McDonald stood at the bottom of the stairs, still in their wrappers. Miss McDonald had one arm around a wide-eyed Jamie. Helen stood shivering only in a chemise. She must've run down the stairs without even stopping to put on a wrapper. And Abigail was behind her, her face tearstained as she held the puppy in her arms.

He took a deep breath to steady his voice and asked low, "Did he touch you?"

Abigail shook her head mutely, her eyes locked with his.

He nodded and looked back to Wiggins, who was gasping for breath on the hall floor. "Get out. Get out of my castle, get off my lands, and make sure you never show your face near me again."

"Ye'll regret this!" the little man rasped. "See if ye don't. I'll be back. I'll take that little bitch—"

Alistair balled his fists and took a step toward him. In a flash, Wiggins was on his feet and running out the castle doors.

He closed his eye, trying to regain his civilized mask, and felt little arms encircle his waist. He knelt, his eye still closed, and wrapped that small body in his arms.

"Never again," he whispered into her hair, so like her mother's. "I'll never let another hurt you again. I promise."

Chapter Eleven

The next evening, Truth Teller let the swallows out of their cage for a third time. The sorcerer had barely run from the courtyard when the monster turned into Princess Sympathy, and Truth Teller approached the cage.

"How can I free you?" he asked.

The princess shook her head. "It is a dangerous task. Many have tried and all have failed."

But Truth Teller merely looked at her and said, "Tell me."

The princess sighed. "If you were to do this thing, you must first drug the sorcerer. In these mountains grows a tiny purple flower. You must gather the buds of this flower and grind them into a powder. When the time comes, blow the powder into the sorcerer's face, and he will be unable to stop you for as long as the light of the moon is upon him. Take his milky-white ring and bring it to me. Lastly, you must have ready two horses, the swiftest you can find, so that we may flee him."

Truth Teller nodded. "I will do these things, I swear. . . ."

—from TRUTH TELLER

Helen watched Alistair enfold Abigail in his arms, and something twisted and broke open in her heart. He held Abigail so tenderly. It was impossible not to make the obvious comparison. Alistair held the little girl like a father would. Except her real father had never held her.

The sight shook her to her core. He'd made love to her as if they were the only ones in the world last night, and now he comforted her daughter with rough tenderness. She realized with a shock that she was falling in love with him, this angry, lonely master of the castle. Perhaps she was already in love with him. And her heart beat faster in near panic. If there was one thing she'd learned in her chaotic, illogical, foolish life, it was this: Love made her make incredibly stupid decisions. Decisions that put herself and her children in jeopardy.

Adding to *that* unpleasant thought was another awful realization. She was still confused—dazed and startled awake from sleep—but she knew in her soul that Alistair had saved her daughter. Saved her when she had failed.

She closed her eyes as a sob shuddered through her body.

"Take this," Miss Munroe said gruffly, draping a cloak over her shoulders. "You look cold."

"I'm such a fool," Helen whispered. "I never thought—"

"Don't castigate yourself until you've spoken to the girl," Miss Munroe said.

"I don't see how I can't." Helen wiped her eyes with her sleeve. "I really don't."

"Mama." Jamie inexplicably shoved himself between them and clutched at her skirts.

"It's all right, Jamie." She gave one last sniffle and determinedly straightened. "Breakfast must be ready. Let's all go get properly dressed, and then we can eat. That'll make us feel better."

Alistair looked at her over Abigail's head. He still hadn't entirely composed himself. His eye glittered with a feral violence. He'd been in the act of killing Mr. Wiggins when she'd reached the hall. Even now she wasn't sure that he would've stopped on his own had she not compelled him to look at her. She shivered. The evidence of this uncivilized, primitive part of him should frighten her. But oddly, instead of making her more fearful, that savage side of him made her feel safe. Safe in a way she hadn't felt since she'd been a child living in her father's house. Back when the complications of adulthood had not yet intruded on her life.

She shivered, aware that she was vulnerable right now—too vulnerable. She was awash in conflicting emotions, and they left her defenseless to him. She needed to get away, if only for a little while, and compose herself.

She swallowed, and taking Jamie's hand, she held the other out for Abigail. "Come, my love. Let's settle ourselves."

Abigail placed her hand in hers, and Helen had to stop herself from squeezing too tightly. She wanted to run her fingers over her daughter's head, look her in the eyes, and see for herself that Abigail was fine, but at the same time, she didn't want to add to her daughter's trauma. Better to calm down and question her gently.

"We'll be back down in a few minutes," she said to Alistair, her voice trembling just a little.

Then she led her children to their room. Jamie had apparently recovered from whatever worry had plagued him. He hurried into his clothes and then sat on the bed with the puppy.

Meanwhile, Helen poured water from the pitcher on the dresser into a basin. She took a cloth, wet it, and gently wiped Abigail's face. It'd been years since she'd helped Abigail dress. Miss Cummings had done the chore in London, and on their journey north, Abigail had mostly been able to get herself ready. But this morning, Helen carefully washed the tearstains from her daughter's face. She prompted Abigail to sit and then knelt at her feet to roll on her stockings, tying the garters over her knees carefully, each movement deliberate and calm. She drew on Abigail's underskirt and skirt, fastening them at the waist.

When Helen picked up the bodice, Abigail finally spoke. "Mama, you don't have to."

"I know, dearest," Helen murmured. "But it's a funny thing that sometimes mothers enjoy dressing their daughters. Can you indulge me?"

Her daughter nodded. Her cheeks had regained the faint color they usually held, and her face was no longer stricken. Helen's fingers fumbled on the laces as she remembered the awful expression on Abigail's face when she'd come to the bottom of the stairs. Dear God, if Alistair hadn't been there . . .

"There," Helen said softly when the bodice was laced. "Hand me the brush and I'll do your hair."

"Can you braid it and put it in a crown?" Abigail asked.

"Of course." Helen smiled. She sat on a low stool. "I'll make you a princess."

Abigail turned around, and Helen began stroking the brush through her hair. "Can you tell me what happened?"

Abigail's thin shoulders lifted, and her head ducked as if she were a turtle withdrawing into a shell.

"I know you don't want to talk about it," Helen murmured, "but I think we must, dearest. At least once. And then, if you wish, we'll never discuss it again. Would that be all right?"

Abigail nodded and took a deep breath. "I woke up, but you and Jamie were asleep, so I took Puddles downstairs. I went with him outside so he could do his business, but then I saw Mr. Wiggins, and I ran back inside with Puddles and we hid."

She paused, and Helen set down the brush to divide the long flaxen hair into three parts. "And then?"

"Mr. Wiggins came in the room," Abigail said softly. "He . . . he shouted at me. He said I was spying on him."

Helen's brows knit. "Why would he think that?"

"I don't know," Abigail said evasively.

Helen decided to let it drop. "Then what happened?"

"And . . . and I cried. I didn't want to—I tried not to, but I couldn't seem to help myself," she confessed miserably. "I hated crying in front of him."

Helen's mouth tightened, and she concentrated on braiding Abigail's hair. For a brief, fierce moment, she wished that Alistair *had* killed Mr. Wiggins.

"Then Sir Alistair came in," Abigail continued, "and he saw me and he saw Mr. Wiggins, and, Mama, he moved so fast! He took Mr. Wiggins by the neck and dragged him from the room, and I didn't even know what was happening until I went into the hall, and then you and Jamie and Miss Munroe were there, and you told Sir Alistair that he must stop." She took a deep breath at the end of this recitation.

Helen was silent a moment, thinking. She finished the braid and set aside the brush.

"Hold the pins," she murmured, "while I do your crown."

She placed the hairpins in Abigail's hand and began wrapping the braid high across her daughter's head.

"Thank you, darling." She accepted a hairpin from Abigail and placed it carefully in the braid to anchor it. "I was wondering if anything else happened in the room where you hid with Puddles?"

Abigail held very still while she did her coiffure, but her eyes were lowered to the pins in her hand.

Helen's heart missed a beat. Something seemed to be clogging her throat, and she had to clear it before going on. "Did Mr. Wiggins touch you at all?"

Abigail blinked and looked up, her eyes puzzled. "Touch me?"

Oh, God. Helen made her voice casual. "Did he put his hand on you, sweeting? Or . . . or try to kiss you?"

"Ewww!" Abigail's face screwed into a mask of appalled disgust. "No, Mama! He didn't want to kiss me—he wanted to *beat* me."

"But why?"

"I don't know." Abigail looked away. "He said that he was going to, but then Sir Alistair came in and dragged him out."

The clog in her throat was abruptly gone. Helen swallowed and asked, to be completely sure, "Then he didn't touch you at all?"

"No, I told you. Sir Alistair came in before Mr. Wiggins could come near me. I don't think he would want to kiss me when he was so angry, anyway."

Abigail looked at her as if she was rather dim.

And Helen had never been so glad in all her life to be thought stupid. She placed the last pin, turned Abigail around to face her, and hugged her, careful not to squeeze as tightly as she really wanted.

"Well, I'm glad that Sir Alistair came in when he did. I don't think we'll have to worry about Mr. Wiggins again."

Abigail squirmed. "Can I look in the mirror?"

"Of course." Helen opened her arms and set her daughter free. Abigail ran to an old mirror over the dresser. She stood on tiptoe, turning her head first one way and then the other to see her crown of braided hair.

"I'm hungry," Jamie announced, bouncing off the bed.

Helen nodded briskly and rose. "Let me dress and we'll see what Mrs. McCleod has for breakfast."

She began her toilet with a considerably lighter heart, though a small part of her brain pondered over Abigail's evasion. If Mr. Wiggins wanted to beat the girl, what was she hiding?

"We have got to find a name for that dog," Sir Alistair muttered to no one in particular later that afternoon. He hitched his old satchel over his shoulder.

He'd paused at the crest of a small hill to watch Jamie and Abigail roll down the other side. Jamie threw himself to the ground and rolled with complete abandon, oblivious both to possible obstacles and the direction his little body rocketed in. Abigail, in contrast, carefully tucked her skirts about her legs before lying down, her arms over her head, and slowly rolled in a straight line down the hill.

"You don't like the name Puddles?" Helen asked. She'd tilted her face to the breeze and looked quite angelic.

Nonetheless, he shot her a dark look. "The animal will die of humiliation once it's old enough to understand its name."

She looked doubtfully at him. "Understand its name?"

He ignored the look. "A dog—especially a male dog— needs a dignified name."

They both watched as the puppy, running excitedly down the hill after the children, tripped on its big paws and rolled to the bottom in a heap of long ears and muddy fur. The dog got up, shook itself, and started back up the hill again.

Alistair winced. "This dog in particular needs a dignified name."

Helen giggled.

He felt his mouth twisting in a reluctant smile. It was a lovely day, after all, and she and the children were safe. For the present, it was enough that Wiggins hadn't touched Abigail with lecherous intent but had merely scared the wits out of her. When Helen had told him, shortly before they'd sat for breakfast, he'd felt an awful weight lift from his chest.

Sophia, who'd also been part of the whispered conversation, had merely nodded and muttered, "Good," before tucking into the porridge, bacon, and eggs that Mrs. McCleod had prepared. Shortly thereafter, she and Miss McDonald had departed for Edinburgh. He'd watched the carriage disappear down his drive with mixed feelings. He'd enjoyed sparring with his sister—he'd forgotten how much he liked her company—but he was glad to have the castle to himself and Helen again. Sophia's eyes were far, far too perceptive.

He'd spent the remainder of the morning in productive work, but during luncheon, Jamie had spoken rather wistfully about the badgers they'd been unable to find the day before. That had led to a suggestion of an afternoon ramble, and now Alistair found himself derelict from his work and hiking the countryside.

"You did say that you'd let the children name him," Helen said now.

"Aye, but I also specified that Puddles was not a name."

"Hmm." Her lips twitched and then firmed. "I haven't thanked you for this morning."

He shrugged one shoulder. "There's no need."

At the bottom of the hill, Abigail got carefully to her feet and shook out her skirts. Miraculously, she had no grass stains on them, though she'd gone down the hill multiple times now.

Helen was silent beside him a moment, and then she stepped closer and took his hand, the action hidden by her skirts. "I am so glad that you were there to protect her."

He glanced at her.

She was watching Abigail with a wistful look in her eye. "She's very special, you know, not at all what I expected in a daughter, but then I suppose we must all accept what God grants us."

He hesitated a moment. It really wasn't any of his

business, but then he said gruffly, "She fears that she doesn't meet with your approval."

"My approval?" She looked at him, puzzled. "Abigail told you that?"

He nodded.

She sighed. "I love her terribly—of course I do; she's my daughter—but I've never understood her. She has these moods, so dark for one so young. It's not that I disapprove of her; it's that I wish I knew how to make her happy."

"Perhaps you don't need to."

She shook her head. "What do you mean?"

He shrugged. "I'm no authority, but perhaps there's no need to try and 'make' her happy. After all, that chore is ultimately one that will lead to defeat. No one can make Abigail happy but herself. Perhaps you need only love her." He looked down into her sad harebell-blue eyes. "And you already do."

"Yes." Her eyes widened. "Yes, I do."

He looked away again and felt the squeeze of her fingers before she dropped her hand.

"Come, children," she called, and started down the hill.

He watched her, her skirts swaying as she descended the hill, her hips moving in a smooth seductive rhythm, a lock of pale gold hair blowing from beneath the wide brim of her hat. He blinked as if waking from a dream and followed those slowly swaying hips.

"Where're the badgers?" Jamie asked. The boy caught his hand, seemingly without thinking.

Alistair tilted his chin forward. "Just over the hill there."

They were surrounded by gently rolling hills covered

in low gorse and heather, the horizon clear as far as the eye could see. Farther to the west, a flock of sheep grazed like dots of down on the green and purple hills.

"But we went that way yesterday," Abigail objected. "Miss Munroe couldn't find the badgers anywhere."

"Ah, but that's because she doesn't know where to look."

Abigail gave him a dubious glance, and he was hard-pressed not to smile at her doubt.

"Puddles doesn't want to walk anymore," Jamie announced.

"How do you know?" Abigail frowned at the puppy, who, as far as Alistair could see, looked perfectly able to walk.

"I just do," Jamie retorted. He scooped the puppy into his arms. "Oof. He's gotten big."

Abigail rolled her eyes. "That's because you gave him the rest of your porridge this morning."

Jamie started to say something rather heatedly, but Alistair cleared his throat. "I found a puddle in the kitchen this morning that I suspect Puddles may have made. Mind you take him outside for his business, children."

"We will," Abigail said.

"Have you thought of a name for him? He can't be Puddles for the rest of his life."

"Well, I thought of George, in honor of the king, but Jamie doesn't like it."

"It's a silly name," Jamie muttered.

"And what is your proposition?" Alistair asked.

"Spot," Jamie said.

"Ah, well, that's—"

"Stu-pid!" Abigail interjected. "Besides, he's more

splotchy than spotty, and Splotch would be an even sillier name."

"Abigail," Helen said. "Please apologize to Sir Alistair for interrupting him. A lady never interrupts a gentleman."

Alistair's eyebrows shot up at this piece of information. He took two long steps, catching up with her and bending his head near hers. "Never?"

"Not unless the gentleman is being extremely stubborn," she replied serenely.

"Ah."

"I'm sorry," Abigail muttered.

Alistair nodded. "Hold the puppy tight, now."

"Why?" Jamie looked up.

"Because the badger sett is right over there." Alistair pointed with his walking stick. The badgers lived in a low mound, covered in gorse. "See the freshly dug earth? That's one of the tunnels."

"Ohhh." Jamie squatted to look. "Will we see one?"

"Probably not. They're rather shy, but they can kill a dog, especially a small one, if they're challenged."

Jamie hugged Puddles to his chest until the puppy squeaked, and whispered hoarsely, "Where do you think they are?"

Alistair shrugged. "Perhaps in their den asleep. Maybe out hunting grubs."

"Grubs?" Jamie wrinkled his nose.

He nodded. "That's what they seem to like."

"Look at this!" Abigail very carefully squatted with her skirts tucked under her rear.

Alistair went to where she pointed and saw a small

black mound. "Oh, well done! You found a badger's scat."

Behind him, Helen made a muffled sound, but he ignored her. He squatted next to Abigail and, taking a twig, poked at the mostly dry scat. "Notice these."

He scraped out a couple black flakes.

Abigail peered closer. "What are they?"

"The carapace of a beetle." He shrugged off his satchel and opened a pocket, rummaging until he found a very small glass jar. He picked up the beetle parts and dropped them in the jar, stopping the top with a tiny cork.

"What's a carapace?" Jamie asked. He was squatting now, too, breathing anxiously through his mouth.

"The hard outer shell." Alistair poked some more and found a thin, pale bone.

"Oh, what animal is that from?" Abigail asked with interest.

"I'm not sure." The bone was only a fragment. He held it up before placing it in another small glass jar. "Possibly a small mammal such as a mouse or mole."

"Huh," Abigail said, and straightened. "Are there other clues to the badgers that we might find about?"

"Sometimes there is debris in the earth dug up by the badger." Alistair picked up his specimen satchel and strolled closer to the burrow hole. A movement in the dark depths made him stop and catch Abigail's shoulder. "Look."

"A baby!" Abigail breathed.

"Where? Where?" Jamie whispered loudly.

"See there?" Alistair bent his head near the boy's and pointed the direction.

"Coo!"

A small black and white striped face peered from the burrow with another jostling for position behind it. The badgers froze, staring for a moment, and then abruptly disappeared.

"Oh, that was nice." Helen's voice came from behind them. Alistair turned to find her smiling at him. "Better anyway than the scat, I think. What shall we search for now?"

And she looked at him as if it were the most natural thing in the world to spend an afternoon with him. To share her children with him.

He shuddered and abruptly turned in the direction of Castle Greaves. "Nothing. I have work to do."

He strode away, not waiting for Helen or the children, aware that his movement looked like he was fleeing from them, when what he fled from was far more dangerous: hope for the future.

AFTER THE WAY Alistair had so rudely cut short their afternoon ramble, Helen had sworn to herself that she wouldn't go to him again. Yet as the hour struck midnight, she found herself stealing through the dim castle halls toward his room. She knew she was playing with a particularly hot fire, knew she was risking both herself and her children, and yet she couldn't seem to stay away from him. *Maybe*, some rash, perpetually hopeful part of her whispered, *maybe he'll open himself to you. Maybe he'll grow to love you. Maybe he'll want you for his wife*.

Silly, childish whispers. She'd spent half her life with a man who'd never truly cared for her, and there was a practical, hard part of her that knew when this thing with Alistair ended, she would have to leave with her children.

But it wouldn't be tonight.

Helen hesitated outside his door, but somehow he must've heard her, though she hadn't knocked. He opened the door, grabbed her arm, and drew her inside.

"Good evening," she began, but he swallowed the last word with his mouth. His lips were hot and so demanding they were nearly desperate. She forgot everything around her.

Then he raised his head and pulled her toward the bed. "I have something to show you."

She blinked. "What is it?"

"Sit." He didn't wait for her to comply but turned to rummage in the drawer of his bedside table. "Ah. Here it is."

He held up a small lemon, no bigger than the tip of his thumb.

She raised her eyebrows. "Yes?"

"I had Mrs. McCleod purchase it last time she bought groceries. I thought . . ." He cleared his throat. "Well, I thought you might wish to use a preventative."

"A preventative for . . . oh." She felt heat invade her cheeks. Actually, since she was newly over her courses, she'd figured that she wasn't fertile at the present moment. But since this was now her third assignation with Alistair, she supposed she would've shortly have had to worry about preventing a pregnancy. It was oddly touching that he'd thought—and acted—on the worry first.

"I've never . . . um, that is . . ." She belatedly remembered that she was supposed to be a respectable widow. Presumably she'd never have heard of preventatives, if

so. In fact, the duke sometimes had used specially made
sheaths, although not usually.

Alistair's cheekbones had tinged a dark red as well. "I
can show you. Just lean back."

She realized what he meant to do and wanted to object. It was one thing to let him see her when they were
intimate, but while he was still dressed and standing, it
was . . . unseemly.

"Helen," he said quietly.

"Oh, all right." She lowered herself to the bed and
stared at the ceiling. She lay horizontally across the bed,
her legs hanging over the side.

She felt him push up the skirts of her wrap and chemise, the slide of silk against her flesh a soft whisper in
the quiet room. He bunched the fabric at her waist, and
then his hands left her. She heard him rummage in the
side table again and then she smelled the sharp scent of
citrus. She craned her head up and saw him holding the
halved lemon. His eyes met hers, and then he knelt on the
carpet beside the bed. She drew in her breath. His warm
hand touched her legs again, and she realized he was urging her thighs apart. She swallowed and parted her legs.

"More," he rasped.

She closed her eyes. Oh, God, he was so close to her
intimate parts. He'd be able to see everything. He'd be
able to scent *her*. She bit her lip and parted her legs still
farther.

"Again," he whispered.

And she did, widening her legs until her thighs trembled. Until the flanges of her sex parted as well, exposing
her utterly to his gaze. She felt his hand slowly stroke up
her thigh.

"When I was fifteen," he said conversationally, "I found a book of anatomy that belonged to my father. It was most instructive, especially in regards to the female form."

She swallowed. His fingers were combing delicately through her hair.

"This"—he spread his broad palm over her mound—"is called the mons veneris. The Mound of Venus."

His fingers trailed down the inside crease of her thigh, almost tickling. She shivered.

"These are the labia majora." He stroked up the other side.

Then something cold and wet trickled over her inner folds. She jumped a little and smelled the lemon, sharper in the air.

She felt him press the curved, slick lemon rind to her flesh. He slid it slowly through her wet folds. "These are the labia minora. But here"—he circled the top of her cleft with the lemon and then, abruptly and shockingly, pressed down—"is a problem."

"A problem?" she squeaked.

"Mmm." His voice had deepened to a near growl. "This is the clitoris. It was discovered by Signor Gabriele Falloppio in 1561."

Helen tried to contemplate his words while he continued to press the lemon so exquisitely against her. Their meaning kept slipping away.

Finally she found her voice. "You mean . . . you mean no one knew of its existence until 1561?"

"That is what Signor Falloppio thought, although it does seem a little, well, unlikely." He emphasized *unlikely* by tapping sharply with the lemon. She gasped. "But there is a further problem besides that one. You see, another Italian anatomist, a man named Colombo, claimed to have made the discovery two years prior to Signor Falloppio."

"I think I feel sorry for these gentlemen's wives," Helen muttered. She was hot, the constant pressure of the cool lemon making her anxious. Aroused. She wished he would just finish and come make love to her.

But Alistair was obviously in no hurry. "Rather you should feel sorry for the wives whose husbands do not believe in the existence of the clitoris."

She squinted at the ceiling. "Are there men like that?"

"Oh, yes, indeed," he murmured. He finally took the lemon away from her sensitive flesh, but now she felt contrarily bereft. "Some doubt there's such a thing at all."

And he slid the halved lemon slowly into her.

She gasped at the sensation. The cold citrus, his warm fingers. He twisted inside her, did something, and then withdrew his fingers, leaving the lemon inside.

"There are those who doubt that a woman feels any sensation at all when stimulated here." He drew his finger up through her folds again until he tapped once more on her clitoris. "I think they are mad, of course, but a scientist always tests his theories. Shall we see?"

See what? Helen thought, but had no time to say, because before she could speak, his mouth had replaced his finger, and she had no way of speaking after that.

All she could do was feel.

He licked carefully, delicately, through the flanges of her sex, as if he wanted to taste every drop of the spilled lemon juice. And when he reached the top, he licked around her bud, in tighter and tighter circles until she was clutching at the sheets on either side of her in trembling ecstasy and had raised her knees to press against him. He took her legs and casually slung them over his shoulders without lifting his mouth from her. Instead, he held her hips more firmly, keeping her from arching away from him. He narrowed his tongue and darted it into her channel, and when she thought she might simply disintegrate from the sensation, he moved up again. He took that sensitive bit of flesh between his lips and sucked on it, gently and persistently.

She couldn't move, couldn't escape his determined lovemaking. She was moaning and panting, unable to control the sounds coming from her mouth. She'd tangled her fingers in his long hair at some point, and that lifeline was the only thing holding her earthbound. She tugged anxiously, inarticulate with need, for him to stop or continue—she didn't know which, and it did not matter.

Nothing was stopping him.

Until light exploded behind her closed eyelids, and pure, almost painful pleasure radiated out from the center he still ministered to. She gasped, feeling tears welling in her eyes.

Feeling as if she'd touched heaven.

He continued to lick softly as she quieted, and then he rose, standing by the bed, examining her almost dispassionately as he shed his clothes.

"I don't believe I shall ever taste a lemon and not think of you," he said conversationally. He stripped his breeches off, and his penis rose, monstrously erect before him. "Think of this."

He prowled up her spent form, his arms on either side of her, his weight making the bed sink beneath her. He took off her wrap and chemise as easily as undressing a doll, and she only watched him, her lids lowered lazily. He shifted and tugged her until she lay on the bed properly, and then he spread her legs again, as wide as he could. He lowered himself onto her.

She flinched slightly at his touch, her flesh still sensitive.

He bent his head until his lips touched her ear. "I don't want to hurt you, but I must be in you now. I can no more refrain than I can stop breathing. Gentle." He said this last because the head of his penis had nudged her entrance. "Relax. Just . . . let me." He pushed an inch or so inside.

She breathed rapidly. She'd never been this sensitized. She felt as if a feather's touch would make her shudder. And what he was introducing inside of her body was no feather. He slid a little farther in. She was very wet, but she was also swollen, ripe with arousal. She turned her head and licked at his jaw.

He froze. "Don't—"

This time she carefully tested her teeth against his skin. No matter how casual his words, he was on a razor's edge—she could tell by how stiffly he held his body—and a wicked part of her wanted to send him over that edge. Wanted to drive him to the brink of insanity.

She scratched her nails down his back.

"Helen," he rasped, "that isn't wise."

"But I don't want to be wise," she whispered back.

That did it. Whatever thread that had held him snapped. He lunged, driving his length into her softness, pummeling her, thrusting into her, panting and uncivilized.

She wrapped her arms about him and held on as he plunged and writhed above her, watching him, watching his strong, scarred face. Even when the edges of her vision blurred and pleasure began to sweep over her in hot beats, she still forced her eyes open, watching, watching.

And he watched her back, his gaze locked with hers, his eye darkening as he neared his crisis. It was as if he strove to communicate something he could not say but could only demonstrate with his body. His lips twisted, his face flushed, and his mouth opened wordlessly, but he kept his eye locked with hers even as he pulsed hot life into her body.

Chapter Twelve

Thereafter, when the sorcerer relieved him from his guard duty, Truth Teller would hunt the mountain for the purple flower. It took some time, for he had only the light of the moon to search by, but eventually he had gathered enough buds to grind them into a powder. Then he set about finding two horses. This proved an even more difficult task, for the sorcerer kept no horses. But one night Truth Teller took what coin he had and hiked all the way down the mountain to a farm in the valley below.

When he awakened the farmer and explained what he wished to purchase, the man frowned. "Your purse is too small. I can only sell you one horse for that amount."

Truth Teller nodded and gave the farmer all the money he had in the world. "So be it."

And he hiked back up the mountain before dawn with only the one horse. . . .

—from TRUTH TELLER

Helen woke in the wee hours of the morning in Alistair's bed. The embers of the fire still glowed in the hearth, but the candle sitting on the table by the bed had long ago guttered out. Next to her, Alistair's breathing was heavy and slow. She'd not meant to fall asleep here. The realization brought her fully awake. She needed to return to her own room and her children.

With that thought, she quietly inched from the bed and padded to the mantel. There was a jar of tapers here, and she bent and lit one in the fire's embers, then lit several candles so she could see to dress. She looked around. Her wrap was half under the bed, but she couldn't see her chemise. Muttering softly to herself, she took up the candle and approached the bed to look. The chemise wasn't under or next to the bed. Finally she leaned over the great mattress, searching for the chemise amongst the bedclothes. She paused as the soft candlelight illuminated Alistair.

He lay sprawled on his back, one arm flung high over his head, the sheets pushed to his waist. He looked like a sleeping god, his muscled shoulders and arms dark against the white sheets. His face was slightly turned toward her, and she saw that he'd taken off his eye patch sometime during the night. She hesitated briefly before leaning closer to examine his exposed face. She'd only seen him without his eye patch on that first night at the door, so long ago now. Then, she'd been overwhelmed with a feeling of horror. That horror had taken precedence in her mind, wiping out any detailed impression.

She saw now that the eyelid on his missing eye had been closed and sewn shut. It was sunken, true, but beyond that, there was nothing more distressing than a normal closed eye would be. The rest of that side of his face was another matter, of course. A deep gouge ran diagonally across his face, starting below the closed eyelid and ending at a point near his ear. Below that was an area pitted and reddened, the skin thickened and leathery-looking, perhaps some kind of burn scar. Smaller white lines were scattered across his cheekbone, obviously the result of knife cuts.

"Not a pretty sight, is it?" he rasped.

Helen jerked, startled, only just missing dripping candle wax on his shoulder.

Alistair opened his eye to regard her calmly. "Are you examining the beast you let bed you last night?" His voice was deep. Rough from sleep.

"I'm sorry," she murmured rather inanely. She saw now that her chemise lay half under his shoulder.

"Why?" he asked.

"What?" She yanked at the chemise, but he lay over most of it, and she couldn't pull it out from under him without ripping the fine fabric.

He didn't move. "Why be sorry? You have the right, after all, to see what your lover looks like under the mask."

She gave up on the chemise for the moment and glanced about distractedly for the wrap instead. Really, it felt quite odd to be having a conversation whilst nude. "I didn't want to seem, well, rude, is all."

He grasped her wrist and pulled her toward him, taking the candlestick from her hand and setting it on the small table by his side of the bed. "It's not rude to want to know the truth."

"Alistair," she said softly, "I must return to my own room. The children—"

"Are most likely sound asleep," he murmured. He tugged at her arm, and she half fell across him, her breasts crushed to the heat of his chest. He leaned up and brushed his lips across hers. "Stay."

"I can't," she whispered. "You know that."

"Do I?" he rasped against her lips. "Someday you'll leave, but right now I know only that it's very early and my bed is very cold without you in it. Stay."

"Alistair . . ." She hadn't seen this side of him before, this gentle, charming lover. He was very appealing like this, and her resolve wavered.

"Is it the eye? I can put the patch back on."

"No." She drew back a little to see his face. Truly, she was no longer shocked by the scars, horrible as they were.

He placed his large hand on the back of her head and gently drew her down. "Then stay a little longer. I haven't had a chance to properly woo you."

She drew slightly away, eyeing him uncertainly. "Woo me?"

A corner of his mouth curled in amusement. "Court. Dance attendance on. Woo. I've been remiss."

"And what would you do if you were to woo me?" she asked, only half in jest. She'd never been wooed, not properly. Surely, he wasn't referring to marriage, was he?

He cocked one arm beneath his head, his mouth still curled. "I don't know. I'm a bit rusty at paying court to a beautiful woman. Perhaps I should compose an ode to your dimples."

Startled laughter puffed from her lips. "You can't be serious."

He shrugged and reached up with his free hand to play

with a lock of hair near her face. "If you can't abide poetry, I'm afraid I'm left with carriage rides and bouquets of flowers."

"You'd bring me flowers?" He was joking, she knew, but a small, silly part of her heart wanted to believe him. Lister had bought her expensive jewels and an entire wardrobe, but he'd never thought to give her flowers.

His beautiful brown eye met her own. "I'm not a sophisticated man, and I live in the country, so you'd have to make do with country flowers. Violets and poppies in the early spring. Michaelmas daisies in the fall. Dog roses and thistles in the summer. And in late spring I'd bring you the harebells that grow in the hills hereabouts. Blue, blue harebells the exact same blue as your eyes."

And that was the moment she felt it: a loosening, a breaking free. Her heart slipped its traces and went racing away, beyond her grasp, beyond her control. Entirely free and racing toward this complex, vexing, and utterly fascinating man.

Dear God, no.

BY THE TIME Alistair rose that morning, it was later than usual, a result of a night spent making love to Helen—which, all things considered, was a wonderfully satisfactory turn of events. If he had the choice of starting his day early or laying abed with his housekeeper, he very much feared he'd choose the latter and happily damn the sunrise.

Right now, though, it was past his usual hour to rise. As it was, by the time he'd shaved and dressed and run down the stairs, he discovered that Mrs. Halifax was engrossed in airing one of the unused bedrooms. One hoped that one rated higher than mildewed linen in one's lover's estimation, but apparently this was not always so. Helen rather distractedly refused an offer of a ramble and then soothed his ruffled male feathers by blushing violently before returning her attention to ordering the servants about.

Alistair continued to the kitchens. He might've not pulled her away from her work, but a woman wasn't entirely indifferent if she went red at a mere glance. He snatched a warm bun from a tray Mrs. McCleod had just taken out of the oven and strode out the back door, tossing the hot bread from hand to hand. The day was brilliantly sunny, perfect for a ramble. Whistling, Alistair went to the stables to get his old leather specimen satchel.

He greeted Griffin and the pony and then went to pick up his satchel, which was lying in a corner. The strong, acrid odor of urine assaulted his nostrils when he raised the satchel. Only then did he see the dark wet spot on the corner.

He stared for a second at the ruined satchel, and then he heard a whimper and swung around. The puppy sat behind him, tongue lolling, entire rear end wagging.

"Dammit." Of all the places in the stable, the yard, the whole, wide world, why, *why*, did the animal pick his satchel to piss on?

"Puddles!" He heard Abigail's high voice call to the puppy from outside.

Alistair followed the puppy from the stables, holding the stinking satchel away from his body.

Abigail was outside, picking up the puppy. She turned a startled face toward him as he came out of the stables.

He held up the satchel. "Did you know he did this?"

The look of confusion told him her answer even before

she replied. "What did . . . oh." She wrinkled her nose as she caught a whiff of the satchel.

He sighed. "This is ruined, Abigail."

A mutinous expression creased her little face. "He's only a puppy."

Alistair tried to tamp down his exasperation. "That's why you are supposed to be watching him."

"But, I was—"

"Obviously not or my satchel wouldn't be full of piss right now." He placed his hands on his hips, watching her, not entirely sure what to do. "Get a scrub brush and some soap, and I want you to clean this for me."

"But it's smelly!"

"Because you weren't doing your duty!" Anger finally overcame his good sense. "If you can't mind him, I'll find someone else who can. Or I'll simply return him to the farmer I bought him from."

Abigail jumped to her feet, the puppy held protectively in her arms, her face red. "You can't!"

"I can."

"He's not yours!"

"Yes," Alistair said through gritted teeth, "he damn well is."

For a moment, Abigail only sputtered. Then she shouted, "I hate you!" and ran from the courtyard.

He stared for a moment at the stained satchel. He kicked it viciously and then tilted back his head, his eye closed. What sort of idiot lost his temper with a child? He hadn't meant to yell at her, but dammit, he'd had that satchel for years. It'd survived all his tramping through the Colonies, even his capture by the Indians after Spinner's

Falls and the voyage home. She should've been watching the puppy.

Still. It was just a satchel. He shouldn't have bellowed at Abigail and made threats to the puppy that he'd never had any intention of fulfilling. Alistair sighed. He'd have to remember to somehow apologize to Abigail later while still making clear that she had to watch the damned puppy more carefully. Just the thought started a throbbing in his temple. Instead of taking his morning ramble, he went to his tower to work, wondering as he mounted the stairs why females, whether young or old, were so hard to fathom.

HE'D YELLED at her.

Abigail ran, trying to hold back tears, with Puddles in her arms. She thought Sir Alistair liked her. She'd begun to think that she liked him back. But now he was angry with her. His face had been stern, his forehead wrinkled in an ugly frown as he'd yelled at her. And the very worst thing was she was to blame. He was right. She *hadn't* been watching Puddles closely enough. She'd let him wander into the stables alone while she looked at a beetle she'd found on the ground. But knowing that she'd been wrong had only made everything so much harder. She loathed being wrong. She loathed admitting her fault and apologizing. It made her shrink inside, like a tiny worm. And because she hated that feeling, because she knew he was right and she was wrong, she'd screamed at him and run away.

She ran down the hill at the back of the castle, toward the river and the small bunch of trees where they'd buried Lady Grey, and it wasn't until she neared the river that she realized her mistake. Jamie was already there, squatting on the bank and tossing sticks into the swirling water. She stopped, panting and sweaty, and thought about turning around and sneaking back to the castle, but Jamie'd already seen her.

"Oy!" he called. "It's my turn with Puddles now."

"No, it's not," Abigail said, though she'd had the puppy all that morning.

"Is, too!" Jamie got up and came toward her, but then halted as he looked at her face. "Are you crying?"

"No!"

"'Cause it looks like you're crying," Jamie pointed out. "Did you fall down? Or—"

"I'm not crying!" Abigail said, and ran into the woods.

It was dark here, and she was momentarily blinded. She felt a branch hit her in the shoulder, and she tripped over a root, stumbling, but she kept going. She didn't want to talk to Jamie with his stupid questions. Didn't want to talk to *anyone*. If only everyone would just leave her—

She ran into something solid, and the breath was jolted from her body. She would've fallen if hard hands hadn't grabbed her. She looked up into a nightmare.

Mr. Wiggins leaned down so close that all she could smell was the stink of his smelly breath. "Boo!"

She jerked, humiliated that she'd let him frighten her, but she *was* frightened. Then she looked beyond him, and her eyes widened in shock. The Duke of Lister stood not three paces away, watching them without any expression on his face at all.

*   *   *

ALISTAIR CAREFULLY FOLDED the letter to Vale. The way the mail carriages ran around here, he was likely to arrive in London before the letter, but it'd seemed a good idea to try and alert Vale, anyway. He'd decided. He would leave Castle Greaves, make the journey to London, and speak to Etienne when the other man's ship docked. Alistair might be gone for a fortnight or more, but Helen could take care of the castle in his absence. He hated travel, hated encountering staring idiots, but he needed to know the truth about Spinner's Falls enough to endure the discomfort.

Alistair was dripping sealing wax on the letter when he heard footsteps on the tower stairs. At first he thought it was the call for luncheon, but the footsteps were louder and quicker. Whoever was on the stairs was running.

As a result, he was already rising with a feeling of vague alarm when Helen burst through the doorway. Her hair was coming down from her pins, her blue eyes were wide and round, and her cheeks had gone quite white. She tried to say something but only bent, gasping, her hand at her waist.

"What is it?" he asked sharply.

"The children."

"Are they hurt?" He started past her, visions of drowned, scalded, or broken little bodies filling his maddened brain, but she caught his arm with a surprisingly strong grip.

"They're gone."

He stopped and looked at her blankly. "Gone?"

"I can't find them," she said. "I've looked everywhere— the stables, the kitchen, the library, the dining room, and the sitting room. I've had the servants searching the entire castle this last hour, and I just can't find them."

He remembered the words he'd yelled at Abigail, and guilt swept through them. "Abigail and I had an argument this morning. She's probably hiding with her brother and the puppy. If we—"

"No!" She shook his arm. "No. The puppy wandered into the kitchen alone two hours ago. I thought at first that the children had neglected him, and I was annoyed with them. I went looking to scold them, but I couldn't find them. Oh, Alistair." Her voice broke. "I was going to scold Abigail—she's the eldest. I was thinking of the words, angry words, I was going to say to her, and now I can't find her!"

Her anguish made him want to pound down walls. If Abigail was merely hiding, he'd have to punish her for the grief she'd caused her mother, whether or not it destroyed any relationship he might have had with the child. Right now, though, he had to do something, anything, to end Helen's pain. "Where did you last see Abigail and Jamie? How long ago?"

He'd turned to the door, intending to go down and handle the search himself, when one of the maids rounded into sight on the stairs, panting heavily.

"Oh, sir!" she panted. "Oh, Mrs. Halifax. The children . . ."

"Have you found them?" Helen demanded. "Where are they, Meg? Have you found my babies?"

"No, ma'am. Oh, I'm that sorry, ma'am, but we haven't found them."

"Then what is it?" Alistair asked quietly.

"Tom the footman said he remembered seeing Mr. Wiggins in the village last night."

Alistair scowled. "I thought he'd left the area."

"That's what everyone thought, sir," Meg said. "That's why Tom was so surprised to see Mr. Wiggins, although he was daft enough not to say so until now."

"We'll go to Glenlargo," Alistair said. "Wiggins is probably somewhere about."

He didn't say that if Wiggins had taken off in another direction, their chances of finding him soon were slim. The knowledge that the manservant might have the children sent ice sliding down his spine. What if Wiggins was bent on some kind of revenge?

Alistair strode to a chest of drawers and opened the bottom one. "Tell Tom and the other footman that they'll be going with me." He found what he was looking for—a pair of pistols—and turned to the door.

Meg eyed the pistols. "He wasn't alone, Tom said."

Alistair stopped. "What?"

"Tom said that he saw Mr. Wiggins talking to another man. The man was very tall and finely dressed, and he carried an ivory cane with a gold—"

Helen gasped and Alistair saw that her face had gone slightly greenish.

"—knob. He wasn't wearing a wig, Tom said. The man was balding," Meg finished in a rush, staring at Helen. "Ma'am?"

Helen swayed, and Alistair put his arm about her shoulders to keep her from falling. "Go on ahead, Meg, and tell the footmen to ready themselves."

"Aye, sir." Meg curtsied and left.

Alistair closed the door firmly behind the maid and turned to Helen. "Who is he?"

"I . . . I . . ."

"Helen." He took her gently by the shoulders. "I saw your face. You know the man Tom saw last night. Right now we have no way of knowing in which direction Wiggins and his accomplice might've taken the children. If you have any idea where they could've gone, you need to tell me."

"London."

He blinked. He hadn't expected an answer quite that definite. "Are you sure?"

"Yes." She nodded. Her face had regained some of its color, but now it held an expression of resigned fatality.

A wisp of unease uncurled in his belly. "How do you know? Helen, who was the other man?"

"Their father." She looked up at him, her eyes grief-stricken. "The Duke of Lister."

Chapter Thirteen

⁓

Truth Teller hid the horse he'd bought outside the
castle walls. He guarded the monster all that day.
In the evening, the sorcerer came as usual, and as
usual, Truth Teller answered his question and left.
But instead of retreating inside the castle, the soldier
hid himself behind the cage of swallows. He watched
and waited patiently until the moon had risen, and
then he ran swiftly to the sorcerer. The sorcerer
turned, startled, and Truth Teller blew the powder
into his face. Instantly the sorcerer transformed into
a little brown bat and flew away, leaving his robes
and ring on the ground behind him. Truth Teller
picked up the ring and offered it to the princess
through the bars of her cage.

She looked at the ring and then at Truth Teller in
astonishment. "Will you not demand a boon from me in
exchange for the ring? My father's wealth or my hand
in marriage? Many men would do so in your place."
Truth Teller shook his head. "I only wish
you safe, my lady. . . ."

—from TRUTH TELLER

Alistair stared at Helen and felt as if the earth shifted and moved beneath him. "The children's father is a *duke*?"

"Yes."

"Explain."

She looked at him with tragic harebell-blue eyes and said, "I was the Duke of Lister's mistress."

He cocked his head to see her better from his good eye. "Was there ever a Mr. Halifax?"

"No."

"You were never married."

It was a statement, but she answered it, anyway. "No."

"Jesus." A goddamned *duke*. His chest was tight, as if held within the grip of a giant, terrible vise. He glanced down at his hands and was almost surprised to see he still held the pistols. He walked to the desk and put them back in the drawer he'd taken them from.

"What are you doing?" she asked from behind him.

He closed the drawer and sat back down behind the desk. He aligned the papers before him with care. Soon he'd have to get back to work. "I should think that was obvious. I'm putting away the pistols, calling off the chase."

"No!" She flew across the room and slammed her hands to the desk. "You can't stop now. He'll have gone to London. If we follow, we can—"

"We can what, ma'am?" Anger was replacing the band about his chest, thank God. "Perhaps you'd like me to call out the Duke of Lister on your account?"

Her head reared back at his sarcasm. "No, I—"

He talked over her, the steam building. "Or simply knock on his door and demand the children back? I'm sure he'll bow, apologize, and meekly hand them over. He can't have wanted them much if he traveled all the way to *Scotland* to take them back."

"You don't understand. I—"

He stood to place his own balled fists on the desk and lean toward her. "What don't I understand? That you whored yourself out? That, judging by the ages of your children, you sold your services for years? That you gave birth to those two sweet babes and made them bastards the same moment they drew their first breath? That Lister is their sire and therefore has every right under the laws of God and man to take them and hold them for as long as he bloody well pleases? Tell me, madam, what exactly do I not understand?"

"You're being hypocritical!"

He stared at her. "What?"

"You've lain with me—"

"Don't!" He leaned close to her, enraged almost beyond bearing. "Don't compare what was between us to your life with Lister. I never paid you for your body. I didn't sire bastards on you."

She looked away.

He straightened, trying to control himself. "Dammit, Helen. What were you thinking to have not one, but two children with him? You've tainted their lives. It's not so bad for Jamie, but Abigail . . . any man interested in her will know she is a bastard. It affects who and how she can marry. Was Lister's money worth blighting your children's future?"

"Don't you think I know what I've done?" she whispered. "Why do you think I left him?"

"I don't know." He shook his head and stared at the ceiling. "Does it matter?"

"Yes." She took a deep breath. "He doesn't love them. He's *never* loved them."

He stared at her a moment, his mouth twisted, and then thrust himself away from the table with a barked laugh. "And you think that matters how? Will you go to a magistrate and plead that your love is truer than his? May I remind you, madam, that you *whored* yourself to him. Who do you think any right-minded person would side with—a duke of the realm or a common whore?"

"I'm not a whore," she whispered in a trembling voice. "I never was a common whore. Lister kept me, yes, but it wasn't what you think."

A part of him ached at the pain he was inflicting on her, but he couldn't seem to stop. And besides, another part of him wanted to inflict the pain. *How could she have done this to her children?*

He leaned a hip against a table and crossed his arms, cocking his head again. "Then explain to me how you were his mistress but not a whore."

She clasped her hands like a little girl giving a recitation. "I was young—very young—when I met Lister."

"What age?" he snapped.

"Seventeen."

That gave him pause. Seventeen was still a child. His mouth tightened a bit before he jerked his chin at her. "Go on."

"My father is a physician, a rather respected one, actually. We lived in Greenwich, in a house with a garden. When I was young, I would sometimes go with him on his visits."

He eyed her. What she described was a lower class than he had imagined her to be. Her father worked as a physician, true, but he still earned his living. She wasn't even gentry. She was leagues beneath a duke in social standing. "You lived with just your father?"

"No." Her eyes dropped. "I have three sisters and a brother. And my . . . my mother. I was the second eldest girl."

He jerked a nod for her to continue.

She was squeezing her hands together so tightly, he could see her nails digging into her skin. "One of my father's patients was the dowager Duchess of Lister. She lived with the duke at that time. She was an elderly lady with many ailments, and Papa saw her every week, sometimes several times a week. I often accompanied him to the residence, and one day I met Lister."

She closed her eyes and bit her lip. The room was quiet; this time Alistair made no move to interrupt.

Finally, she opened her eyes and smiled crookedly, sweetly. "The Duke of Lister is a tall man—Tom was right. Tall and imposing. He looks like a duke. I was waiting in a small sitting room for Papa to finish the visit, and he entered the room. I think he was looking for something—a paper, perhaps, though I can't remember now. He didn't notice me at first, and I was frozen in awe. The dowager duchess was an intimidating old lady, but this was her son, the *duke*. He looked over at me finally, and I rose and curtsied. I was so nervous I thought I'd trip over my own feet. But I didn't."

She frowned down at her hands. "Perhaps it would've been better if I had tripped."

He asked quietly, "What happened?"

"He was kind," she said simply. "He came and talked to me a little, even smiled. I thought at the time that he was being gracious to a nervous young girl, but of course it was more than that even then. He admitted quite freely later that he wanted me as his mistress from the first."

"And you went skipping into his arms?" he asked cynically.

She cocked her head. "It was a bit more complicated than that. Our first conversation was very brief. Papa came down from the dowager duchess's rooms, and we left for home. I chattered all the way about His Grace, but I think I would've forgotten him eventually had I not seen him again on our next visit. I thought it an odd coincidence that I would meet him again so soon when I'd been accompanying Papa to the duke's mansion for almost a year without meeting him. Lister had engineered it, of course. He made sure to enter the sitting room where I waited only after my father had gone to see Her Grace. Lister sat and talked to me, ordered tea and cakes. He flirted, although I was too unsophisticated to realize it."

She walked to one of his display cases and peered inside, her back to him. He wondered if she was hiding her face from him. "There were several such tête-à-têtes, and in between he sent me secret letters and small gifts—a jeweled locket, some embroidered gloves. I knew better. I knew I was not supposed to accept such gifts, wasn't supposed to let myself be closeted alone with a man, but I . . . I couldn't seem to help myself. I fell in love with him."

She hesitated, but he simply watched that curving back. Even at this moment, he could feel desire for her—perhaps more than desire.

"Then one afternoon we did more than talk," she said to the glass case. He could see her reflection, ghostly in the glass, and she looked remote and cool, though he was beginning to realize that the appearance she projected might not be real. "We made love, and afterward I knew that I couldn't go back home with Papa. My world—my life—had changed completely. I knew vaguely that Lister was married, that he had children not much younger than I, but in a way that only fed my romantic fantasy. He didn't mention her often, but when he did, Lister described his wife as cold. He said she had not let him into her bed for years. We could never be together as husband and wife, yet I could be with him as his mistress. I loved him. I wanted to be with him always."

"He seduced you." Alistair knew his voice was cold with suppressed rage. How could she? How could Lister? To seduce a young, sheltered girl was caddish behavior beyond the pale of even the most dissolute of rakes.

"Yes." She turned and faced him, her shoulders back and her head high. "I suppose he did, although I was more than willing. I loved him with all the fervor of a young, romantic girl. I never truly knew him. I fell in love with what I thought he was."

That he didn't want to hear. He pushed away from the desk. "Whatever your motives when you were seventeen, it doesn't change anything now. Lister is the father of your children. He has them. I don't see anything you or I can do."

"I can try and get them back," she said. "He doesn't love them; he's never spent more than fifteen minutes at a time with them."

He narrowed his eye. "Then why take them?"

"Because he considers them his," she said, not bothering to hide the bitter tone in her voice. "He doesn't care for them as persons, only as things he thinks he owns. And because he wants to hurt me."

Alistair frowned. "Will he hurt them?"

She looked at him frankly. "I don't know. They are no more than a dog or a horse to him. Do you know of men who whip their horses?"

"Dammit." He closed his eye a second, but he really had no choice. He opened the bureau drawer again and took out the pistols. "Pack one bag. Be ready in ten minutes. We're going to London."

HE WASN'T TALKING to her. Helen swayed as the carriage Alistair had rented in Glenlargo jounced over a rut in the road. He'd agreed to come with her, agreed to help her find and rescue the children, but it was obvious that he wanted no more to do with her beyond that. She sighed. Really, what had she expected?

Helen gazed out the tiny, rather grimy carriage window and wondered where Abigail and Jamie were now. They must be frightened. Even if Lister was their father, they didn't know him very well, and he was a cold man besides. Jamie would be either very still with fear or nearly ricocheting off the carriage walls with nervous excitement. She very much hoped it wasn't the latter case, because she doubted Lister would take well to Jamie in high form. Abigail, in contrast, would probably be watching and worrying. Hopefully, she wasn't saying much, because Abigail's tongue could be quite tart at times.

But wait. Lister was a duke. Naturally he wouldn't be taking care of the children himself. Perhaps he'd thought ahead and brought along a nanny to take care of the children after he snatched them. Perhaps she was an older, motherly woman, one who would know how to handle Jamie's high spirits and Abigail's sullen moods. Helen closed her eyes. She knew this was all wishful thinking, but please, God, let there be a nice, motherly nanny to keep the children away from their terrible father and his temper. If—

"What about your family?"

She opened her eyes at Alistair's rasp. "What?"

He was frowning at her from across the carriage. "I'm trying to think of possible allies we can recruit to help fight Lister. What about your family?"

"I don't think so." He simply sat staring at her, so she reluctantly explained, "I haven't spoken to them in years."

"If you haven't spoken to them in years, how can you know they won't help?"

"They made it quite plain when I went to the duke that I was no longer a part of the Carter family."

He raised his eyebrows. "Carter?"

She felt her face heat a little. "That's my real name—Helen Abigail Carter—but I couldn't use Carter when I became Lister's mistress. I took the name Fitzwilliam."

He continued to stare at her.

Finally she asked, "What is it?"

He shook his head. "I was just thinking that even your name—Mrs. Halifax—was a lie."

"I'm sorry. I was trying to hide from Lister, you see, and—"

"I know." He waved away her apology. "I even understand. But that doesn't stop me from wondering if anything I know about you is true."

She blinked, feeling oddly hurt. "But I—"

"What about your mother?"

She sighed. Obviously he didn't want to talk about what was between the two of them. "The last time I spoke to my mother, she said she was ashamed of me and that I'd tainted the family. I can't blame her. I have three sisters, all of whom were unmarried when I went to the duke."

"And your father?"

She looked down at her hands in her lap.

There was silence a moment before he spoke again, and now his voice had gentled. "You went with him on his visits to patients. Surely you were close?"

She smiled a little then. "He never asked the others to go with him, only me. Margaret was the eldest, but she said visiting patients was boring and sometimes disgusting, and I think my other sisters felt much the same. Timothy was the only boy, but he was also the youngest and still in the nursery."

"Was that the sole reason he took you?" he asked softly. "Because you were the only child interested?"

"No, that wasn't the sole reason."

They were passing through a small village now, the stone cottages worn and ancient-looking. It may have stood thus for millennia—unchanging, uncaring of the outer world.

Helen watched the village go by and said, "He loved me. He loved all of us, but I was special somehow. He'd take me on his rounds and tell me about each patient—their symptoms, his diagnosis, the treatment and if it was progressing well or not. And sometimes if we were coming home late in the day, he would tell me stories. I never heard him tell them to the others, but when the sun was beginning to glow with sunset, he'd tell me stories of gods and goddesses and fairies."

The carriage came to the last cottage in the village, and she could see a woman cutting flowers in her garden.

She said softly, "His favorite was Helen of Troy, though I didn't like it much because the ending was so sad. He'd tease me about my name, Helen, and say that someday I'd be as beautiful as Helen of Troy but that I should watch myself because beauty wasn't always a gift. Sometimes it brought grief. I never thought about it before, but he was right."

"Why don't you ask for his help?" Alistair asked.

She looked at him, remembering her father in his gray bobbed wig, his blue eyes laughing as he teased her about Helen of Troy, and then she remembered the last time she saw him. "Because when I last spoke to my mother, when she called me a common trollop and said I was no longer a part of the family, my father was in the room as well. And he didn't say anything at all. He just turned his face away from me."

IT WAS HER fault, Abigail thought as she watched Mr. Wiggins snoring in a corner of the duke's carriage. She should've told Mama that Mr. Wiggins knew that they were the duke's children, that Jamie had shouted their secret at the nasty man one day. You couldn't blame Jamie. He was too little to realize why they shouldn't tell. He lay curled against her side now, his hair sweaty and stuck to his forehead from crying. The duke said he couldn't stand Jamie's bawling anymore and had mounted a horse at the last inn to ride beside the carriage.

Abigail stroked Jamie's hair, and he made a funny

little noise and burrowed closer to her in his sleep. You couldn't blame him for crying, either. He was only *five*, and he missed Mama terribly. He didn't say it, but Abigail knew he wondered if they'd ever see their mama again. Mr. Wiggins had shouted at Jamie to shut up after the duke had left. She had worried that he might leap across the carriage and hit her brother, but fortunately Jamie had been very tired by then and had suddenly fallen asleep.

She looked out the window now. Outside, green hills rolled by with white sheep dotted here and there as if dropped by a giant hand. Maybe they wouldn't see Mama again. The duke hadn't said much to them, besides telling Jamie to stop crying. But she'd heard him tell Mr. Wiggins and the coachman that they were on their way back to London. Would he take them to live with him in his house there?

Abigail wrinkled her nose. No, they were bastards. Bastards were to be hidden away, not taken to live with their fathers. So he'd hide them away somewhere. It would make it very difficult for Mama to find them. But perhaps Sir Alistair would help. Even though she'd not minded Puddles and he'd ruined Sir Alistair's bag, he'd still help Mama find them, wouldn't he? Sir Alistair was tall and strong, and she thought he would be very good at finding things, even hidden children.

She was very sorry now that she hadn't minded Puddles better. Her lips turned down, her face screwed up, and a sob escaped before she could stop it. *Stupid! Stupid!* She scrubbed angrily at her face. Crying wouldn't help anything. It'd just make Mr. Wiggins happy if he caught her at it. That thought should've made her control the tears, but they wouldn't stop. They ran down her face whether she wanted them to or not, and she could only muffle the sound in her skirts, hoping Mr. Wiggins wouldn't wake. And some part of her knew why she was crying, even as she wiped at her face.

It was her fault, all of it. When Mama had taken them from London on that awful journey north and she'd first seen Sir Alistair's castle, she'd wished in a secret part of her heart that the duke would come and take them back with him.

And now her wish had come true.

It wasn't until they stopped for the night at a small village inn that the problem of traveling together struck Alistair. A man and woman traveling alone together could only be one of three things: a man and his wife, a man and a blood relative, or a man and his mistress. If anything, their relationship was closest to the last. The thought made Alistair scowl. He didn't like to think himself anything like Lister, yet in a way, had he not used Helen similarly? He'd never even thought about marriage. Perhaps he was as much a cad as the duke.

He watched Helen under his brows. She sat staring worriedly out the carriage window as the hostlers ran to take the horses. Her full color had still not returned from its retreat this morning, and that made up his mind.

"We'll share a room," he said.

She glanced at him distractedly. "What?"

"It's not safe for you to be in a room by yourself."

She gave him an odd look. "It's a small country inn. It seems perfectly respectable."

He could feel his face heat a bit, and his words were rather gruff as a result. "Nonetheless, we'll present ourselves as Mr. and Mrs. Munroe and stay in the same room."

And he ended the discussion by descending from the carriage before she could protest farther. The inn did look respectable. A row of old men sat outside the main door, which was blackened with age. There were a fair amount of hostlers and stable boys milling about and gossiping, and in a corner of the yard, a little boy with tousled brown hair played with a kitten. Alistair felt a pain in his chest at the sight. He wasn't very similar to Jamie, but the boy was of an age.

God, let the children be safe!

He turned back to the carriage to help Helen down, moving his body between her and the sight of the little boy. "Come inside and I'll see if there's a private room to be had."

"Thank you," she said breathlessly.

He offered her his arm in a husbandly way, and the hesitation before she laid her fingertips on his sleeve was so small that in all probability only he saw it. But he did see and note it. He covered her gloved hand with his and led her into the little inn.

As it turned out, there was indeed a small—very small—private room at the back of the inn. They settled at the rustic table next to a tiny hearth, and very soon thereafter a hot meal of mutton and cabbage arrived.

"Are you sure Lister's headed to London?" Alistair asked as he cut into his meat. The thought had begun to bother him the last half hour or so; they might be on a wild-goose chase, haring off to London when Lister might have an entirely different destination in mind.

"He has a country estate—several, in fact," Helen

murmured. She was pushing at the food on her plate, but hadn't taken a bite. "But he spends nearly all his time in London. He hates the country, he says. I suppose he might decide to hide the children elsewhere, but if he came in person to get them, I think he'd want to return to London first."

Alistair nodded. "Your reasoning is good. Do you know where he might take them in London?"

She shrugged, looking weary and depressed. "It could be anywhere. He has a main house, of course—a huge town house in Grosvenor Square—but there are several other properties that he owns."

An unwelcome thought intruded. He carefully broke apart a crusty roll and, with his eye on his task, asked, "Where did he keep you?"

She was silent a moment. He buttered the piece of roll without looking up.

Finally, she said, "He gave me a town house to live in. It was on a small square, quite nice, actually. I had a staff to look after the house and serve me."

"The life of a duke's mistress sounds very elegant. I'm not sure I understand why you bothered to leave him." He raised his eyes as he bit into the buttered bread.

Her face was flushed, but her blue eyes sparked with anger. "Don't you? I don't think you understand much about me, really, but I'll endeavor to explain. I'd been his plaything for fourteen years. I'd borne him two children. And he didn't love me. He never loved me, I think. All the jewels in the world, all the servants and the town house and the beautiful dresses were not enough to make up for the fact that I'd let myself be used by a man who didn't really care for me or my children. In the end, I decided that I was worth more."

She shoved back from the table and stalked from the room, fortunately refraining from slamming the door behind her.

Alistair thought about following her immediately, but some innate male instinct told him it was safer to wait just a bit. He finished his meal in higher spirits than he'd begun it. The knowledge that she no longer loved Lister—if she ever had—was a salve to his soul. He took the plate that Helen had abandoned and went up to the room he'd procured for the night for the both of them.

He tapped softly at the door, half expecting her not to answer—she was very mad at him, after all—but the door cracked almost at once. He pushed it open, entered the little room, and shut and locked it behind him. She had moved across the room after letting him in and now stood at a tiny gabled window, her back to him, in her shift with a shawl thrown over her shoulders.

"You didn't eat any of your dinner," he said.

One elegant shoulder rose in a shrug.

"It's a long journey to London," he said gently, "and you'll need to keep your strength up. Come eat."

"Maybe we'll catch up to Lister before London."

He looked at that slim, brave back, and the tiredness that he'd been holding in check all day nearly overwhelmed him. "He's got a head start. It's not likely."

She sighed then and turned, and for a moment he thought he saw tears sparkling in her eyes. But then she ducked her head and came toward him, and he could no longer see her eyes. She took the plate of food from him but then didn't seem to know what to do with it.

"Sit here," he said, indicating a small chair before the fire.

She sat. "I'm not hungry." She sounded like a small child.

He squatted before her and began cutting her meat. "The mutton is quite good. Have a bite." He proffered a piece on the tines of the fork.

She met his eyes as she accepted the bit of food from him. Her eyes were wet, harebells that'd fallen in a stream.

"We'll get them back," he said softly. He stabbed another piece of meat for her. "I'll find Lister and the children, and we'll get them back, safe and sound. I promise."

She nodded, and he carefully, tenderly, fed her almost all of the plate of food before she protested that she could eat no more. Then she climbed into the single bed, and he stripped to his breeches and snuffed the candles. When he got into bed, she lay facing away from him, still and lonely. He stared at the dark ceiling and listened to her breathing, aware that he was hard and pounding with want. They lay thus for a half hour or more until her breathing roughened, and he realized that she was weeping once more. Then he turned to her without a word and pulled her stiff body into his arms. She shuddered against him, her sobs still muffled, and he simply wrapped his arms around her. After a bit, her body slowly lost its rigidity. She softened and relaxed and cried no more.

But he still lay awake, hard and wanting.

Chapter Fourteen

Princess Sympathy took the ring and put it on her thumb. Instantly, the iron bars of her cage turned to water and splashed to the ground. As her cage disappeared, so did the cage that held the swallows. They burst into the air, circling in joy. Truth Teller gave the princess his worn cloak, for she had no other apparel, and led her to where the horse was hidden. But when she saw that there was only one horse, she stopped.

"Where is your mount?" she cried.

"I had only money for one," Truth Teller replied as he lifted her to the saddle.

The princess leaned down and touched his face. "Then you must lie when the sorcerer returns. Tell him a witch has taken me. He will do you a great harm if he thinks you have helped me!"

Truth Teller merely smiled and slapped the horse's flank, sending the beast galloping down the mountain. . . .

—from TRUTH TELLER

A week later, Helen placed her hand in Alistair's and stepped down from a carriage drawn up in front of the Duke of Lister's London residence. She looked up at the tall, classical building and shivered. She'd seen it before, of course, but she'd never tried to enter it.

"He won't see us," she said to Alistair, not for the first time.

"Nothing ventured, nothing gained."

He held out his arm to her, and she placed her fingertips on his sleeve, amazed at how accustomed she'd become to this in the last week.

"It's a waste of time," she muttered in a feeble attempt to quell her clamoring nerves.

"If I thought that Lister would merely hand over the children, then, yes, it would be a waste of time," he murmured as they mounted the front steps. "But that is not my sole aim today."

She stared up at him. His hair was neatly clubbed back, and he wore a black tricorne and reddish-brown coat. Both were newer than any other article of clothing she'd seen him in before, and she had to admit he looked rather nice—an imposing gentleman.

She blinked and focused her thoughts. "Then what is your aim?"

"To learn my adversary," he replied, and let the knocker fall loudly. "Now hush."

From within the house, footsteps approached and then the door was opened. The butler who stood within was obviously a superior servant, but his eyes rounded when he saw Alistair's face. Helen bit back a sharp exclamation. Why did people have to stare so rudely when they saw Alistair? They acted like he was an animal or an inani-

mate object—a monkey in a cage or a bizarre machine—
and gaped as if he had no feelings.

Alistair, meanwhile, simply ignored the man's rude-
ness and asked for the duke. The butler recovered himself, inquired after their names, and showed them into a
small sitting room before leaving to ascertain if the duke
was available.

Helen sat on an ornate gold and black settee and carefully arranged her skirts. She felt wildly out of place here
in the house where Lister lived with his legitimate family.
The room was done in golds and white and black. On one
wall was a portrait of a boy, and she wondered if it was
a relation of the duke, a son perhaps. He had three sons
by his wife, she knew. Quickly she looked away from the
small portrait, feeling shame that she'd once slept with a
married man.

Alistair was prowling the room like a cat on the hunt.
He stopped before a collection of small porcelain figu-
rines on a table and asked without turning around, "This
is his main residence?"

"Yes."

He moved to peer at the boy's portrait. "And he has
children of his own?"

"Two girls and three boys." She stroked one finger gently over the embroidery on her sleeve.

"Then he has an heir."

"Yes."

He was behind her now, out of her sight, but his voice
sounded quite near when he asked, "What age is his
heir?"

She frowned a little, thinking. "Four and twenty, perhaps? I'm not sure."

"But he's a grown man."

"Yes."

He came back into her sight, wandering to the tall windows overlooking the garden in back. "And his wife? Who is she?"

Helen stared at her skirt. "He's married to the daughter of an earl. I've never met her."

"No, of course not," he muttered, turning away from the window. "I suppose you wouldn't have."

He didn't say it with any condemnation in his voice, but she still felt heat climb up her throat and face. She wasn't sure how to reply and thus was rather relieved when the butler returned.

The man's face was impassive now as he told them that the duke was not receiving visitors. Helen half expected Alistair to demand to see the duke and push past the man. Instead he merely nodded and escorted her to the waiting carriage.

She looked at him curiously after the carriage pulled away. "Was that helpful to you?"

He nodded. "I think so, although what he does next will be more so, I hope."

"What he does next?"

"How he reacts to our presence in town." He looked at her, a corner of his mouth twisting up. "It's like poking a hornet's nest to see what will happen."

"I'd think you'd get a hoard of angry hornets swarming you," she said dryly.

"Ah, but will they attack immediately or wait for another poke? Will they come all at once or send out scouts first?"

She stared at him, bemused. "And poking Lister like a nest of hornets tells you all that?"

"Oh, yes." He looked quite satisfied as he held the curtain open with one finger to gaze out the carriage window.

"I see." She believed him, that somehow he was gaining knowledge in a masculine war, but such Machiavellian mechanisms were too complex for her. She merely wanted her children back, pure and simple. She chided herself to be patient. If Alistair's methods could bring back the children, she could wait.

She could.

"I need to make another errand," he said.

She looked up. "Where?"

"I have to see about a ship at the docks."

"What ship? Why?"

He was silent, and for a moment she thought he would not reply. Then he frowned and glanced away from the window to her. "There's a Norwegian ship that's docking the day after tomorrow, or at least it should be. On it is a friend, a fellow naturalist. I've promised to see him."

She watched him. There was something more here that he wasn't saying. "Why can't he come to see you?"

"He's a Frenchman," he said. His voice was impatient, as if he didn't like her questions. "He can't leave the ship."

"You must be very good friends, then."

He shrugged and looked away from her, not answering.

They rode in silence until they made the hotel where Alistair had purchased a room for them both.

"I'll return shortly," he said before she descended the carriage. "We'll talk then."

She watched as the carriage pulled away, her eyes narrowed, and then she glanced at the hotel. It was quite nice, an expensive establishment, but she had no wish to sit in the elegant room and twiddle her thumbs waiting for him.

She turned to one of the hostlers lounging about the front of the hotel. "Can you find me a sedan chair?"

"Aye, mum!" The boy took off like a shot.

She smiled. Alistair needn't be the only one to keep secrets.

The man who'd followed them from Lister's residence to the hotel continued to trail Alistair after the carriage pulled away. Alistair grunted in satisfaction and let the window curtain fall. The man was on foot, a rough fellow dressed in a buff waistcoat, black coat, and wide-brimmed hat, but the carriages rolled so slowly in London that he could easily keep up. Interesting that Lister wanted to know where he went as well as Helen. The duke had obviously pegged him as a threat, sight unseen.

Alistair's lips curled. As well Lister should.

An hour later, the duke's man was still trailing the carriage when it stopped in front of the dock master's office. Tall ships were crowded in the middle of the Thames, where the channel was deep enough for their hulls. Smaller boats and ships were in constant motion, ferrying goods and people to the anchored ships. The smell of the river was sharp here, part fish, part rot. Alistair jumped down and strode inside the dock master's office, pretending not to notice the follower, lounging now against a warehouse wall. There were several men milling about inside the dock master's office, but everyone fell silent when Alistair entered. He sighed. They would begin talking again, avidly, when he left. It became wearying after a while to always be the most bizarre part of other people's days.

He was able to ascertain that Etienne's ship was still scheduled to dock in London. That was good news. If he must leave his home and go scurrying all over England, then at least he could find out about the Spinner's Falls traitor while he did so. More troubling was the information that Etienne's ship was only docking in London to pick up supplies. The captain wasn't even letting his men have shore leave. The time period when Alistair might visit the ship was very slim—only a matter of hours. Dammit. He would have to check back regularly at the docks to make sure he didn't miss Etienne's ship altogether. Once Etienne sailed, he'd be going around the Horn of Africa. It would be months, maybe years, before Alistair would be able to contact him again.

Alistair left the dock master's office and paused to don his tricorne. He glanced quickly from under the brim and saw that his tracker was still waiting. Good. He leapt into his waiting carriage and banged on the roof to signal the coachman. Hopefully the man was well rested, because he'd be jogging another hour or so before they made the hotel.

Alistair smiled and tilted his hat over his eyes, prepared to use that time in a nap.

*   *   *

"I KNOW HE would not see me before," Helen said patiently to the butler, "but I think he will now. Tell His Grace that I am alone."

The man obviously didn't want to bother his master, but with perseverance and much repetition, Helen was finally able to send the man on his errand. He placed her in the same sitting room she'd inhabited with Alistair not an hour before. Alistair would be angry if he knew she was visiting the duke alone, but she couldn't simply wait passively for Lister to respond. She had to at least try to reason with him. And she knew that if she came alone, he'd see her. She could talk to him, beg if she had to. Abigail and Jamie were the only good things she had to show from a life less than wisely lived. She would do whatever it took to get them safely back.

Half an hour later, when her nerves had stretched taut enough to snap, the Duke of Lister entered the room. She'd turned at the sound of the door opening. Now she watched as he strolled toward her and remembered that first sight of him over a decade before. He'd changed very little in that time. He was still tall, his head held arrogantly erect. He'd gained a small amount of weight about his middle, and she knew that beneath his curled wig his hair had receded, but otherwise he was much the same—an older, handsome man who knew very well the power he held. What had changed was her. She was no longer a green girl over-awed by a man's rank and wealth.

She dipped in a tiny curtsy. "Your Grace."

"Helen." He stared at her, his eyes cold, his pale lips thin. "You have made me very, very angry."

"Have I?" she asked, and she saw a quick flash of surprise in his light blue eyes. She'd never challenged anything he'd said in the past. It was what had made her an exemplary mistress: her willingness to accede to his every wish. "I didn't think you would notice my absence at all."

"Then you are mistaken." He gestured her to a seat. "I'm afraid you'll have to work hard to regain my esteem."

She sat and tamped down anger. "I want only my children."

He sank into a chair opposite her, flicking aside the skirts of his velvet coat. "My children as well."

She leaned forward, unable to stop herself from hissing, "You don't even know their names."

"James, and the girl"—he snapped his fingers as he searched for her name—"Abigail. You see, I do know their names. *Not* that it matters when all things are considered. You knew very well what the price of leaving me would be. Pray don't feign shock now."

"I'm their mother." She tried to keep the pleading from her voice, but it was hard. Impossible, really. "They *need* me, Lister. Let me have them back. Please."

He smiled, his lips spreading without any humor—or indeed any emotion—at all. "Very pretty, but your pleas do not sway me. You've crossed me, Helen, and now you must be punished. Come, now. Agree to move back into the town house I gave you and then I may be more amenable to discussing the children."

She stared, truly shocked. It'd not occurred to her that he might try to blackmail her in this way. "But why?"

He raised his eyebrows in what looked like genuine surprise. "Because I want you, of course. You're just as much mine as the children are."

"You don't want me. You haven't seen me—haven't

made love to me—in years. I know you've taken another mistress, probably more than one."

Lister made a moue of distaste at her mention of the bedroom. "Please, Helen, we needn't be so crass. Never think because I don't visit you as often that I've forgotten you. I'm really quite fond of you, my dear; please believe it. And when you've come back, why, I may find it in my heart to reward you with a small trinket." He seemed much struck with the thought. "Yes, I think sapphire earrings or perhaps even a necklace. You know how I like sapphires on you."

He stood and crossed to her, offering his hand to help her rise.

Helen closed her eyes, trying to beat down panic. He sounded so reasonable, so sure that he'd get exactly what he wanted. And why shouldn't he? Lister was a *duke*. He had gotten everything he'd ever wanted in his life. But not her.

Not her.

She opened her eyes and stared at him, this man she'd loved so long ago, this man who was the father of her children. She placed her hand in his and rose to stand before him. "I'm not coming back."

His eyes became hard and opaque, and his fingers tightened into a vise around her hand. "Now, don't be foolish, Helen. You've already put me out. I don't think you'd like to enrage me."

She caught her breath at the implied threat, twisting her hand, trying to free herself. He let her struggle for a moment more and then abruptly let her go. He stood smiling. She stared at him, wondering if she truly knew him at all. Helen turned and walked from his sitting room and his house. She almost ran down the front steps and into the waiting sedan chair. Once enclosed in the small space, she allowed herself to shake. Dear God, could she do it? If returning to Lister was the only way to get Abigail and Jamie back, could she stand firm against him? No. She already knew in her heart. No.

If she had to choose between her pride and her children, she would concede her pride.

"MAMA," ABIGAIL WHISPERED.

She stood in the duke's house, in the old nursery, and watched as far below a lady who looked very much like her mama ran down the steps and entered a sedan chair. The men lifted the chair and trotted down the street and around a corner.

Abigail still stared out the window, though.

Maybe the lady hadn't been Mama. It was very hard to tell from way up here, and there were bars that prevented her from getting very close to the window, but she hoped it was Mama. Oh, how she hoped!

She turned reluctantly from the window. The duke had brought them to his house, because his real family was away in the country. He'd stuck them up here in the hot old nursery and made Mr. Wiggins and a maid watch over them. The maid was better than Mr. Wiggins, because she mostly sat in the corner looking bored. Mr. Wiggins often looked bored when he watched them, too, but he also teased them. He'd already worked Jamie up into a screaming fit today.

Now Mr. Wiggins had left and the maid nodded off in the corner. Jamie had fallen asleep after his fit. Again. He was sleeping an awful lot, and when he was awake, he was sad. Not even the huge set of tin soldiers interested him. At night Abigail had heard him call Mama's name, and she didn't know what to do. Should she try to run away with Jamie? But then where would they go? And if—

The door to the nursery opened, and the duke came in. The maid lurched to her feet in the corner and bobbed a curtsy. The duke ignored her.

He looked at Abigail. "I've come to check on your welfare, my dear."

Abigail nodded. She didn't know what else to do. She'd hardly spoken to the duke since he'd brought them from Scotland. He'd never hit her or Jamie, but something about him made her very nervous.

He frowned a little, not an angry frown, but one that seemed to mean he was irritated. "You know who I am, don't you?"

"The Duke of Lister." Abigail remembered the curtsy she should've dropped when he entered.

"Yes, yes." He waved his hand impatiently. "I meant who I am to you. You know how I am related to you, don't you?"

"You're my father," Abigail whispered.

"Very good." The duke flicked a smile at her. "You're a bright little poppet, aren't you?"

Abigail didn't know what to say to that, so she was silent.

The duke strolled to a shelf where dolls sat in a row. "Yes, I am your father. I've provided for you all your life. Fed you. Clothed you. Gave your mother a house in which you could sleep at night." He picked up a doll and turned it over, stared at it, then replaced it on the shelf. "You liked the house where you lived with your mother, didn't you?"

He turned and looked at her with the same expression on his face he'd had when he examined the doll. "Didn't you?"

"Yes, Your Grace."

That smile flicked across his face again. "Then you will be happy when you, your brother, and your mother return to that house."

He turned to the door. Maybe he was done talking to her now. But then he seemed to see Jamie asleep in a chair.

He stopped and frowned at the maid. "Why is the boy sleeping at this hour?"

"I don't know, Your Grace," the maid said. She hurried over and shook Jamie awake.

Jamie sat up, his hair rumpled, his face flushed and lined from the chair.

"Good," the duke said. "Boys shouldn't sleep during the day. See to it that he's kept awake until his bedtime."

"Yes, Your Grace," the maid muttered.

The duke nodded and walked to the door. "Behave, children. If you're very good, I shall come see you again."

And he left.

Abigail went to Jamie.

He had begun to whimper at being awakened. "I want Mama, Abby."

"I know, dearest," Abigail whispered, using the tone she'd heard their mother use so many times. "I know. But we have to be brave until Mama comes for us."

She held Jamie against her chest and rocked him a little, mostly to comfort him, but also to comfort her, she admitted. Because the duke was wrong. She didn't want to go back to living in the grand London house. She wanted to return to Scotland. To help Mama clean Sir Alistair's dirty castle. To go for walks with him to look for badgers and to catch fish in his clear, blue stream. She wanted them all to return to Castle Greaves and to live together there.

And she was very much afraid that she'd never see Castle Greaves or Sir Alistair again.

Chapter Fifteen

*Truth Teller looked up and saw that clouds were
moving over the moon. He remembered what
Princess Sympathy had said: that the sorcerer would
only be transformed while the light of the moon was
upon him. Even as Truth Teller turned to run down
the mountain, the little brown bat appeared. The
clouds covered the moon, and the bat turned back
into the sorcerer. He fell to the ground nude and then
stood, powerful and angry.*
"What have you done?" he shouted.
*Truth Teller looked at him and told him what
he must: the truth. "I have drugged you, released
the princess, and loosed the swallows. She has fled
here on a fast horse, and you will never catch her.
Because of me, you have lost her forever. . . ."*
—from TRUTH TELLER

By the time Alistair returned to the hotel, it was early evening. His follower had managed to keep up with the car-

riage all the way from the docks, but once they'd made the hotel, another man had taken his place. A shorter fellow in what had once been a yellow coat leaned against the wall opposite Alistair's hotel. Not that Alistair cared at the moment. He wanted only to get to the room he shared with Helen, retire from all the eyes that stared at him constantly, and perhaps see if he could have a meal brought up so they could dine in private.

He simply wanted to rest.

But the moment he entered the hotel room, he could feel the tension surrounding Helen. He paused a moment in the doorway, eyeing her. She paced by the windows, a short track between the bed and the wall, her brows furrowed and one hand rubbing the other at her waist.

He sighed and shut the door behind him. She'd been anxious when he'd left her here earlier, but not this anxious. What was working her up now?

"I thought I'd order a simple supper to eat in the room if that's agreeable to you," he said as he crossed to a dresser. On the top were a basin and a jug of fresh water. He poured some water into the basin.

Behind him there was silence save for her pacing footsteps.

"Is it?" he asked.

"What?" Her voice was distracted.

"Is it agreeable to you to eat here?" He splashed water on his face.

"I . . . I suppose."

He took a towel and dried his face, turning to watch her. She'd halted by the window, staring down at her feet.

He threw aside the towel. "What did you do this afternoon?"

"Oh, nothing much." Her fair skin blushed, the pretty pink moving up her throat and to her cheeks. She looked quite lovely, but she was lying.

He strolled toward her, examining her. "You didn't go out?"

Her eyes dropped.

And he knew, suddenly and without any doubt. "You saw Lister."

She jerked her head up, her gaze meeting his defiantly. "Yes. I had to at least try to make him see reason."

Scalding hot rage bubbled in his veins, but he held it in check—barely.

"And did he?" he asked gently.

"No," she said. "He's determined to keep the children."

He cocked his head, angling his good eye at her. "And he just let you go, tripping down his front steps and away without so much as an attempt to stay you? Perhaps he even waved his handkerchief in farewell as you left?"

Her blush deepened. "He didn't try to keep me—"

"No, of course not. Why would he when he's gone to all the trouble of kidnapping your children to get you back?"

Her head jerked as if he'd slapped her. "How did you know he wants me back?"

He laughed, the sound harsh and quick. "Don't take me for a fool. A man doesn't kidnap his bastard children when he already has three sons and heirs. I know him. I know his game. He's using them as hostages to get you to return, isn't he?"

"He said I'd never see them again unless I returned as his mistress."

Something inside of him erupted. He felt the release, overflowing the edge of reason into insanity.

"Did you agree?" Somehow he'd crossed the room and seized her arms. "Tell me, Helen. Did you agree to return to him? To let him into your bed? To be his whore? Did you?"

She stared up at him with those damned drowning harebell eyes. "He says I'll never see Abigail and Jamie again unless I return to him. They're all I have, Alistair. My children. My babies."

He shook her once. "Did you agree?"

"I can't never see them again."

"Goddamn you, Helen." His chest was tight with horror. *"Did you agree?"*

"No." She closed her eyes. "No. I told him no."

"Thank God." He pulled her into his arms and brought his mouth down on hers, crushing her soft lips. The thought of her with Lister was driving him beyond control. "Did he hurt you?"

"No," she gasped. "He . . . he gripped my hand, but—"

He grabbed both her hands and saw red welts on the right. Abruptly, he stilled, cradling her delicate fingers in his larger hand. "He hurt you."

"It's nothing." She pulled her hand gently away.

"Did he hurt you—*touch* you—anywhere else?"

"No, Alistair, no."

"He wanted to touch you, I know," he said as he rubbed his hands over her shoulders and to her arms. "He wanted to touch and taste and feel you."

"But he didn't." She placed her palms, cool and soft, on either side of his face. "He didn't touch me."

"Thank God." He took her mouth savagely, thrusting

his tongue into her, wanting to blot the image of Lister from both their minds.

Her acceptance calmed him until he could once again pull away.

"I'm sorry." He closed his eye in disgust at himself. "You must think me a ravening beast."

"No," she said quietly. He felt her soft lips brush over the scarred side of his face. "I think you a man. Only that. A man."

And when she brought her lips back to his, he was able to kiss her gently this time. Sweetly. Worshipping her.

His eye was still closed—perhaps he no longer wanted to see the reality of their situation—so he only felt when she ran her hands over his chest, the pressure light through the layers of his clothing. Her hands descended down toward his breeches, and a primal male part of him waited, breathless, to see what she would do. Her fingers moved over the buttons of his fall, loosening, freeing him.

He reached for her then. "Helen."

"No," she said, quite firmly. "No, let me."

And his hands fell away, because although he was a man of honor, he was by no means a saint. He heard the rustle of her skirts as she knelt, felt her fingers on his throbbing cock, and then the brush of her breath.

He made a heroic effort and tried one more time to dissuade her. "You don't have to."

Her whisper blew across the swollen head of his cock as she said, "I know."

Then her hot wet mouth enveloped him, and he could only groan and brace his legs so he wouldn't fall. God! He'd paid a whore for this once, long ago, but it'd been a disappointment. Then, there had been rough sucking and pulling and he'd barely been able to finish. Now . . . Now there was gentle pressure, the velvet touch of her tongue, and most of all, the knowledge that *she* was doing this to him. He couldn't help himself. He opened his eye and looked down and nearly came on the spot. Her golden head was bent over him, his reddened prick sliding in between her pink lips, her fingers delicate and white against his rude flesh.

She looked up at him, his cock still in her stretched mouth, and her harebell-blue eyes were dark now. Mysterious, feminine, and the most erotic thing he'd ever seen in his life.

He tasted of man and salt and life itself.

Helen closed her eyes, savoring the sensation of Alistair's penis in her mouth. She'd done this a few times with Lister, but she'd found the act distasteful then. Something she'd only performed to please him. What she did now pleased her as well. There was power in holding the most elemental part of a man between her lips, feeling him tremble as she stroked him, hearing his breath come quick and hard as she sucked.

And there was something else. She liked the taste of him, liked licking his smooth head. Liked stroking the soft skin of his shaft and feeling the steely hardness beneath. This was erotic. Primal, and just a little bit naughty. Her breasts were swollen beneath her bodice and stays, her nipples sensitive and pointed. She could feel wetness at the juncture of her thighs, and she pressed them together and sucked strongly on him at the same time.

"God!" he rasped above her.

She felt like the most alluring woman in England at

that moment. She reached carefully, tenderly, into his breeches and found his stones, heavy in their sac. They were like eggs in the softest of leather bags, and she rolled them gently in her hand. She sucked again.

He growled.

She looked up. His head was back, his hands clenched by his sides, and she could feel his thighs, hard and tensed by her head. She could continue this, sucking him until he lost control and spewed his seed into her mouth. The idea was wickedly seductive, and she pursed her lips to draw strongly on him.

But she'd misjudged him. He bent suddenly, scooping her up in his arms so fast she squeaked in alarm. He threw her on the bed, and she hadn't finished bouncing when he landed beside her.

"Enough," he snapped.

He tore at her laces, ripping her bodice from her and flinging it halfway across the room.

"Enough playing. Enough cock teasing. Enough drawing this out."

He pulled her skirts from her and flipped her before she had time to react. He pushed and pulled her until she was on her knees, braced on her elbows, and threw up the skirt of her chemise. He entered her from behind without warning, and she gasped.

Hot and hard. Long and full.

She bit her lip, trying not to cry out at the sensation. He was so right, so perfect. He withdrew a bit, adjusting his hold on her bare hips before slamming back into her. Thrusting fast, thrusting deep. Her arms slid forward under his hard lovemaking, until she caught herself and braced again. Then she closed her eyes and simply felt.

His strong slide against her wet, soft flesh. The heat building at her center.

He stopped suddenly, and she did cry out this time—in disappointment. But he reached beneath her, still sheathed to the hilt in her body, and ran his hands over the tops of her breasts. He pulled a bit, and her nipples popped over the top of her stays, hard and abraded. He pinched them roughly, and she bit her lip, pushing back at his hips.

He laughed, a breathless growling sound, and resumed pounding into her, one hand holding her firm to receive him, the other still teasing her nipples. She groaned and looked down, watching his big, tanned hand playing over her white breasts. The sight made her clench internally, and she exploded suddenly, wrenchingly, her arms giving out from beneath her at the force. Light flew from her center, blinding her and making her limbs weak from pleasure. She collapsed flat on the bed, and he followed her down, still thrusting powerfully, his cock a live thing within her, demanding submission, demanding pleasure.

And she gave it. Without volition. Without conscious thought. Her belly rippling with the orgasm that continued unabated. She panted into the sheets, filling her mouth with the corner of a pillow to keep from screaming aloud.

She felt his upper body lift away from her, causing his pelvis to press into her more heavily. She saw out of the corner of her eye one of his arms braced beside her shoulder. He withdrew. Slowly. In this position, beneath him, with her legs only hip-width apart, the pressure was intense. He was crammed so tightly within her. His cock dragged against her as it retreated from her soft flesh. She closed her eyes, lost in the intense feeling. He pushed back in, just as slowly, and she felt his entire hard length reenter her. This was bliss. This was sensation beyond anything she'd ever experienced before. She could lie like this and submit to him forever, reveling in his hard flesh, his male scent all around her.

"Helen," he rasped. "Helen."

And she felt him jerk against her. He thrust one more time, shoving his entire length into her, and she came again, a sweet, warm, washing wave of pleasure after the intensity of before. He withdrew suddenly, and hot semen splashed her thigh. He was immobile above her, his breath coming harshly, his weight still holding her lower body pinned to the bed. She wished he could stay like this, with his hard body pressing her into the bed, but it was inevitable that he roll to the side.

He slid away from her and stood beside the bed, taking off his clothing, moving slowly as if terribly wearied. He climbed in beside her, nude, and drew her close, and that was better. Wordlessly he fitted her body against his larger, harder one, and tucked her head into the crook of his arm.

She watched sleepily as his chest rose and fell, the beat of his heart slow and steady under her cheek. She wondered what they would do if they got the children back. If he loved her and if they could ever have a life together.

And finally she decided it was all too much to think about right now. So she closed her eyes and went to sleep.

WHEN HELEN WOKE again, the room was nearly dark. Alistair was in the process of gently pulling his arm from beneath her head. The movement was what had awakened her. She made no sound but watched as he stood and found his smallclothes and breeches, sliding them up his long legs. And she remembered something that she'd meant to ask him earlier when he'd first returned to the hotel.

"Where did you go?"

His hands, buttoning the fall of his breeches, stilled at her voice and then resumed their work. "I told you. I went to the docks to see about a ship."

She propped her head in her hand, lying on her side. "I've told you my secrets. Isn't it time you told me yours?"

It was a gamble based on their recent lovemaking. He might still retreat into that hard anger he'd borne toward her for the last week. He might simply pretend he didn't know what she spoke about.

He did neither. Instead he bent and picked up his shirt, holding it in his hands and staring down at it as if he'd never seen white linen before. "Nearly seven years ago, I was in the American Colonies. You know that. It's how I came to write my book. It's also how I lost my eye."

"Tell me," she whispered, not daring to move or breathe lest she break his narration.

He nodded. "My purpose in the Colonies was to discover new plants and animals. The best place to look for undiscovered things is where men haven't already explored—the edges of civilization. But because it's the edge of civilization and because we are at war with France, that was also the most dangerous place to be. Naturally, then, I found it expedient to attach myself to various army regiments. I spent three years thus, tramping where they tramped, collecting samples and making notes when they camped."

He was silent a moment, still staring at the shirt in his hands until he shook his head and looked up at her. "Forgive me; I'm delaying the crux of my story." He inhaled deeply. "In the fall of 1758, I was with a small regiment of men, the 28th Regiment of Foot. We were marching through a thick forest, our destination Fort Edward, where the regiment intended to barrack for the winter. The trail was narrow, the trees oppressively close when we came to a falls. . . ."

His voice broke and trailed away, and a look crossed his face that she'd never seen on him before. Despair. She nearly cried out.

But his face smoothed and he cleared his throat. "Spinner's Falls it was called as I found out later. We were attacked from both sides by the French and a band of their Indian allies. Suffice it to say that we lost." A corner of his mouth twitched in something that might've been a smile. "I say 'we' quite deliberately. In the midst of battle, one is never a bystander. Though I was a civilian, I fought just as hard as the soldiers standing next to me. We fought for the same thing, after all: our lives."

"Alistair," she whispered. She'd seen how he'd touched Lady Grey's dead body, seen him patiently teach Abigail to fish. He wasn't a man who would commit or recover from violence easily.

"No." He waved away her sympathy. "I'm prevaricating again. I survived the battle relatively unscathed with several others, and the Indians rounded us up as captives. We marched for many days through the woods and then we made their camp."

He frowned down at the shirt and carefully folded it. The muscles of his bare arms shifted in the fading light.

"The native peoples in that part of the world have a sort of custom when they win a battle. They take captive the enemy who survives and they torture them; the object is part celebration, part demonstration of the enemy's cowardice. At least that's what I believe the object is. Of course, there may not be a reason at all for the torture. Certainly, there's ample evidence in our own history of peoples delighting in inflicting pain purely for the pleasure of it."

His voice was even, almost cool, but his fingers folded and refolded the shirt he held, and Helen knew that tears were coursing down her face. Had he thought like this as they'd tortured him? Tried to take his mind away from the pain and horror by noting and analyzing the people who had captured him? The thought was too awful to bear, but bear it she must. If he could survive what had been done to him, the least she could do was hear what had happened.

"I'll come to the point." He took a deep breath as if to steady himself. "They took us and stripped us naked. They tied our hands behind our backs and then strung a rope from our bound hands to a stake so that we could stand and move a bit but not go far. They played with a man named Coleman first. They beat him and cut off his ears and threw burning embers on him. And when he collapsed to the ground, they scalped him and heaped burning coals on his still-live body."

She made a sound of protest, but he didn't seem to hear.

He gazed blindly down at his hands. "It took Coleman two days to die, and all the while, we watched and knew we would be next. Fear . . ." He cleared his throat. "Fear does ugly things to a man, makes him less human."

"Alistair," she whispered again, no longer wanting to hear this tale.

But he continued. "Another man—an officer—they crucified and set alight. He made high, terrible screams like an animal as he died. I've never heard the like before or since. When they started on me, it was almost a relief, if you can credit it. I knew I would die; my chore was simply to die with what bravery I could. I never cried out when they pressed burning brands to my face, nor when they cut me. But when they took a knife to my eye . . ."

His hand drifted to that side of his face, and his fingers delicately traced the scars. "I think I lost my mind a little. I can't remember exactly. I don't remember anything before I woke again in the Fort Edward infirmary. I was surprised to be alive."

"I'm glad."

He looked at her. "For what?"

She swiped at her cheeks. "That you survived. That God took away your memory."

He smiled then, a horrible twisting of his lips. "But God had nothing to do with it."

"What do you mean?"

"It made no sense." He waved his hand in a broad sweep. "Don't you see? None of it had any order or reason. Some of us survived and some did not. Some were scarred and some were not. And it mattered not whether a man was good or brave or weak or strong. It was pure chance."

"But you survived," she whispered.

"Did I?" His eye glittered. "Did I? I'm alive, but I'm not the man I was before. Did I truly survive?"

"Yes." She stood and came to him, placing her palm on his scarred cheek. "You're alive and I'm glad."

He covered her hand with his own, and for a moment they stood thus. His gaze searched hers, intent and confused.

Then he turned his head away, and her hand dropped. She felt as if she'd missed something in that moment, but she didn't know what. Bereft, she sat back down on the bed.

He resumed dressing. "As soon as I was well enough to travel, I sailed for England. You know the rest, I think."

She nodded.

"Yes, well. I've lived since that time very much as you first saw me when you came to the castle. I've avoided the company of others for obvious reasons." He touched the patch over his eye. "But a month ago, Viscount Vale and his wife, your friend, Lady Vale . . ."

He trailed away, frowning. "I say, how did you become acquainted with Lady Vale? Was that part of your story made up as well?"

"No, that was true enough." Helen grimaced. "I suppose it does look odd, a mistress like me friends with a respectable woman like Lady Vale. I confess that I know her only slightly. We met several times in the park, but when I fled Lister, she helped me. We are friends, truly."

Alistair seemed to accept that explanation. "Anyway, Vale was one of the men taken captive at Spinner's Falls. When Vale came to visit, he had this odd story. Rumors that the 28th Regiment of Foot had in fact been betrayed at Spinner's Falls by a British soldier."

Helen straightened. "What?"

"Yes." He shrugged and finally laid the shirt aside. "It makes sense. We were in the middle of the forest, and yet we were attacked by an overwhelming force of Frenchmen and Indians. Why else would they be there save that they knew we were to pass that way?"

She drew a sharp breath. Somehow the knowledge that such destruction of life had been *planned*—and by a fellow countryman—made it all the more horrible.

She looked at him with wonder. "I would think that you'd be wild with the desire for revenge."

He smiled, fully and sadly. "Even if we catch this man, bring him to trial and hang him, it'll not restore my eye or the lives of the men lost at Spinner's Falls."

"No, it won't," she agreed gently. "But you do want him caught, don't you? Might it not bring you some peace?"

He looked away. "I have as much peace now as I'll ever have, I think. But I suppose it would be appropriate for the traitor to be punished."

"And the Frenchman, the friend you want to meet, is somehow connected to all this?"

He went to the fire and kindled a taper. With it he lit several candles in the room. "Etienne says there are rumors in the French government, but he does not want to commit them to paper—for his safety and for mine. He has accepted a position on an exploratory ship, though. It docks in London the day after tomorrow before leaving to sail around the Horn of Africa."

He threw the remainder of the taper into the fire. "If I can talk to Etienne, then perhaps this mystery will be solved."

"I see." She watched him a moment more, then sighed. "Do you want to go down for supper?"

He blinked and looked at her. "I'd hoped to have something brought up."

She began unlacing her stays, and his gaze immediately dropped to her bosom. "I had some food and wine delivered earlier." She nodded to a covered basket on a chair. "It's over there. If you think it'll do, we can stay here and not bother with anyone else."

He crossed to the basket and raised the cloth that covered it, peering inside. "A feast."

Helen straightened the bodice of her chemise over her breasts, rose from the bed, and crossed to him. "Sit here, before the fire, and I'll serve you."

He frowned quickly. "There's no need."

"You didn't object to my service when I was your housekeeper." She rummaged in the basket and found a small plum. She offered it to him in the palm of her hand. "Why demure now?"

He took the plum, his fingers brushing against her palm and sending shivers down her arm. "Because you're no longer my servant; you're my . . ." He shook his head and bit into the plum.

"What?" She knelt at his feet. "What am I to you?"

He swallowed and said gruffly, "I don't know."

She nodded and turned her face to the basket so he wouldn't see the tears in her eyes. That was the problem, wasn't it? They didn't quite know anymore what they were to each other.

Chapter Sixteen

At Truth Teller's words, the evil sorcerer flew into a terrible rage. He raised his arms and laid a terrible curse on the soldier, turning him into a stone statue. The sorcerer placed Truth Teller in his yew knot garden, among all the other stone warriors. There he stood, day by day, month by month, year by year as birds came to rest on his shoulders and dead leaves settled at his feet. His still face stared, unblinking, at the garden, and what he thought about I do not know. His very thoughts had turned to stone. . . .
—from TRUTH TELLER

Helen wasn't precisely respectable. This thought only occurred to Alistair as they stood on Lord Vale's front step. He really shouldn't have brought her along on an early afternoon call to a viscount and viscountess. But then again, she'd said that she was friends with Lady Vale, so perhaps the point was moot.

Fortunately, the butler chose that moment to open the

door. After collecting their names, he bowed and showed them into a large sitting room. Very soon thereafter, Vale himself burst into the room.

"Munroe!" the viscount cried, bounding up and seizing Alistair's hand. "Good God, man, I thought it'd take explosives to pry you out of that dratted drafty castle of yours."

"It very nearly did," Alistair muttered, squeezing Vale's hand hard to keep from having his own appendage crushed. "Have you met Mrs. Helen Fitzwilliam?"

Vale was a tall man with hands and feet that seemed too large for his body, like an overeager puppy. His face was long, incised with deep vertical lines that in repose made his countenance look perpetually mournful. In contrast, his habitual expression was almost foolish, jolly and open, which lulled many a man into a false sense of superiority.

Right now, though, Vale's expression had gone curiously flat at Alistair's introduction of Helen. Alistair braced himself. He needed Vale's help, but if the other man chose to insult Helen, he'd defend her and damn the consequences. The tensing of his muscles was instinctive.

But a quick smile flashed across Vale's face, and he leaped forward to take Helen's hand and bend over it. "A pleasure, Mrs. Fitzwilliam."

The viscount straightened just as Lady Vale entered the room behind him. Despite the quiet of that lady's step, Vale seemed to sense his wife's presence at once.

"See who has come to visit us, my lady wife," he exclaimed. "Munroe has abandoned his depressing moors and skipped away to bonny London. I think we should invite him to dinner." He swung on Alistair. "You will come to dinner, won't you, Munroe? And you as well, Mrs. Fitzwilliam. I shall expire of disappointment if you don't."

Alistair nodded curtly. "We'd be pleased to dine with you, Vale. But I'd hoped to discuss a matter of business this afternoon. It's pressing."

Vale cocked his head, looking like an intelligent hound. "Is it, indeed?"

"May I show you my garden, Mrs. Fitzwilliam?" Lady Vale murmured.

Alistair nodded his thanks at Lady Vale and watched the ladies leave the room.

When he turned, he found Vale's too-perceptive eyes regarding him.

Vale smiled. "Mrs. Fitzwilliam is a lovely woman."

Alistair bit back a blunt retort. "Actually, it's on her behalf that I'd like to talk to you."

"Indeed?" Vale ambled to a decanter of liquor and held it up. "Brandy? A bit early in the day, I know, but your expression suggests that we might need it."

"Thank you." Alistair accepted a crystal glass and sipped, feeling the liquid burn as it slid down his throat. "Lister has stolen Helen's children."

Vale paused with his glass raised halfway to his lips. "Helen?"

Alistair glared.

Vale shrugged and sipped his own brandy. "These are the Duke of Lister's children as well that we're discussing, I take it?"

"Correct."

Vale raised his eyebrows.

Alistair shook his head impatiently. "The man has no interest in the children—it's Helen he wants. He's trying to force her back by holding the children."

"And I assume you don't wish her to return to Lister's arms."

"No." Alistair gulped the rest of his glass and grimaced. "I do not."

He waited for Vale to make some snide comment, but the other man merely looked thoughtful. "Interesting."

"Is it?" He paced to a small case of books, staring at the titles sightlessly. "Lister won't receive me. Helen he doesn't mind seeing, but I don't want her anywhere near that bastard. I need to find out where he's keeping the children. I need to find out how to pry them away from him, and I need to be able to talk to the man."

"And do what?" Vale asked quietly. "Do you intend to reason sweetly or call him out?"

"I doubt very much that he'll respond to reason." Alistair glared at the bookcase. "If it comes to that, I have no problem calling him out."

"Not very subtle, old man," the viscount murmured. "You usually have more finesse than this."

Alistair shrugged, unable to explain his emotions even to himself.

"I can't help but wonder what this woman means to you. Is she your mistress perchance?"

"I . . . no." He turned and frowned at Vale. "Did not your wife tell you she had sent Mrs. Fitzwilliam to be my housekeeper?"

"It's quite amazing what a wife will keep from her husband," Vale mused. "My innocence has been crushed since our marriage. But, yes, she did indeed finally deign to tell me why she was looking so pleased with herself recently." Vale splashed more brandy into his glass. "The lengths to which you're prepared to go to please a housekeeper make me wonder about the servant situation in Scotland. Good help must be thin on the ground." Vale widened his eyes and took a drink.

"She's more to me than a housekeeper," Alistair growled.

"Wonderful!" Vale slapped him on the back. "And about time, too. I was beginning to worry that all your important bits might've atrophied and fallen off from disuse."

He felt unaccustomed heat climb his throat. "Vale . . ."

"Of course, this means my lady wife will be near impossible to live with," Vale said to the bottom of his glass. "She does get a trifle self-satisfied when she thinks she's pulled something off, and I'm sure you've realized by now that she sent Mrs. Fitzwilliam to you with a purpose."

Alistair merely grunted at that and held out his glass. Women and their mechanisms were no longer a shock to him.

Vale obligingly refilled it. "Tell me about these children."

He closed his eye and inhaled, recalling their small faces. The last time he'd seen Abigail's face, she'd been red with hurt and near tears. Dammit, he wanted a chance to make that better. Pray God he'd have it.

"There are two of them, a boy and a girl, five and nine, respectively. They've never been away from their mother." He opened his eye and looked frankly at the other man. "I need your help, Vale."

*   *   *

"So the Duke of Lister found you," Lady Vale murmured.

"Yes," Helen said. She gazed down into the delicate dish of tea in her hands.

Lady Vale had ordered a tray of tea and cakes brought into her garden. All around them flowers blossomed, and bees buzzed lazily from bloom to bloom. It was a lovely setting. But Helen had trouble keeping the tears from her eyes.

Lady Vale laid a hand on her arm. "I am sorry."

Helen nodded. "I thought I'd fled far enough away that he would not find me or the children."

"As did I." Lady Vale took a very small sip of her tea. "I think, though, that between my husband and Sir Alistair, there is hope that your children will be returned to you."

"God willing," Helen said fervently. She didn't know what she'd do without her babes, couldn't imagine a life lived without ever seeing them again. "Lister has offered to give them back to me if I return to him."

Lady Vale went very still, her back straight, her light brown eyes clear and focused on Helen. She wasn't a beautiful woman—her face was too plain, her color too ordinary—but her countenance was pleasing. Then, too, she had a new serenity about her since the last time Helen had seen her, a little over a month ago now.

"Will you go to him?" Lady Vale asked quietly.

"I . . ." Helen looked down at the teacup in her lap. "I don't want to, of course. But if it's the only way to see my children again, how can I not?"

"What about Sir Alistair?"

Helen looked at her mutely.

"I noticed . . ." Lady Vale hesitated delicately. "I

couldn't help but notice that Sir Alistair has come all the way to London for you."

"He has been very kind to my children," Helen said. "I think he may've grown fond of them."

"And of you?" the viscountess murmured.

"Perhaps."

"In any case, I think he must have an opinion about the matter."

"He doesn't like the idea, naturally." Helen looked frankly at the viscountess. "But should that even matter? My children need me. I need them."

"But if he can rescue them?"

"And then what?" Helen whispered. "What kind of life might I have with him? I don't want to be another man's mistress and yet there doesn't seem to be any other way that I can be with him."

"Marriage?"

"He hasn't mentioned it." Helen shook her head and smiled slightly. "I can't believe I'm discussing this so bluntly with you. Don't you disapprove of me?"

"Not at all. I did send you to his castle in the first place."

Helen stared at the other woman. Lady Vale had a slight frown between her straight eyebrows, and one hand was rubbing her middle. But at Helen's glance, she looked up and smiled very slowly.

Helen's eyes widened. "You . . . ?"

Lady Vale nodded. "Oh, indeed."

"But . . . but his castle was so filthy!"

"And I take it not anymore," Lady Vale said complacently.

Helen huffed. "Most of it. There are still corners that

I'm not going into without boiling water and good lye soap. I cannot believe you sent me there knowing how awful it was."

"He needed you."

"His castle needed me," Helen corrected.

"Sir Alistair, too, I think," Lady Vale said. "He struck me as a very lonely man when I saw him. And you've performed a miracle already—you've got him to journey to London."

"For my children."

"For you," Lady Vale said softly.

Helen again looked at the teacup in her lap. "Do you truly think so?"

"I know so," the viscountess said promptly. "I saw the way he looked at you in my sitting room. That man cares for you."

Helen sipped her tea, saying nothing. This was so personal, so new and confusing, and she wasn't sure yet that she wanted to discuss it with another, even someone like Lady Vale, who had been so kind to her.

For a moment, both ladies sipped tea in silence.

Then Helen remembered something. She set down her teacup. "Oh! I forgot to tell you that I've finished copying out the fairy-tale book about the four soldiers."

Lady Vale smiled in pleasure. "Have you, indeed? Did you bring it with you?"

"No, I'm sorry. I quite forgot in . . ." She was going to say *in worry over the children,* but she simply shook her head instead.

"I understand," the viscountess said. "And in any case, I need to find someone to bind it for me. Perhaps you can hold it for me and I will write when I have an address for you to send it to?"

"Of course," Helen murmured, but her thoughts had already returned to Abigail and Jamie. Were they warm and safe? Did they cry for her? And would she ever see them again in this life?

The tea suddenly tasted like bile in her mouth. *Please God, let me see my children again.*

"THE EARL OF Blanchard is giving a luncheon party in honor of the king," Vale said. "And Lister is an invited guest."

They were still in the sitting room, and Vale was on his third glass of brandy, though he seemed to show no ill effects.

"Blanchard." Alistair frowned. "Wasn't that St. Aubyn's title?"

Reynaud St. Aubyn had been a captain in the 28th Regiment of Foot. A good man, a great leader, he'd survived the massacre at Spinner's Falls only to be captured and later killed at the Indian camp. Alistair shuddered. St. Aubyn was the man he'd told Helen about—the man who had been crucified and set alight.

St. Aubyn had also been Vale's good friend.

Vale nodded now. "The man who has the title is a distant cousin, a widower. His niece acts as hostess for his parties."

"When is it?"

"Tomorrow."

Alistair stared down into the empty glass in his hand. Tomorrow was when Etienne's ship would dock, but only for a few hours. Would he be able to see both the Duke of

Lister and Etienne in the same narrow period of time? In all likelihood not. If he went to the luncheon, he faced the real risk of missing Etienne's ship. Yet, if he were to weigh the children against information about the Spinner's Falls traitor, the children would clearly win. How could they not? They were life where the traitor was death.

"Is that a problem?" Vale asked.

Alistair looked up to meet the viscount's perceptive gaze. "No." He set aside his glass. "Are you invited to this grand luncheon?"

"Alas, no."

Alistair grinned. "Good. Then you can do something else for me while I invade Blanchard's luncheon party."

Chapter Seventeen

Every night the sorcerer would come to the knot garden and smile and gloat over the soldier he had ensorcelled. But by day, the sorcerer closed himself in his castle and thought up evil schemes.
One day a swallow joined the birds resting upon Truth Teller's stone shoulders. This swallow happened to be one of the number formerly imprisoned by the sorcerer, and somehow the bird must have recognized her savior. Gliding down to the yew hedge, the swallow plucked a single leaf. Then she spread her wings and flew high into the sky, away from the castle. . . .
—from TRUTH TELLER

The luncheon party had already started by the time Helen and Alistair arrived on the Earl of Blanchard's front step. They'd been delayed because Alistair had been waiting for a mysterious message at the hotel. Just before they'd left, a small scrawny lad had brought him a dirty letter.

Alistair had read it, grunted in what sounded like satisfaction, and sent the boy away again with a shilling and another letter, hastily written.

Helen tapped her foot as they waited for the door to open.

"Relax," Alistair growled softly beside her.

"How can I?" Helen said impatiently. "I don't know why that letter was so important. What if we missed the luncheon altogether?"

"We haven't. The carriages still clog the street, and besides, these things go on for hours; you know that." He sighed and muttered, "You should've stayed in the hotel room as I suggested."

Helen glared. "They're my children."

He cast his eye heavenward.

"Tell me again what your plan is," she demanded.

"All I have to do is get Lister to relinquish claim on the children," he said in a maddeningly soothing voice.

"Yes, but how?"

"Trust me."

"But—"

The door was opened by a harried maid at that point. "Yes?"

"Late as usual, I'm afraid," Alistair said in a loud, cheerful voice entirely unlike his normal tones. "And my wife has just now torn a lace or some such. Perhaps you can show us to a room where she can put herself to rights?"

The girl wrenched her horrified gaze from Alistair's face and stood back to let them in. Blanchard House was one of the grandest houses on the square, the interior hall lined with pale pink marble and gilt. They passed a white marble statue of Diana with her hounds, and then the girl opened a door leading to an elegant sitting room.

"This will do excellently," Alistair said. "Please, don't let us keep you from your duties. We'll show ourselves in when my wife is ready."

The maid bobbed a curtsy and hurried away. The occasion of a luncheon honoring the king no doubt involved every available servant.

"Stay here, please," Alistair said. He pressed a hard kiss to her lips and swung toward the door.

And froze.

"What is it?" Helen asked.

On the wall by the door was a huge painting—a life-sized portrait of a young man.

"Nothing," he muttered, his gaze still on the painting. He shook his head and turned to her. "Stay here. I'll return and collect you after I've talked to Lister. All right?"

She had barely nodded when he strode from the room.

Helen closed her eyes and inhaled, trying to calm herself. She'd already agreed that the best plan was for Alistair to talk to Lister by himself. She couldn't change her mind now. She needed to wait and let Alistair try to persuade the duke. The problem was it was so difficult to simply wait.

She opened her eyes and looked about the room, seeking something to distract herself with. There were several groupings of delicate low chairs, their arms painted white and gilt. Large portraits lined the wall, figures dressed in fashions long past, but the most commanding painting was of the young man that Alistair had stared at. Helen approached and peered up at it.

The painting depicted a young man dressed in casual

hunting clothes. He held a tricorne carelessly by his side, and his gaiter-clad legs were crossed at the ankle. He leaned against a large oak tree, a long rifle cradled in the crook of one arm. At his feet, two spotted hunting dogs lay, their heads turned adoringly to the man.

Helen could understand their worshipful gaze. The man was so handsome he was almost pretty, his face smooth and unlined in that first youthful bloom of manhood. His lips were full, sensuously wide, and slightly tilted as if he repressed a smile. His heavy-lidded black eyes seemed to laugh at the viewer as if inviting participation in a naughty joke. His entire form was so full of vigor and life that one almost expected him to leap from the painting itself.

"Fascinating, isn't he?" a voice said from behind her.

Helen swung around, startled. She hadn't heard anyone enter the room. In fact, she'd thought she stood by the only door.

But a young lady had entered by a door paneled to fit into the wall, almost hidden. She curtsied. "I'm Beatrice Corning."

Helen sank into a curtsy. "Helen Fitzwilliam." Pray the other woman didn't recognize her name.

Miss Corning had a fresh, open face, slightly freckled. Her light gray eyes were quite fine and rather frank, her hair a lovely wheat color, pulled into a large knot at the crown of her head. Fortunately, she didn't seem in any hurry to toss Helen out of the house.

"I've always found him rather mesmerizing," she said, nodding to the painting. "He looks so amused at something. So very pleased with himself and the world, don't you think?"

Helen glanced back at the painting, half-smiling. "He probably fascinates all the ladies."

"Maybe he did once, but not anymore," was the reply.

Helen looked at the girl. "Why?"

"That's Reynaud St. Aubyn, Viscount Hope," Miss Corning said. "He should've been the Earl of Blanchard, but he was killed in the Colonies by Indians in the massacre at Spinner's Falls. I suppose I should be grateful—my uncle would never have become the Earl of Blanchard otherwise, and I wouldn't be living in Blanchard House. But I can't find it in myself to be happy at his death. He looks so alive, doesn't he?"

Helen turned back to the portrait. *Alive.* That was the word she'd thought of, too, when she'd seen the lounging young man.

"Pardon me," Beatrice Corning said apologetically, "but I've just realized who you are. You're connected to the Duke of Lister, aren't you?"

Helen bit her lip, but she'd never been very good at lying. "I'm his former mistress."

Miss Corning's lovely eyebrows rose. "Then would you mind telling me what you're doing here?"

HIS PLAN WAS a risky gamble. If he played this wrong, he and Helen might lose the children forever. On the other hand, if he did nothing, they were as good as already lost.

Alistair laid his hand gently on the closed dining room door, took a breath, and pushed it firmly open. The Earl of Blanchard had spared no expense in this royal luncheon. Flowers were massed in vases along the sideboard, sumptuous swags of gold and purple fabric draped every surface, and carved sugar swans sailed the middle of the long dining table.

There were as many servants as guests, and a bewigged fellow near the door held out his hand to halt Alistair. "Sir, you can't—"

"Your Majesty," Alistair called in a deep voice. He made sure his tone carried to the far end of the table, where King George sat next to a florid little man, presumably the Earl of Blanchard. He strode toward the king, moving fast and with enough assurance that no one gainsaid him. "I beg a word, Your Majesty."

Alistair reached the king and bent in a low bow, arms outstretched, leg pointed before him.

"And who are you, sir?" the king asked, and for a moment Alistair felt his heart go still. Then he looked up, and the young king's face lit. "Ah! Sir Alistair Munroe, our fascinating naturalist! Blanchard, bring a seat for Sir Alistair."

Blanchard frowned but snapped his fingers at a footman, who leapt to obey. A chair was brought and set at the right hand of the king.

"Do you know the Earl of Blanchard, Munroe?" The king gestured to his host.

"I haven't had the pleasure." Alistair made another bow. "Forgive me, sir, for bursting into your party so precipitously."

Blanchard's expression was sour, but he could hardly demure now that the king had welcomed Alistair. He nodded curtly.

"And these gentlemen are the Duke of Lister; his son and heir, the Earl of Kimberly; and Lord Hasselthorpe."

The king indicated the men sitting across from him and to his other side.

Hasselthorpe sat to the king's left. He was a distinguished-looking gentleman of middling years. Lister and his son were across from the king. Lister was of an age with Hasselthorpe. He wore a wine-colored coat with a waistcoat beneath that curved over his sloping belly. His heir was a brawny young man who wore his own brown hair clubbed back and unpowdered. He was frowning slightly as if in confusion at Alistair's abrupt entrance. Lister was eyeing Alistair narrowly beneath a curled gray wig.

Alistair bowed and sat. The fact that Lister's heir was present was an unforeseen bit of luck. "I beg your forgiveness, Your Majesty, gentlemen, but the matter I come about is most urgent."

"Indeed?" The king was a fair man with pink cheeks and prominent blue eyes. He wore a snowy white wig and strikingly brilliant blue coat and waistcoat. "Have you finished your opus on the flora and fauna of Britain?"

"I am very near the end, Your Majesty, and if it pleases Your Highness, I beg the favor of dedicating my book to you."

"Granted, my dear Munroe, granted." The king's color had risen in pleasure. "We look forward to reading this tome when it is finished and published."

"Thank you, Your Majesty," Alistair replied. "I hope to—"

But Lister cut him off with a loud cough. "Pleasant as the information of your book's progress is, Munroe, I do not see why you need interrupt the king's luncheon to tell him of it."

A very slight frown appeared between the king's eyebrows. At the far end of the room, the door opened again and a blond young lady entered and seated herself in an empty chair at the table. She cast an inquisitive glance at them.

Alistair turned to Lister and smiled genially. "I do not mean to bore you with the details of my studies as a naturalist. I realize that not everyone is as fascinated by the oddities of God's world as His Highness and I."

Lister's face went blank as he understood his faux pas, but Alistair continued. "Actually, the business I come about involves you as well."

He paused and took a sip of the wine that had been placed at his elbow.

Lister's eyebrows rose. "Do you mean to enlighten us?"

Alistair smiled and set his wineglass down. "Naturally." He turned and addressed the king. "I have been studying the habits of badgers recently, Your Majesty. Amazing what secrets are hidden in even the most mundane of animals."

"Indeed?" The king leaned forward in interest.

"Oh, yes," Alistair said. "For instance, although the badger sow is a creature known for its unpleasant and even aggressive disposition, when it comes to her young, or kits, she shows a pretty maternal side that rivals even the most caring of animals."

He paused to take another sip of wine.

"How extraordinary!" the king exclaimed. "We would never think a lowly badger to hold the higher feelings God has granted mankind."

"Exactly." Alistair nodded. "I myself was moved to sympathy by the plight of a sow when her kits were killed by a hawk. She cried most piteously for her dead children, running back and forth and refusing any sustenance for days. Indeed, I was afeared that she might starve herself to death, so saddened was she by the loss of her young."

"And what has this to do with us?" Lister demanded impatiently.

Alistair turned slowly to him and smiled. "Why, do you not feel a small portion of sympathy for a badger so grief-stricken by the loss of her young, Your Grace?"

Lister sneered, but the king replied, "Any gentleman of true sensibility would, of course, be moved by such devotion."

"Naturally," Alistair murmured. "And how much more moved would a gentleman be by the plight of a lady deprived of her children?"

Silence fell. Lister's eyes were narrowed to mere slits. His son was watching him in dawning understanding, and Hasselthorpe and Blanchard sat frozen. Alistair wasn't aware how much the other gentlemen knew about Helen and Lister and their drama involving the children, but Lister's son at least knew something. He looked quickly between his father and Alistair, his mouth set in a grim line.

"Do you speak of a specific lady, Munroe?" the king asked.

"Indeed, sire. There is a lady formerly acquainted with His Grace, the Duke of Lister, who has recently suffered the loss of her children."

The king's lips pursed. "They are dead?"

"No, thank God, Your Majesty," Alistair replied silkily. "They are only kept apart from their mother, perhaps in honest mistake."

Lister shifted in his seat. His brow had begun to shine with sweat. "What are you implying, Munroe?"

"Implying?" Alistair opened his eye wide. "I do not imply. I merely state facts. Do you deny that Abigail and Jamie Fitzwilliam are being kept at your London town house?"

Lister blinked. He'd no doubt counted on Helen not knowing where he'd hidden the children. Alistair had, in fact, only learned of their whereabouts this morning, via the simple expedient of sending a boy to bribe one of Lister's footmen.

Lister visibly swallowed. "I have every right to keep the children within my house."

Alistair was silent, watching the man and wondering if he saw the trap gaping wide.

The king shifted in his seat. "Who are these children?"

"They are—" Lister began, and then cut himself abruptly off when he finally saw where Alistair had led him. He shut his mouth and glared while Alistair smiled and sipped his wine, waiting to see if the duke was angry enough to throw caution to the wind. If he acknowledged the children in the presence of the king, they would have a claim on him and, more importantly, on his estate.

Kimberly turned to face his parent fully and murmured, "Father."

Lister shook his head as if coming out of a daze, and his face assumed a polite mask. "The children are nothing to me—merely the offspring of a former friend."

"Good." The king clapped his hands together. "Then they can be returned immediately to their mother, eh, Lister?"

"Yes, Your Majesty," Lister muttered, and then turned to Hasselthorpe. "When do you propose to submit this bill to parliament?"

The duke, Hasselthorpe, and Blanchard leaned together in a political discussion, while Kimberly merely looked relieved.

The king waved for more wine and when it was poured, tilted his glass slightly to Alistair and said, "To maternal love."

"Aye, Your Majesty." Alistair gladly drank.

The king set down his glass, cocked his head, and said sotto voce, "We trust that was the outcome you were aiming for, Munroe?"

Alistair looked into the king's amused blue eyes and permitted himself a small smile. "Your Majesty is as perceptive as ever."

King George nodded. "Finish that book, Munroe. We look forward to inviting you to another tea."

"To that end, I'll take leave of this lovely luncheon with Your Majesty's permission."

The king waved a lace-draped hand. "Go, then. Just make sure you don't stay away from our capital so long this time, what?"

Alistair stood, bowed, and turned to leave the room. As he did so, he passed the back of Hasselthorpe's chair. He hesitated, but when, after all, would he have another chance to ask the man?

He bent over Lord Hasselthorpe's chair and said, "Might I ask you a question, my lord?"

Hasselthorpe eyed him with disfavor. "Haven't you already done enough for one afternoon, Munroe?"

Alistair shrugged. "No doubt, but this won't take long.

Nearly two months ago, Lord Vale wanted to talk to you about your brother, Thomas Maddock."

Hasselthorpe stiffened. "Thomas died at Spinner's Falls, as I'm sure you know."

"Yes." Alistair met the other man's gaze without blinking. There were too many questions left to let a grieving brother's anger stand in the way of finding the answers. "Vale thought Maddock may've known something about—"

Hasselthorpe leaned into Alistair's face. "If you or Vale dare to insinuate that my brother was a part of any treasonous activity, I shall call you out, make no mistake, sir."

Alistair raised his eyebrows. He hadn't meant to insinuate any such thing—it'd never occurred to him that Maddock had been the traitor.

But Hasselthorpe hadn't finished. "And if you have any feeling for Vale at all, you'll dissuade him from this course."

"What do you mean?" Alistair asked slowly.

"He and Reynaud St. Aubyn were good friends, were they not? Grew up together as lads?"

"Yes."

"Then I very much doubt Vale would truly want to know who betrayed the 28th." Hasselthorpe sat back, his mouth grim.

Alistair leaned so close, his lips nearly brushed the other man's ear. "What do you know?"

Hasselthorpe shook his head. "I've heard only rumors, ones bandied about in the higher ranks of the army and in parliament. They say the traitor's mother was French."

Alistair stared into the other man's watery brown eyes

for a moment, and then he swung around and walked swiftly from the room. Reynaud St. Aubyn's mother had been French.

HELEN WAS TURNING a hand-bound book over in her hands when Alistair entered the sitting room. She dropped the book from nerveless fingers and stared at him.

"He's denied claim to the children," Alistair said at once.

"Oh, thank God." Helen closed her eyes in relief, but Alistair took hold of her elbow.

"Come, let's leave. I don't think it wise to tarry."

Her eyes flew open in alarm. "Do you think he'll change his mind?"

"I doubt it, but the faster we act, the less time it gives him to think about it," Alistair muttered as he hustled her to the sitting room door.

Helen's gaze fell on the portrait of Lord St. Aubyn. "I should write Miss Corning a note."

"What?" He stopped and frowned at her.

"Miss Corning. She's Lord Blanchard's niece and quite nice. Do you know she binds books by hand? She told me."

Alistair shook his head. "Good Lord." He again started striding to the front door, so fast she had to trot to keep up. "You can write her a letter later."

"I shall have to," she murmured as they got in the carriage.

Alistair banged on the carriage roof, and they started forward with a lurch. "Did you tell her who you were?"

"I was in her home," Helen said. She felt heat invade her cheeks, because she knew that Alistair meant her connection to Lister. She tilted her chin. "It would've been rude to lie."

"Rude maybe, but there would've been less chance of you being thrown from the house."

Helen's gaze dropped to her hands in her lap. "I know I'm not respectable, but—"

"You're plenty respectable to me," he growled.

She looked up.

He was still frowning, scowling really. "It's just other people." He glanced away and muttered quietly, "I don't want to see you hurt."

"I came to terms with what I am—what I made myself—a long time ago," she said. "I can't change the past or how it affects me and my children now, but I can decide to live my life despite my terrible choices. If I was afraid of being hurt by others and what they say to me, I would have to live all my life in hiding. I won't do that."

She watched as he thought that over, still not meeting her eyes. That was the problem still between them, wasn't it? She'd made her choice about how she would live her life.

He still had not.

She glanced away, out the carriage window, and then frowned. "We're not going to Lister's house."

"No," he replied. "I hope to catch Etienne's ship still in the harbor. If we hurry and luck is with us, I might be able to."

But when they arrived at the docks a half hour later and inquired about the ship, a rather grimy fellow pointed to a sail disappearing down the Thames.

"You've missed her, guv," the fellow said, not without sympathy.

Alistair tossed a shilling at the man for his help.

"I'm so sorry," Helen said when they'd once more entered the carriage. "You missed your opportunity to talk to your friend because you were rescuing my children."

Alistair shrugged, looking moodily out the window. "It couldn't be helped. Had I to make the same decision again, I wouldn't change my mind. Abigail and Jamie are more important than any information I could've gotten from Etienne. Besides"—he let the curtain fall and turned to her—"I'm not sure I would've liked the news he might've given me."

Chapter Eighteen

*Now, Princess Sympathy had long ago made it
safely back to her father's castle, but still she
worried. Had her rescuer, Truth Teller, escaped the
sorcerer? Worry for the soldier so filled her thoughts
that in time she no longer ate or slept and spent
entire nights pacing. Her father, the king, became
concerned for her welfare and sent for all manner
of healers and nurses, but none could tell him what
was wrong with the princess. Only she knew of Truth
Teller, of his bravery, and of her secret fear that he
had not escaped the sorcerer's clutches.*

*So when a swallow flew in her window one night
and presented her with the leaf from a yew bush, she
knew exactly what it meant. . . .*

—from TRUTH TELLER

"Do you think he's really Sir Alistair's friend?" Jamie
whispered to Abigail.

"Of course he is," she said stoutly. "He knew Puddles's name, didn't he?"

Abigail knew better than to go with a strange man. But when the tall man with the funny face had burst into the duke's nursery, he'd seemed to know exactly what to do. He'd ordered the footmen to leave and had told them that he was Sir Alistair's friend and that he would take them to Sir Alistair and Mama. Most importantly of all, he'd said that Sir Alistair had told him Puddles's name. That had settled it in Abigail's mind. Better to go with a stranger than to stay in the duke's prison. So they'd followed the tall gentleman, sneaking down the back stairs and into a waiting carriage. Jamie had seemed happy for the first time in days. He'd nearly bounced out of the carriage seat as they'd driven away.

Now they sat side by side on a satin settee in a very grand room. They were alone, since the gentleman had left for some reason, and only now did Abigail think about all the terrible things the funny-faced gentleman might do to them if he *wasn't* Sir Alistair's friend.

She was careful, of course, to keep her fear from Jamie.

Jamie squirmed now and said, "Do you think—"

But he was interrupted by the opening of the door. The gentleman came in again, followed by a straight-backed lady. A small terrier dog rounded the lady's skirts, gave one sharp bark, and raced toward them.

"Mouse!" Jamie cried, and the little dog leapt straight into his arms.

Abigail recognized him then. She and Jamie had met Mouse, the dog, and his mistress at Hyde Park. She rose and curtsied to Lady Vale.

That lady stopped and inspected Abigail while Mouse bathed Jamie's face with his pink tongue. "Are you well?"

"Yes, my lady," Abigail whispered, and a great weight lifted off her heart. It was going to be all right. Lady Vale would make it so.

"We ought to send for some tea and biscuits, Vale," Lady Vale said. She gave a very small smile, and Abigail smiled back.

And then something even more wonderful happened. There were loud voices in the hall and Mama rushed in.

"My darlings!" she cried, and went to her knees, her arms outstretched.

Jamie and Abigail ran to her. Mama's arms were so warm. She smelled so familiar, and suddenly Abigail was crying into Mama's shoulder, and they were all hugging, even Mouse. It was wonderful, really.

They stayed like that for a long time before Abigail saw Sir Alistair. He stood by himself, watching them with a small smile on his face, and her heart gave a happy hop at the sight of him, too. Abigail stepped back from Mama.

She dried her eyes and walked slowly to Sir Alistair. "I'm glad to see you again."

"I'm glad to see you, too." His voice was deep and gruff, but his brown eye smiled at her.

She swallowed and said quickly, "And I'm sorry that I let Puddles make water on your satchel."

He blinked and then cleared his throat and said quietly, "I shouldn't have yelled at you, Abigail lass. It was but a satchel." He held out his hand. "Forgive me?"

For some reason, her eyes filled with tears again. She

took his hand. It was hard and warm and large, and when she held it, she felt safe.

Safe and as if she were home.

AN HOUR LATER, Alistair watched as Helen and the children said their farewells to Lady Vale outside the Vale town house.

He turned to the viscount, standing and watching beside him. "Thank you for rescuing them for me."

Vale shrugged carelessly. "It was no trouble. Besides, you were the one who realized that if you and Mrs. Fitzwilliam went to the luncheon at Blanchard House, it would draw away your watcher and perhaps leave Lister's town house with fewer guards."

Alistair nodded. "But it was still a risk. He might've had a much larger force guarding the children."

"Might've, but as it turned out, he didn't. As it was, the only one who put up any fight was your old manservant, Wiggins." Vale looked at him rather sheepishly. "I do hope you don't mind that I knocked the fellow down the stairs?"

"Not at all," he replied with a grim smile. "I only wish he'd broken his neck in the fall."

"Ah, but we can't have all our wishes, can we?"

"No, we can't." Alistair watched as Helen smiled and shook hands with Lady Vale. A lock of golden hair blew across her pink cheek. "In any case, I do owe you, Vale."

"Think nothing of it." The viscount scratched his chin. "Any chance Lister will come after them again?"

Alistair shook his head decisively. "I doubt it. He renounced them in the presence of the king—and his heir. If nothing else, it's in Kimberly's vested interest to keep his father from acknowledging his bastard children in any way. If the rumors are true, Abigail and Jamie aren't Lister's only children out of wedlock. I'm afraid Kimberly will have quite a chore on his hands, making sure his father doesn't give away the unentailed parts of his inheritance to various bastard half siblings."

"Indeed." The viscount grunted and rocked back on his heels. "By the way, I heard that Hasselthorpe was at the luncheon. I don't suppose you got a chance to speak to him?"

Alistair nodded, his gaze on the carriage. "I saw him and briefly spoke to him."

"And?"

He hesitated only a fraction of a second. As Hasselthorpe had pointed out, St. Aubyn had been Vale's greatest friend. And besides, the man was dead now. Let the dead take care of the dead.

Alistair turned to meet Vale's eyes. "He knew nothing pertinent. I'm sorry."

Vale grimaced. "It was always a long shot, anyway. Hasselthorpe wasn't even there. I 'spect we'll never know now."

"No." The ladies had parted, the children and Helen turning to the carriage. It was time to go.

"It's just . . . ," Vale said quietly.

Alistair looked at him, at his long lined face, his wide, mobile mouth, his extraordinary green-blue eyes. "What?"

Vale closed his eyes. "Sometimes I still dream of him, Reynaud. On that goddamned cross, his arms widespread, his clothes and flesh alight, black smoke rising in the air."

He opened his eyes, bleak now. "I wish I could've brought to justice the man who put him there."

"I'm sorry," Alistair said, because it was the only thing he could say.

A moment later, he shook hands with Vale, bowed to Lady Vale, and entered the waiting carriage. The children waved good-bye enthusiastically as the carriage rumbled down the street.

Helen watched them, smiling. She looked across the carriage to Alistair on the opposite seat, with the smile still on her face, and he felt it like a physical blow. She was so lovely, so loving. At some point it must occur to her that he was nothing but an ugly misanthrope with only an equally ugly castle to his name. He'd not even discussed with her whether or not she wished to accompany him back to Scotland. Perhaps once there she'd change her mind, see Castle Greaves for the provincial place it was, and leave him. He should discuss it with her, find out what her plans for her future were, but the truth was that he didn't want to precipitate a heart-search on her part. If that made him a coward, so be it.

The children chattered for the next hour or so as they bumped and rolled out of London proper. Jamie did most of the talking, describing their kidnapping and the long carriage ride to London with the perfidious Wiggins. Alistair noted that the boy hardly mentioned his father at all, and when he did, it was always as "the duke." The children didn't seem to hold any filial regard for their father. Perhaps that was just as well.

Just outside of London, the carriage rambled into a small inn yard and halted.

Helen leaned forward to look outside the window. "Why are we stopping here?"

"A small bit of business," Alistair replied evasively. "Wait here, please."

He jumped from the carriage before she could bombard him with any more questions. The coachman was just descending his box. "A half hour you said, sir?"

Alistair nodded at the man. "That's right."

"Juss enough time for a pint, I reckon," the man said, and went into the inn.

Alistair looked about the yard. It was a quiet little inn with no other carriages. Only a dogcart with a dozing mare stood on one side under the stable eaves. A gentleman came out of the inn. He put up a hand to shield his eyes from the glare of the sun and then caught sight of the carriage and Alistair. He let his hand drop, then walked slowly toward Alistair. The gentleman wore a gray bobbed wig, and as he approached, Alistair saw that his eyes were a bright harebell blue.

The gentleman looked past him to the carriage. "Is she—?"

Alistair nodded. "I'll be in the inn. I've told the coachman we'll stop for a half hour. It's up to you if you want to use all of that time."

And without waiting to see what the man would do, Alistair strode to the inn.

"WHAT IS HE about?" Helen muttered under her breath as they waited in the carriage.

"Perhaps Sir Alistair has to use the necessary," Jamie said.

That made her eye her son suspiciously. Jamie was five

years old, but apparently a five-year-old boy's bladder wasn't very large because—

A single knock came at the carriage door. Helen frowned. Surely Alistair wouldn't knock at his own carriage? Then the door swung open, and she entirely lost her thought.

"Papa," she whispered, her heart in her throat.

She hadn't seen him for fourteen years, but she'd never forget his face. There were a few more lines about his eyes and forehead, his bobbed gray doctor's wig looked new, and his mouth was more pinched than she remembered it, but it was her papa.

He stared at her but didn't smile. "May I come in?"

"Of course."

He climbed in the carriage and sat across from them. His coat, waistcoat, and breeches were black, making him very somber. He didn't seem to know what to do now that he was in the carriage.

Helen put her arms around her children. She cleared her throat so that she might speak clearly. "These are my children. Abigail, who is nine, and Jamie, who is five. Children, this is my father. Your grandpapa."

Abigail said, "How do you do, sir?"

Jamie merely stared at his grandfather.

"Jamie." Papa cleared his throat. "Ah. Well."

Papa's Christian name was James. Helen waited to see if he'd say anything more, but he seemed a little stunned.

"How are my sisters and brother?" she asked, her tone formal.

"All married, Timothy just last year to Anne Harris. You remember her, don't you? Lived two houses down, had a terrible fever when she was but two years old."

"Oh, yes. Little Annie Harris." Helen smiled, but it was bittersweet. Annie Harris had been only five—Jamie's age—when she'd left home to live with Lister. She'd missed an entire lifetime out of her family's daily life.

Her father nodded, on firmer ground now that he had something familiar to discuss. "Rachel is married to a young doctor, a former student of mine, and expecting her second child. Ruth married a sailor and lives in Dover now. She writes often and comes to visit every year. She has but one child, a girl. Your sister, Margaret, has four children, two boys, two girls. She had a babe stillborn two years ago, another boy."

She felt tears closing her throat. "I am sorry to hear it."

Her father nodded. "Your mother fears that Margaret still grieves."

Helen took a fortifying breath. "And how is my mother?"

"Well enough." Papa looked at his hands. "She does not know I've come to see you today."

"Ah." What more could she say to that? Helen glanced out the window. A dog was napping in the sun on the inn doorstep.

"I should not have let her send you away," Papa said.

Helen turned to stare at him. She'd never guessed that he hadn't been completely in agreement with Mother.

"Your sisters were not yet married, and your mother worried for their futures," he said, and the lines on his face seemed to deepen as she watched. "Also, the Duke of Lister is a powerful man, and he made it plain that he expected you to go to him. In the end, it was simply easier to let you go and wash our hands of you. It was easier, but it wasn't right. I've regretted my decision for many years now. I hope you can forgive me someday."

"Oh, Papa." Helen went to the other side of the carriage to hug her father.

His arms were strong when they wrapped around her. "I'm sorry, Helen."

She pulled back and saw that there were tears in his eyes.

"You can't come home, I'm afraid. Your mother will not budge on that point. But I believe she'll look the other way if you write me. And I hope that I can see you again someday?"

"Of course."

He nodded and stood, briefly touching Abigail's cheek and the top of Jamie's head. "I need to go now, but I'll write you in care of Sir Alistair Munroe."

She nodded, her throat swelling.

He hesitated, and then said gruffly, "He seems like a good man. Munroe, that is."

She smiled, although her lips trembled. "He is."

Papa nodded and then he was gone.

Helen closed her eyes, her hand at her trembling mouth, on the very edge of breaking down in tears.

The carriage door opened again and rocked as someone climbed in.

When Helen opened her eyes, Alistair was scowling at her. "What did he say? Did he insult you?"

"No, oh, no, Alistair." And she got up for the second time and crossed the carriage to kiss him on the cheek. She drew back and looked into his startled eye. "Thank you. Thank you so much."

Chapter Nineteen

Princess Sympathy gathered all the magical things she could—spells, potions, amulets that were said to convey power—for she knew that if she were to face the sorcerer, she would need to be armed. Then she set off at night, all alone and without telling anyone in her father's castle. It was a long and dangerous journey back to the sorcerer's castle, but Princess Sympathy had her courage and the memory of the man who had saved her to guide her.

At last, after many weary weeks, she arrived at the grim black castle just as the sun rose on a new day. . . .

—from TRUTH TELLER

It took over a week to return to Castle Greaves. A week in which Helen and Alistair shared one tiny inn room after another with the children. She wouldn't let them out of her sight, and he would've thought less of her if she had. Which was perhaps why, the very moment the clock struck nine on the night they returned, he was out of his room and pacing toward hers.

There was an urgency to his step not entirely explained by delayed lust. He wanted, *needed*, to reestablish his relationship with Helen. To make sure that all was the same as before the children had been stolen. He needed her on some basic level, and he didn't want their time together to be over yet. He admitted this weakness to himself, and it only sped his steps.

Then, too, he was aware that she no longer had an external reason to stay with him at Castle Greaves. She had no need of employment, at least for the foreseeable future. Not with the cache of jewels she'd shown him one night in an inn. Lister, the bastard, had provided enough pearls and gold to last her a lifetime if she were frugal. And with Lister's guns spiked, she need no longer hide from him, either.

Which begged the question, When would she leave him?

Alistair shook the depressing thought away, halting at Helen's door. He gave the door a faint scratch. In a moment, it opened and she stood there in her chemise.

He stared at her mutely and held out his hand, his palm uppermost.

She glanced behind her and then took his hand, stepping into the hallway and shutting the door. He clutched her hand, probably too tightly, and led her quickly back to his rooms. He was already monstrously erect and aching with the need to claim her. He seemed to have lost whatever vestiges of civilization he'd ever had.

He'd barely closed his own door behind them when he swung her into his arms and brought his mouth to hers.

Tasting her. Consuming her. *Helen*. She was soft on the surface, but underneath he could feel the strength of her muscles and bones, the strength of her core.

He thrust his tongue into her mouth, demanding satisfaction, and she complied, sweetly sucking. Yielding to him, though he knew it was an illusion. He ran his hands over her shoulders, down her gently curving back to her hips. He filled his palms with her rounded buttocks and squeezed.

She broke the kiss, gasping, and looked at him with wide eyes. "Alistair—"

"Shh."

He picked her up, her weight solid in his arms, and he was glad to play the conqueror. In his arms she was helpless to escape.

"But we need to talk," she said, her face solemn.

He swallowed. "Not yet. Just let me . . ."

He lowered her gently to his big bed, and her golden hair spread over his dark coverlet, an offering any god would be pleased with. He was no god; he didn't deserve her, but he'd take what he could for as long as he could.

He stripped off his banyan and crawled, naked, over her form. With those harebell-blue eyes, she watched him come up over her. Wide and impossibly innocent. Dark now and a little sad. She raised her hand and brushed it carefully, tenderly, over his scarred cheek. She didn't speak anymore, but her eyes, her expression, the very gentleness of her touch sent ice into his veins.

He leaned down and kissed her so he wouldn't have to look into those eyes anymore. He drew her chemise up over her legs, feeling them shift restlessly beneath him, feeling the brush of her bush against his belly. He lifted his head briefly to draw her chemise over her head and throw it aside, and then he lowered his nude body to her nude body and kissed her once more.

Men talked of an afterlife filled with heavenly bliss, but this was the only bliss he wanted, in this life or the next: to feel Helen's bare skin beneath his own. To delight in the soft cushions of her thighs cradling his. To press his hard cock into the velvet of her belly. To smell her intimate, womanly scent mingled with the scent of lemons, and to feel the warmth of her skin. Oh, God, if ever there was a chance of paradise for him, he'd relinquish it, and gladly, to stay right here in Helen's arms.

He traced the faint bumps of her ribs, the indent of her waist, the curve of her hip, until he came to the center of her. She was wet, her curls drenched already, and he gave thanks because he wasn't sure he could stand a moment longer outside of her. He grasped his cock and guided himself to her warmth, to her softness.

To home.

She was tight, despite her wetness. He clenched his jaw and thrust into her in small shoves, parting her folds, burying himself deep. She held him and he closed his eyes to keep from spilling too soon. He felt her arms slide around him, and she pulled his face down to hers. She kissed him with a moist, open mouth and spread her legs, wrapping her calves over his hips. He moved then—it was that or die. Sliding, grinding, pushing his flesh into hers. Making love to her. She continued to kiss him without any haste, her mouth accepting his tongue as her body accepted his cock.

This was all he wanted. This was heaven.

But his body had to speed up, the imperative to plant

his seed overtaking the luxury of a slow coupling. He raised himself on his arms to intensify his thrusts. He watched as her heavy eyelids drifted closed, her face flushing a deep pink. Her breath was coming short, but she'd not yet crested. He held his weight on one hand and with the other searched for that small bit of feminine flesh that would send her over the edge. He found it, hiding in her slippery folds, and he gently pressed, slowly circled. Her arms fell from his shoulders, and she flung them over her head, grasping the pillow with both fists. He watched her, diddling her pearl and humping her hard, and when he saw her toss back her head, he felt it, too. The churning explosive start of his orgasm.

He pulled out just in time, spilling on her thighs. His heart was pounding, his breath coming short. He rolled to the side so he wouldn't crush her and just lay there a moment, his arm over his head, exhausted. He was drifting into sleep, in fact, when she moved, nestling against him and running her fingers over his chest.

"I love you," she whispered.

His eye snapped open, and he stared sightlessly at the ceiling of his bedroom. He knew what he should say, of course, but the words wouldn't come. He seemed struck mute. And now it was too late. Too late. Their time together was over. "Helen—"

She sat up next to him. "I love you with all my heart, Alistair, but I cannot stay with you like this."

SHE'D THOUGHT HERSELF in love before, when she'd been young and very naive. That had been the infatuation of a girl overawed by a man's rank and worldly possessions. This love she felt for Alistair was entirely different. She knew his faults, knew his bad temper and cynicism, but she also gloried in the best parts of him. His love of nature, the gentleness he hid from most of the world, his uncompromising loyalty.

She saw both the worst and the best, and she saw all the complicated parts in between. She even knew that there were pieces of him that he still kept hidden from her, pieces she wished she had the time to discover. She knew all this, and she loved him despite or because of it. This was a mature woman's love. A love that was aware of both his human foibles and his nobility.

And she also knew, deep in her heart, that this love, however wonderful, wasn't enough for her.

He'd gone still beside her, his great chest damp with the sweat from their lovemaking. He hadn't said a word when she confessed her love, and that fact nearly made her break down. In the end, though, whether or not he admitted loving her was beside the point.

"Stay with me," he rasped. His expression was stern, but in his eye was desperation.

It nearly broke her heart.

"I can't live like this again," she said. "I fled Lister because I realized that I was more than a man's convenient plaything. I *have* to be more—for myself and for my children. And although I love you a thousand times more than I ever loved Lister, I will not repeat my mistake."

His beautiful eye closed, and he turned his face away from her. His hands clenched into fists above his head. She waited, but he did no more, neither speaking nor moving. He might as well have turned to stone.

At last she rose from the bed and picked up her chemise from the floor. She put it on and went to the door.

She glanced back one last time, but he still hadn't moved. So she opened the door and slipped from the room, leaving him—and her heart—behind.

Alistair retreated to his tower the next morning, but nothing was the same. The treatise on badger behavior that had interested him before was now patently ridiculous. His sketches, his specimens, his journals and notes, everything in the room seemed pointless and useless. Worst of all, the tower windows overlooked the stable yard, and he could see Helen supervising the loading of her bags into the dogcart. Why had he even bothered rising this morning?

His brooding thoughts were interrupted by a knock at the tower door. He scowled at the door, debated ignoring the knock, and eventually yelled, "Come!"

The door opened and Abigail poked her head in.

Alistair straightened. "Oh, it's you."

"We wanted to say good-bye," she said, her voice exceedingly serious for a child of nine.

He nodded.

She came in, and he saw that Jamie was behind her, holding a squirming Puddles in his arms.

Abigail clasped her hands in front of her, reminding him very much of her mother. "We wanted to thank you for coming to London to rescue us."

Alistair started to wave this aside, but apparently she wasn't finished.

"And for teaching us to fish and letting us dine with you and showing us where the badgers live." She paused, looking at him with her mother's eyes.

"Quite all right." Alistair pinched the bridge of his

nose between forefinger and thumb. "Your mother loves you, you know."

Her eyes, so like Helen's, widened as she stared at him mutely.

"She loves you"—he had to stop and clear his throat—"just the way you are."

"Oh." Abigail looked down at the toes of her shoes and frowned fiercely as if to keep from weeping. "We also wanted to thank you for letting us name your dog."

He raised his brows.

"We've decided on Badger," she explained gravely, "because he went with us to the badger sett. Besides, we can't call him Puddles forever. It's a baby name, really."

"Badger is a very good name." He looked down at the toes of his boots. "Mind you walk him every day and see that he isn't fed too much rich food."

"But he isn't ours," she said.

Alistair shook his head. "I know I said that Badger was my dog, but I really got him for you."

She gazed at him with the same damned determined eyes that her mother had used on him the night before. "No. He isn't ours."

She gave a little push to Jamie, who was looking quite miserable. The boy came forward with the puppy and held him out to Alistair. "Here. He's yours. Abby says you need Badger more than us."

Alistair took the squirming, warm little body, completely nonplussed. "But—"

Abigail marched right up to him and yanked on his arm until he bent. Then she wrapped her skinny little arms around his neck and half strangled him. "Thank you, Sir Alistair. Thank you."

She whirled and caught her startled brother's hand and dragged him from the room before Alistair could think of a reply.

"Dammit." He stared down at the puppy, and Badger licked his thumb. "What am I to do with you now?"

He strode to the window and looked down in time to see Helen help the children into the dogcart. Abigail glanced up once, he thought in his direction, but she hastily looked away again, so perhaps he was wrong. Then Helen climbed in, and the footman driving the cart gave the reins a shake. They all rolled away, out of the stable yard, out of his life, and Helen never once looked back.

His body urged him to run after her, but his mind chained him where he was. Keeping her would just delay the inevitable.

Now or tomorrow, he'd always known that Helen would leave him.

Chapter Twenty

The sorcerer opened his doors to Princess Sympathy readily enough, but when she told him what she'd come for, he laughed. He led her to the yew knot garden and pointed to where Truth Teller stood, immobile and cold.

"There is your knight," the sorcerer said. "You may work what little magic you know to save him, but be forewarned: I give you only this day. If he is still a man of stone when the sun sets, I will make you his stone bride and together you both shall stand in my garden for all eternity."

The princess consented to this poor bargain, for she had no other choice if she were to make Truth Teller a man of flesh and blood again. All the hours of that day she performed the spells and incantations that she had brought with her, but when the sun's rays began to fade, Truth Teller was still stone. . . .

—from TRUTH TELLER

Three days later, Alistair was woken by a commotion downstairs. Someone was shouting and carrying on. He groaned and shoved his head beneath his pillow. Rising early was no longer a priority in his life. In fact, he had no priorities at all. Might as well stay abed.

But the commotion grew louder and closer, like an advancing midsummer's storm until—ominously—it was right outside his bedroom door. He'd just flung the covers from his head when his sister crashed into his room.

"Alistair Michael Munroe, have you lost your mind?" Sophia blasted at him.

He clutched the bedsheets to his bare chest like a startled maiden and scowled at his sister. "To what do I owe the honor of this visit, dear sister?"

"To your own stupidity," Sophia said promptly. "Do you know I met Mrs. Halifax on Castlehill in Edinburgh just yesterday morn, and she said that you and she had parted company?"

"No," Alistair sighed. Badger had woken with the commotion of course, and the puppy came bumbling over the bed to lick his fingers. "Did she tell you that her name isn't really Halifax?"

Sophia, who'd been pacing the room, stopped, her expression alarmed. "She's not a widow?"

"No. She's the former mistress of the Duke of Lister."

Sophia blinked, and then scowled. "I thought she might still be married. If she's left Lister, who she was before hardly matters." She dismissed Helen's scandalous past with an impatient wave of the hand. "What matters is that you dress at once and go to Edinburgh and apologize to that woman for whatever boneheaded thing you've said or done."

Alistair eyed his sister, now vigorously drawing the curtains. "I'm appreciative of the fact that you assume the rift is my fault."

She only snorted at that.

"But what," he continued, "do you think I should do once I apologize? The woman won't live here."

She turned to face him and pursed her lips. "You asked her to marry you?"

Alistair looked away. "No."

"And why not?"

"Don't be a fool, Sophia." His head was aching, and he just wanted to go back to sleep—perhaps forever. "She's been the mistress to one of the richest men in England. She's lived in London or near the capital all of her life. You should've seen the jewels and gold Lister gave her. Perhaps you hadn't noticed, but I'm a disgustingly scarred, one-eyed man who is nearing his fourth decade and living in a dirty old castle in the middle of nowhere. Why the hell would she want to marry me?"

"Because she loves you!" Sophia nearly shouted.

He shook his head. "She might say she loves me—"

"She admitted it to you and you did nothing?" Sophia looked scandalized.

"Let me finish," Alistair growled. His head was pounding, his mouth tasted of the ale he'd drunk the night before, and he hadn't shaved since Helen left. He just wanted to get this over with and go back to bed.

His sister pressed her lips together and waved a hand impatiently for him to continue.

He inhaled. "She might think she loves me now, but

what future would she have here with me? What future would I have if she grew tired of me and left?"

"What future do you have now?" Sophia retorted.

He raised his head slowly and looked at her. Her expression was fierce, but her eyes were sad behind their round spectacles.

"Are you looking forward so much to spending the rest of your life alone?" Sophia asked quietly. "Childless, friendless, without a lover or helpmeet to even talk to in the evenings? What life is this that you're protecting so desperately from Helen's defection? Alistair, you must have faith."

"How can I?" he whispered. "How can I when at any moment everything might change? When I might lose everything?" He traced his scars. "I can no longer believe in happy futures, in good luck, in faith itself. I lost my *face*, Sophia."

"Then you're a coward," his sister said, and it was like a slap.

"Sophia—"

"No." She shook her head and held out her hands to him. "I know it will be harder for you than most. I know you have no illusions left about happiness, but goddamn it, Alistair, if you let Helen go, you might as well kill yourself now. You'll be giving up, acknowledging not that happiness is capricious, but that you have no *hope* of happiness."

He drew in a painful breath. His chest felt as if shards of glass were buried there, breaking, shifting, cutting into his heart. Making him bleed.

"You can no more change your face than she can change her past," Sophia said. "They're both there;

they'll always be there. You must simply learn to live with your scars as Helen has learned to live with her past."

"I have learned to live with my face. It's *her* I'm worried about." He closed his eye. "I don't know if she can live with me. I don't know if I could bear it if she couldn't."

"I do." He heard her walk closer. "You can bear anything, Alistair. You already have. I once told Helen that you were the bravest man I've ever known. And you are. You've had the worst happen to you, and you view life with no illusions. I can't even imagine the courage it takes for you to live day to day, but I'm asking you now to find an even greater courage."

He shook his head.

The bed dipped, and he opened his eye to see her kneeling by his bed, her hands clasped before her as if in prayer. "Give her a chance, Alistair. Give your *life* a chance. Ask her to marry you."

He rubbed his hand down his face. God, what if she was right? What if he was throwing away a life with Helen out of pure fear? "Very well."

"Good," Sophia said briskly, and rose to her feet. "Now get up and get dressed. My carriage is waiting. If we hurry, we can get to Edinburgh by nightfall."

HELEN WAS SHOPPING on High Street when she heard the scream. It was a beautiful, sunny day, and the street was crowded. She'd decided once they reached Edinburgh to stay for a bit and buy Jamie and Abigail some new clothes. Jamie's wrists were beginning to stick out from the cuffs of his coat. Her mind was taken up with fabrics and tailors and the scandalous cost of a small boy's shoes, so she didn't immediately turn to see what the problem was.

At least not until the second scream.

She looked then and saw several paces away a young pretty woman fainting gracefully into the arms of a startled gentleman in a dashing dark crimson coat. To the side stood Alistair, scowling at the girl, who'd obviously taken dramatic fright at his face.

Alistair looked up and saw her, and for a moment his expression went blank. Then he was making his way through the crowd to her, his gaze never leaving her face.

"It's Sir Alistair!" Abigail exclaimed, finally seeing him.

Jamie strained at Helen's hand. "Sir Alistair! Sir Alistair!"

"What are you doing here?" Helen asked when he was in front of them.

Instead of answering, he sank to one knee.

"Oh!" She placed a hand over her heart.

He held out a bunch of sadly wilted wildflowers, scowling at them. "It took longer to get to Edinburgh than I thought it would. Here."

She took the limp wildflowers, cradling them as if they'd been the finest roses.

He looked up at her, his brown eye steady and focused exclusively on her face. "I said if I ever courted you, I'd bring you wildflowers. Well, I'm courting you now, Helen Carter. I'm a scarred and lonely man, and my castle is a mess, but I hope someday that you'll consent to be my wife despite all that, because I love you with all my poor battered heart."

By this time, Abigail was nearly jumping up and down with excitement, and Helen knew tears were in her own eyes.

"Oh, Alistair."

"You don't have to answer now." He cleared his throat. "In fact, I don't want you to answer yet. I'd like to have the time to properly court you. To show you that I can be a good husband and that I have some faith in the future. *Our* future."

Helen shook her head. "No."

He froze, his gaze fixed on her face. "Helen . . ."

She reached down and stroked his scarred cheek. "No, I can't wait that long. I want to be married to you right away. I want to be your wife, Alistair."

"Thank God," he breathed, and then he was on his feet.

He pulled her into his arms and gave her a quite improper kiss right there on High Street, in front of God, the gaping crowd, and her children.

And Helen had never been happier.

SIX WEEKS LATER . . .

Helen lay back on the big bed in Alistair's room—*their* room now—and stretched luxuriously. She was, as of ten o'clock this morning, officially Lady Munroe.

They'd had a small ceremony with only family and a few friends, but Papa had been able to attend, and Lord and Lady Vale had come, and really they were the only ones who mattered, anyway. She'd noticed that Papa had even gotten a tear in his eye as she'd come out of the little Glenlargo church.

He was their guest now for a week or so and was a floor below in a newly appointed room. Abigail and Jamie were exhausted from the excitement of the day. They were in the nursery a floor above with Meg Campbell, former housemaid, now raised to the exalted rank of nursemaid. Alistair was already talking about hiring a governess for the children. Badger had doubled his size in the last month and a half and was probably asleep in Jamie's bed, though the dog was supposed to sleep in the kitchens.

"Admiring your new curtains?" Alistair's rough voice came from the door.

She looked over and smiled at him. He was lounging against the doorframe, one hand held behind his back. "The blue's so lovely in here, don't you think?"

"I think," he said, advancing toward the bed on which she lay, "that what I think has very little influence on the decorating of my castle."

"Really?" She widened her eyes. "Then no doubt you won't mind if I have your tower painted puce."

"I have no idea what color puce is, but it sounds entirely revolting," he said, and put one knee on the mattress. "Besides, I thought we'd agreed that you might do anything you wished to the rest of the castle as long as you left my tower be."

"But—" she started, intending to tease him further.

He laid his mouth against hers, stopping the words in a long kiss.

When next he raised his head, she gazed up at his dear face dreamily and whispered, "What have you got behind your back?"

Alistair propped himself on one elbow beside her. "Two gifts, one small, one a little larger. Which would you like first?"

"The small one."

He held out his fist and opened it to reveal a lemon. "Actually, this is a gift that comes with a condition."

She swallowed, remembering when last they'd used a lemon to prevent conception. "What is that?"

"You may have it only if you wish it." He raised his gaze to hers, and she saw a hesitant hope there. "I'm quite happy to continue as we are, with just Abigail and Jamie, for as little or as long as you want. But if you wish to forgo this"—he rolled the lemon between his fingers—"that would make me very happy as well."

Silly tears flooded her eyes. "I think, then, that I prefer we use this lemon for lemonade."

He didn't reply, but the ardent kiss he pressed on her was eloquent. The prospect of having a shared child sometime in the future delighted him as well.

When she could catch her breath, Helen said, "And the other gift?"

"More of an offering, really." He brought a bunch of wildflowers out from behind his back. "At least they're not wilted this time."

"I adore wilted flowers," she said.

"I am a lucky man to have such an easily pleased wife." He sobered. "I would like to give you a wedding present soon. Perhaps a necklace or a new dress or a special book. Think about it and let me know what you'd like."

She'd been the mistress of a duke. She'd had jewels and gowns showered upon her once, and they hadn't brought her happiness. Now she knew better.

Helen reached up and traced the scars on his cheek. "There's only one thing I want."

He turned his head to kiss her fingers. "And what is that?"

"You," she whispered before he lowered himself to her. "Only you."

Epilogue

Princess Sympathy lifted her eyes to the sky and saw that she had failed. Soon she would join her champion in a stony sleep. Despairing, she wrapped her arms about Truth Teller's cold stone waist and kissed his frozen lips.

And then a strange thing happened.

Color and warmth rushed over Truth Teller's gray face. His limbs turned to flesh and blood, and his mighty chest heaved, drawing breath.

"No!" cried the sorcerer, and raised his hands to bespell both Truth Teller and the princess.

But a crowd of swallows suddenly appeared and swarmed about his head, diving at his eyes and plucking at his hair. Truth Teller drew his sword and with one swing, cut the sorcerer's head from his body.

At this, the swallows suddenly dropped to the ground and became men and women who bowed before Truth Teller. Long ago they had been servants of the castle before the sorcerer had stolen it from a prince and bespelled them. At the same time, the statues of knights and warriors turned once again into living men, for they had once been fellows who had tried and failed to rescue the *princess. They dropped to their knees as one man and pledged to make Truth Teller their lord and master.*

Truth Teller thanked the servants of the castle and the knights most solemnly, and then he turned to the princess. He looked into her eyes and said, "I have a castle, servants, and men now, where before I had only the clothes on my back. But I would renounce them all to hold your heart, for I love you."

Princess Sympathy smiled and placed her palm against Truth Teller's warm cheek. "There is no need to renounce your newfound wealth. You already have my heart and have held it since that day you gave me the sorcerer's ring and wanted nothing in return."

And she kissed him.

"There's enchantment in
Hoyt's stories that makes you
believe in the magic of love."
—*Romantic Times BOOKreviews Magazine*

Don't miss the next

delightful installment in

THE LEGEND OF THE

FOUR SOLDIERS

series

To Desire a Devil

Available in November 2009

Please turn this page for a preview.

Chapter One

Few events are as very boring as a political tea. The hostess of such a social affair is often wildly desirous for something—*anything*—to occur at her party so as to make things more exciting.

Although perhaps a dead man staggering into the tea was a little *too* exciting, Beatrice Corning reflected later.

Up until the dead-man-staggering-in bit, things had gone as usual with the tea she was hostessing. Which was to say it was crashingly dull. Beatrice had chosen the blue salon, which was, unsurprisingly, blue. A quiet, restful, *dull* blue. White pilasters lined the walls, rising to the ceiling with discreet little curlicues at their tops. Small tables and chairs were scattered here and there, and an oval table stood at the center of the room with a small vase of late Michaelmas daisies. The refreshments included thinly sliced bread with butter and small, pale pink cakes. Beatrice had argued for the inclusion of raspberry tarts, thinking that they at least might be *colorful,* but Uncle Reggie—the Earl of Blanchard to everyone else—had balked at the idea.

Beatrice sighed. Uncle Reggie was an old darling, but he did like to pinch pennies. Which was also why the wine had been watered down to an anemic rose color, and the tea was so weak that one could make out the tiny blue pagoda at the bottom of the teacup. She glanced across the room to where her uncle stood, plump bandy legs braced, hands on hips, arguing heatedly with Lord Hasselthorpe. The force of his ire had made Uncle Reggie's wig slip askew. Beatrice calmly gestured to one of the footmen, gave him her plate, and began slowly winding her way across the room.

Only a quarter of the way to her uncle, she was stopped by a light touch at her elbow and a conspiratorial whisper. "Don't look now, but His Grace is doing his famous imitation of an angry codfish."

Beatrice turned and looked into twinkling sherry-brown eyes. Lottie Graham was only a hair over five feet, plump, and dark-haired, and the innocence of her round, freckled face was entirely belied by the sharpness of her wit.

"He isn't," Beatrice murmured, and then winced as she casually glanced over. Lottie was quite correct, as usual—the Duke of Lister did indeed look like an enraged fish. "Besides, what does a codfish have to get angry about anyway?"

"Exactly," Lottie replied as if having made her point. "I don't like that man—I never have—and that's entirely aside from his politics."

"Shh," Beatrice hissed. They stood by themselves, but

there were several groups of gentlemen nearby who could overhear if they'd wished. Since every other man in the room was as staunch a Tory as the Duke of Lister, it behooved the ladies to hide their Whig leanings.

"Oh, pish, Beatrice, dear," Lottie said. "Even if one of these fine, learned gentlemen heard what I'm saying, none of them have the imagination to realize we might have a thought or two in our pretty heads—especially if that thought doesn't agree with theirs."

"Not even Mr. Graham?"

Both ladies turned to look at a handsome young man in a snowy white wig in the corner of the room. His cheeks were pink, his eyes bright, and he stood straight and strong as he regaled the men about him with some story.

"Especially not Tom," Lottie said, frowning at her husband.

Beatrice tilted her head toward her friend. "But I thought you were making headway in bringing him to our side?"

"I was mistaken," Lottie said lightly. "Where the other Tories go, there goest Tom as well. He's as steadfast as a titmouse in a high wind. No, I'm very much afraid he'll be voting against Mr. Wheaton's bill to provide for retired soldiers of His Majesty's army."

Beatrice bit her lip. Lottie's tone was almost flippant, but she knew the other woman was disappointed. "I'm sorry."

Lottie shrugged one shoulder. "It's strange, but I find myself more disillusioned by a husband who has such easily persuaded views than I think I would be by one whose views were entirely opposite but passionately held. Isn't that quixotic of me?"

"No, it only shows your own strong feeling." Beatrice linked her arm with Lottie's. "Besides, I wouldn't give up on Mr. Graham so easily. He does love you, you know."

"Oh, I do know." Lottie examined a tray of pink cakes on the table nearby. "That's what makes the whole thing so very tragic." She popped a cake into her mouth. "Mmm. These are much better than they look."

"Lottie!" Beatrice protested, half laughing.

"Well, it's true. They're such proper little Tory cakes that I'd've thought they'd taste like dust, but they have a lovely hint of rose." She took another cake and ate it. "You realize that Lord Blanchard's wig is crooked, don't you?"

"Yes," Beatrice sighed. "I was on my way to setting it right when you waylaid me."

"Mmm. You'll have to brave Old Fishy, then."

Beatrice looked and saw that the Duke of Lister had joined her uncle and Lord Hasselthorpe. "Lovely. But I still need to save poor Uncle Reggie's wig."

"You brave soul, you," Lottie said. "I'll stay here and guard the cakes."

"Coward," Beatrice murmured.

She had a smile on her lips as she started again for her uncle's circle. Lottie was right, of course. The gentlemen who gathered in her uncle's salon were the leading lights of the Tory party. Most sat in the House of Lords, but there were commoners here as well, such as Tom Graham. To a man they'd be outraged if they found out that she held any political thoughts at all, let alone ones that ran counter to her uncle's. Generally she kept these thoughts to herself, but the matter of a fair pension for veteran soldiers was too important an issue to neglect. Beatrice had seen firsthand what a war wound could do to a man and how it might affect him for years after he left His Majesty's army. No, it was simply—

The door to the blue salon was flung savagely open, cracking against the wall. Every head in the room swiveled to the doorway, where a man stood. He was tall with impossibly wide shoulders that nearly filled the doorway. He wore some type of dull leather leggings and shirt under a bright blue coat. Long black hair straggled wildly down his back. An overgrown beard reached halfway up his gaunt cheeks. An iron cross dangled from one ear, and an enormous unsheathed knife hung from a string at his waist.

He had the eyes of a man long dead.

"Who the hell are—" Uncle Reggie began.

But the man spoke over him, his voice deep and rusty, as if he hadn't spoken in so long he'd almost lost the power. *"Où est mon père?"*

He was staring right at her, as if no one else in the room existed. She had stopped, mesmerized and confused, one hand on the oval table.

He started for her, his stride firm, arrogant, and impatient. *"J'insiste sur le fait de voir mon père."*

"I . . . I don't know where your father is," Beatrice stuttered. His long stride was eating up the space between them. He was almost to her. No one was doing anything, and she'd forgotten all her schoolroom French. "Please, I don't know—"

But he was already on her, his big, rough hands reaching for her, and Beatrice couldn't help but flinch. It was as if the devil himself had come for her, here at this boring tea.

And then he staggered. One brown hand grasped the table as if to steady himself, but the little table wasn't up for the task. He took it with him as he collapsed to his knees, the vase of flowers crashing to the floor. His angry gaze was still locked with hers, even as he sank to the carpet, until his black eyes rolled back in his head and he fell over.

Someone screamed.

"Good God! Beatrice, are you all right, my dear? Where in blazes is my butler?"

Beatrice heard Uncle Reggie behind her, but she was already on her knees beside the fallen man, unmindful of the spilled water from the vase. Hesitantly, she touched his lips and felt the brush of his breath. Still alive, then. She took his heavy head between her palms and placed it on her lap so that she might look in his face.

She caught her breath.

The man had been *tattooed*. Three stylized birds flew about his right eye, savage and wild. His commanding black eyes were closed, but his brows were heavy and slightly knit as if he disapproved of her even when unconscious. The beard had never been trimmed and was at least two inches long, but she made out the mouth beneath, incongruously elegant. The lips were firm, the upper a wide, sensuous bow.

"My dear, please move away from that . . . that thing," Uncle Reggie was saying. He had his hand on her arm, urging her to get up. "The footmen can't remove him from the house until you move."

"They can't take him," Beatrice said, still staring at the impossible face.

"My dear girl—"

She looked up. Uncle Reggie was such a darling, even when red-faced with impatience. This might very well kill him. "It's Viscount Hope."

Uncle Reggie blinked. "What?"

"Viscount Hope."

And they both turned to stare at the portrait near the door. It was of a young, handsome man, the former heir to the earldom. The man whose death had made it possible for Uncle Reggie to become the Earl of Blanchard.

Black, heavy-lidded eyes stared from the portrait.

She looked back down at the living man. Though closed she remembered his eyes well. Black, angry, and glittering, they were identical to the eyes in the portrait.

Beatrice's heart froze in wonder.

Reynaud St. Aubyn, Viscount Hope, the true Earl of Blanchard, was alive.

THE DISH

Where authors give you the inside scoop!

♥ ♥ ♥ ♥ ♥ ♥ ♥ ♥ ♥ ♥ ♥ ♥ ♥ ♥ ♥ ♥ ♥

From the desk of Elizabeth Hoyt

Gentle Reader,

Whilst researching my latest novel, TO BEGUILE A BEAST (on sale now), I came across the following document which was written in a Suspiciously Familiar hand. I append it here for Your Amusement.

THE GENTEEL LADY'S GUIDE TO CLEANING CASTLES

Written for the Express Purpose of Guiding the Lady of Quality who may, through no fault of her own, be hiding under an Assumed Name in a Very Dirty Castle Indeed.

1. If at all possible, the Genteel Lady should choose a very dirty castle not inhabited by a Male (one cannot use the word Gentleman!) of a foul and disagreeable disposition.
2. Even if the Male in question is rather attractive otherwise.
3. An apron, preferably in a becoming shade of light blue or rose, is important.

4. The Genteel Lady should immediately hire a large and competent staff—even if it is against the express wishes of the Disagreeable Male. Remember: if the Disagreeable Male knew anything about cleaning, his castle wouldn't be in such a deplorable state in the first place.

5. Tea is harder to make than one might imagine.

6. Beware birds' nests hiding in the chimney!

7. The Genteel Lady should never deliver the Disagreeable Male's luncheon to him in his tower study by herself. This may result in the Lady and the Male being closeted together—alone!

8. Should the Genteel Lady dismiss the Above Advice, she should not under any circumstances participate in a Passionate Embrace with the Disagreeable Male.

9. Even if he is no longer Quite So Disagreeable.

10. Finally, the Genteel Lady should never, ever engage in an Affair d'Coeur with the Master of the Castle. In doing so she puts not only her virtue in peril, but also her heart.

Yours Most Sincerely,

Elizabeth Hoyt

www.elizabethhoyt.com

♥ ♥ ♥ ♥ ♥ ♥ ♥ ♥ ♥ ♥ ♥ ♥ ♥ ♥ ♥

From the desk of Annie Solomon

Dear Reader,

Everyone always asks me where I get my ideas. Sometimes I get them straight from the newspaper. Or a song lyric might start an idea rolling. Places often give me ideas, especially if they're new to me. But in the case of my latest, ONE DEADLY SIN (on sale now), the idea for the book came from a tour guide to Iowa.

My brother was moving, which was sad because we live next door to each other, and also happy, because it meant he was taking a job that was exciting and challenging and something he always wanted to do. As a parting gift, someone had given him a guide to interesting places in Iowa, and while flipping through it one day—trying to ignore the boxes that were piling up in his living room—I happened across a famous midwestern legend about a monument in an Iowa cemetery. A monument that supposedly turned black overnight because the man buried beneath it was guilty of crimes of the heart.

That got me thinking. What if the person buried beneath the angel was innocent? What if someone wanted to prove it? What if proving it cost that someone his or her life?

That's the nugget that got me started on Edie Swann, the tattooed, Harley-riding heroine of ONE DEADLY SIN.

They say you can't go home again. For Edie, going home is murder. Out to revenge her father's long-ago death, she's caught in her own trap by a maniac who wants to see the sins of the past paid in full. With Edie's blood.

You can check out an excerpt on my Web site, www. anniesolomon.net. You'll also find more on the legend that started the story circling in my head. And while you're there, don't forget to check out my blog for behind-the-scenes stories in the life of a writer.

Happy Reading!

Annie Solomon

♥ ♥ ♥ ♥ ♥ ♥ ♥ ♥ ♥ ♥ ♥ ♥ ♥ ♥ ♥ ♥

From the desk of Lillian Feist

Dear Reader,

Have you ever had a crush on a rock star? Have you ever watched *American Idol* and your heart began to pitter-patter as you saw a performer belt out a song, straight from his gut? Have you ever stared at a musician's fingers as he strummed his guitar and thought, "Wouldn't it be fabulous to be tied up by that rock star as he did wicked things to me?"

Or maybe that's just me.

It all started when I heard Robert Plant. I'd never even seen him, but when I listened to him sing I fell in love with his voice. He sounded so soulful, so sexy. I wondered why he wanted someone to squeeze his lemon, but my mom assured me it was because he liked a citrusy tea. Being thirteen, I believed her. It didn't stop my crush, though. I'd just lie on my bed, listening to Led Zeppelin, in bliss. And when I caught sight of Plant onstage, swinging his hips in those low-slung jeans, I was toast. I never got over my fascination with musicians, and I suspect few of us do.

Enter Mark St. Crow, the hero in my May release, BOUND TO PLEASE. Mark's a hot, tattooed musician with a tendency to, well, tie women up and do wicked things to them. Of course, I couldn't make his life easy so I made Mark fall for Ruby Scott, an event planner who longs for stability and all the things Mark's lifestyle could never allow. Oh, I admit it was fun torturing them both (even though they sometimes liked it) and while I did so I got to live out my not-so-secret rock-star crush, with a heavy dose of spicy romance thrown in.

I hope you enjoy BOUND TO PLEASE! You can find out more information about me and my writing at www.lillianfeisty.com.

Lilli Feisty

Want to know more about romances at Grand Central Publishing and Forever? Get the scoop online!

GRAND CENTRAL PUBLISHING'S ROMANCE HOME PAGE

Visit us at www.hachettebookgroup.com/romance for all the latest news, reviews, and chapter excerpts!

NEW AND UPCOMING TITLES

Each month we feature our new titles and reader favorites.

CONTESTS AND GIVEAWAYS

We give away galleys, autographed copies, and all kinds of fun stuff.

AUTHOR INFO

You'll find bios, articles, and links to personal Web sites for all your favorite authors—and so much more!

THE BUZZ

Sign up for our monthly romance newsletter, and be the first to read all about it!